The Dollfuss Directive

Augustine Campana & Marco Di Tillo

The authors wish to thank everyone who believed in and encouraged the writing of this book, especially Jean Campana and Dr. Jane Leon for their astute advice and unflagging support.

For author information and other titles, visit **campana-ditillo.com**

Cover Image Credit: Piazza San Marco, Venice (creativemarket.com)

Library of Congress control number on file with the publisher.

ISBN 13: 978-1-7360446-0-5

Printed in the United States of America

Imprint of Skyway Press, LLC

For Jean

Table of Contents

Chapter One

Wednesday, 2 May 1934

Vienna, Austria

It was a warm spring day in Vienna's *Volksgarten* and Captain Sepp Karper was sweating in the woolen dress uniform he had chosen for this special occasion. Ignoring the glorious gardens, statues, and monuments around him, he hurried for the shade along a tree-lined walkway, his sword softly clanking against his thigh as he strode. Once out of the bright sun, he picked up an abandoned copy of a *Wiener Tagblatt* newspaper from a bench and began scanning it for a hint why Chancellor Engelbert Dollfuss had summoned him. Articles about the constitutional changes that had created a new Austria, the recent pact with the Vatican, and the installation of Prince Ernst Starhemberg as vice chancellor failed to provide a clue. He tossed the periodical aside, unaware that, within the hour, he would be ordered on the most challenging and crucial mission of his life.

With the Dollfuss question left unanswered, Sepp checked his wristwatch. Finding he was nearly thirty minutes early, he took a deep breath full of the scent of budding roses and allowed the splendor of the park to enter his consciousness. Once a refuge for Napoleon's retreating troops, the *Volksgarten* was now a haven for idle pensioners, prim ladies, doting nursemaids with their infant charges, and frolicking children. In the distance, a brilliant white sculpture caught his eye. It honored Empress Elisabeth, wife of Emperor Franz-Joseph. Known as "Sisi," she had died at the hands of an anarchist in 1898. Sepp's head filled with a memory of his mother's tearful face as the empress's funeral cortege passed by them on its way to a requiem mass.

Barely two years later, typhus took the loving woman who was the center of his life. At eight years old, he was left in the severe service of his father, a butcher and weekend woodworker, who had little time for his son other than insisting that he have a good Catholic education at the seminary of Hollabrunn.

Drawn to the likeness of the ill-fated royal, Sepp approached the memorial's reflecting pool. There, a group of boys chattered and splashed as they sailed their carved wooden boats and comical plastic ducks.

"Look here!" shouted an arriving youngster proudly holding up a crude vessel fashioned from a handbill. "I made it myself from a paper I found!" With hope and determination on his face, he set the craft on the water. "Off to sea, my good ship!"

As the flimsy boat bobbed atop the ripples, a husky, older lad carrying a satchel grabbed the boy by the scruff, plunged his head into the water, and held it there.

Sepp covered the few meters to the pool in seconds and pulled the bully away, breaking his hold on the youngster who came up gasping and coughing.

"I'm here, Peter. It is alright. Mama is coming," cried a woman rushing toward them.

"What the hell do you think you're doing?" Sepp demanded of the older lad.

"He needs a lesson, that one!" answered the young brute as he wiped his hands on his shirt. Pulling one of the flyers from his pouch, he held it up to Sepp's face. "No one destroys the property of the National Socialists."

Emblazoned with a large Nazi swastika, it read, "Austrian patriots, the hour has come to reject the impostor Dollfuss and join us today. The future glory of Austria can only come from a union with Germany. Heil Hitler!" Details of a meeting time and place followed.

Sepp grabbed the flyer, crushed it into a ball, and presented it on his palm. "The National Socialists have been outlawed. You are a felon, and this is rubbish."

"I and others like me are the true future of Austria," the bully countered as he grabbed the crumpled flyer from Sepp's hand. "*Anschluss* will happen, and you and your uniform will mean nothing.

Hitler will return the land of his birth to Germany, and we must be ready for that great day."

"You are an ignorant fool. I could arrest you," Sepp warned as his hand went for the sword's grip. He pulled the weapon partway out of its sheath and pointed to the satchel. "Give me that."

The bully flung the case at Sepp and ran off shouting, "I am right! You will see! We, too have swords—and guns."

Seeing that the offended youngster was being comforted by his mother, Sepp put the satchel under his arm and headed for the *Ballhaus.* Named for the tennis facility that once sat there, it was now the seat of the Austrian government. A cigarette later, he showed a guard his credentials and handed him the bag of flyers. "Please dispose of this trash, Sergeant."

"Yes, Captain," the guard responded as he accepted the satchel and nodded to a corporal. The young soldier reported to Sepp and escorted him to a salon on the ground floor.

The room was elegantly spartan with sideboards along its walls and a simple oak meeting table surrounded by leather chairs at its center. Mindful of his military creases, Sepp remained standing. He was checking the shine on his boots when Vice Chancellor Prince Ernst Rüdiger Starhemberg entered.

Supremely confident, the prince was trim and almost as tall as Sepp. The epitome of 1930s fashion, he wore a tailored gray suit with a vest, and a blue tie knotted under the rounded collar of his white shirt. His left lapel held the badge of the Fatherland Front, a defense organization that he and Engelbert Dollfuss had founded. It was a conglomeration of right-wing politicians, Catholic clergy, and elements of the *Heimwehr*, the home guard of which he was also a past leader. Aside from Dollfuss's confessor, Starhemberg was the chancellor's most trusted advisor.

"Captain Karper," the prince said, acknowledging Sepp's greeting and crisp nod. "I am happy you are early. We must chat." He sat and motioned for Sepp to do the same.

Sepp took a seat and offered, "May I congratulate you on your appointment as Vice Chancellor, Highness."

"Thank you, but there is no need for such formality, especially among those I consider friends."

“I am most honored, sir.”

“Please excuse the fact that we chose not to meet in our offices. You see, the chancellor and I do not want to attract undue attention.”

“Certainly,” Sepp accepted, still unclear why he was there.

“You know,” Starhemberg went on, picking up the thread of Sepp’s reference to royalty, “Chancellor Dollfuss is warming to the idea of allowing a Habsburg return. It could lend a greater air of legitimacy to his government and help us discourage Hitler’s annexation attempts.”

“I just experienced that very threat in the *Volksgarten,*” Sepp confided. “A Nazi youth was posting propaganda and terrorizing some boys. I had no choice but to step in.”

“As you once did for our dear chancellor at Hollabrunn,” Starhemberg said, reminding Sepp of an incident from his school days.

“We were classmates, and I couldn’t stand by and watch those bullies attack the little guy. I’m surprised he ever mentioned it to you.”

The prince smiled. “He has told me quite a lot, including how you again saved his skin defending against an entire company in the terrible war.”

“I was a lowly corporal, and he was my lieutenant.”

“To your great credit, you earned the rank of captain. Was it your marksmanship?”

“That and some fortunate circumstances managed largely by my friend. All in all, the military has been good to me. It has been my life.” Starhemberg said nothing, giving Sepp a chance. “Sir, may I ask why I am here?”

The handle of one of the tall doors clanked, and Starhemberg replied, “I believe you are about to find out.” He stood and Sepp did the same.

A guard held the door open for a small man in a brown business suit, his neatly trimmed mustache hovering above a bow-like mouth. The soulful eyes of Engelbert Dollfuss held an undeniable tinge of steel. A war hero, he had gained office by forming a coalition of Christian socialists, agronomists, and right-wing members of his Homeland Front. In March 1933, soon after Hitler’s rise to power in

Germany, Dollfuss dissolved the Austrian parliament and outlawed the Communist Party. A few months later, intent on keeping his country independent, he banned the Austrian National Socialists.

"Ernst," Dollfuss nodded to Starhemberg then went to Sepp with open arms. "My dear friend." He reached up on tiptoe and gave the captain an awkward hug. "It has been months since our last contact." Stepping back, he indicated a chair. "Please, sit."

Starhemberg also took a seat as the diminutive chancellor settled into an armchair that was low enough for his feet to reach the floor. "I'm glad to see you looking so well, and most punctual, just as you always were. Would you like a refreshment?"

"No, thank you. I am fine," Sepp assured.

"Perhaps a bit of schnapps?" prompted Dollfuss.

"I avoid alcohol, Excellency."

"Yet another trait from the old days. Well then, let me get to the point." His face went dark. "Not many are aware, because we do influence the press, but things are not good." He leaned forward in his chair. "Three months ago, we were able to contain the factory riots." He frowned. "Today, I doubt we could do the same."

Sepp nodded grimly. "I have seen the internal reports."

Dollfuss continued, "The National Socialists are growing in number and becoming more dangerous as their patron Hitler secures a firmer grip on his adopted country. He sends weapons and his hooligans to help, and I believe a civil war could come at any time."

Sepp frowned. "Such a conflict could take months."

"Hitler is far too impatient for that," Starhemberg offered.

"In fact, Sepp," the chancellor went on, "at the first spark of such an outbreak, the Germans would likely sweep us out in days. It could happen, unless …"

Dollfuss held the pause and Sepp prompted, "Sir?"

"We need to do something about Hitler now before the pot boils over. This is why I am calling upon you."

"I am now no more than a paper shuffler."

"You are a patriot, Sepp, and it is a time for patriots," Dollfuss corrected.

"What would you have me do?"

"We want you to develop and carry out a plan to kidnap Hitler.

Bring him here, and we shall intern him for life in the mountains of Tyrol. Lacking their charismatic leader, the Nazis will make no further gains in Germany or here, and their movement will eventually wither on the vine."

Sepp said nothing and looked to Starhemberg for a reaction. Receiving only a shrug from the prince, he asked, "Where would I go to do this? Germany? Is he coming to Austria?" A realization struck. "Ah! The Italy meeting. Is it definite?"

"Set for Venice, according to our sources," Dollfuss responded. "That is where Hitler will disappear."

Starhemberg explained, "On June fourteenth, Hitler will meet Mussolini for the first time."

"I see," Sepp replied, his mind shifting into high gear.

"You know Benito is my friend," Dollfuss added. "I went to Rome recently and signed formal statements of amity between our two countries. I also made an accord with the Vatican."

"Yes," Sepp agreed, "I read of it earlier."

"Both the Pope and Mussolini want Austria to remain independent."

"Confidentially," added the prince, "I believe the Italian regards Hitler as a fool and a dangerous madman."

"Then, why meet with him?" asked Sepp.

"*Il Duce* is quite crafty." Dollfuss referred to Mussolini by his fascist title of leader. "One reason he has held power since the early twenties is that he has mastered strolling both sides of the street."

"Hitler probably has no idea what Mussolini thinks of him," added Starhemberg. "He regards the Italian as a prophet who shares his views."

"Does he believe he can get the *Duce* to support the annexation of Austria?" asked Sepp.

"That is likely Hitler's aim," replied the prince. "It will keep him from attempting anything before Venice."

"What about afterward?" Sepp asked.

"There must not be an afterward," proclaimed Dollfuss.

Sepp locked eyes with the chancellor. "Why not eliminate him right off and be done with it? Cut the head off the snake."

"I cannot condone anything so final as killing." Dollfuss reached out to Sepp. "Like me, you have served at Mass and are still a good Catholic. Yes?"

Sepp looked down at the floor.

"Have you not also kept your faith?"

Sepp shrugged. "I could do better."

"We should never abandon our beliefs or our fear of God and always ensure that the laws of the state correspond to His commandments. I would not ask you or anyone to kill a man, not even a lunatic like Hitler. It is different in battle or dealing with violations of the law, but it is not in me to order a murder. He will be taken to Tyrol to live out his life quietly. No one will hear anything more of him." The face of the chancellor lit up with a wry smile as he snapped his fingers. "Like sorcerers, we shall make him disappear."

"I am a soldier, and I will do whatever is asked of me."

"Just as I had expected." Dollfuss stood. "And now, I must go prepare for a radio speech." As Sepp and Starhemberg both rose, he continued, "Later, my sweet Alwine and I are off to the opera for a special performance of Puccini's *La Bohème*." He eyed Sepp. "Perhaps you would like to join us. I can arrange for an additional ticket," adding with raised brows, "or two."

Sepp shook his head, "Oh, no sir. While I would enjoy seeing *Frau* Dollfuss again, my distaste for opera has also stayed with me."

"Can I assume there is still no woman in your life?" Receiving no response, Dollfuss urged, "Sepp, you need someone. Without her, you are incomplete. There is nothing so satisfying as a loving wife and family." He turned to the prince. "Ernst, I think I am making our friend uncomfortable, so I shall leave." Before exiting, he added. "I rely on you both to develop a plan and keep me informed of your progress."

Starhemberg waited for the door to close. "An interesting idea; however, you understand things are not always what they seem."

"Sir?"

"Dollfuss reveres you as a trusted agent, but we also know you as a fine marksman. In our discussions, I supported using you with the hope that it might come to this." He paused then spoke slowly and precisely, "Your true mission is to kill Hitler in Venice."

"But the chancellor's wishes?"

"We both know it would be impossible to kidnap Hitler, and the idea of keeping him on ice in Tyrol is pure fantasy."

"I don't understand," Sepp responded. "Does he know of this?"

"He does not want to know. Part of your mission is to provide our chancellor with a clear conscience for the confessional."

"I see."

"You will follow my orders and mine alone. Assassination is your mission. Is that clear?"

Sepp nodded. "I take it I am not expected to survive."

"That will be up to you. You have seen worse, and I know you are resourceful." The prince patted Sepp on the back. "We do have assets in Italy that may be able to help. If so, you will be informed, should it come to that. After all, we can't have a known Austrian turn up dead in the aftermath. Be assured of our help in developing a scheme for the mission, but you will be on your own."

"I work well alone." Sepp took a deep breath. "I prefer it."

"We shall discuss this further tomorrow morning. Eight o'clock at the Ministry of Defense, the *Vaterländischen* Front."

"Isn't that where Major Fey keeps an office?" Sepp asked.

"That building, yes, however, we will not discuss any of this with Fey." Starhemberg frowned. "He and I have never been on the best of terms, and since yesterday, when I replaced him—well, you can imagine." He ushered Sepp to the door, "There is someone else there you need to see." Regarding Sepp's uniform, he added, "And, please, you needn't be so conspicuous."

"Yes, sir. Until tomorrow."

* * *

Sepp entered his apartment on the second floor of 10 Hintzerstrasse and immediately began changing his clothes. He was removing his shirt when a chill ran through him as he realized this would be the first time he used his deadly skills as a marksman since the war.

He put on comfortable slacks and a shirt and, falling back on his usual escape, he loaded his Meerschaum pipe, lit it, and picked up a book-marked novel about the expansion of America's new frontier. One of his diversions was losing himself in tales of the gold frenzy in California; the cattle drives north along the Chisholm Trail; and lawless towns such as Dodge City and Tombstone. The experience often left him wondering what it would be like to have been a part of all that. He sometimes fancied himself a lawman the likes of Bat Masterson or Wyatt Earp, confident that he could handle a gun as well as any of them.

Despite his attempt at relaxing, the order to kill Hitler kept scratching at his brain. He considered going to the training center where he enjoyed sparring with the up-and-coming fighters. Maybe one of his regular visits to the gun range would do. Deciding that neither promised to ease his bother, he pulled a scribbled note from his billfold. "I hope she's there."

Suddenly, anticipation filled him as he considered the prospect of seeing someone who had always been a source of comfort and understanding. And, there was the intimacy.

He had covered the four kilometers to the Josefstadt district in just over thirty minutes and located the address along Florianigasse. He rapped on one of the black doors, half expecting his signal to go unanswered. He was wrong. It opened on a familiar gray-whiskered face with sad, blue eyes gazing at him through horn-rimmed glasses.

"Mr. Karper! This is a surprise! Madam will be elated."

"Jacob, how good it is to see you. The pleasure is mine, I promise."

"Come in."

As he was beckoned into a rococo foyer, Sepp added, "I received her note about the move from Berlin, but wasn't certain when it might happen."

"We arrived only days ago after a rushed departure. She was forced to leave many of her things behind. Just as well, though, this house is much smaller than the situation we enjoyed there."

"I am sorry to hear it. She has such treasures."

"All the same, sir, we a grateful to be here and not in a camp somewhere."

Sepp looked around at the two hallways leading off the foyer. "Where?"

"Madam is in the sitting room, her usual location at this time of evening."

Sepp smiled, "Sipping her brandy, no doubt."

"Quite so." Jacob led the way through a marbled corridor, its walls covered with modern paintings.

Sepp paused at a portrait of a woman at a table wearing a revealing red dress and pouring a glass of wine. The style was severe, but the face was quite familiar.

Jacob offered, "She sat for Otto Dix. It's one of the few works by him still in circulation."

"What happened?"

"Confiscated. The Nazis seized most of them because they consider Dix a degenerate. So many no longer enjoy peace in Germany now, Mr. Karper—especially Jews. Madam was right to leave."

"Tell me, how is she? I mean, really."

"Not well, sir. She never fully recovered from the cancer. Months in Baden-Baden had promise at the start, but finally did little to offer a cure. She had to return to hospital in February."

"What do the doctors say?" Sepp asked.

Jacob shook his head, "They sent her home to die. That's when she decided to return to her beloved Vienna. They say she may have months or possibly a year."

Sepp grimaced. "Damn!"

"Excuse me. I will inform her she has a guest."

Sepp put his finger to his lips. "Don't tell her who. I want it to be a surprise."

"As you wish." Jacob nodded as he opened a large, white door.

While Sepp waited, he put the dark thoughts of her demise out of his head and allowed warm memories to flow in—the thrilling adventures, the friendly competition, the ecstatic lovemaking.

When Jacob beckoned him, Sepp took a deep breath, forced a smile, and entered a cozy chamber of draperies, tapestries, and gold-framed mirrors. A leather armchair faced the fireplace, and an elegant hand on the end of a slender white arm caressed a snifter of amber brandy. In profile, he saw the beautifully coiffed platinum hair, the classic straight nose, and eyes locked in a stare at the crackling fire.

"Come reveal yourself. Let me see you." She pointed the cigarette holder in her other hand at a chair opposite hers. When Sepp did as he was told, her face burst into a bright smile, her red lipstick framing porcelain-white teeth. "Sepp! What a lovely surprise!" Her voice had not lost its sensuality.

"Katy, it is so good to see you. Believe me, I have thought of you often and most fondly. Oh, more than that. The truth is, I still love you and …" he shrugged, "well, you know." He bent over, kissed her lightly on the lips and gave her a tender, careful hug, feeling the frailty of her once dangerously sexy body.

Katherine Hermann, born in Vienna to a French mother and a German-Jew father, had been a double agent during the big war, spying for both the allies and Germany. She hated conflict and would make reports to one side or the other depending on what best suited her at the moment. As the hostilities progressed, she came down on the side of the allies. Known to the intelligence gatherers by the code name "Venus," she and Sepp met when she was on the Eastern Front in Ukraine. She was there feeding erroneous information to Germany about the plans of General Aleksei Brusilov, a hero of one of the battles that marked the beginning of the end for Austro-Hungary as a force.

Sepp had been reassigned from the Tyrolean component to the infantry as a sniper and shipped east. In June 1916, his unit was vanquished when Brusilov's surprise offensive caught them off guard and rolled over them. After weeks moving from one assignment to another, by late August, when defeat loomed, Sepp was wounded in his right side. Fighting to stanch the loss of blood, he worked his way out of the battle zone rather than risk capture. He escaped to Kovel, where Katherine found him near death in a ditch. While she nursed him back to health, they became close.

At the time, he was twenty-four while she was almost thirty, but age hadn't mattered. Neither had their allegiances. What would guide their relationship for the rest of their lives was the spark of romance that ignited a flame of passion each time they met. When the war ended, Sepp began a climb to the rank of captain with the National Security Ministry. At the same time, Katherine relocated to Munich, where she worked for British intelligence as the seeds of Nazism were beginning to sprout in the soil of the German psyche.

"My love, you see, the years have taken their toll." She sucked on the cigarette holder and let out a cloud of light gray smoke.

"Schatz," he asked softly, "wouldn't it be time for you to give that up?"

Disregarding his question, she set down her cigarette holder and glass and wrapped the blanket around her shoulders. "Put another log on the fire, will you?"

He complied, and she beckoned him. "Come closer, please. I want to look you properly in the eyes."

He moved to the arm of her chair. "Is this better?"

"Much." She nuzzled into him. "You could always please me. Caressing every inch of me, you took me to heaven. Whoever said to get there, one must die? All you need are Karper's strong hands to forget everything."

"It has been a long time, Katy."

"Has it? My heart doesn't feel so. My desire doesn't either. You know, passion has always ruled with us."

"I know," he said hoarsely.

The two looked into each other's eyes and silently savored the moment. As it passed, she asked, "Well, my dear, why are you here? Why now?"

He stroked her hair. "Business. A crucial assignment that I'm trying to make sense of."

"You mean trying to rationalize."

"Something like that. I must murder someone."

"You killed dozens in war. Why is this a problem?"

"The target is an important person."

"How important?"

"Very. An ex-patriot Austrian."

"Oh, God! Not that one!"

"Uhm …"

"You will be doing the world a favor getting rid of that Jew hater." She retrieved her drink and took a sip. "When?"

"Next month, he will meet with *Signor* Mussolini in Venice."

"Ah, wonderful Venice, Queen of the Adriatic." Her eyes lit up. "The bell tower! Is that it?"

"Possibly. No details yet. It's only been a few hours."

"You know, I have a nephew there: Maximilian Klemperer,

a dressmaker—'couturier,' as the French call them. He occupies a small *palazzo* I used."

"Impressive."

"I don't own it, Love. The state controls most of those buildings. This one was a shelter for the infirm during a time when I was doing surveillance work. Once again, I was riding two horses—Austria and Italy. The Italians wanted my presence in Venice and made a deal with the owning agency to let me use the upper floors as quarters and for my work."

"And your nephew? Is he also in the business?"

"No, he is simply a dress designer, but he can be counted on if you need him." She again gazed for a long second into Sepp's eyes. "It is so good to have you here. I can't tell you what it has done for my spirits."

He leaned in and kissed her cheek. "I wish I could be with you longer, dear Katy."

"You can't. I know that. Not now that he's gaining power." Her tone was professional, and her words precise. "You need help, and I think I can offer it." She paused to catch her breath. "Max is not an agent, but he knows Venice well. He now has the entire *palazzo* since the shelter fell into disuse two years ago. The lower floor is for his business, but there is plenty of room above. You and your team are welcome to it."

"I'm working alone."

She smirked. "Of course you are." After another sip, she asked, "Do you have a plan for smuggling in a weapon?"

"I'm not sure about that either."

"Max has connections." She patted his hand. "Before you go, I will give you the particulars for contacting him." She held up her glass, "Now, I could use another splash. Join me, or are you still a teetotaler?"

"I'm afraid so," he reached for the bottle of Napoleon brandy on a side table. "Maybe next time."

Chapter Two

Thursday, 3 May 1934

Vienna, Austria

Wearing a business suit for his meeting with Prince Starhemberg, Sepp descended the stairs to the ground floor of his apartment house. As he passed by the open door of landlady *Frau* Olga Adorf's flat, he could smell the cabbage soup she was eternally preparing. It reminded him how desperately he wanted to avoid the nattering woman. That hope was shattered when he found her scrubbing the entryway—sloshing water onto the marble floor while screeching an inharmonious version of *"Ach du lieber Augustin."*

Sepp grimaced, remembering how he had enjoyed performing the same song at Hollabrunn with one Engelbert Dollfuss. Surprisingly, little Engel had a mellow alto voice that harmonized well with Sepp's youthful tenor. Passing the brush-wielding woman, he mumbled a terse greeting, put his head down, and attempted to move on.

"Good morning, Captain Karper. You're up early!" she said with a crooked smile. "And, no uniform."

"Yes." He forced a grin, baring his clenched teeth, and hastened for the door.

"Have you heard the news?" she quickly asked.

"I have heard nothing."

"It's all over the building. Mrs. Rottmaier seems to have gotten pregnant again. "

"Rottmaier?" He paused his escape.

"You know. The family on the fourth floor! Her husband is an agent at the post office."

"I don't think I do."

"You must." she insisted. "The little bald man with the grumpy scowl who apparently is a master of the bedroom," she said with a leer. "They have four sons and a daughter. The next would be the sixth child. Does that not seem a bit too many in these difficult times?"

"Maybe." He made a show of checking his watch. "Oh, the time. You must excuse me, but I have an appointment."

As he opened the door, she called after him, "They say children come from heaven. Maybe so, but they are also coming from that bedroom. You know perfectly well what I mean. After five children, it would be best to read a good book or sleep. What do you think, Captain Karper?"

The door closed on her last words, and out on the sidewalk, he inhaled a much-needed breath of fresh air. At a newsstand, he bought a copy of *Wiener Zeitung* and quickly scanned it. The political news was a regurgitation of events he already knew about. As expected, the review of *La Bohème* was glowing, and lastly, the sports page gave the initial schedule for the World Cup football matches starting in Italy on 27 May.

Joining the flow of other Viennese starting their workday, he passed one of the cinemas in the district. The movie playing there was a musical titled, "Waltzes from Vienna." He made little of it until noticing it was the work of Alfred Hitchcock, a man notorious for his suspense movies. Shaking his head, he mused that even a talented filmmaker wasn't always able to choose the work he did. At that moment, he felt an odd kinship with the director.

A few minutes before 08:00, Sepp entered the lobby of the Ministry of Defense. He barely had time to survey his surroundings before he saw the prince standing down a corridor by an open door and waving to him.

The meeting room had an oval table, a few simple chairs, and the lingering aroma of stale smoke. Starhemberg checked the hallway before he closed the door. "So, Captain, how did you sleep? Not well, I expect."

"Yes, sir. I have had many thoughts and concerns about this assignment."

"Surely, you are used to such things by now."

"Sir, this is not a mission I can take easily in stride."

"Sepp, you are a warrior. It cannot be so different."

"This is political, and he's the German chancellor."

Without warning, the door opened, and there stood Major Emil Fey. His uniform was decorated with medals while his face wore a scowl.

"Well, dear Vice Chancellor," he said as he closed the door behind him. "It is so good to have you here in my home. To what do I owe this honor?"

Starhemberg indicated Sepp. "The captain is here for a special assignment."

"I see. Something worthy of your office and possibly the chancellor himself?" Fey turned to Sepp. "Captain Karper, I believe Dollfuss would like to eliminate *Herr* Hitler. Something I agree with as I detest the man. Would your special assignment have anything to do with that?"

Sepp looked straight ahead and did not respond.

Fey shot Starhemberg a withering stare. "Does he even know why he is here, Ernst?"

"It is precisely what we were about to discuss."

"I see." Fey scowled as he concluded, "And, you don't need me for this discussion, do you."

The prince smiled, "Emil, let me assure you, this is nothing so important as to be worthy of your concern."

"Yet, it is worthy of yours." Fey went to the door. "I find it quite interesting, Captain Karper, that you are one of Austria's finest marksmen."

Starhemberg and Sepp both said nothing.

Before exiting, Fey added, "Whatever you are about, do it well and honor the patriots."

Starhemberg broke the ensuing silence. "Sepp, I must apologize for this. I do not want Fey to know anything because he is not a man of finesse. He is more the bull in the crystal shop, and his methods could threaten everything."

"Yes, sir."

"You must be careful not to raise his suspicions any further. He has a network of informants. Make no unnecessary contacts."

"Absolutely, sir."

"We are aware that you visited Katherine Hermann yesterday. A former agent."

Sepp said nothing.

"That must stop. For now, your life is on hold until this is over, understand?"

"Yes, sir." Sepp felt an emptiness inside as hopes of seeing Katherine soon again faded.

"Good." The prince smiled, satisfied. "Now, we move on to someone you need to see." He opened the door and checked the hallway. "Come quickly."

Starhemberg hustled to a long, descending staircase that led to an austere corridor lined with a series of unmarked doors. He stood by one. "Go on in. I must get back before that old hound Fey wonders where I have disappeared to. Meet me in that same room when you are finished here."

Sepp did as he was told and continued through a small entryway and into a dim, musty smelling chamber.

"Good morning Captain Karper," came the greeting from behind a desk cluttered with papers, phones, a coffee cup, and ashtray.

The voice was familiar, and as his eyes adjusted to the low light level, Sepp recognized the greeter. "Captain Joscht?" Seeing the man's rank, he corrected, "Excuse me, Colonel Joscht, is that you?"

"In the flesh, such as it is, my friend," Joscht said with arms outstretched. "It has been a long time."

"Yes, sir," Sepp agreed as he shook the hand the colonel shot at him across the desk.

Paul Joscht was a man Sepp had fought under on the Russian front until the Austrian army was defeated. Joscht was a captain known for his skills as a strategist and an expert in arms and explosives. He would call upon Sepp when there was an essential and often particularly tricky task for a marksman. Sepp was on one such mission when the captain was wounded and left for dead behind enemy lines.

Having assumed Joscht had been one of the thousands of casualties of the Russian campaign, Sepp never knew that, like himself, his commander had survived and later accepted a promotion and a position with the Ministry of Defense. Now the head of a covert operation code-named *Steinschlag,* he was responsible for thwarting potential assassination attempts and conspiracies against the state.

"Please, let's dispense with the formality," suggested Joscht as Sepp took a seat. "I am Paul, and you are Sepp, two old army mates who saw the worst of it together."

Sepp nodded and Joscht continued, "Now that the prince has handed you over to me, let's not waste any time. First, the serious consideration of what you would like to drink. Coffee? Tea?"

"Coffee, please, black."

Only when Joscht stood and moved away from his desk did Sepp see his disability, one requiring a cane.

Joscht carried a tray holding mugs of coffee and utensils back to the desk and flashed a mock scowl. "Stop staring at me like that. Have you never seen someone serve coffee?"

"I apologize, sir … Paul. I didn't know. I wasn't even sure you had made it back." Sepp's face flushed.

"This was after the war. I lost a left leg below the knee due to my own foolishness. I was careless while neutralizing a land mine. Cautioning others against something over and over again somehow made me arrogant and lax. Not worth talking about. Besides, we have grand plans to discuss." He raised his cup, "To Austria!" Sepp joined in the toast.

Attacking the business at hand, Joscht provided an overview of the latest secretly acquired information about the Venice meeting.

"Hitler arrives in Italy on the morning of fourteen June," he announced.

"Will he be traveling by rail?"

"One would think, but not so. Meeting Mussolini face-to-face for the first time, Hitler is about impressing him. He and his staff will travel aboard Junkers Ju-52 tri-motors and land at the Nicelli airfield on the Venice Lido."

"What about Mussolini?"

"He'll be there waiting to receive him, accompanied by his entourage. After a brief welcome and review of the honor guard, they will go for lunch to the Grand Hotel on the main canal, which is where the German chancellor will stay. We learned that Mussolini will continue on to *Villa Pisani* in Stra, where the first of the formal talks will be held."

“I don’t understand. Why move it out of Venice? Aren’t there enough palaces and fine hotels there?”

“We thought it strange, as well.” Joscht sipped his coffee. “Apparently, it was arranged by *Il Duce* himself.”

“But why?” wondered Sepp as he set down his cup and saucer.

“We can only guess. Napoleon once owned the place, so maybe the Italian wants to impress Hitler with its opulence. Or, perhaps he wants to charm him to have an advantage when pressing his terms.” He shook his head, “We both understand war and battle. It is always a matter of defeat or be defeated. Statesmanship is more the realm of imagery and impression.”

Sepp offered his box of cigarettes to Joscht, who selected one and lit it. “Will their discussions have to do with the continuing independence of Austria?”

“That’s the crux of it. A failure there could mean a terrible fate for our country.” The colonel set his cup aside. “It’s precisely why we need to take the mad German out of the equation. We can’t afford to leave it to chance.”

“I agree, but Dollfuss has insisted that we not kill Hitler. He looked into my eyes and told me so.”

“I am certainly not in a position to countermand him or Starhemberg,” Joscht responded. “Maybe, through the prince’s connections with the Italians, he knows something we don’t.” He let a long moment pass before making his way to a closet door. “Come, this way.”

Joscht opened it and turned a small, obscure lever in the rear. A panel slid away, revealing a passageway that led to a brightly lit chamber lined with long, wooden tables. There, uniformed staff workers were reviewing documents, checking maps, and working at an array of communication devices.

Immediately, some of the men snapped to attention, but Joscht waved off any further show of formality. He and Sepp took stools at a table by a large wall map of Venice. Through another door, Sepp could make out hundreds of labeled cartons arranged on shelves marked with letters of the alphabet. From the section with a “V,” the sergeant pulled two boxes and brought them to their table.

“As you had requested, Colonel,” said the soldier as he removed the box lids. "Please advise me if you need anything further."

"Thank you, Heinsel, that will be all for now."

With a click of his heels, the sergeant left.

Searching the first box's contents, Joscht came up with a set of photostats. "That's the proposed schedule for the visit," he explained. "Close to final, I would say as it came from Himmler's office."

Sepp stood and examined the copies that included penciled revisions and notes in the margins, some indicating minutiae such as whether smoking would be allowed at specific meetings. It read as follows:

THURSDAY, 14 JUNE
h. 10:00 – Arrival at the Nicelli airport, Venice
h. 10:15 – Welcoming ceremonies.
h. 11:30 – Transfer to the Grand Hotel - luncheon
h. 16:00 – Private meetings at Villa Pisani
h. 18:00 – Concert or tour
h. 20:00 – Dinner - German Consulate
FRIDAY, 15 JUNE
h. 10:00 – Military review in Piazza San Marco
h. 12:30 – Luncheon and meetings - Alberoni Golf Club
h. 16:00 – Tour
h. 18:00 – Speech - Italian Head of State, Piazza San Marco
h. 20:00 – Chancellor hosts a reception
SATURDAY, JUNE 16th
h. 08:00 – Ceremony and departure from Nicelli airport.

As he read, Sepp consulted the map showing the waterways, streets, plazas, alleys, churches, and other large buildings. His tactical mind evaluated where and when Hitler might be most vulnerable. Quickly, it became clear that the best chance of getting off a fatal shot would come during the day, outdoors, among a large, noisy crowd. The trip to the hotel on the Grand Canal might present an opportunity, but the military parade and Mussolini's speech in the *piazza* stood out. Recalling Katherine's comment, he told Joscht, "The bell tower is an excellent vantage point."

"We reached the same conclusion." Joscht laid out a dozen

photographs of the square, taken from various angles. "We expect Mussolini and Hitler will be on an open stand during the military review. Later, the Italian will greet the people from a balcony. If tradition holds, it will be in the Napoleonic Wing. We assume Hitler will be at his side, a clear shot from the tower."

Sepp studied a picture of the bell tower, then a photograph taken from the tower loggia toward the far end of the square and the Napoleonic Wing. "How far is it to the balcony?"

"Well within range." The colonel searched a stack of papers and pulled a sheet. "According to this, considering the angle, it is roughly one-hundred and fifty meters."

Sepp's brow furrowed. "But how the hell do I get a rifle up there, and for that matter, how will I gain access to the tower? Security is sure to be tight."

"I believe I have a workable plan. It won't be easy, but we would both worry if it were."

"Let's have it," said Sepp.

Joscht extracted more papers and pictures, one of which was a print of an ancient scene in the bell tower. "Galileo!" he announced. "Demonstrating the telescope to the Doge of Venice."

Sepp's eyebrows shot up. "What?"

"August will mark the three hundred and twenty-fifth anniversary of Galileo's demonstration. It took place in that tower. Well, an older version of the tower, but no matter." Seeing he had Sepp's attention, Joscht continued. "You, my friend, will be an astronomer and Galileo expert from the University of Vienna. You arrive early in June to begin arranging for a re-enactment of that event, and a replica of Galileo's telescope will be your ticket to the tower. And …"

"Wait!" Sepp interrupted, "What about the rifle? I can't shoot anyone with a telescope."

"Patience, my good Captain. I will get to that."

"Okay, let's say I spend the next month boning up for my role as this professor."

"And, growing a beard," Joscht added. "We want you to look the part of one Alex Höbling."

Sepp unconsciously rubbed his chin. "Anything for Austria, but how does a foreign professor get approval for all this?"

"You go first to Florence. There, you will meet with a Father Tucci, a priest who is sympathetic to our cause."

"Not Guido Tucci, is it?"

Joscht nodded, "Yes, do you know him?"

"My God," Sepp erupted in a smile. "I grew up with him. He was just a kid living here in Vienna. His father brought the family here to find work. We had some interesting times together in Venice."

"Tucci's transplant took well; he is quite loyal to Austria. Oddly, he never mentioned your friendship."

"That's him all over! Introspective to a fault. He entered the priesthood around the time I went off to war. Poor eyesight, you know." Sepp stroked his face. "We saw each other over the years, and the last I knew, he was posted in Venice. Why must I see him?"

"Many in the Church also fear Hitler."

"Ergo, the Vatican deal, but why Tucci?" Sepp shrugged. "I still don't understand."

Joscht patted his shoulder. "You were right about Venice. Tucci was lately an important member of the staff of Archbishop Pietro La Fontaine, the Patriarch. He has since moved to Florence to serve there. Well-respected in the archbishop's office, he has contacts who can arrange for your access to the tower. Moreover, he is quite a Galileo aficionado." Seeing Sepp's face full of doubt, he continued, "Plans are rather sketchy at this point. He will explain what you need to do to acquire the necessary documents."

"Why would the Church allow a tribute to a man they consider a heretic for his views regarding the center of the universe?"

"Everyone from the Pope on down knows his findings are correct. The Church has a difficult time admitting it. Maybe this celebration will break the ice a bit."

"Okay, I go to Florence first."

"Correct, and while there, Tucci will help you obtain a copy of the telescope."

"What about the rifle?" Sepp reminded.

"It can be concealed in the scope's carrying case."

"Then on to Venice," Sepp offered. "A few days early, yes?"

"The sooner, the better. By the fourteenth, the police there should regard you as a fixture and have little need to track your comings and goings." Joscht extracted two more photos from another folder. "These are possibly the most important images of all." He handed Sepp two close-up pictures of Adolf Hitler—one a profile and one full face.

"My God!" Sepp exclaimed. "I've seen news films and photos of him, but never anything this clear."

"As a matter of protocol, nothing leaves this room. You must commit anything you find useful here to memory. I recommend you purchase guidebooks, maps, and whatever other common items you might need. Remember, you are a professor out to honor Galileo. In effect, nothing more than a tourist." He swept his hand over the documents and pictures. "Well, there it is, my friend. Can it work?"

"Risky, of course, but a fine rifle makes a wonderful equalizer." Sepp regarded Joscht. "And, if killing becomes impossible, is the Dollfuss abduction plan a viable second choice?"

"It may be. Our goal is to stop Hitler one way or the other. More details will be decided over the coming weeks. For the moment, you will become Professor Alex Höbling, an astronomy expert." Joscht paused, sensing Sepp's skepticism. "Look, I know the fact we seem to be subverting Dollfuss may smack of treason. I assure you it isn't. The chancellor is a realist with a conscience, and we must try to respect that."

"Will I be completely out of touch?" Sepp asked. "What if plans change?"

"For the most part, you are on your own. If the need arises, an agent will contact you."

"How will I know him?"

"He will speak a phrase to which you must respond. If the phrase is not exact, do not trust him. If you do not answer properly, the agent will assume the mission has been compromised. He may even kill you."

Sepp's eyes narrowed. "In German or Italian?"

"Latin, so there will be no mistake. *"Domine non sum dignus ut intres sub tectum meum,"*

"Lord, I am not worthy that you should enter under my roof," Sepp translated.

"Precisely! It is proclaimed during mass at every holy

consecration."

"Then, my response must be, *"Sed tantum dic verbo et sanabitur anima mea*—only say the word, and my soul shall be healed."

"Wait!" cautioned Joscht, "This is crucial. The phrases are to be abbreviated and said in reverse order to preclude a chance response. Your contact will speak only the second part, *'Sed tantum dic verbo,'* and you must respond with the opening portion, *'Domine, non sum dignus.'*"

Sepp put his hand to his temple, "Those words were burned into my brain as an altar boy. I could never forget them."

"I said it would be easy." Joscht smiled. "Now, let's discuss your cover."

"Exactly how do I become an astronomy and Galileo expert in a month?"

"A perceived expert," corrected Joscht. "Starhemberg is arranging for Doctor Kasimir Graff, director of the university observatory, to tutor you personally. He is yet another German who has tasted Nazism and detested the experience."

The seemingly simple plan filtered through Sepp's brain as he pored over the documents, pictures, and maps before him. He concluded that whatever the future held, it would not be easy. He slowly began accepting the reality that the ultimate sacrifice may be required to ensure the success of his mission.

Rome, Italy

The sunny sky above *Palazzo Venezia* suggested leisurely walks in the *Janiculum* gardens or pleasant trips to the lake at *Castel Gandolfo*. None of these were options open to the man sitting behind the desk in the far corner of the vast *Sala del Mappamondo*—the Hall of the Globe. The spacious office lent an air of power and majesty, but for Benito Mussolini, it was a chamber of solitude and remoteness from the outside world. As usual, he was spending the day ensuring that the country was stable, and his fascist ship of state was sailing on an even keel. It had been twelve years since his 1922 march on Rome and takeover, and the challenges of realizing his dream of reborn Roman glory seemed to multiply daily.

The hands of an ornate wall clock were approaching eleven. It had been three hours since *Il Duce* began depleting the waiting rooms outside his office of diplomats, engineers, ministers, architects, lawyers, police officers, generals, priests, industrialists, and artists. They all wanted something. Mussolini strode out onto the balcony from which he regularly made speeches to energize and bring hope to the Italian masses. With his hands on his hips and chin jutting out, he breathed in the aromas of the city as the din from the *Piazza Venezia* rose to fill his ears. Closing his eyes, he imagined he could hear a familiar melody coming from the nearby *Gran Caffé Faraglia*. The place and its music, once a tradition of the art nouveau establishment, had failed due to the security measures put in place by his zealous chief of state police, Arturo Bocchini. As a lover of Faraglia's cuisine and unique ambiance, he regretted that, for the sake of his safety, the café had been forced out of business. He shrugged, concluding, "Such is the price of security. Caesar was a trusting fool."

Il Duce took a final deep breath and returned to his chair, where he idly inventoried the desktop: a bronze inkstand, a clock-barometer, a flowered porcelain container for his pencils. He smiled when his eyes fell upon a framed portrait of Rosa Maltoni Mussolini, his mother, who had died of meningitis in 1905. The grin broadened when he eyed a more recent addition: a small trinket depicting a cottage with the inscription, "A refuge for your heart." The gift, from 22-year old Claretta Petacci, was quickly secreted away whenever his wife Rachele came to his office. Happily for him, such visits were rare, and the alluring signorina was usually close by, keeping herself available.

The table also held three phones, an intercom, and a gold button, which Mussolini was about to press when there were rhythmic raps on the chamber door by the fireplace along a nearby wall. It was not the entrance visitors were allowed to use. He purposely had them walk the twenty meters to his desk so he could evaluate them as they approached.

"Yes, Quinto. Come in," he boomed.

Il Duce's valet, Quinto Navarra, entered carrying a tray holding a delicate cup and saucer and a silver carafe. "Ready for your coffee, sir?"

"Absolutely!" he smiled. "Once again, you anticipate me."

"It is quite hot, Excellency. Please, be careful," said the valet as he placed the tray on the table.

"Always, the same warning," Mussolini said with a grin.

"Is there anything else I can bring you, sir? A roll, perhaps?"

"Nothing to eat, but please ask Osvaldo to join me and have him bring my file of personal letters."

"Yes, sir." The valet left.

The Italian dictator savored a few sips of coffee, stroked his nearly hairless pate, and glanced at his schedule, considering how he might lighten his day and make time for a needed diversion. A moment later, his secretary, Osvaldo Sebastiani, forty-five, round-faced with a pleasing countenance, entered carrying a brown file folder tied with a black ribbon.

"Thank you, Osvaldo." *Il Duce* accepted the package and donned his reading glasses. Undoing the ribbon, he opened the folder arranged in sections by month. "I must refresh my memory of a certain letter."

"Sí, Duce."

As Mussolini pulled a sheaf of papers from the July section, an envelope dropped into his lap. Recognizing the handwriting, he opened it and smiled at the photograph of a stately white horse. It was written in the hand of the man who had made him a present of the animal, Engelbert Dollfuss, then the Director of Austrian Agriculture. He showed the photo to Sebastiani. "*Aprile* was the best gift I had received in many years."

Continuing his search, Mussolini found the document he sought. Under the letterhead of the National Socialist Party of Germany, neatly typed words said it originated in Berlin, Germany, on 12 July 1931. He waved it at Osvaldo. "The epistle of a scoundrel." He worked his way through the original text, relying on the German he learned while a laborer in Switzerland. "Listen to this," he spoke the sycophantic lines aloud as he interpreted.

"Your Excellency was so kind to send me a signed photograph. As you will discover in the enclosed, I have reciprocated in kind. The feeling of agreeability towards the National Socialist movement, manifested by Your Excellency in his dedication, is likewise and for a long time reciprocated by an equal consideration for the Fascism established by Your Excellency. The spiritual relationship which exists between the foundations and principles of Fascism and those of the movement initiated by myself give me great hope that, once National Socialism will have gained its victory in Germany, as I am certain will happen, an alliance will be good for our two great nations. I pay my respect, and I wish all the best to Your Excellency and Fascist Italy that Your Excellency so effectively leads. Please, accept my portrait as an expression of my most earnest admiration and highest reverence for one I so admire. Yours devoutly, Adolf Hitler."

Mussolini stared at the photograph of the unlikely man who had somehow managed to become the German chancellor at the start of 1933. "This is the worst excreta of all excreta!" He continued, "How dare this insignificant little creature compare himself to me? How dare he believe that the slightest harmony could ever exist between us?" He stood and tossed the letter and photo aside. "Five times in his slobber of admiration, he called me Excellency. Five! And each time, the word insulted me deeply." Mussolini raised his fist. "Now that he has acquired the power he coveted for so long, the bastard wants to meet with me. He wants to ruin my reputation in front of the world. He'll try, but I shall never allow it. Never!"

"Of course not, *Duce.*"

"Get me Cerruti in Berlin immediately!" Mussolini ordered.

"*Sí, Duce.*" The aide hurried off.

The Italian leader went to a window attempting to soothe his ire in the breeze moving the sheer curtains. Instead, the more he considered the impertinence of the German pretender, the hotter he became. He would speak frankly to Cerruti, a good man and a worthy representative of Italy. Still, *Il Duce* placed little trust in any diplomat, believing them circumspect and never as direct and to the point as he desired.

He had appointed Vittorio Cerruti ambassador to Berlin in 1932. As Adolf Hitler and his Nazis gained influence, Cerruti understood that the re-emergence of Germany as an industrial and military power could either work for the benefit of Italy or against it. He was encouraged that *Herr* Hitler courted Mussolini like an amorous suitor seeking a meeting, a quest that promised to be fulfilled soon.

Circumstances had changed. Hitler was garnering support for the annexation of Austria, and Mussolini, the man Winston Churchill had referred to as "the Roman genius" in advancing his brand of national socialism, was determined not to permit it. He grumbled to himself, "That impression of Chaplin's Little Tramp is threatening everything. He wants to take Austria and eliminate my friend Dollfuss. What else does the bastard want? Who else does he want to get rid of? Are there no limits? I shall refuse to appease him at every turn." He walked to a stand holding a large globe and spun it to Europe. "Once the Nazis take Austria, we will share a border and are certain to be their next target."

The ringing phone interrupted his grim assessment.

"That will be Ambassador Cerruti, Excellency," said Sebastiani as he entered.

Mussolini grabbed the handset and shouted into it. "Vittorio, you must do something! Listen to me. I want you to tell that half-ape that he must not get too excited—he must moderate his expectations. That I have agreed to meet with him doesn't mean we are equals, and it is certainly no indication he has gained my esteem."

"I'm not sure I can say such a thing, *Duce,*" a hesitant voice replied.

"No, damn it, but God knows how much I wish you could."

"I beg your patience, Excellency. The situation is delicate."

"Delicate my ass. He has hungered for this meeting, and I intend to take advantage of that fact."

"*Duce,* I have met with Doctor Goebbels himself and given him the terms you stated previously. In good faith, we developed a schedule for the visit. You should have received a copy."

"I have read it. Hitler expects to come to our beloved *Italia* and be welcomed with honors."

"Just as any chancellor on such a diplomatic mission, sir."

"Yes, but has the dumb bastard not realized that requesting a meeting location of Venice and not Rome diminishes the entire affair?"

"*Duce*, he feels privileged to be meeting you for the first time. He requested Venice to reduce world attention."

"Vittorio, let me assure you, we will receive him with great pomp: military parades, tours, and elegant lunches and dinners. He'll have it all. However, when we meet privately, I will make my demands for allegiance to Versailles and an independent Austria."

"Yes, Excellency."

"And, I will make it clear that he covets Austria at great risk. Then, my utter humiliation of him will come on the second day when in *Piazza San Marco*. I speak to my people. The schedule shows it as a greeting, but I will make certain Hitler is there to view my address to an adoring crowd. He will be forced to observe my power. I can picture how the worm will squirm with rage and envy when the excited citizens honor me with their cheers and applause."

"I am certain it will be most impressive indeed." Cerruti's words were stiff and cool.

"Then there it is," concluded Mussolini. "Until next time." He hung up the receiver and told Sebastiani, "That will be all for now, Osvaldo." His secretary left, and as Mussolini sat back in his chair calming himself, there was a tapping at the door Sebastiani had exited.

"What now?" he grumbled.

"May I?" asked a soft, seductive voice. The face peering in awakened passions of another sort. With a spring in his step, he went to greet the young woman with a tender hug.

Claretta Petacci was startlingly attractive, with short, curly black hair, dark eyes, and a shapely figure complemented by firm, generous breasts. A throat illness contracted in childhood had left her with a sultry voice.

Utterly charmed by this girl who was twenty-nine years his junior, Mussolini found her as tempting as the most luscious *dolce* he could imagine. Proceeding slowly, he was determined not to make her one of the willing beauties available to him. His Claretta was unique, and despite his growing desire, he had kept their relationship platonic.

He led her to the window overlooking the square and pointed to the sky splattered with cottony clouds. Softly, he spoke of his hopes for her and the promise of a deeper relationship. When the moment passed, he brushed the lips of the girl with his own, and she walked away quietly. The view of her supple body caught in the sunlight kindled in him a flame that would not go out on its own. He grabbed the phone. "Osvaldo, send one of my special guests. Surprise me."

Chapter Three

Monday, 7 May 1934

Rome, Italy

Prince Starhemberg arrived on the afternoon train alone and dressed well below his usual sartorial standard. After a spine-jolting taxi ride, he checked into a second-rate hotel on *via Rasella,* not far from the *Trevi* Fountain. He registered as Klaus Hofner, the name on the official Austrian passport he showed the desk clerk.

Noting he had plenty of time before his appointment, Starhemberg decided to walk rather than risk his life again in a Roman cab. He made his way to *via Barberini* and on to *via del Tritone,* one of the broadest, most stylish streets in the city. It was also one of the busiest, with noisy trams running down its center to and from *Piazza Barberini,* smoke-belching automobiles, carriages, and hordes of sweaty bikers challenging the area's hills. A right on *via dei Due Macelli* led the prince directly to *Piazza di Spagna*, the square at the base of the Spanish Steps. He was still early, but as he had not eaten since breakfast on the train, he headed for Babington's Tea Rooms. Opened some forty years earlier by two British women, it was a meeting place for English-speaking tourists and locals.

Looking down her nose at his attire, a hostess in Victorian dress delivered Starhemberg to a table in a back corner. There, a smiling waitress presented the establishment's bill of fare. "Good afternoon, sir. How may I serve you today?"

"I believe I will have a pot of Earl Grey with scones and cream."

"Earl Grey is one of our most popular teas, although we do have dozens of others," the waitress said.

"I have sampled many, but I always return to this one. I enjoy the flavor of bergamot. Quite apropos here in Italy."

"A moment, please."

As she left, Starhemberg wondered if he hadn't tipped his hand by revealing more of his aristocratic tastes than he should have.

The thought faded when the snooty hostess returned with a note of respect in her voice. "Excuse me, sir, you have been requested elsewhere. If you will, please come this way."

She led him into a windowless room with several tables, all of which were empty except for one. The prince wasn't sure because of the slouch hat and dark glasses, but he assumed that the man at the lone occupied table was Count Galeazzo Ciano, Mussolini's son-in-law, and an old friend.

"Ernst," said the count, "welcome back to *Roma*." As he stood, he doffed the hat. His muscular body was draped comfortably in a tailored tan suit, a white shirt accented by a dark silk tie, and gold cufflinks. A well-to-do, worldly man, he was the son of Admiral Costanzo Ciano, a decorated hero of the war to end all wars.

Ciano claimed to have joined the Fascist Party in 1921 and a year later to have participated with the fascist militias in the infamous march on Rome. In truth, this was a product of *Il Duce's* propaganda mill, made up well after the fact. His actual accomplishments included the practice of journalism for several newspapers, such as *"Nuovo Paese," "Tribuna,"* and *"Impero."* He also had an interest in theater, for which he wrote a few dramas. In 1925, he graduated from university with a law degree, which he set aside when he chose instead to enter politics.

Diplomacy seemed a perfect choice and, despite his youthfulness, he was posted in South America and China. In 1930, after marrying Mussolini's daughter Edda, he and she left for the Italian consulate in Shanghai. When they returned to Italy in 1932, he became Mussolini's confidant and trusted advisor.

Starhemberg, older and of higher social standing than Ciano, was a true Austrian aristocrat; however, the conversation between the men took on the ease and frankness of two allies.

"Galeazzo, how did you know I had arrived?" asked Starhemberg as they both sat. "I came early and didn't expect …"

"My driver was watching for you."

"I see. So, how are you, my friend?" asked the prince.

"Always busy, keeping up with my dynamo father-in-law. It is challenging to be close to such power." The smile on Ciano's face faded. "*Duce* can be quite demanding."

"I understand this well," agreed the prince.

"Your trip here? Not in luxury class, I should guess."

Starhemberg shrugged, "The price of my assumed identity; however, I did break up the trip with a stopover in Florence. It's one of my favorite places to visit."

"Will you return today?" asked Ciano.

"The albergo where I am stopping is accommodating enough, so I plan to stay over."

Ciano shrugged. "I would gladly host you, but things being what they are, I'm afraid you must suffer the indignation of your charade."

"All for a good cause," the prince replied. "Although I must say, on the way here, if it had not been for my attire, I would have investigated the Bulgari salon."

"Bulgari!" Ciano threw up his hands. "My Edda's favorite shop. Her love for it is taking us to the poor house."

"Just the same, it is good we are here together. We have some important things to discuss."

"To be sure, my friend. Would you like something before we begin?"

"I did have an order of tea and scones coming."

"It may never get here. I told them not to disturb us." Ciano put on the dark glasses and went to the door where he called out to have someone bring the gentleman's order and requested the same for himself." He confided as he returned to the table, "I come here whenever I can get away. It seems we Italians are not the only ones who can arrange such a warm and welcoming room." He cupped his hand beside his mouth and leaned forward, "I keep it from *Il Duce* as he has no great love for the English."

"I gathered as much from an interview I read in the Times."

Ciano's face again darkened. "And now he has agreed to meet with Hitler, and this may create a problem for Italy and your country as well."

"Look, Galeazzo, we are of one mind on this. I know Hitler well. I walked beside him and was part of the putsch in '23. At the time, the Nazi tenets made some sense to me. What turned me was their mad obsession with racial purity and their manic hatred of Jews. They blame them for the outcome of the war and every ill imaginable. I don't agree with any of it. This scientific proof they claim about the Aryan master race is so much rubbish. Fascism works, but given that obsession, Nazism is doomed. Based on all I know of him, I have concluded Hitler is quite mad, and we need to do something about him, or Austria will be absorbed, and God knows what will happen to France, Poland, and the rest of Europe."

There was a tap on the door. "Come," Ciano called as he again donned the glasses. The waitress entered with a large tray and served their tea and scones. Placing cozies over the pots, she left. The two men continued their conversation in between bites of food and sips of tea. "Mussolini is for peace," said Ciano. "He has had great success here and is, for the moment, content. Versailles is also uppermost in his mind because it appears Hitler will never honor it."

"Hitler has always thought the surrender came too soon and never agreed with the terms of the treaty," said Starhemberg. "I believe if he takes full power in Germany—we know Hindenburg is dying—there will be war, and Austria will cease to exist."

"Someone must nip it in the bud, as they say."

"We are prepared to do precisely that," assured Starhemberg. "For the good of Austria, and Europe."

"What are you saying? Assassination?"

"Venice presents a perfect opportunity."

"*Duce* would never agree," said Ciano flatly.

"He must not know."

"My father-in-law is dead set against having anything happen to the chancellor of Germany on Italian soil." Ciano drank some tea. "Look, Ernst, concern for your homeland is well placed, but *Il Duce* believes he can sway Hitler away from carrying out annexation. Would it not be better to solve this with diplomacy rather than bullets?" The prince frowned as Ciano continued, "At least we must give it a chance of working."

Starhemberg countered. "Dollfuss wants to kidnap the bastard and keep him isolated until he's in his dotage. A preposterous plan with only the slightest chance of success, and more potential bloodshed than with a nice clean rifle shot."

Ciano sowed the seeds of compromise. "What if the meeting goes as *Il Duce* hopes and he turns the German wolf away from your door? There may be no need for any of this."

"How will we know?"

"I will be right there by their sides much of the time. Believe me, I will be able to judge whether *Duce* is succeeding."

"And, if he fails," Starhemberg pressed, "you must tell us so, no matter the consequence."

"Yes, but I need to be assured that, if the meeting is succeeding, you will cancel the attempt."

"Absolutely, we will end immediately if it proves unnecessary."

As he shook Starhemberg's hand, sealing their agreement, the count added, "Oh, and there is one more thing to recognize."

"What's that?" asked the prince as their clasp broke.

"If there is an assassination, Mussolini will want an instant resolution. Your marksman will be killed."

"That would be a most bitter pill to swallow, Galeazzo. The man is something of a hero. He saved Dollfuss during the war."

"This too is war, and it may have such consequences," Ciano reminded.

Starhemberg said reluctantly, "He must not be identified as an Austrian."

"Of course not," Ciano agreed. "Maybe a Marxist Slav."

"Okay then," Starhemberg consented and drank the last of his tea.

"I must say, Ernst, I have always known of your cunning, but today you impress me as a master. I'm happy to be your friend and not your enemy."

"My dear count, at the same time, you revealed yourself as a most tactful and effective diplomat." He looked down at his empty cup. "Maybe a spot more of tea," he said as he removed the cozy and poured.

Ciano went for his pot. "I believe I will join you."

Chapter Four

Sunday, 13 May 1934

Rome, Italy

Villa Torlonia, a magnificent estate on *via Nomentana*, had been leased in 1925 for a single lira per year to Benito Mussolini as his family home. It was a few kilometers from the official residence of *Palazzo Venezia*, but for *Il Duce*, the two locations would remain worlds apart. Unlike the dynamic urban center of fascist power that was the *palazzo*, the villa was a place of serenity, surrounded by a landscape replete with varieties of trees, flowering gardens, fountains, faux temples, and Egyptian-style obelisks. It presented a scene of aristocratic family life with diversions such as a tennis court, a stable, and a riding course. Long pathways wound through beautiful gardens, and there were indoor facilities for fencing and exercising, musical performances, movie watching, and receiving and entertaining visitors.

The villa was for Rachele, their three sons, and one of their two daughters. However, unlike the *Palazzo Venezia*, it presented few opportunities for *Il Duce's* affairs. While regular visits by his paramours were impossible, the self-proclaimed lothario did enjoy the occasional tryst away from *Casino Nobile*, the primary residence. A favorite hideaway was the *Casina delle Civette*—the House of Owls. Another was the less-private orangery, with its wall of glass that heightened the risk and excitement of his sexual adventures. Mussolini would also find targets of opportunity among the adoring women who had passed the rigors of security to observe demonstrations of his equestrian skills or the power of his tennis forehand.

While in residence, *Il Duce* kept to a full schedule of diversions aimed at fighting off the ennui attending his time there. This day began with a shave and hair trim administered by Giuseppe Sciarretta, one of his presidential guards who had been a barber in his youth.

As he sat being fussed over in a tall, cherry wood chair, Mussolini looked out the large open window and took in the view. Among the trees and gardens, he spotted several of his guards stationed along the outer paths. Off to one side, his son Romano was having a Sunday tennis lesson with the young master Dogi Cavallotti. Watching with a father's loving eyes, Mussolini wondered about the boy's future. In his heart lived the hope that the lad would one day become a capable and inspiring fascist.

When Sciarretta had finished, he held up a mirror for his boss to check his work. Mussolini rotated his head back and forth, and seeing all traces of his stubborn whiskers gone, smiled and nodded a sign of dismissal. Once the cloth had been removed from around his neck, he went into the bathroom and washed his face with almond Viset soap.

Ten minutes later, the Italian leader descended the central stairway wearing boots, jodhpurs, and a white, sleeveless shirt emphasizing his barrel chest and muscular arms.

"Good morning, Excellency," greeted Sebastiani.

"What have you for me today?"

"*Signor* Bocchini awaits you in the study."

"Already?"

"He arrived early and seemed impatient to speak with you."

"He must wait a while longer. This morning I ride *Aprile*." Mussolini strode to the door, but before exiting, he turned back.

"And, Osvaldo."

"Yes, Excellency?"

"Tonight, I'd like to watch Charlie Chaplin's 'City Lights.'"

"But sir, you have seen it twice in the past month!"

"And tonight will be the third time! Have Quinto set it up and notify my family; although, I doubt they will come. It seems I am the only real fan of the Little Tramp."

"As you wish, Excellency," Sebastiani hesitated. "Sir, there is another movie I believe you might prefer first."

"Another?" replied *Il Duce*, eyebrows raised at his secretary's seeming impertinence.

"Produced by your son Vittorio."

"He has made a movie?"

"Yes, sir, with the camera you gave him. He wrote it himself, and it includes his classmates and even some of your guards."

"So, my agents have been distracted making this movie?"

"Off duty, sir."

"And, what is the title of my son's epic?"

"The Terrible Sheriff."

"Do you know the plot?"

"An American-style western."

"I believe the title tells me that," he chuckled.

Undaunted, Sebastiani continued, "Vittorio says he wants it to be a surprise, but I thought I would mention it since you have other plans."

"Is it long?"

"I do not believe so, sir."

"Well, then, it is decided." Mussolini folded his arms before him. "We shall see the film of my son Vittorio. Later, Quinto may project Chaplin's."

"As you wish, sir."

Mussolini exited through the tall, windowed doors on the villa's east side and walked apace to the stables where a groom awaited holding the reins of the white horse given him by Dollfuss.

"Salvatore, she looks quite fine this morning," the Italian leader said as he mounted up. Once he adjusted himself in the saddle, he rode off, at first in a trot, then breaking into a gallop. He circled the riding track once and headed for the jumps, where he demonstrated impressive equestrian proficiency.

Meanwhile, in a private study, Arturo Bocchini gazed out a window as he awaited the man who had made him one of the most respected and influential men in Italy. Since 1926, Bocchini had headed both the *Polizia di Stato*, the general police force, and the more covert OVRA, the Organization for Vigilance and Repression of Anti-Fascism. Many considered him second only to Mussolini himself, having proven his worth to fascism by bringing down nonconforming deputies and dissidents, including one of the founders of the Italian Communist Party. He also went after crimes by wayward party members, stopping them before they had a chance to undermine the fascist movement. For his work, Mussolini deeply trusted this provincial man with peasant roots like his own.

Now, at fifty-four, he fought to maintain his patience as he fidgeted with the dark suit he wore and adjusted and readjusted the white handkerchief flowing from the breast pocket. A small voice from behind gave him a start.

"My father is out riding. He is excellent at it, right, Mr. Arturo?" said the young lad standing at the door of the study, holding a tennis racket and smiling.

"Well, hello Romano," Bocchini greeted the six-year-old. "How was your tennis lesson?"

"I don't know, Mr. Arturo."

"Oh, why is this?"

"I think I am not good at sports." The boy frowned. "Not like my brothers. They are the athletes."

"And you?"

"I make music."

"Music is fine also. Piano, isn't it?"

"Yes," Romano replied as he made a gesture of playing.

"Really? And what pieces do you prefer? Verdi? Rossini?"

"Oh, no, sir. I like hot jazz."

"You mean that foolish American clatter?"

"Jazz is not foolish, Mr. Bocchini. Not at all. Why would you say that? Why?" Upset, the little visitor disappeared from the doorway.

Bocchini shook his head and took a seat. Retrieving a silver case from his pocket, he selected a *Sovrana* cigarette and lit up. Time ground by as he repeated the process twice again until he decided he needed to act. Determined, he went to the horse track where he watched Mussolini make one last round of jumps before heading for the stable. Bocchini was having another cigarette when his boss emerged and came his way.

"Arturo, tell me about the arrangements for Venice." *Il Duce* demanded as he approached.

"Good morning, Excellency," Bocchini said, not mentioning his boss's tardiness. "I assure you, we are preparing the highest security possible. Unprecedented!"

Mussolini's face darkened. "Arturo, do you know why for me the number seven has never been good?"

"Seven, *Duce*? I have no idea. I always considered it lucky, as the seven virtues of man."

"The claptrap of Christianity," the fascist leader grumbled. "I remind you there are also seven deadly sins. It worries me because, so far, there have been six attempts on my life. Do you recall?" He proceeded to list them. "In 1925, there was the deputy Tito Zaniboni; in 1926, we had the crazy Irishwoman Violet Gibson, the anarchist Gino Lucetti, and the young Anteo Zamboni. And then two other anarchists in 1931 and 1932: the Sardinian Michele Schirru and the other fool who emigrated to Belgium, Angelo Sbardellotto. Have I not remembered them accurately?"

"Your memory is perfect, *Duce*," said Bocchini. "But if I may say, only the last two occurred since I took over in 1926. And, both Schirru and Sbardellotto were apprehended almost immediately."

"You were effective. This time you have to be perfect because there will be two targets. One assassin could kill the German monkey and me."

"Sir, I believe Hitler will have his own protection."

"Who knows how effective it will be. They are new to this game. I rely on you to protect us both, and I absolutely do not want a chancellor harmed while visiting Italy." Mussolini's stern gaze brightened into a smirk. "Although it is a tempting idea. It could solve all my concerns—for the Versailles Treaty, for the French, and for Austria and my little friend Dollfuss. However, world opinion would turn against fascism, and that we cannot have. Hitler must return to Berlin in perfect health. I will convince the German bastard using the strength of my persuasion and not the threat of a weapon. Do we understand each other?"

"Do not be concerned. Every moment of the Venice meeting will have my greatest attention."

"I expect you to eliminate any possible threat beforehand." With a dismissive wave, Mussolini signaled the meeting was over and, as Bocchini started down a path to his car, *Il Duce* added, "Arturo."

“Yes, sir?”

“I am happy to see you have come outdoors to have your cigarette. Rachele hates the smell of smoke in the house. I can stand it, but not she. Good day.”

Mussolini turned and walked in the direction of a group of spectators at the track railing.

Bay of Naples, Italy

The S.S. Roma, arriving after a five-day voyage from New York, had its main promenade, lido, and forward decks awash with animated, chatty passengers. Among the sightseers was Martha Markham, a red-haired beauty in her mid-thirties. Made a young widow when her husband, Ronald, committed suicide after the 1929 stock market crash, she was left to face the future with her two children. One of them, her five-year-old daughter Melissa, stood by her side—a doll with strawberry blonde hair and Delft-blue eyes. The child grasped the strap of a box camera as she steadied it on the deck railing. She checked the image in the viewfinder and slowly pressed the shutter lever. It clicked, and she looked up at her mother with great delight. “There! I’ve made a picture of that big mountain.”

“So you have, Lissa. It is a volcano called Vesuvius,” Martha told her.

“A volcano?” the girl’s eyes grew large. “Will it interrupt on us?”

“Oh, I doubt it. It always seems to want to e-rupt,” she pronounced the word slowly for her daughter’s benefit, “but it seldom does so any more.” Martha stroked Lissa’s hair and squatted before her. “Besides, we won’t be here for long.” She looked the girl in the eyes. “You know I will always keep you and Brian safe.” Her reassurance included her son, who was five years older than Melissa and attending a New England military school.

Melissa’s lower lip quivered, and she gazed down at the deck. “I know that, Momma. It’s just that there should be two of you.”

Martha hugged her. “I understand, sweetheart.” They said nothing for a long moment before the child returned to her camera. Martha opened a leather carrying case at her feet. “Now, I will see if I can also capture something.” She proceeded to pull out a Kodak Retina

117 camera that had been a surprise gift from her parents during the bon voyage party at the family home at Georgetown, Connecticut. She already had an array of professional cameras befitting her career as a freelance photographer; however, her father, Congressman Andrew Hughes, had assured her this one was special. It was light and portable, but what made the camera unique was its use of sealed film cartridges. The innovation eliminated the need to load and unload film in a dark room or under a cover. The gift had included two dozen thirty-six shot rolls of Kodak 135 film.

She opened the Retina's front panel, extended the bellows, and was about to take several shots when she spotted Aldo Donelli heading her way. The swarthy young man with an athletic gait was a member of the U.S. soccer team she had met during the passage. Known to all as "Buff," he looked quite natty in his blue blazer, striped tie, and light trousers.

"Good afternoon, Mrs. Markham," he said with an easy smile.

"Mr. Donelli." She nodded and surveyed him briefly. "You ready to attack the next leg of your trip?"

"Absolutely. And, please, make it 'Buff.'"

Melissa chimed in, "Hello, Mr. Buff. You do look different than when we see you exercise and run around the ship."

He went down on one knee and kissed the little girl's cheek. "Today is special, Lissa. We leave the boat and go to Rome by train for the games."

"I hope you win. I shall pray for it," said the tyke.

"We'll do our best." He patted the child's head and stood. He flushed a bit as he eyed Martha's camera. "Mrs. Markham, I have come to ask a favor of you."

"What's that, Buff?"

"We were wondering if you would take some pictures of our group." Again, he eyed the Retina. "We have cameras. Well, some of the guys do." He smiled his way through a pause. "None as nice as yours."

"It would be an honor." She thought for a moment. "As a matter of fact, I can even give you the roll of film so you can have it developed."

His brows shot up, "You can do that?"

"Come, let's join the others and I'll show you." She picked up the carrying case, took Melissa's hand, and started off to join the team members a few dozen paces away.

Walking alongside her, Donelli gushed, "Gosh, you have been really swell about this. I hope we'll get to see you again. Maybe on the train or in Rome."

"Lissa and I are staying aboard for Genoa. It's closer to our destination of Florence."

"*Firenze*," he said. "I've read how beautiful it is." His face glowed with the smitten look of a student for an adored teacher. "Maybe we will see you there if we win and get into the quarter-finals."

"That would be wonderful," she said brightly before realizing she might be encouraging the young man. "Winning, I mean."

When the photo session was over, she and Melissa bid the team good luck and Godspeed. Martha couldn't help smiling over the puppy dog look in Donelli's eyes as they parted.

Chapter Five

Wednesday, 16 May 1934

Berlin, Germany

The *Schöneberg* district, famous for its cabarets, avant-garde theaters, and trendy bars, was once frequented by free-thinkers, artists, and intellectuals. With the assumption of power by the Nazis, clubs like the famous Eldorado, where Marlene Dietrich had entertained, came under the heavy hand of Nazi Minister of Propaganda, Joseph Goebbels, and his so-called "alignment of culture." Hitler's regime began controlling artistic production and purging cultural organizations of Jews and those who were deemed politically or artistically suspect. The works of authors such as Bertolt Brecht, Lion Feuchtwanger, and Alfred Kerr were considered dangerous and unceremoniously burned. At the same time, the Nazis exploited the propaganda value of art celebrating their Aryan heritage, of which, according to them, real Germans were the purest expression and, therefore, entitled to guide the destinies of all peoples.

Consequently, theater companies were forced to stage the works of German authors such as Goethe and Schiller, as well as new dramas extolling the virtues of National Socialism.

One such company, performing at the Luitpold Theater located on a small side street close to *Winterfeldtplatz*, was headed by forty-six-year-old Wilfred Metzger. His current production, which he had written and staged himself, depicted the plight of the Aryan family of Peter Wald, a merchant whose life was destroyed by the greedy demands of an evil Jewish loan shark.

Despite the play's perfect "alignment" with the style of the work proposed by the Nazi leaders, ticket sales were dismal. As one partisan review had stated, the Berlin public was neither impressed by nor drawn to the piece. Most of the meager audiences consisted of party faithful, sympathizers, and members of Hitler's *Schutzstaffel*—the dreaded *SS*—none of whom ever paid admission.

As Metzger played the final scene of the ponderous drama with his wife, Sabine, he could not help but notice how, while she held him to her bosom, she stared longingly at the blond SS officer sitting in the front row. Being almost twenty years her senior, he had expected bouts with jealousy, but he would be damned if he allowed himself to be made a fool.

His wife's dalliances dominated Metzger's thoughts as he sat before a mirror removing his stage makeup. When the door latch clicked, he smiled, expecting Sabine. Instead, a tall, round man with a long cigar in his mouth entered scowling. Simon Neumann disliked everything about the theater he had inherited from his father—everything but the income it produced and his regular assignations with the young actresses and chorus girls.

"Where is my money?" Neumann demanded. "You are long overdue!"

"Please, Simon, I need more time. You'll see. People will start to come. Spread the news of this beautiful drama, and they will come."

"The news has already spread, Wilfred. The whole town now speaks of you."

"Really?" Hope lit up Metzger's face.

"Would you like me to read what they wrote last Saturday in *Der Stürmer*?" Neumann grumbled.

"Yes, yes, I do," replied Metzger with wide-eyed expectation.

"The two best things about the new drama of Wilfred Metzger playing at the Luitpold Theater are …" Neumann tossed the paper at Metzger. "Shit, you can read it. The only two things they liked were your wife's tits and legs."

"They said that?"

"In so many words," Neumann said with a smirk. "That's really four things, isn't it? But you get the idea. Your drama is unspeakable dross! Pay your bill and close the show, or I'll close it for you. A month's rent by tomorrow." He left, slamming the door behind him.

"Fucking Jews!" Metzger said in a low voice as he wiped the

remaining residue from his face and went to the backstage area. It was deserted except for the gray-haired wardrobe mistress sitting by the exit.

"Emma, have you seen Sabine?" he asked.

The old lady's eyes darted everywhere except at him as she answered, "She left, *Herr* Metzger."

"Tell me."

She paused and swallowed. "Your wife came out of her room with an SS major. He was carrying her bag." The old woman pulled an envelope from her apron. "She asked me to give you this."

He already knew the contents. She had left him.

Back in his dismal apartment, Metzger poured a bit of milk for his cat and a glassful for himself. As he sat pondering his future, there was a knock on the door.

"Go away," he called out, determined to avoid any visitor, especially that Shylock Neumann.

"*Herr* Metzger, please let me in," said an unfamiliar male voice.

"I do not want to see anyone."

"This is a police matter."

He opened the door on a tall man wearing a light brown raincoat over a gray suit.

"Is this about my wife?"

The man shook his head. "Allow me to introduce myself. I am Hans Seeler, captain of police."

"What do you want with me?"

Seeler put his hand on Metzger's shoulder. "You must come."

"Where?"

"I can't say, sir. Please hurry. Someone important awaits you."

Metzger backed away. "But who?"

"I'm sorry, I can't tell you that either."

A ten-minute ride in the back of a speeding Mercedes ended at a nondescript building with no identifying plate on the door and no number.

Seeler got out of the car and rang the bell. Immediately, the lock clicked, and he held the door open for Metzger. "This way," he said firmly.

Up two flights of stairs, they arrived at a bourgeois-style apartment with oak parquet flooring, large, oriental rugs, gold-framed paintings, and a mirror in the otherwise drab foyer. Proceeding down the hallway, they came to a dimly lit room where a man sat in the shadows behind a desk.

"Sir, *Herr* Metzger," announced Seeler.

"Well done, Captain," came a voice from the dark. "You may go. I will ring when our guest is ready to leave."

As Seeler went to the door, the voice asked, "Do you know who I am, Mr. Metzger?" A figure moved into the light.

The actor instantly recognized his host's almost cherubic face with its small, insufficient mustache over a pouting mouth, and round, frameless nose glasses. Before him stood one of the most feared men in the Nazi hierarchy, Heinrich Himmler."

Immediately, Metzger rendered a stiff Nazi salute. "Herr *Reichsführer!* Excellency, it was a great honor to have you attend the premiere of my drama and visit us backstage."

"I was about to pour a little cognac," said Himmler, going to a side table with decanters and glasses. "Will you join me?"

"Thank you, sir, but I never take spirits," the actor replied nervously.

"I see," Himmler smirked and held up a crystal decanter, "Mineral water, perhaps? I don't care to drink alone."

"I would love some. Thank you."

Himmler returned to the desk with the drinks, and as they raised their glasses, Metzger said, "To the *Führer*."

"To the *Führer,*" Himmler repeated the toast usually reserved for Nazi gatherings before taking a swallow of the mellow amber liquid. "So, Wilfred, if I may … "

Metzger nodded at Himmler's familiarity.

"You are a member of the party, yes?"

"Yes, sir. For four years."

"Do you not wear the emblem?" Himmler pointed to the swastika pin he had on his tie below the knot.

"I can't, you see." Metzger's tone grew more insistent as he added, "There are so many God-damned Jews. They control all aspects of theater, and they would never work for me or with me if they knew." He added sheepishly, "I deeply apologize, Herr *Reichsführer*."

"Relax." Himmler held up his hand, "Doctor Goebbels is in a similar situation. His propaganda movies would be impossible without their Jew directors. We have allowed the bastards to permeate every aspect of our lives." He took another swallow of the cognac and continued. "And, this brings me to the reason you are here."

Metzger nervously drank some of the water.

"Has anyone ever told you that you bear a striking resemblance to the *Führer*?" Himmler asked.

"Some honor me so, but I don't see it," answered Metzger, careful not to reveal that the recognition came most often when he mimicked Chaplin's tramp.

Himmler leaned forward and locked onto his eyes. "I know you are in financial difficulty with the play." He raised both hands off the desk, adding matter-of-factly, "And, I am also aware of your marital situation. It is most difficult to keep a young wife."

Metzger lowered his head glumly. "Impossible. It is impossible, sir. This evening, she left me." He strained to again hold his tongue and not say that Sabine had run off with one of Himmler's officers.

The *Reichsführer,* who had arranged for the SS officer to lure Metzger's wife away, offered, "I have wonderful news. I am about to present you with a life-changing opportunity."

Chapter Six

Friday, 18 May 1934

Vienna, Austria

Shortly after the meeting with Colonel Joscht, Sepp began a daily ritual that took him to the observatory at the University of Vienna. His goal was to become confident enough with the subjects of astronomy and Galileo to carry off a convincing cover as a professor.

Each morning, for almost two weeks, he made the seven-kilometer trip from his apartment by bicycle or on foot. Today, at Graff's request, he left his house after dark and chose to use the *stadtbahn*, the municipal railway line. At *Stadtpark,* he caught a train that took him close to the observatory. As he approached the domed structure for his final tutorial, Sepp realized he would miss the man who had been such a gracious mentor.

Born in Germany, and no lover of Nazism, Professor Kasimir Graff came from the University of Hamburg in 1928 to assume the directorship in Vienna. He shared much of his encyclopedic knowledge of astronomy with Sepp, altering his daily routine with little apparent effect on his investigation of the cosmos. Typically, after their sessions, Graff would return to his passion of annotating planetary maps and recording stellar radiation.

This evening would be different because the professor had told Sepp they would be using the powerful telescope together. Sepp's pace increased in anticipation, and as he entered the building, he was met by Graff, a distinguished-looking man with short-cropped hair and a neat mustache.

"Good evening, Captain. I considered you might arrive early."

Sepp smiled, surprised that the astronomer had left his sanctuary to greet him. "Good evening, Professor."

"Well," Graff's eyes danced as he continued, "I do have something quite special for you tonight since this is your graduation, as it were." He led the way to the main room where the primary scope was housed.

On the way, Sepp commented, "Professor, in my line of work, I usually don't care for surprises, but this is one I should look forward to very much."

"I promise not to disappoint, Sepp." Graff's mustache curled up at the edges in a smile. "All the studying of charts, theory, and the contributions of men like Galileo now comes to this. You see, if conditions are right, we may observe the giant red spot of Jupiter, the intensity of the star Vega, and explore our fellow voyager, the moon." He opened a door and led Sepp in. "Unfortunately, due to the planetary positions, we will not be able to view the rings of Saturn or the canals of Mars as I would have wished, but let us save them for another time."

Sepp watched the shutter of the dome slide open on a blanket of stars.

Graff accessed the clockwork mechanism in the telescope's base and explained, "This will keep us aligned." Checking the view, he made an adjustment before inviting his student to have a look.

In the eyepiece, Sepp saw a powerfully bright, pulsating light.

"That is Vega, one of the most intense objects in the night sky. It is in the constellation Lyra," Graff explained.

Sepp came away from the eyepiece. "Professor, it is quite interesting to me that astronomers use the constellations, mixing astronomy with the unscientific art of astrology?"

"In a way, this is correct. However, the symbols, established centuries ago, are an effective way of keeping track. We use them as maps, for convenience only."

"I see. So, you look for Libra, and there you find Vega."

"Lyra," corrected Graff.

Sepp grimaced. "Is there a trick to remember which is which?"

"Lyra is a harp, so think of bright music, and it will stand for Vega, the bright star. Libra has no star so intense. It is a scale of equilibrium."

"Aha!" Sepp nodded. "I am sorry, professor, but for me, the stars are all simply lights in the sky. We really can't see detail."

Graff put his hand on Sepp's shoulder, "They hold vast amounts of information not visible to our eyes, but perhaps we had better move on to something more definite."

With that, the professor repositioned the telescope to a lower, southerly point and re-focused the eyepiece. "We should be able to see the red spot and the moons of Jupiter. Galileo himself discovered four," Graff said then added wistfully, "We owe him much."

For more than two hours, the men took turns at the scope's eyepiece. Graff would zero in on what he wanted to show Sepp, then surrender the view to his student. When the session ended, they parted as friends, with Graff sending best wishes to Prince Starhemberg, and Sepp promising he would one day return to learn more. Before Sepp left, Graff assured him that he would protect his cover should a question ever arise.

On his way back to *Währingerstrasse* station, the stars and planets he had been observing seemed to follow him. He stood on the platform considering walking all the way home when a train arrived. From a window seat, he watched idly as the shadowy scenery drifted by. They stopped every few minutes at stations along the way: *Nussdorferstrasse, Friedensbrücke, Rossauerlände, Schottenring.* As they pulled into *Schwedenplatz,* short of his final destination, Sepp could take no more. He dashed out of the car, and as he walked along a path by the *Donnaukanal*, once a branch of the Danube that flowed into the city, something caught his eye. There was an unusual amount of activity along a stretch of brightly lit shoreline among rows of moored merchant boats and stacks of wooden containers.

Approaching the site, Sepp saw what he recognized as a movie camera mounted on a wooden tripod. The cameraman was filming a couple at the edge of the canal. An attractive, sandy-haired man in a neatly tailored suit was doing all he could to control an agitated woman of the night. She shrieked in his face, and he grabbed her by the waist and tossed her into the water like a bundle of twigs. Flailing wildly, she fought to keep the current from carrying her away.

Meanwhile, the assailant watched hands on hips and making

no effort to rescue her. A silver-haired man Sepp surmised was the director shouted into his megaphone, "Keep rolling! This will make the movie a hit."

The cameraman obeyed the order, and Sepp could see the woman was losing her battle with the current. She had stopped struggling and was no longer moving her arms or legs.

With the lifeless body being carried downstream, Sepp raced to the shore, tore off his jacket, stepped out of his shoes, and dove into the water. With a succession of powerful strokes, he caught up with the drowning woman and desperately fought the current as he grabbed her. He never heard the staccato shouts of "cut, cut, cut" coming from the shore.

Instantly, the woman revived and shrieked, "Stop, you dumb ass! Let go of me!"

"I will save you!" Sepp tried pulling her to him, but she wriggled out of his grasp and swam easily to the shore where there awaited a host of cast and crew. A second man with a megaphone bellowed, *"Bastardo stupido!"*

Sepp swam to the shore and was lifted from the canal by a massive brute who set him down in front of the angry shouter.

"What the hell did you think you were doing?" ranted the man.

Wiping his face and shaking water from his hair, Sepp explained, "I thought I was saving a drowning woman."

"Look, mister genius," he grumbled, throwing down the megaphone. "Did you not realize we are filming a movie here?"

"I did," Sepp ran his hands down his trouser legs, squeezing out small cascades of water. "But the man in charge!" He pointed to the first megaphone man. "Him, the director, was doing nothing for her and letting her drown."

"Precisely!" exclaimed the stout man. "He was playing the role of an evil man, for this movie, *'Il male è come il male fa.'*

"Evil is as evil does," Sepp translated as the tirade continued.

"He is not the director, I am. He is an actor doing and saying what he is told to do and say." He grabbed Sepp's arm, spun him away from the canal, and pointed back beyond the bright lights. "Look, there. What do you see?"

Sepp squinted into the glare. "Another camera," he said in a low voice.

The big man who had pulled him from the water stepped forward. "My camera with real film in it, which is now worthless."

"Bruno here is the actual camera operator," the director added, "filming the wonderful scene you destroyed."

"I saw her drowning, and no one was doing anything for her."

The director scowled. "So, you had this urge to play the hero, and your meddling has cost me money and time."

"Wait, Marcello." The actress Sepp had rescued approached wearing a dressing gown and her hair wrapped in a towel. She curled her arm around Sepp's waist and squeezed familiarly. "He is a hero of sorts."

"Some hero!" the director grumbled

"Why not use the scene with him in it?" she suggested, running her hand down Sepp's thigh. "He saves me, and we have a romance."

"Hold on!" Sepp pulled out of her grasp. "I don't want to be in this or any movie." Considering what it might do to his upcoming mission, he added, "I am a member of the Austrian state police. It is not possible."

"Ornella Masi," said the actress. "Maybe you have seen my films."

Sepp's brow furrowed. "I can't say that I have, Miss Masi, but I'm certain they are wonderful. Clearly, I find your acting quite convincing."

"And, this," she indicated the director, "this is *Signor* Marcello Martone, our glorious leader."

Sepp slicked his wet hair back. "I apologize for ruining your filming, *Signor* Martone. I am Captain Sepp Karper, and I wish there were some way I could make this right."

"Captain," the actress repeated as she reattached herself to Sepp. "I love military men. So gallant."

The director stepped in. "Captain Karper, do not worry. It often takes many tries to make a good scene." Martone screwed up his mouth thoughtfully. "However, in this case, I am on a most limited schedule." What he said next sent a shiver up Sepp's spine. "You see, I have an important assignment in Venice in a matter of a few weeks. A historic meeting." He beat his chest. "Me, a common Jew. They asked me to film it. A command performance, one might say."

The actress fawned, "Oh, but they had no choice. Are you not the finest in all of Italy?"

"I am." Martone pulled up from a slouch. "And, I know a winning scene when I see one. Maybe we can use it with an actor with the captain's looks and stature to complete the role." Martone considered his own words for a moment. "Yes, that is precisely what we shall do!" He turned to Sepp. "You will need to sign an agreement, but I assure you, no one will know it is you who played the hero."

Sepp shrugged. "Okay, but you understand this must be a guarantee."

"Of course," the director assured him. "We will use nothing closer than several yards. Your face will be indistinct. We do it all the time with stunt people."

"It is a shame," the actress added, "we will not have any scene of intimacy together. Maybe …"

Sepp's mind filled with concern for what this unexpected Venice connection might mean. "Well, *Signor* Martone, I am glad the damage I caused can be fixed, but now, I must go." He looked down at the arm clinger. "It was a pleasure meeting you, *Signorina* Masi. I will make a point of seeing a movie of yours soon."

"You have me here now." As she said it, the robe opened slightly, revealing the evenly tanned skin of her breasts. "And, you can't leave like that. You are all wet." She snuggled him. "I would give you my robe, but you see," she whispered, "I have nothing on under it." Her eyes were hungry as she smiled up at him.

"I'm fine," he assured her as he wriggled out of her grasp.

She pulled the towel from her head. "Let me at least dry you with this." She proceeded to wipe his hair and face, and Sepp detected the scent of vanilla, citrus, and the odor of canal water.

She worked her way down his chest. He wriggled away and stepped out of reach as she reached his waist. "I must be going."

With that, the amorous vixen settled for a peck on the cheek, and after shaking Martone's hand and retrieving his jacket and shoes, Sepp was off with the stars and moon once again in pursuit.

Chapter Seven

Thursday, 24 May 1934

Rome, Italy

Count Ciano paced back and forth before Mussolini's desk then stopped at its center and addressed his father-in-law. "You must go, *Duce*."

"I see no value in attending this qualification round for losers."

"Excellency, it is a unique opportunity to informally chat with the American ambassador and find out more about the point of view of Roosevelt concerning the situation in Europe. Above all, we do not know how the American president regards Hitler."

"Everyone knows the monkey will be a problem."

Ciano folded his arms, mimicking a classic Mussolini pose. "Not everyone, *Duce*. You see it clearly, but does Roosevelt? He is a potential benefactor against the Germans. What would happen if he were to become their ally?"

"All right, you win!" Mussolini relented, regretting he would have to forego a pleasant afternoon with his Claretta. "Notify ambassador Long. I will be happy to join him at the stadium."

An official state car escorted by four motorcycles pulled up at the entrance of the *Palazzo Venezia*. The vehicle, driven by *Il Duce's* personal chauffeur Ercole Boratto also carried Achille Starace, the suave, heavy-browed Secretary of the National Fascist Party. As the Italian head of state arrived, he greeted three of the riders by name.

Entering the vehicle, he asked the driver, "Boratto, where is Effernelli today? Is he not well?"

"Excellency, his wife has given birth, and he took time to be with her," replied the driver.

"Aha! That day has finally arrived," Mussolini said, smiling.

"A strong boy, I hope. Italy needs such men to secure a healthy and powerful future."

"A girl, sir. I'm sorry," muttered Boratto, shyly.

Mussolini made a face, shrugged, and turned to Starace as the motorcade set out. "Are they any good, these Americans?"

"Against the Mexicans, maybe. Otherwise, no threat, *Duce*. I went to see their practice at *Campo Testaccio*, the field the *Roma* team has made available to them."

"And?" The Italian leader motioned for more information.

"Their coach, Mr. Gould, has some crazy ideas. For one, rather than practicing football, or soccer as they call it, he had them playing baseball."

"Baseball? This Gould sounds odd, but if his method works, expect other teams to begin training the same way. We live in a world of imitators."

"The American sport is not like football, *Duce*. It requires different techniques." He shrugged, "Maybe they will learn from the players loaned by the *Roma* team."

"We loaned them players?"

"You see," Starace explained, "when the Americans arrived, they were short three players—only nineteen, and to make two full teams, they need twenty-two. And *Roma* was so kind."

With raised eyebrows, Mussolini asked, "Which players?"

"Stagni, Pasolini and Fulvio Bernardini."

"This Bernardini. Isn't he Roma's most reliable player?"

"That's him," Starace agreed.

"The Americans already have players of Italian descent."

"Yes, several." Starace consulted a note taken from his inner breast pocket. "Joe Marinelli, with grandparents in Viareggio, Tommy Florie, with parents of Padula, near Salerno and finally Aldo Donelli, the one they call 'Buff,' his family comes from Lucca."

"Buff?" repeated Mussolini, intrigued. "He sounds like a tough guy. I like tough guys. I will be interested to see this Buff."

As the car arrived at the National Fascist Party Stadium, Mussolini instructed Starace, "Achille, if Ambassador Long mentions world affairs in any context, please keep silent. I do not want to discuss fascism and diplomacy today."

"As you wish," was Starace's clipped reply.

Nearing the entrance, they could hear the muted roar of a crowd of over 10,000; quite a large turnout for an early elimination round, but word of the Italian leader's appearance had contributed to the game's popularity. As Mussolini came into the stadium, all present stood cheering and shouting. When he acknowledged their greeting with a straight-arm fascist salute, they began chanting, *"Viva Il Duce! Viva Il Duce."*

Mussolini walked briskly to the stands where United States Ambassador Breckinridge Long awaited him. The distinguished-looking fifty-three-year-old diplomat with a benevolent attitude toward fascism and Mussolini was pleased to see the head of the Italian government. Since he had taken office less than a year earlier, Long had made confident reports back to the Secretary of State and the President about the situation in Italy, to which Roosevelt usually reacted positively.

For his part, Mussolini had observed with great curiosity the workings of the Roosevelt administration and had written articles about it. Referring to FDR's book "Looking Forward," he wrote, "Many have wondered in America and Europe whether fascism is a part of the doctrine and practice of the American President."

The undercurrent of the talk with Long was Hitler's rise to power and its effect on continental Europe, the British Empire, and the United States. Mussolini made it clear that he considered America a potential ally.

True to his word, Starace concentrated on the game and did not insert himself into the conversation. He simply watched the match, which had the United States up by one point over Mexico at the end of the first half thanks to the two goals by Buff Donelli.

Mussolini congratulated the ambassador on the U.S. team's early success before moving the conversation to a more personal level. "How's your president? Is he well?"

"Very much so, Excellency. He is a most dynamic and motivated man who accomplishes what he sets out to do, despite his physical short …" Long caught himself.

"Do not worry, Ambassador. I am aware of the problem with his legs. He does well to conceal it in public. We all hide our shortcomings before the people." *Il Duce* swerved back into the subject of Hitler when he declared, "I believe the German has more to hide than most." He stared at Long. "What does your president think of him?"

"I'm not sure I know, Excellency. He has never said publicly." Long shrugged and added, "Our policy toward Germany is hands-off. If Roosevelt has concerns, he is reluctant to show them."

"We often also hide our apprehensions. It all has to do with Hitler."

"Him, his policies, and the entire Nazi movement, I'd say. They appear to have a tightening grip on their country, and Hindenburg is too old and sickly to do anything about it."

"Roosevelt has said this?" asked Mussolini.

Realizing he was in diplomatically dangerous waters, Long immediately assumed a cautious tone. "Excellency, these are merely surmises on my part. We are all unsure of Hitler's motives. His seeming obsession with power and his pronouncements on the purity of the Aryan people are certain to concern any president."

In *sotto voce*, Mussolini confided. "You can report to Roosevelt that I do not consider Hitler a great threat. If he moves on other countries, there will be someone to stop him. That someone will be me leading the fascist armies."

The conversation was cut short by the roar of the crowd accompanying the start of the second half of play. It did not begin well for Mexico when one of their defenders committed a serious foul and was ejected from the field. Donelli took advantage and scored his third goal.

As the game drew to a close, Ambassador Long turned to the Italian Prime Minister. "Thank you for joining me today, Excellency. It appears it will be a surprising win for my country, and we had some interesting conversations. May I come to see you after you meet with *Herr* Hitler and get your thoughts and conclusions?"

"Certainly, Ambassador Long," *Il Duce* replied genially. "You are always welcome. And, I promise to be candid. I am here to bar the way of that deranged corporal—for Italy, for Europe, and the whole world!"

Starace, let out a whoop as, in the waning minutes of play, Donelli made the longest goal of the day.

Mussolini exclaimed proudly, “This Buff! He has scored four times in all.” He nudged Long. “Football is in the blood of all Italians.”

Chapter Eight

Friday, 25 May 1934

Washington, DC

The room lacked decoration save for the portrait of Abraham Lincoln above a fireplace mantel at one end, several unimaginative sconces along an inner wall, and neatly draperied windows. A long, rectangular table offset to one side was surrounded by eleven studded leather chairs occupied by some of the most influential politicians in America: President Franklin D. Roosevelt, Vice President John Nance Garner, and members of the cabinet. Most were smoking, including the president, his Camel cigarette securely installed in its ivory holder.

With the business of state concluded, Roosevelt looked about at the stares and wrinkled foreheads, knowing they were waiting for him to end the meeting and get on with the day. He held up his hand. "I apologize, but I must ask you to stay awhile longer. Now that we've finished the formal meeting, and it was mercifully brief, thanks to all of you, I want to add several postscripts." He paused for a moment, scanned their faces, then continued. "First, thank you for sitting still for the photographer earlier. I'm sure you may have guessed something was up when you saw me without my rolling apparatus."

There were a few murmurs and awkward smiles as he continued. "I also want to alert everyone to the latest plans for the renovation of the White House. It will begin in July, and it's certain to be disruptive, but I believe we will see major improvements in the end." He grinned broadly. "I plan to be away for most of it." He let the chuckles subside before continuing. "Now, I need a favor, and it must stay strictly off the record."

The vice president and assembled cabinet members paid keen attention whenever they heard the "off the record" phrase. Although he didn't usually share many confidences with the cabinet, they knew FDR meant what he said.

Roosevelt leaned forward and clasped his hands before him, all traces of a smile gone. "I have a growing interest in the upcoming meeting between *Herr* Hitler and Premier Mussolini." He looked directly at Cordell Hull, his Secretary of State, seated to his right.

Hull took the cue. "Yes, Mister President. We are aware of it, but believe there is no cause for concern. Like you, the German chancellor has been in office for barely more than a year, and he is reaching out to a fellow fascist he admires. It was inevitable, sir."

"Inevitable or not, I think it needs our attention, unofficially. Let me make clear I have mulled this thing ever since we got wind of it, but I don't want to appear to be getting involved in German or Italian politics." FDR surveyed the faces looking back at him. "What has brought me to this point is my concern that this Hitler fella sounds more and more like he plans to toss aside the Versailles Treaty. I want to be certain Italy is not leaning to support such a move. If anything, I would like the two countries kept at loggerheads."

"Mister President," Hull advised, "the Italian is head and shoulders above Hitler in prestige and power. We were surprised to learn he had agreed to the meeting."

"That means they are both after something, thus, the source of my apprehension. Germany may again be industrializing, and an alliance with the likes of Italy could give the Nazis the impetus to move on their neighbors." Roosevelt used the chair's armrests to adjust himself in his seat. "As you are all well aware, with the tenuous economic conditions here and around the world, we don't need another war in Europe or anywhere. The American people sent me here to make this country prosperous again, not to get embroiled in a conflict."

The Secretary of War, George Dern, chimed in, "Mister President, your fears are not without foundation. By all indications, Germany's neighbors are getting jittery. We see it in Austria, for example, where their chancellor, Dollfuss, has been voicing his fears quite openly."

"This is yet another topic we think will be broached during the meeting," Hull said. "But Italy and Austria are close, and we don't expect a liaison between Mussolini and Hitler to develop."

FDR nodded. "All the same, I want a presence on the scene when they meet." He looked questioningly at Hull.

"June fourteenth for two days in Venice, sir," Hull reported.

"We haven't much time, and I would like to take the pulse of the situation." Roosevelt winked. "On the QT."

"Mister President," Claude Swanson, Secretary of the Navy, spoke up. "I believe our intelligence boys can handle it."

Recalling his stint as Assistant Secretary of the Navy, FDR replied, "Claude, I know firsthand the fine job your people do, but I don't want this raised to that level." His head bobbed as he added, "Not until I know what's what." Turning back to Hull, he asked, "Cordell, can you do anything?"

The older man shook his head. "Mister President, I like to think we are diplomats, not spies."

"Exactly! And I don't want a spy." FDR tapped the table with his index finger. "I also don't want to rely on the newspapers. We all know how reporters can be manipulated, and these dictators are masters at that." He sat back. "I want what Doctor Freud calls an alter ego. Someone to be my ears and eyes," adding paradoxically, "but in no case shall I take notice." He again looked around the table. "Suggestions?"

As the group pondered the request, at the far end of the table, Secretary of Labor Frances Perkins, the first woman to ever hold a US cabinet position, raised her hand. With no one in the boys' club offering anything constructive, she spoke up in her full-bodied feminine voice. "Mister President, I believe I have just the person."

With raised brows, FDR responded, "Frances, tell me."

"Sir, someone who would fill the bill perfectly."

Roosevelt nodded. "Trustworthy, with no direct ties back here."

"Exactly, but I wouldn't want to commit to anything until I can make inquiries. May I have a day or two?"

"Fine, but time is short. I'll leave it up to you. I don't need to know the details. I am only interested in results."

"Yes, sir, I understand," she replied.

The president regarded the others. "Not a word of this." He pushed back slightly from the table, signaling the end of the meeting. As they left, each cabinet member indicated an assurance of secrecy. The president remained seated until an aide brought in his wheelchair, which was actually a sawed-off kitchen chair mounted on a carriage with four wheels—two large bicycle-type to the front and two smaller ones in the rear. FDR waved off the young man's offer to help him onto the chair and shot a "come hither" head jerk at Postmaster General, James Farley, a close friend and the man credited with his rise to power. Farley took the seat Hull had occupied.

"Jimmy," said the president after the room had cleared, "I don't want to make anything of it, but I'd like you to keep an eye on what Frances comes up with for this Venice meeting. Let's not give her the idea I don't trust her, because you know I do. I just need to feel comfortable no matter who is arranging it."

"Gotcha. I'll see that she keeps me posted. We work well together." Farley winked.

"I'm counting on it. Now, I have another small favor to ask."

"What's that?"

"I received this lovely note of thanks from Generoso Pope, our friend in New York. Remember how his donations and articles in his *Progresso* newspaper helped bring in the Eye-tie vote."

"Of course."

"Well, he was exceedingly grateful for our making Columbus Day a federal holiday, so I would like you to look into doing something special for the occasion. Maybe you can work with Fiorello."

Farley balked, "But ..."

FDR went on, "I know the mayor is on the other side of the fence, but he's proven himself an affable fellow who knows how to play the game. Maybe a brief tribute to Generoso during the opening.

"As you wish, Mr. President," Farley replied, knowing it would be a waste of time to debate the point.

Roosevelt raised himself up on the arms of the chair. "Give me a hand here, won't you."

With that, Farley helped FDR onto his rolling apparatus.

Chapter Nine

Sunday, 27 May 1934

Dresden, Germany

The Bellevue, the city's premier hotel, was a stopping place for many of the world's elite, including the cream of the dwindling European aristocracy as well as the *nouveau riche* from America. Over the years, its proximity to the city's cultural center also made it a favorite home away from home for artists, performers, dancers, and composers such as Richard Strauss. On this day, the fabled hotel's most prominent guest was Germany's Chancellor.

Adolph Hitler pushed aside intricate lace curtains and gazed across the *Theaterplatz* to the *Semperoper*, Dresden's state opera house. He would open the 1934 theater season and attend a production of *Tristan und Isolde* by Wagner, his favorite composer. "This is fine, Doctor," he said to Joseph Goebbels. His propaganda minister nodded from one of the room's overstuffed chairs, his gray suit matching his dour expression.

Hitler continued, "I love Dresden, and this trip is particularly satisfying. The opera will be most pleasing, as always, and tomorrow I will be addressing the locals of the *Sturmabteiling*."

As the German chancellor relished a rare moment of contentment, his eyes wandered beyond the grand opera house façade to the outline of the Holy Trinity Cathedral. Its edifice was imposing, but most striking were the dozens of sacred statues adorning its roof line, silhouetted against the bright sky. He allowed himself to fantasize about being so honored one day, not as a mere saint, but as the savior of the German people. The lofty thought was interrupted by a low rapping on the door.

"Yes, yes. Come."

A husky, senior SA officer entered carrying a leather case. He was Hitler's adjutant and bodyguard, Wilhelm Brückner. "The latest dispatches, *mein Führer*."

"So, Willie, what of this Venice trip?"

"Excellency," the big man calmly produced a paper as he approached the chancellor. "*Reichsführer* Himmler reports that the terms of the Italy trip are set. As you had previously approved, you will arrive by airplane on fourteen June and depart early on sixteen June." Brückner handed a paper to Hitler, "*Mein Führer,* the final details for the visit are here.

Hitler glanced at the document and turned to Goebbels. "Why is Himmler attending to such particulars?"

Breaking his silence, Goebbels responded, "Excellency, it will have to do with security concerns. He has been going on about such matters for days."

"Doctor Goebbels is correct," offered Brückner. "The *Reichsführer* says he is worried that you will be in a foreign land and greatly out of his purview."

The German chancellor looked accusingly at Brückner. "And I suppose you share his concerns."

"Sir, I will be with you every moment, yet I fear what could happen."

Hitler scowled. "It is a diplomatic undertaking, and the Italian prime minister is in full control. He understands how much he requires my friendship and the power of the German state. He will see to my safety."

Goebbels advised, "There are elements in Italy beyond Mussolini's control. This is why …"

Hitler cut him off with a dismissive wave. "Himmler sees threats everywhere. You yourself have also heard him going on about the growing danger from Röhm and the SA. He imagines the stormtroopers who were so important to my rise are now turning against me." He stared at Goebbels. "Do you know of any evidence of this among the SA?"

The propaganda minister shrugged. "I only see what you see, Excellency."

Meanwhile, Brückner sheepishly handed a sealed letter to the man he was sworn to protect.

"What is this?" asked Hitler.

"Also, from the *Reichsführer*."

As he opened and read it, Hitler's face reddened until the pressure building inside him had to escape. "I will not hear of such a thing!" he roared.

Brückner winced and said nothing.

Squinting at Goebbels, Hitler added, "It is the *Doppelgänger* issue again. He wants to use a double, and I will never allow it. Do you not agree?"

"*Führer,* there are occasions where it could be acceptable," Goebbels replied.

The chancellor pounded a fist into the palm of his other hand. "Standing next to the leader of Italy is not one of them."

Brückner asked, "Excellency, may I arrange a telephone call to Berlin?"

"No. Have *Frau* Schroeder come in. I wish to dictate my response so that the words are not mistaken. *Doppelgänger,* indeed!" He then turned back to the window and searched for the calm he had experienced, but it was gone.

As Brückner headed for the door, his boss had one further request.

"Wait!" Hitler walked from the window and patted his stomach, "For this afternoon's meal, I believe I would favor some of that tasty stuffed squab. You know, prepared in the manner I enjoy so well."

"Yes, Excellency. As in Hanover, where it was a specialty of the Lucas woman, the Englander."

Hitler dismissed Brückner's comment with, "Surely, Dresden chefs can do as well."

The adjutant nodded and left as Hitler returned once again to the window.

Chapter Ten

Monday, 28 May 1934

Vienna, Austria

Sepp Karper sat at his kitchen table, reviewing a stack of postcards of Venice and marking a tourist map. He turned over a picture of the Grand Hotel, wrote the number four on its back, and recorded the same numeral on the route along the Grand Canal. Three other numbers represented *Piazza di San Marco* with its bell tower, Nicelli airfield, and Alberoni Golf Club, both of which were on the Lido. He puffed on his pipe as he thumbed through the cards until coming upon one depicting *Palazzo Contarini del Bovolo's* peculiar winding staircase. He grabbed a magnifying glass and was searching for its location when there was a rapping at his door. He quickly folded the map and answered it, expecting to see *Frau* Adorf on one of her monthly rent-collection visits. He was wrong.

"Hello, Captain Karper,"

"Major Fey, what are you … I didn't realize you knew where I live.

"I had the address, and as I entered, this older woman with endless information about you gave me your flat number."

"She's the building busybody." Sepp let a grimace fade as he continued. "Is there something you need of me?"

Fey entered and looked around. He pointed to Sepp's divan. "May I?"

"Yes, of course. Please. Can I get you something to drink?"

Fey waved him off. "Information is all I require."

"Yes, sir." Sepp sat on the arm of his easy chair. "What would you like to know?

Fey grinned stiffly. "About your trip to Venice."

"Yes, sir, I …"

"Do not attempt to deny it," Fey said flatly. "I know you have made purchases of travel brochures and postcards of that city."

"They are for a pleasure trip, sir. I have always wanted to revisit that wonderful place." His stomach tightened with concern that Fey might see what was on his kitchen table.

"Next month, is it?" Fey asked. "Possibly around mid-June?"

The Florence detour gave Sepp a way out. "Oh, no, sir. Earlier. I will be leaving soon and expect to return before then."

"So, it has nothing to do with the meeting of Hitler and Mussolini."

"No, sir. Strictly a lark on my part. A break from my hum-drum duties," Sepp assured.

"Not at the insistence of our dear vice chancellor?"

Drawing upon various facts about his preparations, Sepp cobbled together what he hoped was a plausible story. "I have been studying astronomy—a kind of hobby. The prince knew I would be going and asked me to consult with a professor at the Vienna observatory who is interested in learning more about Galileo's demonstration of his telescope to the Venetian doge."

Fey stroked his chin. "Yes, I know of your visits to the observatory."

Sepp's mind screamed, "Bastard!"

Fey continued. "And, you say you will return here when?"

"If all goes as planned, sir, by 13 June."

"Well," Fey smiled dryly. "It seems I have obtained what I came for." He stood and looked around. "Perhaps you might show me the rest of your lovely flat."

Sepp blocked the view into the kitchen. "I apologize, but the place is an embarrassing mess. May I invite you and Frau Fey for dinner after I return? I am a fair cook and should enjoy your company." He held an arm out, herding the major toward the door.

"As will we." Fey turned almost cordial. "Until sometime after the thirteenth." He opened the door, adding as he left, "Soon after."

"Of course," Sepp agreed as a mixture of relief and concern ran through him.

Chapter Eleven

Tuesday, 29 May 1934

Rome, Italy

Enzo Noschese, a ferret-like man with pleading brown eyes and a parrot beak for a nose, fidgeted impatiently with his glass of Cinzano and soda as he eyed the establishment's front doors. Due to its proximity to the United States State Department's mission, the *Osteria Vicenzo* was a hangout for American diplomatic staffers unaccustomed to *riposo*, the afternoon nap of the Italians. It was, therefore, the shifty reporter's daily source of overheard conversations he could use for his weekly feature on foreign affairs in *Il Messaggero*, the Roman weekly he had worked at for the past twelve years.

Nursing his third drink, the reporter watched the passing tourists enjoying the near-perfect Roman day. A glance at his wristwatch told him it was past three-thirty. *"Finito,"* he muttered, draining the glass. He was about to leave when he saw coming his way a shapely brunette in a tailored suit accompanying a man he knew well. He was John Ravelli, an assistant to American Ambassador Breckinridge Long.

Ravelli and the woman acknowledged the proprietor's familiar *"Sera"* greeting and took a table within earshot of the reporter.

"John," the brunette said, "I still don't understand why you must leave in such a hurry. We've had this spring ball planned for months. I was counting on you."

Ravelli took her chin in his hand, "Please, Ann. You know I wouldn't go if it weren't damned important."

Noschese inched his chair closer and strained to hear their conversation.

She took Ravelli's hand in hers. "I've been in this business long enough to know that precious little in diplomacy moves this fast. And yet, you need to race off to Florence. Is it a sudden passion for the Renaissance?"

He touched his finger to her lips. "Please, the order came directly from …" He stopped. "Let me just say that you are the only other person in the office who even knows about this. You must swear to keep the secret."

Ann raised her pinky, "Promise."

"Besides," he added playfully, "You know my favorite piece of art is here in Rome."

Smirking, she asked, "You sure you don't mean your favorite piece of ass?"

"Never in a million years," Ravelli reassured her as he signaled for a bottle of *spumante*.

When the waiter arrived with the wine, Noschese heard Ravelli explain, "It will be a quick trip."

The reporter took out a pad and pencil and made a note.

"I don't like it," Ann shrugged, "but I suppose I have no choice. You realize, of course, you will be in my debt."

He kissed her hand affectionately. "There's no place I'd rather be, except maybe in your bed."

She slapped his hand playfully, "Take it easy, Casanova."

Ravelli raised his glass of bubbly. "Here's to you, my love. I'll be back before you know it." They clinked glasses, and each took a sip. "I'm sure one of the other guys would be happy to accompany you to the party."

"None of them is you," she said, sticking out her lower lip. "You wouldn't have time for a quick trip to our little hideaway now, would you?"

"I'm afraid not. Let's make our moments here as romantic as we can, okay?"

"I suppose … "

As their conversation had settled into a drone of irrelevant coos and romantic ramblings, Noschese made his way to the door.

Ravelli spotted him. "Oh God, that damned Noschese has been watching us. I hope he didn't hear anything."

"You didn't say much." She smirked as she scanned the bill of fare.

* * *

The newsroom of *Il Messaggero* was cluttered with oak desks butted front to front, their tops littered with notes, papers, and books. Noschese sat across from arts and theater reporter, Mario Mosconi, a chubby cherub with pink cheeks. His fingers were poised over the keys of his typewriter as he searched for a precise phrase for his review of a new film by Alessandro Blasetti.

"Aha!'" exclaimed Mosconi, "complex yet satisfying cinema."

"Hey, Mario," interrupted Noschese. "Are you certain this is the latest?" he asked as he waved a railway timetable at his desk partner.

"Absolutely, Enzo. I travel there often. That particular schedule has not changed in some time." He gestured with both palms to the ceiling. "But why take the train to Florence?"

"I'm not, but I need to know the schedule of trains arriving there. I expect to motor up."

Mosconi leaned back and reached into a drawer and handed his cohort a map of Italy. "When I drive, I take the route up through Viterbo, then Siena. I would say a journey of six or seven hours if you are lucky. The train may be much faster."

"My roadster will do," Noschese countered as he opened the map. "Besides, I need flexibility. I may have to go on to Venice for Mussolini's meeting with the German."

"You'll need a gondola," Mosconi chided with a grin.

"I understand Mussolini will be staying at *Villa Pisani* in Stra. My auto gives me an advantage over the other press vultures." He glanced at a wall clock showing twenty-five minutes after four. "I can still make it to Florence tonight."

"Why are you in such a hurry?" Mosconi asked then added, "Sorry, I know, I ask too many questions." He reached for his book of phone numbers and scribbled on a pad. "I usually stay at the Hotel *Stella d'Oro*. It's small, but the accommodations are good, and the food and service are first rate." He handed Noschese the note. "Mention my name."

"And, they will no doubt throw me out."

"Maybe yes, maybe no," The fat man shrugged and chuckled.

Berlin, Germany

Adolf Hitler's office in the Reich Chancellery was tastefully decorated with a large oil painting over the fireplace next to entry doors and several comfortable chairs. The long opposite wall held a line of cabinets with windowed doors and polished drawers. Offset from the room's center, the chancellor sat behind a square-cornered walnut desk. In front of him, tan armchairs held Joseph Goebbels and Heinrich Himmler.

"So, *mein Führer*, shall we go ahead with it?" asked Goebbels.

Smirking, Hitler quipped, "Yes, and won't *Putzi* be surprised." He used the nickname meaning "cute" in referring to the six foot, four inch Ernst Hanfstaengl, a member of his inner circle known for his insightful and often humorous observations, as well as his piano playing and composing. In February, Hanfstaengl had gone to Rome, ostensibly to promote a propaganda film about Hitler's 1932 presidential bid called *"Hitler über Deutschland."* He also met with Mussolini in an attempt to convince the Italian dictator to host the German chancellor, suggesting the city of Venice since Hitler loved Wagner, who died in a Venetian *palazzo*. Hanfstaengl considered the Nazi party to which he belonged a mob of unruly thugs and cowboys. Educated at Harvard, their very existence did violence to his refined sensibilities. Believing a meeting with Mussolini would demonstrate to the German chancellor the need for decorum and civility, he carefully seduced *Il Duce* to the proposal with flattery and cajoling. However, when he returned to Berlin with news of the meeting, Hitler pooh-poohed the idea, claiming he was much too busy. In fact, the chancellor longed for such an opportunity and had set the meeting wheels in motion with Goebbels, Himmler, and his staff, giving strict instructions that Hanfstaengl should not find out.

"I knew what Putzi was after. He wants to control me," declared Hitler. "Fortunately," he added with a pleased grin, "he will be off to America for a reunion with his college cronies while I am in Venice.

He can read about it in the press."

"A fine ploy, *mein Führer*," said Goebbels.

Himmler adjusted his glasses on his nose, his brow knitted as he leaned forward in his chair. "Excellency, I fully agree that this first meeting with *Il Duce* is important both politically and personally; however, there are risks."

Hitler taunted, "Do you believe the Italians aim to harm me?"

"I see a larger threat coming from within our party."

The chancellor hunched over the desktop and demanded, "The Röhm obsession again. Is that what this is about?"

Himmler continued, undeterred, "Sir, we have clear information he may attempt a takeover in your absence. He has tasted the power you earned for the party, and I believe he thinks he can replace you."

Ernst Röhm had established himself as head of the SA, the stormtroopers who used street-fighter tactics to help the Nazis gain power. Although he was once close to Hitler, Röhm's blatant homosexual lifestyle had become a problem for the *Führer.*

Hitler nibbled on his pinky nail then gestured for more information.

Goebbels' stony gaze told Himmler he was on his own. "He has said as much and is garnering the support of his queer playmates."

The chancellor banged the desktop. "Do you have proof of this?"

"Irrefutable."

"I have tolerated his deviant ways because he was productive and important to the cause, but once the old man dies, and I assume full power, things will change." Hitler referred to President von Hindenburg's failing health.

Himmler agreed, "Yes, sir, but I believe Röhm may strike in Venice where he will have the perfect opportunity to blame any harm to you on the Italians or some radical hooligans."

The logic of Himmler's words prompted Goebbels to conclude, "It does begin to make sense, *mein Führer*."

Hitler shook his head. "What then? Am I to cancel the trip?"

Goebbels tactfully suggested, "Placating Röhm and his SA cronies before Venice could avoid the appearance of a dark cloud over the meeting."

"I will consider seeing him tomorrow." Hitler pointed to Himmler, "And, you will keep your eye on the lot of them."

"*Mein Führer*, I believe I have proposed a way to limit your exposure to danger."

Hitler's face reddened. "I want no more talk of this double."

Goebbels said, "The idea is impossible!" He pulled the meeting agenda from his jacket pocket. "There are several occasions when the *Führer* will be standing next to Mussolini before large crowds. Times when he would be most vulnerable. Attempting a charade so close to the Italian could sabotage the entire event."

Hitler calmly folded his hands before him and said, "I agree with Doctor Goebbels. It is absolute folly."

"Excellency," Himmler persisted, "May I introduce someone, and then, perhaps you will take a more positive view of my suggestion."

Hitler scowled.

Himmler begged, "Please, may I be allowed to do my job, *mein Führer?*"

Hitler's nod sent Himmler out the door. As it closed behind him, the German Chancellor leaned back in his chair and folded his arms on his chest. "Huh! A *Doppelgänger*, indeed."

"There is not another like you, *mein Führer.*" Goebbels's obsequious tone calmed the Nazi leader.

A moment later, a man entered dressed in a military uniform and wearing a red armband with a swastika emblem. It was Adolf Hitler.

"Mein Gott!" exclaimed the chancellor as Himmler followed close behind the double. "Except for the uniform, I am looking into a mirror. Is this a trick? A magic illusion?"

"Indeed," said Goebbels, uncharacteristically animated.

Himmler smiled and prompted the man to step forward. "I present Wilfred Metzger, *mein Führer*."

Metzger approached and came to heel-clicking attention as he executed a perfect salute.

The chancellor came around the desk for a closer inspection of the soldier. His nose was slightly wider, and his complexion a half shade darker than Hitler's, but the resemblance was striking.

"So, Herr Metzger, how old are you, and why do you wish to put yourself in harm's way for me?"

"*Mein Führer*," the double began, the pitch and modulation of his voice closely matching Hitler's mellow baritone, "I am forty-six years of age and dedicated to you and the National Socialist cause. The Fatherland can survive the loss of a poor actor like myself, but never you. I do this gladly."

Goebbels asked, "An actor? Should we know you?"

"Possibly, Herr *Doktor.* I have appeared most recently in an approved drama at the Luitpold Theater."

Hitler examined Metzger closer. "The look is mine, but the voice. Is this my voice as well?"

Himmler responded, "It too is quite similar, *mein Führer*, save for speech patterns. I would like your permission for him to act your shadow, to learn such things, and much more as he serves possibly as a bodyguard or aide."

"How can this be?" Hitler asked.

Himmler nodded at Metzger, and the actor ran his fingers through his hair, sweeping it straight back. He then peeled off the false mustache and donned a pair of gold-rimmed spectacles. He was no longer a Hitler look-alike.

The chancellor frowned and again inspected the actor. "Make the arrangements. I find Herr Metzger here most intriguing." He beat a fist into his palm. "But I agree to nothing!"

Goebbels sat up in his chair. "The parade next Sunday, we can test Metzger there."

Himmler jumped in, "After he has spent time with you, Excellency, a final trial would be most appropriate."

Hitler grunted and nodded.

Chapter Twelve

Wednesday, 30 May 1934

Florence, Italy

Villa Donati sat on a hillside along *via di Santa Margherita a Montici,* overlooking the city that was the epicenter of the Italian Renaissance. The Donatis, a family of Sephardic Jews of Spanish heritage, had been part of the Florentine scene since the time of the Medici. Despite their history of contributing to the culture as artists, merchants, doctors, and financiers, before the unification of Italy, the Donatis were confined to a ghetto. They and other Jews of similar proficiencies, breeding, and financial means were finally emancipated in 1865 when ghettos were abolished.

Young Giuseppe Donati having, by age twenty-one, become a respected and sought-after goldsmith, established the hillside villa. He brought his parents and younger sister, Elena, to live there after marrying his sweetheart, Francesca.

Afternoon sunlight beaming through the intricate lace curtains of the windows traced patterns on *Signora* Francesca Donati, née Carlucci, a slight, pale woman in her late 70s, busily tatting an intricate doily. As she had each day of the four years since her husband's death, she wore a black dress of mourning. A painting of David and Goliath attributed to the workshop of Sandro Botticelli hung behind the settee where she sat. It was one of the many major pieces of art adorning the nine primary rooms of the house. Paintings were a passion of Giuseppe, her *"Pepi mio,"* who found it an amusing irony that so much Florentine art featured scenes depicting the lives of Jews.

As she worked her threads and shuttle, Francesca's thoughts turned to times before they were married when she and *Pepi* climbed this same hill, and he would speak of his vision of a home where they sat. Her thoughts jumped back to a warm June day in 1873 when they joined a throng along a nearby roadway to watch as men prompted teams of oxen drawing a huge wagon. It carried a bronze copy of Michelangelo's David to its place of honor in the middle of the broad *piazzale* named for the Florentine master.

The old woman's reverie ended when Lucia, her maid, carried in a tray of coffee cups and fruit tarts. "Where did he go?" she asked.

"*Americani*, they are as impatient as children. When I said she might not be home for an hour or more, he said he would return later and left. He did not even allow us to be cordial. An Italian name, but no manners. Adopted, I suppose."

Lucia shrugged. "And, what do I do with these? They are fresh from the oven."

"Set them down for me to enjoy." The elderly lady smiled coyly.

"*Signora* Donati, you are not to have such things. Remember the doctor's warning."

"I must be allowed an occasional treat. Otherwise, what does a long life matter? I am sure little Lissa would love one as well. Please, invite her."

The sound of a motor and the crunch of wheels on the driveway's gravel announced the arrival of an automobile. Moments later, Martha, the redhead from the S.S. Roma, entered festooned with camera equipment and toting a bulging rucksack.

"Ah, Bellezza," said the old woman brightly, "You return early."

"*Sí, Nonna,* I have had a full day. Florence is a lovely place, but it holds more than my camera can capture." Martha put down her things and hugged her grandmother, kissing her on both cheeks. "My days melt into one another until they all seem the same."

"This day is different. You had a visitor. *Un americano*."

"An American? Are you positive?"

"The man has an Italian surname and speaks the language beautifully, but I am sure of it. Just as I was always certain when they came to do business with your grandfather." She added wistfully, "They loved his intricate work in gold."

Martha took a seat next to her grandmother. "How could he even know I'm here? Did he say what he wanted? Could it have something to do with Brian's school?"

"Who knows? He gave no reason and would not wait. Americans know no patience." She indicated the tray. "Eat something. Lucia made them, and they are still warm." She gazed at a wall clock. "I expect your visitor will …"

"Mama, Mama!" Melissa interrupted Francesca, who, with clasped hands, turned her eyes to the ceiling.

"Lissa!" Martha hugged the bright-eyed, fidgety little girl who had dashed in from the veranda. "Why so excited?"

"You must come outside now and see my *farfalla*."

"A butterfly? You caught one?" asked Martha.

"Oh, no. Great-grandma said it might kill him. He is big, with yellow and black stripes, and he stays near the purple flowers. I wait for him to land so I can pet him. Come, we must hurry before the *farfalla* flies away."

As Martha and Lissa went out the doors, a bell sounded down the hallway.

"I will go," Lucia called out and shortly returned carrying a gray fedora as she showed in John Ravelli.

"*Signore*," Francesca greeted him. "So, you have returned. She is here now."

He said gently, "I thought that might be her auto. Very good, *Signora* Donati. May I speak with her?"

Francesca nodded to the maid and indicated the veranda.

As Lucia started for the doors, Ravelli said, "That will be fine. I will see her there, if I may."

"As you wish," said Francesca as she waved off Lucia.

Ravelli went through the doors and was immediately taken with the stunningly attractive woman and the animated little girl exploring the blooms of a large potted lilac bush at the other end of the balcony.

"Hello," said Martha. "You must be the visitor grandmother mentioned."

"John Ravelli, at your service."

"I see." Martha eyed him cautiously. "And what sort of service might that be?"

He smiled and gazed down at the child, prompting Martha to

remind, “Lissa, say hello to Mister Ravelli.”

The little girl curtsied. “Hello, Mister Ravelli. We are watching for my *farfalla*. Would you like to join us?”

Ravelli smiled and went down on a knee to greet her. “You are most kind, but I’m afraid I don’t have time for butterflies right now. Maybe another day.” He arose and looked at Martha. “Now, I must speak with your mother.”

“Lissa honey, please sit with great-grandma, and we’ll do our butterfly watching a little later. Maybe you can capture him with your camera.”

“I would like that, Mama.” Happily, Lissa went back inside.

Martha regarded Ravelli with more than an ounce of skepticism as he began his explanation. “Mrs. Markham, I am here on an important mission. Possibly, one of great consequence.”

“It sounds ominous.”

“Not at all, I assure you. Anything but that.” He paused, choosing his words. “First, let me say I am not on official business.”

“What kind of business are you here on, and for whom?”

“The person I represent is of no consequence.” Once again, he paused and measured out his next sentence. “A certain matter has raised some concern at the highest levels of our government.”

“You do mean the United States government, don’t you?” He nodded, and she continued, “I have heard this kind of talk before. You must know my father is a congressman and was in diplomatic service for many years.”

“Certainly, and I also know your background. Mrs. Martha Markham: your brilliance at Vassar as Martha Hughes, your marriage, and your husband’s tragic death.”

Her face stiffened. “My God! Who are you?”

“As I said, it is of no importance. Please, allow me to get to the heart of the matter.”

“Go on.”

“Next month, there will be a most important event in Venice. The German Chancellor Adolf Hitler and Benito Mussolini will meet face-to-face.”

“So, what does it have to do with me?”

“There is interest and some concern about this meeting, but the

American government can in no way recognize it officially."

"I see. This is one of those 'off the record,' situations." Her demeanor warmed a bit as she recalled her father speaking of President Roosevelt's penchant for keeping certain things out of the public consciousness.

"Precisely," he responded, relieved by her instant grasp of the circumstance. Flashing a quick smile, he continued, "And, this is where you come in. We would like you to be a, shall we say, casual observer."

"Well, I am about as unofficial and casual as they come."

"You are perfect for the task in many ways. You are an American here in Italy, you speak the language, and you already have the cover of an itinerant photographer."

"Cover? Itinerant?" The concern returned to her face. "Yes, I'm just so perfect."

Ignoring her sarcasm, he continued, "A word of caution, though. We cannot provide any support whatsoever. I hope you understand we must remain uninvolved. How you get to Venice and what you do there are up to you, so long as, shortly after the event, we receive a full report describing your experience and what you observed. We are especially interested in the interactions of Mussolini and Hitler and how they appear to get along. Photos, particularly candid ones, would be most welcome. After it is over, you won't need to contact anyone. I will find you."

"So, I'll be watching them, and you'll be watching me, is that how it works?"

"Not quite. Maybe from a distance. But for you, I am not there and will not intervene. Be careful not to take any action that provokes a reaction. If you get into a bind, you are on your own. Please, take your pictures, keep your eyes and ears open, and record your observations. That is all we ask."

"Has my father been informed?"

"The congressman has been briefed and said he was certain you would consider it an honor."

"June," she confirmed.

"Fourteenth through the sixteenth. There will be reimbursements at some point, but mainly you will have the satisfaction of knowing you helped protect the country and the futures of children like Melissa and your boy. He's off at military school in Connecticut, isn't he?"

"My God, you are thorough. Yes, he'll be coming here shortly."

"When it is over, you can get on with your," he surveyed the surroundings, "rather comfortable life."

"Right now, I don't feel so comfortable. I need time to consider this," Martha said as she ushered Ravelli inside.

"Certainly," he agreed. "I will contact you in a day or two."

She paused. "Not here. I'll be working at either *Santa Croce* or later, the academy."

"Excellent. I know both well."

As they entered the house, a yellow and black swallowtail butterfly flew over the railing of the balcony and alit on the lilac blossoms. Melissa, who had been watching at the window, scurried past them on her mission to touch the delicate insect.

From his Fiat roadster parked up along the way past the Donati house, Enzo Noschese watched through a spyglass as John Ravelli emerged and entered the taxi awaiting him in the drive. The reporter started the car's engine and followed the cab.

* * *

The small bar in the *Hotel Supremo* was nearly deserted save for a few tourists and an older woman nursing a fruity, cream-colored libation at one of the small tables. John Ravelli sat at another, idly twirling his cocktail glass by the stem, watching the green olives in his martini trying to keep up with the momentum of the spin. He concluded it was a little like his own life, where he was always striving to stay even with what was going on around him and never fully succeeding. A day ago, he was about to enjoy a romantic evening with his special girl when he was plucked away for this mission. The cloud of self-pity he was snuggling into evaporated with the sound of his name coming from a source he was in no mood to deal with.

"*Signor* Ravelli, how are you?" Noschese called as he approached the table. "It is a fine coincidence, no? Meeting here in *Firenze?*"

"Enzo! Why are you following me?"

Noschese shrugged. "You are always of interest, *signore*."

"You will be sorely disappointed."

"Why are you in Florence? I saw you go to the villa on the hill earlier."

"You what?"

Noschese pulled up a chair and sat. "I ask in the *vicinato*, the neighborhood, and find out it is the home of an old goldsmith. He is *morto,* but the wife, she lives there. Why see the wife of a dead goldsmith?"

"Look, Enzo, there was personal business. If you must know, their granddaughter is a visiting American, and she needed some assistance. It was nothing to concern you." Ravelli took a pull on the Martini.

"I see. And, you are on your way to Venice for the big meeting of *Il Duce* and the German, yes?"

"Wrong!" Ravelli said stiffly. "I return to Rome in the morning. I have no interest in it, and Venice isn't in my purview."

Noschese said nothing for a few moments, his eyes surveying Ravelli's face for an indication of a lie. "I am so sorry for my assumption, *signore*. You see, I am going to Venice, and I thought we might travel there together. I have my auto."

"I need to return to my work in Rome," Ravelli assured him. "Look, Enzo, I know you have a job to do, and you must do it rather well. Except …"

"Yes, except what, *signore*? Do I displease you?" Noschese asked, his eyes resembling those of a pleading rodent.

"At times," Ravelli answered. "Such as when you call my office and pretend to be me and fool my staff into giving you information. That displeases me very much."

"But *signore,* I am …"

"I know," Ravelli cut him off, "only doing your job." His face hardened. "Look, I too have a job to do. You must respect that."

"Certo!" replied Noschese. "You have my deepest *rispetto*, my friend."

Vienna, Austria

Sepp Karper, sporting a tweed jacket, a neat beard, and a pair of horn-rimmed glasses, arrived early at the *Westbahnhof* rail station. Booked on an overnight train to Italy, he searched for an escape from the noisy center tracks and bustling boarding platforms. Settling for a table in an enclosed restaurant area, he perused a late edition of the Vienna *TagBlatt*. Disregarding the bland headlines, he paged through on his way to the sports section for the latest World Cup results. Suddenly, a familiar countenance on the obituary page screamed at him. Katherine Hermann had died! The woman he loved and with whom he had shared the devastation of war and the elation of ecstasy was gone.

The instant pain that filled him was laced with deep regret over not being able to see his Katy again after that single visit almost a month ago. He was so devastated he wanted to run away from everything—his solitary life, his humdrum daily routine as a researcher, and, most of all, this terrible assignment. He wished he could race out of the station and keep on running, but he knew it wasn't in him, and it would violate everything his Katy had ever believed of him. The words of Chancellor Dollfuss echoed in his brain: "You are a patriot, Sepp, and it is a time for patriots." He had never felt so alone.

Chapter Thirteen

Thursday, 31 May 1934

Florence, Italy

The white, pink, and green marble façade of *Santa Croce* basilica was bathed in the light of a new day, while inside, the *Castellani* Chapel glowed with dim candlelight illuminating its altar and the cycle of frescoes adorning the walls. Father Guido Tucci, graying and gaunt, with intense dark eyes enlarged by thick glasses, was concluding the first mass of the day. He covered the communion chalice with the paten, pall, and purificator, then genuflected. Turning to the group of faithful in attendance, he announced, *"Ite, missa est."* The mass was over, and after thanking God, the congregation began to disperse.

In the church's nave, Martha set down her cameras by one of the basilica's octagonal columns and knelt before the tomb of Niccolò Machiavelli, not to pray, but to unload her rucksack. Unlike the more magnificent monuments of the pantheon of famous Italians, this one had but a single figure of a mourner, a political allegory sitting atop a sarcophagus, and holding up a cameo of the Florentine historian and philosopher. It was this work of simple beauty before which Martha laid out her equipment. As she went about it, light from the clerestory played in her hair, firing it with orange and gold highlights. She was unaware of the man approaching from the central aisle.

He came within a few feet of her, paused, and cleared his throat.

She turned, startled and tight-lipped.

"Good morning, Mrs. Markham. Please excuse this interruption." His smile was genuine and disarming.

"Mister Ravelli, I thought I would have more time," she said as she got to her feet.

He moved closer and said in a near whisper, “I had hoped so, but things have changed. I must return to Rome this morning. It would simplify things greatly if I could have your answer now.”

She folded her arms before her as she regarded the designs on the basilica’s floor. After a moment, she shrugged. “I guess my dad was right about me. I love our country and will do anything I can to help.”

“Wonderful.” His bright countenance faded. “I remind you, what you do and how you do it is up to you and completely unofficial.”

“I do understand. I am to be only an observer.”

“Remember, when I go out that door,” he said, pointing to the main entrance, “you will not hear from me again until it is over. If you are contacted by anyone identifying himself as me, please ignore him.”

* * *

Slightly more than a kilometer from Santa Croce sat the Basilica of *Santa Maria Novella*. A magnet for tourists and pilgrims, the church’s sculptures, paintings, and carvings also attracted art enthusiasts and students. Among the most notable works were the frescoes by Domenico Ghirlandaio and the representation of the Holy Trinity by the fifteenth-century artist known as Masaccio, whose figures set in perspective influenced the birth of the Italian Renaissance.

Across from the rear of the basilica sat its busy namesake railway station and the *Piazza della Stazione* bustling with people and conveyances. Passengers and their well-wishers arrived and departed on foot, in trams or taxis, and horse-drawn rigs varying from leather-appointed carriages to crude carts.

Father Guido Tucci stood by his black Lancia Augusta sedan, observing the ebb and flow of travelers.

Across the way, Enzo Noschese consulted a railway timetable as he watched John Ravelli exit a cab and enter the railway station. “The ten fifty to Rome. It must be.” He headed for the terminal entrance.

Meanwhile, arriving from Bologna, Sepp Karper was trying to detrain; however, he had the misfortune of getting trapped behind a large woman and her unruly brat who stubbornly insisted on sitting down every few steps and refusing to budge. The flustered mother was ineffectual in her attempts to keep the boy from stalling the flow of passengers trying to reach the carriage exit.

In no mood for the childish game, Sepp picked up the imp and carried him along the aisle and down the steps. He wriggled and shouted until Sepp deposited him on the platform. Receiving a toothy grin from the grateful woman, the Austrian visitor went for his luggage before heading to the main concourse. As he exited the station, he paused and pulled out a note with the address of the hotel Tucci had arranged and continued toward the taxis in the *piazza*.

"Hey, Karp, over here."

Sepp stopped and spotted his friend-turned-priest motioning to him. "Tucci, you old dog." They met, and the two mates shook hands before they ended up in an awkward embrace, back-patting, and huge smiles.

Noschese exited the terminal, having confirmed Ravelli's departure, and spotted a priest and a man he thought he recognized.

"I hardly knew you. What's with the getup? And the glasses?" asked Tucci. "What happened to your perfect vision."

"My new look," said Sepp. "This is a surprise. I wasn't expecting to be picked up."

"I provide this service for all visiting spies," Tucci responded a bit too loudly.

"Hey, watch it!" Sepp looked around, checking to see if anyone overheard the comment. "My God, that collar hasn't made any difference."

"Oh, it's changed me alright, more than you'd know. I'm not the same man I was. Man? More a foolish kid when we were reveling in Venice." As the priest took Sepp's bag from him and put it on the rear seat of the car, he asked, "How are things in our Austria these days?"

"Tense, as you might guess. You've spoken with the prince, have you not?"

"I have, and as your friend and a priest, I worry they have you on the path to perdition."

Getting into the auto, Sepp assured him, "I do what I am ordered to do."

Tucci's glasses accented the skepticism in his eyes. Reacting, Sepp added, "I didn't ask for this. Honest, I spend most of my time at a desk."

"Why now?" asked the priest.

"For Austria and possibly all of Europe."

Tucci revved the engine and slipped the lever into first gear. "Last time, when they killed Archduke Ferdinand, it started a world war."

Sepp stroked his beard and volleyed back, "This could have the opposite effect. Stopping a maniac." He stared at Tucci's profile. "Look, I can explain."

"Not now, I have a baptism."

"Okay, we can discuss it later."

As the priest paused the Lancia at the direction of a policeman in the middle of the *piazza*, Noschese pulled up three cars behind.

When they were allowed to continue, they left the square and entered the *Piazza dell' Unità Italiana.*

"Is this your first visit to Florence?" Tucci asked.

Sepp nodded, "Right. I've been to Rome several times and Venice once. You remember?"

"My period of confusion and doubt, before I saw the light."

"Those women were …"

"Okay, enough!" The priest cut him off and added with mock concern, "Get behind me, Satan."

Sepp returned to the question at hand. "In any case, you're right about me never being in Florence."

"Good, I'll be your guide."

Sepp gave the priest a friendly pat on the shoulder. "It makes perfect sense. Guido the guide, like the character in Dante."

And so began the priest's commentary on each historic façade and point of interest on the way to Sepp's hotel. As they proceeded into *Piazza di Santa Trinita*, Sepp expected to hear about the column at its center or the brownstone church with a grand entry door to their right, but the priest pointed straight ahead.

"We are coming to the Trinity bridge, built 500 years ago." They paused once more for cross traffic. "The designer followed Michelangelo closely. It has some beautiful sculptures, but we will not cross it today." He pointed to the left. "Your hotel is that way."

As they turned, an ancient bridge came into view. Sepp exclaimed, "Hey, the *Ponte Vecchio*! It's in every Florence pamphlet."

"And, for a good reason," Tucci said, adding as he steered the car to the curb, "We have arrived at Hotel *Vecchio Vista*. Small, but comfortable with a great view of the river and bridges. A bit up past the old bridge is the *Uffizi* museum if you are interested in art. Beyond that, it is an easy walk to my church." He was waiting for Sepp to get out of the Lancia.

"Hold on!" Sepp insisted. "Look, give me a chance to tell you about it."

"Please, not now, Sepp. I must prepare for the sacrament, and I shouldn't disappoint the parents. Come to *Santa Croce* in the morning. I have some things there about Galileo, which may surprise you." He put his hand on Sepp's shoulder. "I am opposed to any sort of killing, but in the end, I respect you and trust your motives, whatever they are."

"I knew I could count on you," Sepp said as he got out of the car and stood leaning in from the open door.

Tucci pulled up the brake lever and prompted, "You need to get some rest. I'm sure the train ride was no cakewalk."

"Yeah, hours on end being jostled and jangled, breathing smoke and soot. It was nearly as bad as banging around in an army troop lorry."

The priest chuckled as he reached into the back seat. "I remember your Dollfuss story about him driving such a vehicle with you in back." He retrieved Sepp's bag, and as he handed it to him, added, "Maybe later you can walk to the *Piazza della Signoria.* It's close. Everything here is close. The *piazza* is where the David statue depicts his meeting with the giant Goliath. Might be an appropriate inspiration for you." The priest winked and grinned. "The square will be deserted while the big football match is on at the stadium this afternoon."

"I thought it was yesterday." Sepp had never made it to the sports pages.

"It ended all even, one to one. So, this afternoon, the teams play again—Italy and Spain."

"Maybe I'll go watch," Sepp said with a yawn. "Or, I may need to settle for listening on the wireless." He shot out his hand. "Until tomorrow, *Ciao."*

"Sí, a domani." Tucci responded as Sepp closed the car door."

Heading for the hotel, Sepp heard, "Excuse me. Hello." The man following him was vaguely familiar. "Remember me? Enzo Noschese. We met in Rome. The security conference last Summer."

Sepp immediately went on the defensive. "I am sorry, but I have never been to Rome. I'm afraid you have mistaken me for someone else."

The reporter shrugged, and his face twisted into a scowl. "I was so sure …"

"Sorry," Sepp said, holding up his luggage. "I really must be getting along." He continued toward the hotel door leaving the reporter standing there.

Noschese strolled to the *Ponte Vecchio* muttering, "I know I am right."

Berlin, Germany

Adolf Hitler sat at his desk looking up at Wilfred Metzger, who was standing before him. Sporting a short beard and wire-rimmed glasses, the would-be double bore only a slight resemblance to the German chancellor, who wore a light business suit and a dark expression.

"Look, Metzger, you have been with me for almost two weeks, watching me like a hawk. You must know by now even how I wipe my ass. Enough!"

"*Mein Führer,* I only do as the *Reichsführer* directs," Metzger apologized. "Your own words tell us that, 'the strength of a political party lies by no means in a mentality of the individual members, but rather in the disciplined obedience with which its members follow their intellectual leadership.'"

"You speak my words as well as I do."

"Excellency, as an actor, I have a gift for memorizing."

Hitler glared. "So, is this simply a part you play?"

"No *mein Führer*, in this case, I believe and live the very essence of your writings." Hitler's stone-faced stare prompted Metzger to continue. "I have read and reread your book often and never with a thought of becoming your *Doppelgänger*, but to better understand you and your ideas."

The chancellor squinted one eye. "Oh, really? And what have you learned?"

"Excellency, that you are a complex, thinking man who has struggled to rise above your meager beginnings to form a party that will lead Germany to greater glory through the cleansing of society."

"So, what have you gained from this knowledge?" Hitler asked as he pushed a persistent lock of hair out of his eyes and added, "I would say, nothing as you remain poor and alone in life."

"Sir, you have shown me what is possible. I am a stronger member of the movement, and I am dedicated to your ideals and ready to take on whatever life may offer me. I commit myself to you and the cause."

"The streets overflow with others who speak as you do. They are followers in need of a leader." Hitler slapped his palm on the desk. "If you intend to emulate me, you must show me you can lead."

"I believe I can," Metzger insisted. "I have lived every moment with you through your writings: as a boy in Braunau, as a youth attempting to climb out of the shadow of his father, and as a man dedicated to the reemergence of the Fatherland." The actor's face flushed. "As a player of roles, I have lived your life through your writings."

"So, you think you can replace me!" Hitler frowned and folded his arms on his chest.

Stunned, Metzger assured, "Never, *mein Führer*. Reading *Mein Kampf* would convince anyone of that." He shrugged. "I only wish to be near you to learn from you and to protect you if it should ever come to it."

"Himmler must know you can't possibly stand in for me for any of it." Hitler smoothed down his mustache with his thumb and index finger.

"Possibly, at a distance?" Metzger ventured.

The response came with a clenched fist. "Not at all! Never!" He settled himself and continued. "Himmler claims I will be in danger for the entire trip, and he wants you as a substitute whenever I appear in public. Impossible!"

Frowning, Metzger said softly, "Yes, Excellency."

"You may go now." Hitler indicated the door. As Metzger went for it, he added, "You amuse and interest me, *Herr* Metzger. I will inform *Reichsführer* Himmler that you may stay on here as an aide, nothing more."

Metzger saluted and left as the *Führer* returned to his chair, smiling candidly.

New York Harbor

Flying the flag of the Commander-in-Chief from its mainmast, the heavy cruiser USS Indianapolis, carrying more than a hundred dignitaries and guests, sat stationary, delayed by dense fog for almost two hours.

Below, under the eight-inch guns of the ship's second forward turret stood President Franklin Roosevelt, his trousers hiding the leg braces that supported him as he gripped the railing. At his side were Secretary of the Navy, Claude Swanson, and former Navy secretary and ambassador to Mexico, Josephus Daniels. A lifelong sailing aficionado, Roosevelt knew well that fog could end any endeavor on the sea, even in a safe port such as New York. Easing the moment, he quipped, "Even the mighty United States Navy must give way to the whims of Mother Nature. Fog is as capricious as any female."

Earlier, his wife Eleanor had stood by his side along with their son and daughter-in-law for a photograph. Staying long enough for cameras to capture the tender scene, the First Lady was soon off to hobnob with the other guests.

Although FDR and his wife had stayed together for political reasons, they had not lived as husband and wife since 1918. That was after Franklin returned from a trip to Europe, and Eleanor discovered proof of his love affair with Lucy Mercer, her former personal secretary. In his luggage, Eleanor found a pack of love letters Lucy had written to her husband while he was abroad. The Washington rumor mill had buzzed about the relationship, but the compliant press took little notice. They also conveniently ignored FDR's more recent liaisons that included a renewed alliance with Lucy.

Eleanor weathered it all by throwing herself into nurturing social programs that were part of her husband's New Deal, traveling extensively, and having several romantic dalliances of her own in the process.

As the cabinet members came for a photograph with the president, James Farley whispered into FDR's ear, "I have news. Let's find some time later."

Roosevelt nodded, and the photo session continued.

The fog dissipated, and from his post on the bridge, Captain John Smeallie grumbled, "It's about time!" The ship creaked as it moved forward, and cheers went up from the guests and the crews of both the Indianapolis and her accompanying cruiser the USS Louisville. A similar reaction came from among the hundreds of thousands who had gathered to watch the review of the Navy armada from steamships, tour boats, private vessels, and along the New York and New Jersey shorelines.

The presidential vessel made it to the reviewing position, and the parade of ships of the U.S. Naval fleet finally began. It was led by the battleship USS Pennsylvania, the fleet's flagship, which took its place alongside the Indianapolis as the USS Louisville passed in review. On it and on each of the ships that followed, uniformed sailors saluted the president, and bands played patriotic music as they passed. Many rendered 21-gun salutes. FDR acknowledged it all with a wave and a broad smile. The review of the 96 ships and their complements of forty thousand men was capped off with a sky filled with planes launched from the aircraft carriers Lexington and Saratoga. Following the aerial display, the Indianapolis led the flotilla up Ambrose channel and back into the harbor.

During the return trip, FDR relaxed in an easy chair under an awning and held forth with the various civilian and military guests on hand for the occasion. When there was a lull in the succession of presidential tête–à–têtes, James Farley pulled up a chair beside him.

"What have you got, Jimmy?" Roosevelt asked.

Farley leaned in. "Your alter ego, she's in play for Venice."

"She?" FDR blurted a bit too loudly. Grimacing and lowering his voice, he continued, "I never expected …" He rubbed his chin. "Frances. I might have known."

Farley explained. "The woman is the daughter of Congressman Andrew Hughes of Connecticut, a former ambassador.

"I've known Andy since he was at State," FDR recalled.

"Frances says she met the daughter at a Christmas party and took to her instantly. Apparently, she is bright, a Vassar graduate, and thanks to her Italian mother, she speaks the language fluently. And, she's a photographer."

"Not for a newspaper, I hope." The president frowned. "This would never stay under wraps, and it needs to."

"No, strictly freelance," Farley assured him. "Mostly artsy things for National Geographic."

Roosevelt gave a slow nod, "Okay, she sounds capable, and they won't be expecting a woman. When will she leave? You know time is short."

"That's the thing. She is already over there in Florence," Farley said with an assuring smile. "At the home of her mother's family."

"How was it arranged? I don't want a hint of this out anywhere."

"Very discretely. Frances first discussed it with the woman's old man and got his consent. He's a good guy, as solid as the Rock of Gibraltar, and she believes the daughter is a chip off the old block. It turns out Andy had a protégé who is assigned to the embassy in Rome. A model of discretion, he'll notify the daughter. Neither Ambassador Long nor Cordell has been read in on any of it."

"Damn it!" FDR exclaimed, his face full of concern. "That's still one more person who can throw a monkey wrench into this operation, and he's a diplomat to boot!"

"In this case, he's only a messenger, Mr. President," Farley said calmly. "Andy tells me the guy is an up and comer we can trust."

FDR leaned closer. "Okay, but it's her choice to accept or not. I don't want her taking risks. She is to act merely as an observer, nothing more."

"Absolutely. I know you like a book, Frank, and the messenger has been informed of every one of the wishes and precautions you just mentioned."

"Fine, let's not say any more about it," said FDR as he watched the New York skyline grow in the distance.

Chapter Fourteen

Friday, 1 June 1934

Florence, Italy

The day was unlike any promised in the travel brochures as the Tuscan sun, usually seen ascending above the towers and steeples of the city, was nowhere in sight. Gray skies and a steady rain wrapped Florence in gloom and masked the city's festive soul. In the drenched *piazza* in front of *Basilica di Santa Croce*, a street sweeper worked to remove the sopping debris left behind by the previous evening's crowds celebrating Italy's football win over Spain. The few others who had ventured out took refuge under black umbrellas as they went on their way.

Leaving his chore incomplete, the sweeper wheeled his barrel to the base of the statue of Dante Alighieri, climbed the steps to the basilica's main doors, and entered. Meanwhile, from the right, a woman in a floral dress and kerchief held an umbrella in one hand and a bulging sack gripped in the other as she waddled across the square. She called out to a thick-set man in a white apron leaning in the doorway of a small bar, *"Federico! Quando finirà questa pioggia?"*

The barman looked skyward and shrugged resignedly. "Only God knows when the rain will end." Taking advantage of a slight lull in the downpour, he began collapsing colorful umbrellas and removing the chairs and tables he had set out earlier. Maybe later the skies would clear, but for now, he would relax with a coffee and newspaper and consider an early *riposo*. As he worked, he paid little attention to the taxi that cut through the *piazza* and stopped at the cloister entrance on the right side of the church complex directly behind the Fiat 520 sedan of Martha Hughes Markham.

Sepp, looking rested and quite scholarly as he exited the cab, tugged the collar of his tan trench coat up to the brim of his fedora and hustled up the steps to the basilica's entrance. Doffing his hat as he passed through the vestibule, he proceeded into the dimly lit nave of the cavernous church. Immediately drawn to the bright glow of lights to his right, he was unaware of the slim man in a raincoat and soft woolen hat who had entered a few paces behind him.

As he walked to the lights, Sepp was drawn to the red-haired woman setting up equipment before one of the church's splendid monuments. He recognized it from photos as the tomb of Michelangelo Buonarroti, whose bust sat atop a marble sarcophagus. Three dolorous figures surrounded it before a wall decorated with frescoes representing some of the master's works. As the redhead stooped to move a stand by its base, Sepp considered her shapely form and concluded she could have posed for any of the three lovely mourners. *"Buongiorno, signorina,"* his words echoed in the vast open space.

She looked up. *"Buongiorno signore. Come la posso aiutare?"*

Struck by her beauty and vivacity, Sepp suddenly became unsure of his command of Italian as he asked, *"Lei parla tedesco o inglese?"*

Her smile dimmed, and she shook her head. "I'm not good at German," she said with a frown, "but English is my native tongue. Did you need some information about the memorials here? There are brochures in that stand." She pointed to a wooden rack along the wall.

"Oh, no, I am here for another reason. I was only curious about you." He indicated the light stands. "I mean, what you are doing."

"I am about to capture some images."

"A photographer! A woman photographer?"

"Is it so unusual?" she asked coolly.

"No, not at all," he replied with as much sincerity as he could muster. "Only a bit unexpected."

"Why does someone with no interest in art or architecture visit Santa Croce?" she asked.

"I am here to see Father Tucci," Sepp answered cautiously.

"Karp, are you bothering this lady?" called Tucci, coming up behind him.

Sepp immediately jumped on the priest's words, "Excuse me, Father Tucci? I am Professor Alexander Höbling. We have an appointment." He shot a furtive look at the priest.

Catching his slip, Tucci responded, "Ah, yes, my mistake, professor. You bear a great resemblance to a friend of mine. Please call me Father Guido, you know, like Guido the guide."

Sepp barely contained a guffaw. "Well, Father Guido, I have come to speak to you about Galileo. I understand you are quite an expert on the great inventor."

"Some say so." Tucci retrieved a handkerchief from his cassock sleeve and cleaned his glasses. "I am a simple priest merely intrigued by the man." He took Sepp's arm. "Come, we can talk in my office."

Tucci led Sepp toward the other side of the church, and as they passed the center aisle, he faced the main altar and genuflected. Owing to his childhood training, Sepp copied the move.

In a voice purposely loud enough for Martha to hear, Sepp announced, "Well, Father Guido, this is a grand church, and these tombs are most impressive."

"Let me show you the memorial to Galileo himself."

As they strolled, Sepp asked, "He is called a heretic, yet the Church honors him in this historic basilica. Why are you permitted to study him?"

They stopped in front of the tomb and Tucci replied, "Some say Galileo was the first modern scientist, for his methods as well as his insights and ingenuity. This is nineteen thirty-four, and we know so much more now. I honestly believe he will someday be vindicated. However, the Holy See moves at a snail's pace. Meanwhile, I explore him just as he explored the great ocean of space."

Sepp noted how each of the monument's sculptures, Galileo and the two figures representing philosophy and geometry, gazed up to the ceiling. The astronomer was depicted with one hand on a globe representing the universe, and the other grasping a telescope. It reminded Sepp why he was there. "The telescope there is small."

"It's art. The one I believe you want is considerably larger." He ushered Sepp back to the central aisle and added, "I'm sure you've seen the lithograph of the demonstration for the Doge many years ago."

"That's why I asked."

"Come, it's in my office."

As they approached the grand main altar, the pair went by sparsely populated pews of the faithful who knelt saying their rosaries, or sat back, contemplating their petitions to the deity. At one, Enzo Noschese kneeled, hat off and head lowered, eavesdropping on their conversation.

At the altar, Sepp paused and reflected upon the magnificent crucifix hanging above him. It was the basilica's namesake Holy Cross created by the artist Cimabue in the thirteenth century.

Meanwhile, once she had locked her Folmer-Graflex Autoflex camera onto its tripod, Martha watched the pair exit the church.

Tucci's office was stark with unadorned walls, except for a badly faded fresco, a bronze crucifix, and an ancient painting on wood of Saint Francis of Assisi kneeling in prayer. A dark oak table with a single center drawer, three chairs, and a painted wooden cabinet at the wall comprised the place's meager accouterments.

"Have a seat, old man," said Tucci as he sat behind the pitiable desk. "I've given this a great deal of thought and concluded that I must walk a narrow line here. I will not go against my vows or my conscience."

Sepp shrugged. "I wouldn't ask you to."

Tucci smiled, "In that case, I am ready to help. Austria is my second home, and I love her people, especially good friends like you and the prince."

"Starhemberg is a friend?"

"From my time in Venice. He visits Italy quite often and has been here for my grand tour." The priest gazed into space for a moment. "Well, be that as it may. Let's talk about what did you call it, your duty?"

"Mission. Look, you already know about Galileo's demonstration of his telescope to the Doge of Venice. I want to recreate that, and to do so, I need a passable duplicate of his instrument."

From behind his cabinet, Tucci produced a large print of the 1858 Bertini painting of the 1609 event. "You mean this. It shouldn't be a problem."

"Good! I also need help with a Venice connection. To make the re-enactment authentic, I must have access to the bell tower loggia."

"The demonstration for the Doge took place in August."

"The twenty-first." Seeing Tucci's look of skepticism, Sepp went on, "but I need time to make sure I duplicate it as accurately as possible."

"Karp, what kind of fool do you take me for?" Tucci said sternly. "I could begin to accept what you are saying if you were, in fact, a professor from the university. But I know you as a sharpshooter with the Austrian security service wanting to be up in the bell tower while Mussolini and Hitler are in the *piazza*." Tucci leaned over the desk. "You need to tell me exactly what's what."

Sepp avoided his friend's persistent stare.

"Look," Tucci went on, "let's treat this as a confessional. I can't give you absolution for something you plan to do, but I am bound never to reveal what you tell me."

"Okay, okay, you were right. But it's the German I'm after. Austrians have great respect for *Il Duce.* Chancellor Dollfuss is counting on him to keep Hitler at bay. As insurance, he came up with a plan to abduct Hitler so we can put him on ice in Tyrol." He moved in closer. "But Starhemberg ordered me to get rid of the mad Nazi altogether."

Tucci sat back, "I can't say I disagree."

"Then, do you still want to help?"

"I can't do that either. I won't accompany you over this Rubicon you seem determined to cross, but maybe I can help identify the rocks where you may step safely."

"Such as?" Sepp asked with raised brows.

"The Galileo cover story." Tucci proceeded to pull out three leather-bound books from the cabinet behind his table. "You are welcome to look these over. They are recently discovered letters and writings the experts say are in the master's own hand, written while he was in exile here. They will provide insight into a most complex man. Things that even seasoned scientists do not understand about him. They cannot leave here, but you may read them if you wish while I take care of some of my endless pastoral duties."

Sepp briefly thumbed through one of the books and looked at the priest with a blank stare.

"Ah, yes!" The priest opened the table drawer and handed Sepp a small stack of papers, "I have translations of the more important sections."

Sepp happily accepted the sheaf.

"Next, I offer you something that more directly affects your mission." He returned to the cabinet and served up a bound folder. Opening it to a bookmarked page, he ran his finger down a list of names. "Someone you can speak to in Venice."

Sepp's brow wrinkled, "I thought that would be you."

"I can do nothing directly, but I can contact Monsignor Virgilio Monaco and tell him about your re-creation and need for the tower." He got a pad and pencil from his drawer. "I knew him quite well during my days there. The good Monsignor is the archbishop's planner for such events. He may have some suggestions, and I think it better for you to meet and finalize this face-to-face." He carefully transcribed Monaco's name and office number on a slip of paper and handed it to Sepp.

"Very good." Sepp was glad to be making some early headway.

"Finally," Tucci went on, "I can help with the telescope."

"And, there is still the matter of a rifle," Sepp added. "We plan to conceal it in the telescope case." Seeing Tucci's dark stare, he clarified, "Look, if you feel uncomfortable with it, I have someone I can see in Venice."

"Your contact wouldn't happen to be an old flame, would she? I had heard rumors she was living in some *palazzo*. You know how the clergy love to gossip." The priest cut himself short when he saw Sepp's face turn ashen. "My God, man, what is it?"

Sepp wiped his tearful eyes. "She's gone … a few days ago." The words caught in his throat.

"Okay," suggested Tucci. "Let's take a break. Some wine?"

"No," Sepp insisted. "I need to put all that behind me and get this done."

"As you wish. The rifle in the telescope case. Have you thought about an alternative?"

"Such as?" Sepp was still fighting to control his emotions.

Tucci shrugged. "A rifle and a telescope all-in-one."

"You mean a rifle attached?"

"No, a rifle inside, giving the appearance of only the telescope."

"Is this possible?

"The fit will be a challenge because the Galileo telescope was not so big around, but I believe I have someone who can do it. It can certainly help get you past security in Venice." Tucci reached into his drawer again and held up a sketch of the concept. "I drew this earlier when I put two and two together about what you might be scheming." He pointed to the drawing. "Unlike the Galileo original, the gun barrel protrudes slightly, but can be made to appear as the spine of the telescope. The firing mechanism can be completely enclosed."

"Why, you old ..." Sepp's face was full of amazement. "You've been stringing me along."

The priest shrugged. "I may go to hell for this, but I hate the bas ... er, chancellor just as much as you do." Again, referring to the drawing, he added, "It doesn't show a great amount of detail, but I'm certain the man I have in mind can make it all—the complete package. He is here in Florence, but I met him in Rome when I was a liaison for the Swiss Guard, and they used his services for their, shall we say special requirements." Reading skepticism on Sepp's face, he explained. "Not for telescopes, but powerful aiming scopes for rifles. Not so different from what you need."

"When can we see him?"

Tucci checked his watch. "Later today, let's say at three. I'll pick you up at your hotel." He stood, "Meanwhile, enjoy the reading, and I'll return later." He left Sepp reviewing the Galileo books and papers.

As the morning wore on, Martha was about to complete coverage of the final memorial on her list, that of Gioachino Rossini. The tomb, a more recent addition to the church, had been erected just after the turn of the century. Because things had gone so well, she hoped to have time to photograph some of the basilica's art and architectural details. She planned to finish in time to go to the *Academia di Belle Arti* where Michelangelo's original statue of David was on display.

Father Tucci returned to his office just as Sepp was finishing with the last of the Galileo translations. "Well, what did you think?"

“A bit boastful and hard-headed, but his mind is amazing. He’s all over the map, and well beyond the astronomy he is known for.”

“Like most gifted artists and thinkers, a complex man. He truly belongs among our memorials here, don’t you agree?”

They spent time discussing Galileo’s so-called heretical ideas and concluded that the intractability of Holy Mother the Church was a mystery. When there was no more to say on the subject, Sepp shook Tucci’s hand and went to the door.

“The basilica has many great pieces of art. Don’t forget to consider more than the ginger you were ogling when I arrived.” Tucci nudged him and winked.

“I had planned to,” assured Sepp. “This whole place takes me back to the days when we studied the Church’s memorials. I have always looked forward to seeing them in real life.”

“Enjoy your tour,” Tucci said as he ushered Sepp back into the main church, “See you in a few hours.”

Having taken her eighth photo of the basilica’s main altar, Martha transferred the septum holding an exposed photographic plate to a black bag before returning it to the camera. Concentrating on arranging her next shot, she was unaware that Sepp had re-entered the church. Once she had extended the legs of the tripod as far as they would go, she set the camera at the highest extension, at a level with the gold-trimmed polyptych of the Virgin Mary and saints. Carefully climbing a step stool used by servers to reach tall candles, Martha looked into the camera’s viewfinder to finalize the composition and focus of the shot. She was about to press the shutter release when Sepp’s voice boomed from behind. “Hello again.”

His ill-timed greeting nearly knocked her off the stool and almost toppled the camera. As she fought to balance herself, he steadied the stool and reached up, offering his hand. She accepted it and climbed down, fuming.

“Well, that was utterly thoughtless of you!” she glared, hands on hips.

“I am sorry, miss. I didn’t mean to alarm you.”

“It’s missus. My God, are all you Germans so pushy? Couldn’t you see I was …”

Sepp covered her words with, “I am truly sorry. It was my mistake, and I am Austrian."

"German, Austrian, what's the difference?"

"Perhaps, you will allow me to atone for my sin in some way. Maybe I can assist you."

Martha's face softened. "I am almost done here and could use a hand gathering up my gear."

"Just call when you need me. I know little about cameras, but I certainly can help with the packing."

"You aren't a typical tourist, are you? They're always in a hurry."

"I am here on business from the University of Vienna, and for now, it has been seen to."

"Didn't I hear you use the title 'professor'?"

"Yes, Alex Höbling from Vienna. I have come for a consultation about the scientist Galileo. The priest is an expert."

"I see." She stuck out her hand, "Martha Markham," she said as he shook it, letting herself be charmed by the warm, dry grasp of the handsome Austrian. After all, maybe they were different from those awful Germans. As an afterthought, she added, "Didn't I hear Father Tucci call you by another name?"

Ready with a reply, Sepp explained, "Apparently, I resemble one of his old friends."

Satisfied, she returned to her work, and Sepp headed for the central aisle.

He explored other tombs and memorials of the basilica, unaware his every move was being observed. After Martha captured the remainder of her shots, she allowed the professor to help pack up.

As they carried her gear through the vestibule and out the main door, they were met by bright sunlight, which had breathed life back into the city. The *piazza* was busy with vendors, tourists, and Florentines going about their daily business.

Sepp and Martha loaded the back seat of her car, and she went to the driver's door of the vehicle.

"So, that's that," she proclaimed.

"Look," Sepp said, glancing about, "It has become such a lovely day. Certainly, not one to be wasted. Is there something I can get you for the trouble I caused?"

“Well,” her vision of the next hour or so had changed. She said coyly, “I do enjoy stopping at that café,” indicating Federico’s bar where tables and colorful umbrellas were again out on the sidewalk.

“Then, we must go,” Sepp said, offering his arm.

“Buongiorno,” came the greeting as they took seats at a table under a large red and white umbrella. “Ah, *Signora* Markham, what can I bring for you and the gentleman?”

“Buongiorno, Federico,” Martha replied and looked to Sepp.

“Caffe’ per favore,” Sepp responded as he decided to enjoy this happy interlude.

Martha screwed up her mouth and thought for a moment. “Today, I choose *Caffe’ Americano,* and one of the delicious rice tortes I love.”

“Sí.” Federico grinned. *“La torta di riso.”* Adding with a hopeful grin, “Maybe you also enjoy a nice *panino*. All fresh this morning.”

She looked at Sepp, and they both nodded. “Bring my favorite one.”

“I’ll have the same,” Sepp agreed, figuring the favorite sandwich of a beautiful woman had to be tasty. “Do you come here often?”

“Lately, quite. Somehow, my path usually ends up at Federico’s. In Florence, nothing is that far. It seems no matter what museum or church I visit, I always manage to find my way here.” Sepp nodded as she twisted an errant strand of hair on her index finger, “Federico likes to flirt, and I make it easy for him. Italian men are all such little boys.”

He clucked his tongue. “Naughty, naughty.”

Martha sat up in her chair and folded her hands before her. “So, tell me more about your study of Galileo. Why here, when he was from Pisa?”

“He was, but he did quite a bit of work in Florence and was even confined here after the debacle with the Church.”

“Is that why you came?”

“That and for his telescope.”

Martha brightened. “Interesting. Camera lenses are much like telescopes.” She slid into more questions. “Will you be here long? Did you watch football?”

“I’m here for a few days, maybe a week, and no to the latter.

Although I did play a bit as a young boy, the game never consumed me as it does so many children. My thoughts were always elsewhere.

"You mean, the ether of the universe."

"Exactly." She was making his pretense easy for him. "You see, my real work is in Venice, where I must prepare for an event marking an anniversary of Galileo's demonstration of his instrument to the Doge."

"Venice," there it was again. For the second time in two days, it seemed to be beckoning her. "What a coincidence," she said, almost gleefully. "I have to be in Venice myself to photograph the monuments there and possibly cover the Hitler visit." That was it. Despite some lingering doubts, she admitted to herself that she had fully committed to the FDR mission.

Federico arrived carrying a tray with the two coffees, *panini*, and a rice torte. He set the cups before Martha and Sepp, then laid out two spoons and two forks, adding with a wink, "I bring if you wish to share."

As the friendly server left for another table, Sepp took a bite of *panino* and found it quite delightful. He sipped his coffee and asked, "When are you going there?"

She held up her hand. "I didn't realize how famished I am. Let's hold the small talk for now. I'm hungry."

They ate in silence, savoring the fresh, crusty bread filled with prosciutto, tomato slices, and mozzarella cheese, ordering more coffee in the process.

Martha devoured a forkful of the sweet, grainy rice dessert and pushed the plate toward the man who was fast becoming a friend. "Please, try some. It's *delizioso*."

He sampled a modest piece then asked, "Are you on a schedule?"

"I need to get my photographs to the Geographic by the end of June, so I get to set my own."

"A liberated woman." He cocked his head. "I find it refreshing." Looking down into the remaining black liquid in his cup, he leaned her way and asked, "Do you mind if I smoke?"

"The pipe of a professor, I suppose."

The Amneris box he pulled from his jacket pocket told her

otherwise.

"In that case, I only mind if you don't offer me one."

"A free spirit, too!" He opened the box toward her.

As she selected a cigarette, she could smell the aroma of its strong tobacco. "If our first lady can smoke in public, so can I."

"And, a rebel to boot," he observed as he lit them both. "You do surprise me."

She shrugged, "Sometimes, I surprise myself." She pushed the torte toward him again, but this time he refused.

"I am quite satisfied with this," Sepp said, draining his coffee.

When Martha polished off the last of her treat, Sepp pushed back his chair, pulled out his purse, and laid some lira coins on the table. "I need to see about my train reservations to Venice."

He started to rise, but her "Wait" caused him to settle back down.

"You can add impetuous to that list of my traits." She looked squarely at him. "How would you like to join me on a drive to Venice? We can make the trip in less than a day."

"I wouldn't want to impose, and I'll have this rather cumbersome telescope."

"The car has plenty of room, and it should fit right in with my gear. Besides, it is better than taking it on the train. The railway situation in Bologna is a mess."

Sepp realized he would not only have the company of this fascinating woman, but he also could avoid the hassle of transporting the Galileo copy. "In that case, I accept your gracious offer." As he said it, he silently vowed to do everything he could to keep Martha from the turmoil that surely lay ahead for him.

Federico picked up their empty plates and cups and said, "*Signora* Markham, I must tell you I close tomorrow. I go to Milano for the next match of *calcio*—the football. *Italia* meets Austria, and my cousin there has tickets for the game."

Martha responded, "Thank you for telling me. I will miss my Sunday visit, but I wish your team good luck."

The barman nodded and left, and Martha turned again to Sepp. "I read where the Italian team beat the Americans by a score of seven to one. I would feel embarrassed, except this game of football is different than the one we play in the states."

"For you, this is soccer."

She got up, and he did the same. "Can I drop you somewhere?"

"I think I'll walk over to the David statue. My taxi passed it on the way this morning, but it was raining." He stretched. "Besides, I feel I have been sitting for too long."

"The David in *Piazza della Signoria.* You know it's a copy."

"I had heard, but since sculpture is not exactly my element, I shouldn't be able to differentiate. Two similar nebulae would have hundreds of variations, but statues?" Sepp delighted in his impromptu comparison.

"The original was moved to the Academy of Fine Arts about sixty years ago to protect it from the elements. You must see the real one, professor. I am going there next. Come with me, and I shall explain the nuances."

He looked at his watch. "It does sound quite interesting, but I am afraid I have no time now."

From several tables away, Enzo Noschese, hat pulled down obscuring his face, watched as they stood and came his way. As they passed him, the reporter overheard Martha ask, "So, professor, have you never seen any of what Florence has to offer?"

"Only in photographs. My visit here is barely a day old."

She latched on to his arm. "It's settled then. I must show you as much as possible in the few days you have. The Academy, the *Duomo*, the *Bargello*, *San Lorenzo*, and of course, the *Uffizi*.

Sepp paused a few paces past Noschese's table. "I much appreciate your offer. However, today I have an appointment at three."

She tugged him onward, "Then, we must set a schedule."

"Goodbye, Mrs. Markham, and sir," Federico called from the doorway as he wiped off a serving tray.

"*Ciao,* Federico," Martha called back, and Sepp echoed her words as they continued into the *piazza*.

Noschese paid for his mineral water and went swiftly to his car. Seeing that Martha was alone as her Fiat exited the square, he scanned the *piazza* and spotted Sepp walking toward the far end.

* * *

Bright highlights tinged the cottony clouds set in a Tuscan-blue sky as Father Tucci drove across the Trinity Bridge. Awaiting the priest and Sepp on the other side was the *Oltrarno,* where many local artists and artisans lived and plied their skills. Following the *lungarno* upriver, then over a winding cobbled byway, they arrived at an area below Fort Belvedere. The priest turned into a side alley and stopped before a large brown door and a quaintly decorated window full of carved wooden toys, trinkets, and game pieces. The sign told them they were at the shop of Reinhard Tropp *Giocattolaio*—toymaker. In smaller German lettering, it said, *"Der Spielzeugmacher."*

"Here we are, Kar … er, professor," announced Tucci.

"A toy shop! Are you joking?"

Before the priest could respond, the door opened, and out came a man with an angelic face, a shock of white hair, and round eyeglasses. Wearing work clothes and a leather apron, he resembled a beardless version of Thomas Nast's Santa Claus. Grinning, he called out, "Greetings, Father Tucci. It is so good to see you."

As they exited the car, the priest replied, "Reinhard, it is wonderful to see you as well."

Tropp hugged his friend whose cheeks glowed with delight. "Father, it has been too long since your last visit. I have been saving some fine schnapps for you."

"I am sorry I don't get over here more often. The work of God you know."

Tropp waved off the apology, "I'm afraid I don't get to *Santa Croce* nearly often enough." Seeing a look of practiced disappointment cross the priest's face, he pointed up the hill, "I do attend *San Miniato*."

Tucci smiled and backed away, extending an arm toward Sepp. "Reinhard Tropp, I want you to meet my great friend. This is prof …"

"Of course," Tropp cut him off. "*Herr* Karper."

"You know me?" Sepp asked, nonplussed, as he shook Tropp's hand.

"Certainly! A fellow Austrian who is quite famous in my world. The beard is new, but your face has not changed." He squinted. "The glasses? Has your vision failed?"

"Oh, these," Sepp took them off. "Part of my charade. I'm under cover as Professor Alexander Höbling of the University of Vienna."

"I see," responded Tropp. "Your secret is safe with me, I assure you."

Tucci patted his buddy on the back, "Best not to leave those off. Didn't you say someone recognized you already?"

"Right out of the blue." Sepp put on the glasses.

"We all must play our roles." Tropp waved them in. "Come, gentlemen." He stood back and allowed the two visitors to enter the shop. As they did, two boys who had been playing with a ball in the street waved, *"Ciao, Petto!"*

As Tropp returned the greeting, Tucci explained, "He must put them in mind of Collodi's woodcarver because, to many, he is their own Geppetto, the maker of Pinocchio."

"Interesting," said Sepp, taking in the room full of carved items in various phases of completion, all lined up in rows and set in neat piles.

His look of wonder prompted Tropp to explain, "You didn't expect me to have all my wares on display, did you? What would people say?" He then led his two visitors past bins of doll heads, hands, and feet, followed by partially assembled trucks, cars, and wooden chess pieces. They came to a dark area where there stood a massive wardrobe, its Florentine decoration barely visible through the decades of built-up hand oils and grime. He opened the two doors, tugged on a floor panel, and turned an electric switch, illuminating a wooden ladder leading below. "This takes us to my other workshop." He stepped back and directed them to the ladder. "Please."

Sepp was about to follow the toymaker's instruction when Tucci grabbed him by the elbow. "Wait," he said. "I really must get back." The priest reached into his pocket and retrieved the sketch he showed Sepp the day before. He handed it to Tropp. "This is a rough idea of what I believe the professor needs." He looked to Sepp. "I'm sure you can fill in the details."

Sepp patted his friend's back, "Absolutely."

Tucci said his goodbyes, and moments later, Sepp and Tropp descended to the basement.

Meanwhile, outside, Enzo Noschese observed the priest get into his car and drive away, alone. He did not follow.

From the base of the ladder, Sepp surveyed the gunsmith's shop. "Wonderful," he proclaimed, breathing in the musty coolness. The walls were lined with shelves and racks full of complete weapons and gun parts, all carefully organized. Off to the left sat a long, rough-hewn workbench with two vises, an electric lathe, an anvil, an array of hand tools, and bins of small metal bits and pieces.

"What's this?" When Sepp stepped closer to examine the micrometers and calipers, on the wall, he noticed a clipping of an article with a photograph of him aiming a rifle.

"You see, I do know of you," Tropp grinned. "I have arranged to receive Austrian periodicals. They are out of date, but I am in no hurry to hear of the demise of our country. Over the years, there have been articles about you and your expertise with a rifle."

"I avoid such notoriety. In the army, I am anonymous. Just another soldier fortunate to possess a God-given skill. It's all simply a matter of my hands aiming precisely where my eyes lead them."

"Fine enough to compete in the Olympics, yes?"

Sepp nodded, "They wanted me to go, but as fate would have it, it was never to be."

Tropp shook his head. "Such a pity."

Sepp continued with a fuller explanation. "The first time I qualified was in 1920, but Austria didn't participate that year. In 1924, I had a terrible bronchial ailment and never even tested for the team."

"So, you missed out on the games in Paris."

"Missing Paris was bad, but the worst of it was when Austria failed to send a shooting team to Los Angeles two years ago. I believe that's when this photo was taken." He pointed to the article.

"Too bad." Tropp moved to the large workbench.

"Now, my dreams as an Olympian are over."

"Be consoled that you continue to use your skill for the homeland." Tropp's cherubic face turned serious. He laid out Tucci's drawing. "Let's see what we have here." He eyed the paper carefully. "I have made many rifles with scopes, but never a rifle within a scope." He ran his fingers through his hair. "It will be difficult." Scratching his head, he added, "However, I enjoy such challenges."

As Sepp stepped closer to the bench, he heard a rustling and squeaking. He had disturbed what he discovered to be an obese rat.

A sense of fear rooted in his early childhood overtook him, and he jumped back.

"What is it?"

"I hate those little bastards," Sepp shouted as he grabbed a hammer lying by the anvil. Stooping, he took two wild swipes at the brown and gray creature and missed both times.

"Your eyes and hands are not so effective at this," Tropp said as he pulled a cord over the bench, and instantly a brightness filled the room, sending the rat scurrying. "But it is just as well. The light will keep him away for a time. He fears you as much as you fear him."

"Why not set traps and kill him?"

"It is not in my nature to destroy another being."

"Reinhard, you make weapons."

"If I made pencils, would I then be responsible for the rubbish passing for good writing these days?"

Sepp acknowledged Tropp's logic with a grunt.

The toymaker went to a cabinet where he pulled open a wide, flat drawer containing a variety of plans and drawings. From among them, he produced a diagram of a telescope. "You see, I have done something similar in the past. It was not a weapon, but the design can be adapted. However, it cannot be exact," explained Tropp. "With the rifle internal to the scope, I will have to make certain adjustments. The instrument will be larger than the one usually depicted to accommodate the mechanism you require. I believe I can use the workings of a *Steyr-Mannlicher* M-95, a rifle I am sure you know."

"Yes," Sepp responded. "I own one, with a scope. And I used the M-1895 during the war."

"A fine weapon, but it and the added weight of the telescope will require sturdy support. I suggest a floor stand for more stability. A table stand is often shown; some paintings describe it differently: a longer scope with a tall stand, so we are safe. I will follow a copy of the painting that best suits our needs."

"Please, as close as you can make it."

"Who will know?" asked Tropp rhetorically. "None of the paintings were contemporaneous, and you, my dear professor, are the expert. They will believe what you tell them."

"I'm counting on it."

Tropp continued, "The magazine will be limited to maybe one or two rounds and one in the chamber. "

"I shall need only one," said Sepp confidently. "The second can be fired for misdirection."

Tropp continued describing his vision for the weapon. "A series of prisms and mirrors will make it a working telescope. It will be quite convincing to anyone who looks into it. It will also allow you to move in on your target. Galileo's was eight power. This one I expect will be closer to twenty. Focus on the exact center of the field of view, and your shot will be true. I shall calibrate it precisely and add crosshairs to guide you."

Sepp stroked his beard. "Will I be able to use the rifle separate from the scope?"

Tropp shrugged. "That adds yet another design challenge, but it can be done."

"This 'mechanism' as you call it, is it overly complicated?"

"We shall see."

"How long will it take to construct?"

"A week, possibly less. I have or can manufacture everything except for the optical parts, which I will order directly. This work is all I will do until it is complete." Tropp promised. "I, too, want a free Austria."

Sepp patted the toymaker's back. "You are most gracious, *Herr* Tropp." He looked around for the rat before stepping to the ladder.

Tropp did not follow, but reached into a cabinet over the bench and produced two glasses and a bottle. "Before you go, we have a drink. It is the way here." He poured a half glass of a light wine for each of them. "To success!"

"Success," Sepp agreed then took a small swallow and set the glass down. "Now, I will leave you to your work."

"May I drive you?" Tropp asked.

"Oh, that will not be necessary. My hotel is not far, and I enjoy a walk." He again headed for the ladder.

"Wait!" Tropp pointed to a door at the far end of the room. "This way. It is for my special customers." He accompanied Sepp to the door that opened onto an alley. "Go right here and then left to descend to the river."

They shook hands, and Sepp left Tropp promising to make the finest "toy" he had ever fashioned.

Noschese checked his watch. It had been well over an hour since he had last seen Karper. He returned to focusing on the toy shop door. A minute later, it opened.

Tropp emerged and waved to the children playing in the street. He beckoned, inviting them to join him. As they disappeared into the toy shop, Noschese rolled his Fiat slowly past the shop, straining to peer inside. He saw no sign of Sepp.

Chapter Fifteen

Sunday, 3 June 1934

Milan, Italy

The announcer for the Italian Radio Station, E.I.A.R., watched the crowd filling the stands, nodded to his technician, and began his commentary. "This is Nicolò Carosio reporting from San Siro Stadium, Milan, where we hear there has been a record for gate receipts for this semi-final match of the World Cup. Two long-time football rivals, Italy and Austria, will face off to determine who will advance to the championship game in Rome next week."

Austrian Chancellor, Engelbert Dollfuss, seated in a special section at midfield about halfway up in the grandstand, scanned the access stairway expectantly. Next to him, Prince Ernst Starhemberg offered, "Engel, he said he would come, and I believe him. Did he not specifically invite us?"

"He did. When the games first began, we promised if Italy met Austria, we would both attend." His soft eyes scanned the prince's face. "I verified this with him only two days ago, and we know how dedicated he is to supporting football. It has become the sport of fascism."

"Not for him, personally." Starhemberg reminded.

"I believe his two favorites are horseback riding and fencing."

"And," the prince raised his index finger, "his preoccupation with women may account for his absence."

"Still, he is a man of his word. I expect he will be here."

The announcer proclaimed, "Here we go! Come on, Italy!" just as a security guard captain approached them.

"Excuse me, Excellency."

Dollfuss looked up. "Yes, what is it?"

"Our office has received word, sir. A most important matter has detained *Il Duce,* and he will not be able to attend the game today. He sends his regrets and says he will contact you soon."

"I see," Dollfuss replied tersely. "Thank you for informing me."

The guard saluted and left, and Dollfuss turned to his compatriot. "I don't know what to think. Who has such urgent matters on Sunday?"

"Anything I say may do a disservice to the leader of this fine country," Starhemberg responded as he turned to watch the battle on the field.

Although his national team was playing, Dollfuss was too distracted to act the spectator. Dark thoughts crowded his mind: Was Mussolini forsaking an old friendship in favor of a relationship with the German? Would *Il Duce* withdraw his support for Austrian independence in favor of acquiring more power from an alliance with Germany?

As the game progressed, the Austrian chancellor's concern grew. Could he no longer rely on the man he considered a friend? He nudged the prince. "I must ask you," he said, his voice barely rising above the din of the crowd. "Do you believe he is setting Austria adrift?"

"It is possible, but not likely."

"Why, then, did he not come? Does he not wish to be seen by the world sitting here next to us?"

The prince patted Dollfuss's knee. "Maybe he did not feel well. Maybe he chose to spend the day with his family or one of his whores. Who knows what motivates the man at any particular time?"

"Maybe! Maybe! Maybe!" Dollfuss repeated. "How can we know? What can we do?"

"First, we do know he will host Hitler in less than two weeks. Mussolini is strong in his position while the German is an upstart awarded the chancellorship to calm the masses. So, we must believe your friend has good motives for the meeting and sees the chance to gain from it. All indications are he is going to defend the interests of Austria and the terms of the Versailles treaty."

Dollfuss considered Starhemberg's words before concluding, "If this is all true, then we must succeed with our plans for Hitler."

Starhemberg nodded. “Yes.”

“The abduction!” Dollfuss said firmly.

“As you wish, Excellency.”

“Ernst, what is your wish?”

“Maybe a more final solution.”

Dollfuss shook his head. “I will not condone murder.”

Starhemberg pressed, “Isn’t that how we have suppressed the communists and Nazis? Is it not the means by which you gained power?”

The Austrian chancellor slumped down. “Please. I have paid dearly for what I allowed to happen. Not even the grace of the confessional relieves me of the burden of guilt I carry.” He sat up. “I will not permit such a cold-blooded solution, especially of a man representing an entire country who has taken no direct action against us. I fear my soul would not survive. Abduction is the only way.” He grabbed the prince’s sleeve. “You must see to it. Karper must succeed, but can he do it alone?”

“A resource in Italy will be available to assist when the time comes.”

Dollfuss went silent, lost once again in his thoughts.

Chapter Sixteen

Tuesday, 5 June 1934

Florence, Italy

Stella d'Oro, the albergo recommended by Mosconi, was small but stylish and situated in an alley between *via del Corso* and the *Bargello*. Inside, room 301 was dominated by a large, wooden wardrobe next to a neatly upholstered chair, a disheveled bed, and a small table holding a tray with a coffee pot and rolls. In his underwear, revealing his skinny arms and chicken-like legs, Enzo Noschese stood by the window sipping from a cup decorated with the hotel's crest as he planned his next moves regarding Sepp Karper. Rays of morning sunlight played off the basilica's cupola and reflected from the golden orb and cross atop the dome's lantern. It reminded him of the photos he had seen of the torch held high by Lady Liberty in New York harbor. "America. I must go. I would be respected there." He pondered what it would be like to live in the land of tall buildings, speeding cars, burgeoning industries, and Hollywood glitz. He would give anything to consort with one of those platinum blonde actresses whose images had invaded the theaters of Rome and titillated him so often.

Shaking his head, he reminded himself, "Work must come first." Setting the coffee cup on the tray, Noschese went to the wardrobe where he retrieved his notepad from a jacket pocket. Returning to the bed, he read the entries carefully, recalling the circumstances of each recorded event beginning with the diplomat's trip to Florence.

Below the 29 May entry, "Ravelli, *Firenze treno stanotte*." He had written the following:

"29 May - Motor to Florence. Hotel *Stella d'Oro*.

30 May - R at Villa Donati - villa of a goldsmith. Old widow, red-haired woman, small girl. R. visits, leaves, returns, leaves again.

At bar, R claims he is on personal business - denies interest in Venice.

31 May - Novella station - R off to Rome K met by priest taken to hotel *Vecchio Vista.* I question K—uses cover of professor Alex Höbling

1 June - K at Santa Croce as a Professor Höbling—meets with priest who drove him from Novella station. Father Tucci. Redhead from Villa Donati at SC to photo tombs. Later K done with Tucci, helps redhead pack equipment then to Federico's bar. Her name: *Signora* Markham (SM). American?

1 June - Priest and K to small toy shop (Austrian? German?) Priest leaves, K disappears. Later in his hotel bar.

2 June - K again meets with priest with SM at *Accademia di Belle Arti* - view David - SM tour guide. *Piazza della Signoria - Palazzo Vecchio - via dei Calzaiuoli* (walk) to *Duomo.* Later, *Uffizi*—overhear discussion—Caravaggio. he likes, she hates 'too harsh.' Both love Botticelli, coffee at Federico's - SM orders Americano - stroll the *lungarno* and supper at *Trattoria Giovanni* Small, few tables - observed from outside - romance possible?"

Noschese scribbled at the bottom of the page, "All as expected." Adding with an underline, "Except for the woman?" He tossed the pad aside, bit off a piece of a roll, and gulped his coffee.

* * *

Sepp Karper had a spring in his step as he crossed the *Ponte Vecchio*, it's shops shuttered awaiting the arrival of the gold merchants and the leather and art vendors. At the end of the bridge, he turned left under the Vasari corridor and followed the street along the Arno as he began the trek up to *Herr* Tropp's shop.

Not fifty paces behind him, Enzo Noschese crept his car along the roadway. When he saw Sepp bear right up *via dei Bardi*, he concluded, "Aha! The toymaker. Good!"

Tropp greeted Sepp with, "*Ach*, Herr *Professor. Guten Morgen.* Everything is in order and ready to go."

"*Morgen, Herr* Tropp. Quite fine." replied Sepp before adding in a lower voice, "I have a friend coming here later. She will help me transport the instrument to Venice, but she knows nothing."

"I understand," the toymaker patted his shoulder, "It will remain no more than a copy of a historic telescope to the uninformed. However, for you, it is most reliable and lethal. Come, let me show you." He headed for the wardrobe and waved for Sepp to follow. "I have also fashioned a sturdy box and a stand," the toymaker declared proudly.

In the basement, Tropp went over the telescope with his customer. "The original was wood, covered with leather, but for our purpose, I used a metal tube of aluminum for weight and strength, covered with a similar hide."

"I see," Sepp said, marveling at the toymaker's artistry.

Tropp continued, "As I told you, it is slightly larger than the original, which was less than a meter in length. This one is some twenty percent longer, broader, and the eyepiece and objective lens are bigger to accommodate the weapon. I also needed room for a special prism to erect the image, making it right side up." Tropp stared expectantly at Sepp. "Well?"

"It looks much like the one in the picture to me," Sepp concluded.

"Because it is proportional and will appear so to any curious guard or inspector." Tropp's eyes sparkled. "Now, here is the most important thing." With his thumbnail, he pulled open a small lever on the side of the tube. "This readies the weapon, places crosshairs in the lens, and reveals the muzzle. You will see a bulge in the lower part of the tube. Don't worry. It is the barrel stretching the leather. Once you find the target in the eyepiece, you pull carefully on the lever, and it will fire. There is no return mechanism, so you will need to push it forward to move the second round into the chamber." As Sepp looked in the eyepiece, Tropp added, "You have two chances—no more."

Sepp nodded. "One more than I will require."

Tropp pointed to a small latch, "And, should you need to separate it from the scope, you pull on this firmly. The body opens, and you will have your rifle. Be sure to unfold the small stock."

Sepp's one-word appraisal: *"Wunderbar!"*

"A final caution," added Tropp. "Jostling it may affect the calibration."

Sepp asked, "Won't firing it have the same effect? I mean the recoil."

"I have compensated for that in two ways. You see, the barrel is mounted so that it acts as a piston, canceling out much of the recoil. Secondly, the ammunition is not conventional. It is much like a small rocket that I have manufactured myself. Respecting Herr Newton's law, I decided to eliminate the burst of energy at the point of firing and extend it over the flight of the projectile, which gains speed as it goes. There is little action at the muzzle, thus little reaction."

"And, that is taken care of by the piston effect," concluded Sepp.

"Precisely," the toymaker replied with a wink.

"Ingenious!"

"So," Tropp went on. "Another threat to calibration is in transporting it." He pointed to the box. "I have installed ample padding to help keep it safe." He picked up the folded stand lying in the box. "The telescope will mount easily on this stand and provide secure support."

"Fine work!"

"Anything for Austria! And, please remember, if you remove the rifle, it will be difficult, maybe impossible, to reinstall. Certainly, time-consuming."

"Sir, I do not wish to question the weapon's accuracy, but I would like to fire it."

"Come this way." He led him to a ceiling-to-floor wall panel. "I have tested it and provided two rounds for you to try. That leaves two missiles of the five I was able to make." He pulled the panel open. "You are welcome to use my private range and see for yourself."

Tropp turned a light switch, illuminating a long corridor with various targets along the way.

"Fantastic!" exclaimed Sepp. "This must have been a challenge to build."

Tropp smiled. "I never had to. It is part of an abandoned tunnel system leading to Fort Belvedere. It was the primary reason why I located my shop here."

Sepp entered the tunnel while Tropp retrieved the telescope and set its stand atop a mark on the passageway's floor. "There," he said. "This is two-hundred meters from the most distant target. I think that should give you a proper test."

"Fine," Sepp agreed as he put his eye to the lens, deployed the trigger mechanism as Tropp had instructed, and took aim.

Tropp stepped back and watched as the first of the deadly projectiles sped to the target. A few heartbeats later, a second one escaped the rifle's muzzle.

Sepp trotted toward the target, calling back as he went, "I had it all perfectly aligned in the crosshairs." Moments after he got there, he shouted, "A great triumph, my friend!"

Tropp was all smiles when the marksman returned with two holes in the bull's eye. "Now, it will take time for me to reload and recheck it. Please, feel free to go to meet your friend."

Sepp checked his watch. "I don't expect her for another twenty minutes or more."

From up the street, Noschese sat in his car observing, discouraged that nothing had happened at the shop since he had arrived. He was about to quit his surveillance when a familiar redhead drove by and stopped in front of the toy shop.

Martha entered Tropp's establishment and found the professor and the toymaker waiting for her by a long, narrow box sitting on one of the workbenches.

She greeted them brightly, *"Buongiorno."*

Sepp stepped forward. "Mrs. Markham, may I introduce Herr Tropp, the wonderful toymaker."

Her smile melted the formality as she extended her hand. "Please, call me Martha."

Tropp bowed. "And, you must call me Reinhard."

Sepp added, "To the children, he is *'Geppetto,'* like the father of Pinocchio."

She looked around the room, "I can see why." Walking between the tables, she was examining the bins of Tropp's carvings when something in an out-of-the-way box caught her eye. "Oh, my!" she exclaimed. Reaching into it, she extracted a small, wooden spinning toy with a distinctive square shape and a large Hebrew letter on each side. “Dreidel!” she held it up like a child who had just opened a present. “We played it on Chanukah.”

Sepp shot Tropp a surprised look, and the toymaker shrugged. “I have meant to move those to my basement,” he said sheepishly. “Things Jewish are not so fashionable these days.”

“But you told Father Tucci you attended Mass,” Sepp said incredulously.

“I am Catholic, and I do, but I respect the traditions of those who gave us the very roots of our religion,” Tropp answered. “Persecution has no limits, and for me, the handwriting has been on the wall for years. It has become indelible since the rise of the Nazis. That Austrian bas …” He cleared his throat and eyed Martha. “Excuse me. He is coming to Italy, and I dread what that might mean.”

Sepp put his hand on Tropp’s shoulder. “None of us knows what the future holds.” He then turned to Martha and patted the box containing the telescope. “Let’s get this to your car.”

Noschese watched as the Markham woman held open the Fiat’s rear door and Sepp deposited a long box on the back seat. As she took her place behind the wheel, the reporter wondered, “Could it contain a weapon?” He continued observing as the Austrian professor went back to the shop and returned carrying a small package.

They drove off and left Noschese pondering what he had witnessed. “He is definitely a threat.” He started the engine. “I don’t understand about the toys or where she fits in, but he is up to something.”

* * *

Villa Donati glowed a stunning burnt orange in the afternoon beauty light as the Fiat sedan entered the driveway.

Martha announced, “Here we are.”

“My God, the place is a *schloss*,” Sepp observed.

“I did say grandfather was a successful goldsmith, didn’t I?”

“Successful, indeed,” Sepp agreed then frowned. “So, now I am to meet your grandmother.”

“Does it concern you?”

“New people are always uncomfortable for me,” he admitted in a low voice. “I am much more at ease at the eyepiece of a telescope.”

"My God," Martha reacted, "How did you ever get up the gumption to ask me for coffee?"

"You made it easy. It was as if I had known you for years." He looked her in the eyes. "I am sorry. I have said too much." He grabbed the package from the seat. "Here, Reinhard asked me to give you this."

She tore open the brown paper and exclaimed, "The *dreidel*! How thoughtful."

From a vantage point above the villa, Noschese watched happenings that made little sense to him. Why was Karper at the same villa Ravelli had visited? Bursting with curiosity, he saw the man carry the box into the house. Nothing more happened for several minutes until they both appeared on the balcony, along with a tubular contraption mounted on a stand.

"Un cannocchiale!" exclaimed Noschese. "What is he doing with a telescope?" It began to make sense to him when he saw a young girl join them. "Aha, to amuse the child!" he concluded as he set aside the field glasses and slumped down in his seat.

"Mommy says the telescope brings things closer. Is that right, Professor Höbling?" asked Melissa.

As he checked to ensure the small latch Tropp had demonstrated was in the safe position, Sepp responded, "Yes, Lissa, in a way."

"You mean it can move things?"

"What your mom meant is it will make what is far away appear closer." He swung the telescope so that it was overlooking the Arno and zeroed in on the dome of the Cathedral of *Santa Maria del Fiore*. "Here, have a look." He grabbed a chair and stood the child on it, holding her steady while she peered into the instrument.

"It is closer!" came her amazed reaction. "Mommy, come and see."

Martha obliged and peered at the cupola that seemed more than twice as large as with the naked eye. "My goodness, isn't it amazing?"

Signora Donati arrived on the balcony and was immediately invited to the telescope by her great-granddaughter.

The old woman then took her turn. "Oh, my!" Her reaction was for the benefit of her granddaughter, having had her first look through a telescope many years earlier. "This is the best I have ever seen. Isn't it wonderful, child?" She backed away. "Now, you must sit, and we will have something nice in honor of our guest."

Lucia carried in a large tray of assorted pastries, which she placed on the linen-covered top of the wrought iron table at the center of the balcony. She disappeared for a moment while everyone took their seats at the table then returned with cups of coffee and a glass of milk for Melissa.

Bored and disappointed, Noschese released the emergency brake and let his car coast quietly down the hill.

Rome, Italy

At his desk in the Headquarters of the *Polizia di Stato* in Rome, Arturo Bocchini was taking a stack of incident reports from the previous day out of a large folder when the phone rang. He frowned and picked up the receiver.

"Bocchini." He listened to the mellow, masculine voice in the earpiece.

"Yes, but Lorenzo, why are you bothering me with this?" He paused. "I see. Anonymous? A man? May I remind you of the problems some of these unidentified callers have caused in the past." With raised, pleading eyes, Bocchini muttered, "Why me, Lord?" A second later, another response refocused him. "He what! The country's security?" He paused and rubbed his face. "Alright, put him through, and have someone discover where the call is originating."

Bocchini barely had enough time to take a pad of paper and pencil from a side drawer before a raspy voice sounded in the earpiece. "Yes, national importance, but may I know with whom I am speaking?" Another pause, then, "I see, you are concerned for your safety. Please, tell me the details."

Bocchini scribbled notes as the caller communicated his message.

"In Italy? Sir, many Austrians are living here, and others have come for the football." The chief of state police shook his head in disgust. "In Florence, an agent named Karper in disguise? As what?

A professor from Vienna? Possibly armed."

The chattering over the receiver became more insistent.

"What about this redhead with him?" Bocchini asked. "An American, you say?"

The pencil lead broke from the intense pressure of his hand. Until finally, one word captured his attention. "Hitler? Are you certain?" The response was short and convincing. "I will have someone check into this immediately."

He pressed the receiver cradle twice. "Lorenzo, I need you to follow up on some information. It may be nothing, but it concerns Venice." As his aide entered, he asked, "Did you learn the origin of the call?"

Lorenzo replied, "Only that it came from somewhere in the north."

Venice, Italy

The phone line connected directly to state police headquarters rang insistently at the desk of Antonio Marino, police Inspector General for the Veneto region.

"Pronto," said Marino.

"Antonio, my friend," Bocchini's voice was genial. "You know I have ears everywhere, but I also trust my instincts, and they are telling me disturbing things concerning this meeting in Venice. I smell a rat, and when it stinks as it does, I worry."

"Yes, sir, and I have made provisions. We have ample resources to protect the two leaders," Marino assured him.

"It is not enough! I want an extra measure of precaution. Someone with intuition as keen as mine. Someone who works outside the usual channels and can dig for and discover the truth—the unexpected threats; the secret plots; the figures in the shadows."

"Sir. I know your preferences and have been considering them. I believe I have precisely the man for the job!"

"You anticipate me well," complimented Bocchini. "Who is this mastermind?"

"Luigi Petrin."

"He's a drunkard!" Bocchini exclaimed. "Are you mad?"

“Sir, he is better tipsy than most sober. And, when he is kept away from the bottle, which I will ensure, no one can match him.”

“You realize, you are putting your neck on the block if he fails.” During the silence that followed, he added, “Just the same, I will have a portfolio of the latest information and my concerns delivered by courier.”

The line went dead, and Marino wiped the sweat from his brow. “Shit!” he grumbled, blotting his face. “The bastard had better not fail.” He would be counting on an inspector from the local Venice force who was as reliable as the winter weather of Abruzzo.

He opened a dossier on Inspector Luigi Petrin. It was a patchwork of success stories and reports of unseemly behavior. Petrin, 48, might have one day become general inspector or head of police administration if he hadn’t fallen in love with the bottle, and his wife hadn’t fallen out of love with him. However, when it came to the science and art of investigation, nobody was better than a sober Petrin. He had solved more cases throughout the Veneto than anyone in the past twenty years.

Marino thumbed through the folder and stopped when he came upon a synopsis of Petrin’s first stellar case. In 1920, before the fascists had assumed power, Detective Petrin sniffed out a robbery at the Rialto Bank, saved tellers and patrons from harm, and single-handedly captured the culprits when he jumped from a canal bridge onto their speeding boat. It was, Marino mused, the sort of stuff of American gangster movies, and because of it and other similar cases, Petrin had become a legend within Veneto law enforcement.

Once the inspector general completed his review of the Petrin folder, he gazed out an office window weighing his next move. He grabbed the phone handset. “Get me the Venice police chief.”

Shortly, Luigi Petrin sat before Marino, enduring the pain of a bruised right cheek, the result of a drunken discourse with an Irish tourist. Adrenaline spawned by the inspector general’s summons had cleared his mind enough for him to focus on Marino’s words.

“Damn you, Petrin, listen carefully. I am about to offer you one final chance to redeem yourself.”

“What do you mean by that, sir?”

“I mean, if you fuck this up, I’ll see you are assigned to canal patrol permanently."

"I wouldn't mind. A chance to meet lovely tourists."

"Petrin!" the inspector general erupted, "Stop pissing around! I am responding to a special request from Bocchini himself, and if we get it wrong, we are all in the shit. He was clear about it." His stare locked onto Petrin. "I need assurances if we are going to go forward with this." Silence saturated the room. "Well, man. What do you say?"

"About what? You have yet to explain what you want."

"The visit you dunce! *Il Duce* and the German chancellor will be here in nine days, and I need someone I can rely on for their protection."

"The *carabinieri* handle that," replied Petrin, struggling to stay on track and speak sensibly. "Also, *Duce's* bodyguards and the state police. Besides, the Germans will bring their own security."

"We are responsible for their protection," Marino clarified. "In any case, I expect all units will take a predictable course and practical measures to guard the dignitaries. I need someone with honed instincts who can work the streets and canals, uncover threats, and warn us of less obvious hazards. My question is, are you this person?"

"Isn't that up to you, sir?"

"Wrong, goddammit!" Marino wrung his hands in frustration. "I called you here because I think you can be the best man for the job if you can stay sober for the entire visit. No drinking, no carousing, no brawling. Can you keep your wits about you and your focus sharp?"

"For how long?" asked Petrin.

Marino wiped his hand over his face before taking two papers from a folder and sliding them across the desk. "The program calls for three days. Fourteen June through midday on the sixteenth. You will not touch a drink from today until it is over."

As Petrin read the draft of the planned visit, Marino lit a small, dark, twisted cigar and blew smoke to the ceiling. "Well?"

A surge of excitement and challenge brought mental clarity to the inspector. "Sir, I see many deadly opportunities." He laid the pages on the desk in the direction of Marino and pointed to line entries. "Look here. They are in the open air of the *piazza* twice for at least thirty minutes." He moved his finger down the page. "Again, here at *Stra*, and the *palazzo* of the Doge." He waved his hand over the papers. "And, other times, they will be vulnerable."

Marino added, "The program does not say it all. They always stray." He puffed on the cigar and continued. "You see, what you have pointed to are the obvious threats. The security forces will no doubt cover such things." He looked Petrin directly in the eyes. "I need you to discover and deal with the unexpected. Plots that are not so apparent."

"Fine, sir. Thinking like the killer, for example, in the *piazza*, the tower is too obvious and difficult to access. I would operate from within a crowd. I'd mingle with the people just as the murderers of kings and heads of state have always done."

"Luigi, you know every corner, every sewer, every dark niche, and all the felons of the clammy city. That's what we need from you, your knowledge and great instincts. Keep surveillance discreet and inconspicuous. Request whatever help you need: men, resources, anything. Above all, you must stay completely sober and clear-headed."

"Yes, sir. I understand fully."

Florence, Italy

Free in the city of art and beauty, Noschese let the rest of the day slip by while he strolled *Piazza della Signoria* and visited the *Uffizi,* where he was drawn to the paintings and statues depicting mythology rather than those based on religious accounts. At day's end, stimulated by the mythic allegories and nudity he had seen, he hungrily toured the city's risqué nightspots—the ones with the word "jazz" flashing over their doorways.

Arriving back at his hotel in the wee hours, he removed his shoes and fell onto the bed, still wearing his street clothes.

Chapter Seventeen

Wednesday, 6 June 1934

Florence, Italy

Groping through the fog of the previous evening's excesses, Noschese dragged himself out of bed, scanned his latest notes on the comings and goings of Sepp Karper and *Signora* Markham, and performed his morning ablutions. Noting that it was already after nine, he dressed as smartly as his limited travel wardrobe allowed and began another day of surveillance. Once again, he was a man on a mission. Thirty minutes later, he parked his roadster in *Piazza Santa Croce* and went directly to Federico's.

"Buongiorno," the affable proprietor called out as the reporter approached.

Noschese returned the greeting and gazed around, searching the half-empty tables. Intently focused, he ignored Federico's excited comment that Italy would soon be competing in the football finals in Rome.

"Has the redhead been in today?" he asked.

"*Signora* Markham. No, I am afraid not. I expect she and her professor friend have left on their trip."

"Trip? What trip?" Noschese asked.

"To Venice. They each have business there."

"Damn!" Noschese exclaimed as he rushed out the door and sprinted to his car.

The Road to Venice

It was a lovely spring morning in the Apennines as Martha's

Fiat 520, loaded with luggage, camera gear, and Sepp's telescope, traveled the highway that was once a Roman route between Florence and Bologna.

Driving through the village of *Fontebuona*, some twenty kilometers from the renaissance city, Martha said pensively, "I have a feeling I forgot to do something before we left."

"Do we need to go back?" asked Sepp.

"I don't think so," she replied. "I'll remember it sooner or later Probably later, and if I don't, it means it wasn't important."

"Certainly," Sepp agreed. "We can't afford the delay. I calculate we will not arrive in Venice until evening as it is." He leaned over and checked the car's speedometer, "You are doing well."

"I know this road, but I never overdo it. My children are uppermost in my mind."

"A wise sentiment, indeed. You do love your *kinder*, don't you?"

She nodded, and the conversation moved on to favorite travel adventures and places they would like to see. Martha was also quite good at relating anecdotes about some of the sites they went past.

It was almost eleven o'clock when the challenge of the *Futa* Pass presented itself. As the car climbed, its motor labored, but Martha, expertly managing the gearshift, maintained speed at each switchback, and succeeded in conquering the 915-meter summit.

For hours, the car climbed each hill only to be met by another more challenging one after it. Leaving Tuscany, they were a few kilometers into the province of *Emilia-Romagna*, when she pushed the accelerator to the floor as they ascended Mount *Oggioli.*

"Come on, old girl, you can do it," she coaxed, working the gearshift and the accelerator, but to little effect. The engine's laboring grew increasingly worse until the vehicle's speed dropped to a crawl.

"I can get out and carry some of the baggage up the hill if you think it would help." Sepp offered as he flicked cigarette ashes out the passenger side window. "It could lighten the load considerably."

"That is most kind of you, Professor Alex," Martha replied, "but my old warhorse has never let me down." Suddenly a blast of smoke and steam, accompanied by huffing and wheezing noises, emanated from the engine compartment. Like a tired mule no longer able to carry its burden, the car whimpered and died, refusing to go another meter.

"Oh, hell!" exclaimed the frustrated driver as she yanked the emergency brake. "I guess there's always a first time for everything."

"Scheisse!" Sepp shouted before sheepishly apologizing for his outburst. "Excuse me, but it appears we may not make it to Venice today."

Unfazed, Martha grumbled a profanity of her own, tramped to the engine compartment, and threw open the flap. A seething mess greeted her as oily brown water and steam escaped from around the top of the engine block.

"Looks like the head gasket has given way," observed Sepp, who had come up immediately behind her.

When she turned to him, their faces brushed, and as he stepped back, wisps of her hair caught in his beard. "Automobiles fascinate me," he said awkwardly. "For you as well?"

"I did keep a tractor running on my uncle's farm in Pennsylvania for two summers." She stared at the engine and asked. "Any advice?"

"A rope or chain might be in order. I think I saw something in the boot?"

Regarding him with a mischievous look, she tried breaking the tension. "You aren't proposing we try to haul this beast to Venice, are you?"

"Not at all," adding as he looked back down the road, "but the lorry we passed earlier might do."

Martha opened the latches on the box sitting above the rear bumper, lifted the lid and took out two pieces of luggage. "We're in luck!" she exclaimed as she held up the end of a coil of sturdy jute rope.

Checking a section of the road three or four curves behind them, Sepp declared, "I believe help may be a minute or two away."

"Okay, you stay out of sight," Martha instructed. As Sepp got back into the car, she laid the rope by the front bumper and ran a finger comb through her hair. "I'll take care of this."

As a stake-bed vehicle from the 1920s approached, Martha stepped into the roadway and waved.

The driver, a brawny young man wearing tradesman clothes, stopped alongside the Fiat and smiled. *"Signorina,* may I be of assistance?"

"Maybe you can tow my car to the next town for repair," replied Martha.

"Certainly. It is not far, and my truck is powerful." He got down from the cab, removed his cap, and bowed. "Santino Fusco, at your service."

Ignoring protocol, she offered her hand for him to shake. "I am Martha Markham."

Fusco took it by the tips of her fingers and gallantly kissed it, "A pleasure, *Signorina* Markham."

"Signora," she corrected as Sepp appeared from the other side of the car.

"Ah, I see. This is your husband?"

Martha quickly clarified, "I am a widow. You see, my husband …" She stopped and smiled sheepishly.

Fusco shrugged, as with a wave and a smile, Sepp announced in passable Italian, "I am Professor Alexander Höbling."

"Swiss?" Fusco asked, trying to place the man's accent.

"Austrian,"

The truck driver turned to Martha. "Americana, yes?"

"Yes. We have business in Venice and need to arrive there soon. We had planned for today. Can you help with the car?"

Fusco nodded, "I will tow you to an excellent mechanic in Monghidoro. Famous here. In 1929, he participated in the *Mille Miglia*, my country's important auto race."

"Excellent," said Martha going for the rope. "Then let's get to it."

Fifteen minutes later, the truck rolled onto a gravel driveway in front of three sets of garage doors with a single tall pump for dispensing gasoline off to the side. The sign over the center door said it was the Monghidoro garage of one Erno Liberatore.

"This is it," Fusco announced to Martha, who was sitting beside him. He pressed the horn button twice, and shortly, one of the doors opened, and there appeared a thin, fortyish man in coveralls. Carrying a wrench in his greasy hands, he brightened when he saw the truck driver. *"Ciao, Santino!"*

"Buon Pomeriggio, Erno," replied Fusco. They came down from the truck's cab, and Sepp got out of the Fiat.

"It looks like you have trouble," the mechanic said as he gestured at the car.

"*Sí,"* Fusco agreed, as Martha and Sepp joined them, "these travelers need your help, as they must get to Venice today."

"Something terrible happened as we made our way up one of the hills," Martha explained.

"Signorina," he said with a polite smile, "They are always a challenge." Turning to Sepp, he asked, "Sir, is this your automobile?"

"It belongs to the *signora*," Sepp said quietly.

Seeing the surprised look on Erno's face, Martha confirmed, "It is mine, and we need it fixed."

Erno eyed her up and down. "Then, I shall have a look." He went to the car and opened the engine compartment.

"We think it might be the gasket," Sepp said.

As Martha joined them, Erno looked in silence for a moment then turned, concluding, "The stains of oil and water tell me it is a gasket, but the trouble can be much deeper if it ran for any time in this condition. Maybe a scored cylinder, a piston damaged. Who knows?"

"Can you fix it?" asked Martha.

"First, I must examine it further. Then, if it can be repaired, I will either have the parts or need to get them so I can do my work."

"And how long will it all take?" Martha asked.

"Due giorni, tre giorni," he replied with a shrug.

"Two or three days is an unacceptable delay," Sepp reacted. "We will pay extra."

"*Signore*, I appreciate this, but I can only go as fast as I can go, and I have other work in front of yours."

The two beleaguered travelers looked to Fusco, who re-entered the conversation. "Erno, my friend. Surely, you can help these travelers in need. Remember the good Samaritan."

The mechanic thought for a moment. "Maybe, I will see to you first, once I know what the problem is. Leave it and return in two hours. Then, I will tell you what I can do and how soon."

"Fine," said Martha. "We will come back." She addressed Fusco. "Santino." He beamed at her use of his Christian name, "Where can we find some food in the meantime?"

She looked at Sepp, who agreed. "Right! I have a hole in my stomach." He produced his package of cigarettes, looked at it, and put it back in his pocket, mumbling, "These don't taste so good anymore."

"Maybe you saw on the way here." Fusco pointed back down the road. "There is a fine restaurant. It is early, but they accommodate the needs of tourists. And," he added proudly, "it is a nice *albergo* where you can stay, if necessary." He smiled at Martha, "I can take you, but then I must continue with my deliveries. It is an easy walk back here."

"I will come there," Erno volunteered. "To tell you what I have found."

"It would be most appreciated," she said and smiled brightly at the mechanic.

"Then, it is settled," Fusco declared as he untied the rope from the truck's bumper.

After the men pushed the broken Fiat into one of the garage stalls, Sepp went to retrieve the luggage and gear from the car, but Erno waved him off. "There is no need for that, *signore.* No one touches anything here; you have my word."

Feeling uneasy, Sepp and Martha squeezed into Fusco's truck cab, and off they went. With his mind relieved that help had been found, Sepp was becoming more and more aware of the warmth of Martha's thigh on his leg. He was enjoying it a bit too much when the deliveryman announced, "We are here. The *Locanda Monghidoro.* A fine place to eat and stay. Many tourists do." He accompanied the couple into the inn where they found the manager, who was also the waiter, and occasional chef of the *cucina,* which was mainly the realm of his wife. "*Ciao*, Dante, I have guests for you," Fusco announced.

The balding, mustachioed man in an apron, dark vest, and trousers put down the glass he was polishing and came to them. "*Signora e*

Professore," Fusco said gallantly, "this is my cousin Dante Cirluzzo." The man nodded and smiled as Fusco added, "He will be a fine host and see to all your needs." He addressed Dante, "I must go now. Their car has broken down and is at Erno's for repair."

Cirluzzo smiled. "Your car is in most capable hands, and we here will do our best to erase your bad experience." He held out his arm in the direction of tables in the brightly decorated room. "Please, this way."

As Fusco said his goodbyes and went to leave, Sepp called out, "Wait!" and caught up with him. "I want to give you something for your trouble. You have been most kind."

The deliveryman held up his hand, "*Signore*, it is not necessary."

"Of course, not for you," Sepp agreed. "But for me." He pressed two twenty lire notes into Fusco's hand. *"Grazie mille."*

Fusco accepted the money with a smile and a tip of his hat, then hurried out the door.

Minutes later, an ebullient Dante Cirluzzo came to the table carrying a platter that included a variety of cheeses, olives, pickled peppers, and slices of *Mortadella di Bologna*. "It is early in the day," he said as he set the large plate in the center of the table, "but you must have a good meal for your trip."

True to his word, Cirluzzo served tasty *tagliatelle con il ragu,* followed by *misto di bolliti,* and topped off with a dessert of *tiramisu*.

The stranded travelers ate with great relish, and by the time they were enjoying cups of coffee, Erno appeared. Without coveralls and neatly turned out in a dark suit, white shirt, and tie, he removed his bowler as he approached the table.

"I have good news with not so good news," said the mechanic. Directing his words at Sepp, he continued, "You see, *signore*, you were correct. The head gasket has been destroyed, but this is simply a matter of replacing it."

"And the bad news?" asked Martha.

"As I feared, *signorina*, one piston has a crack. It will destroy the motor if it is not replaced."

"Do you have the part?" asked Sepp.

Erno shook his head. "I must go to Bologna."

"It's not far, is it?" asked Sepp. Seeing Erno shake his head, he added, "Then there may be some hope of completing the repair today."

Again, Erno shook his head. "I am afraid not. Maybe by sometime tomorrow or early the next day, if I can obtain the part, and we work many hours."

Sepp pressed him. "You have served in auto racing. Surely …"

"*Signore*," Erno cut him off with a smile. "It is much faster to replace an entire engine than to repair a single piston and cylinder. And, no, I do not have a replacement for your engine."

"I see," Sepp accepted the explanation and looked at Martha as they both became reconciled to the fact they would be spending at least one night in Monghidoro.

Sepp said to Erno, "We will stay here, but have to collect our luggage. Will it be a problem?"

"Not at all, *Signore.* Francesco is there, and he will be happy to help you. I can take you if you would like."

"I think we could both use the walk," Martha said.

"Then I shall be on my way." Erno arose, nodded to Sepp and Martha, and left the table as Sepp waved for Dante.

"How may I help?" asked the waiter.

"We will need accommodations for the night," Sepp said.

Dante's eyes darted from him to Martha and back again.

Martha met his gaze. "Separate rooms."

"As you say, *signorina.*" Dante smiled stiffly. "I will have them prepared immediately."

The stranded friends enjoyed the walk back to Erno's garage, chatting about the day's events as they went. Once there, assistant mechanic, Francesco, helped them retrieve their luggage and gear and delivered them back to the hotel.

It was after four in the afternoon by the time they settled into their rooms, and Martha was ready for a nap. Sepp attempted the same, but after a restless hour, he gave into the gnawing thought that this delay could jeopardize the timing of his entire mission. He returned to the garage to have a look at the damage for himself. There, Francesco was using a winch to raise the engine off its mounts and cradle it on a wooden stand. The engine's head was off, and it was clear that one of the four pistons was damaged. Sepp was watching the mechanic remove the oil pan when Erno's car pulled into the garage driveway.

"Francesco, you have done well," Erno said as he arrived carrying two parcels: one large, the other narrow and flat. Setting them down, he joined the others at the stand. "*Signore*, do you see the problems of which I spoke?"

"Clearly," Sepp answered. "It would not have gone far in such condition. We can be thankful that we are not stranded somewhere in the mountains."

"Precisely," Erno agreed as he slipped into his coveralls. "If all goes well, tomorrow you will travel in an automobile you can trust. For tonight, enjoy the hospitality of our wonderful village." He added with a wink, "Also, the company of your lovely companion."

Sepp did not respond; however, reassured the repair work was in good hands, he intended to do precisely that. Upon his return to the inn, he knocked on Martha's room door and was happy to find her up.

"Are you ready for more adventure?" he asked.

The nap had rejuvenated her playful spirit, and she responded as she struck a pose, "Why, Professor, whatever do you have in mind?"

Her mock provocation brought a flush to Sepp's cheeks. "I thought we could see some of the sights and try some more local cuisine."

"Oh, is that all," she said with a wink. "Well, I guess I'll have to settle."

Thrown a bit off balance by the comely American's flirtation, Sepp was careful not to get caught up in her enticement. Until his mission was complete, he knew he must ignore such diversions, regardless how tempting.

As it happened, they did walk, actually hike, into the hillside village. There, with the help of the locals and a small guidebook from the hotel, they set about exploring the historic place.

Venice, Italy

The building sat a few hundred meters from *Piazza San Marco,* near the confluence of two not-so-grand canals. Moored in a slip in front, a polished speedboat with the words "Hotel Mocenigo" emblazoned in gold on its side rolled in the churning current.

Five centuries of the incessant lapping of canal water and exposure to the elements had taken their toll on the Gothic façade. However, its interior was expansive and expensively appointed with a décor that included classical paintings, elaborate wall hangings, and sets of imposing walnut doors. The great hall, library, and dining room had frescoed ceilings by the celebrated artist Giambattista Tiepolo, while the common areas and guest quarters carried forth the same themes.

The establishment reflected the character of its owner, Carlo Mocenigo, a swarthy man with heavy brows and blue-green eyes. In his fifties, he was the last heir of one of his family's sixteen lineages of nobility. Among his forebears were soldiers, statesmen, patrons of the arts, and, since the fifteenth century, seven Venetian doges. His vast wealth allowed him to spare no expense in making each of his five Venetian hotels luxurious. Of them, this was his crown jewel in which he had reserved a large section of the top floor as personal living quarters for himself and his beautiful, young wife, Claudia.

Behind a large desk in a paneled office, Mocenigo sat reviewing one of the six thick ledger books that dominated the desktop. As he went over accounts of his holdings, the positive totals brought a smile to his face. Business was thriving, and he was sure it would get even better during the upcoming visit of *Il Duce* and the German chancellor.

Content that all was well; he allowed his thoughts to drift to a subject which had lately dominated most of his waking hours—his exquisite Claudia. He was a man who needed to be in control and on top of every eventuality. With scant evidence to support his suspicions, he had become concerned with his wife's fidelity. Closing the final ledger and setting it aside, he picked up his glass of *Amarone* wine and regarded the mahogany shelves lining the back wall of the room. There were hundreds of books, most of which had been passed down through generations of his family. They included classical Italian writings such as an early manuscript of Dante's *Divine Comedy,* ancient tomes such as a Gutenberg Bible, and bound copies of historically significant documents. He took a long swig of the wine, set the glass down, and went to a section of volumes bound in dark leather. Selecting one titled *Codice di Diritto Processuale Penale*—Italian penal code, he searched the index for a specific topic: crimes in defense of honor. Turning to Article 587, he read carefully:

"*He who causes the death of a spouse, daughter, or sister upon discovering her in illegitimate carnal relations and in the heat of passion caused by the offense to his honor or that of his family will be sentenced to three to seven years. The same sentence shall apply to whomever, in the above circumstances, causes the death of the person involved in illegitimate carnal relations with his spouse, daughter, or sister.*"

A cruel smile spread across Mocenigo's lips as he went to a section with stacks of bound newspapers and pulled "*Corriere della Sera*, 1920 to 1929." Searching the popular Italian journal, he found an article on a 1928 murder of an unfaithful wife, Carmela Cimarosa. She had been killed by her husband, Annibale Mazzone, for her adulterous behavior. Defense attorney Joseph Casalinuovo's closing statement cited the law Mocenigo had just read. The lawyer's argument was so convincing the judge granted all possible leniency for the sake of honor and sentenced Mazzone to three years' probation. The wife-killer was released from prison immediately.

As Mocenigo weighed his options, there was a knock at the door.

"Yes," he said, expecting a visitor he had summoned earlier.

Standing in the doorway was Rubina, her pretty face shining with freshness. The gray maid's dress and black service apron she wore outlined supple hips and ample breasts.

"Is it the correct time, sir?" she asked timidly.

"Of course, my dear," replied Mocenigo, "and, throw the latch." His hand went to his crotch. "I have been thinking about you."

"Really? Something lovely, I hope."

"Come closer and let me tell you." He stood.

When Rubina went to him, Mocenigo enveloped her in his arms and stroked her seductively. The girl undid her top buttons and presented herself to him, allowing him to kiss her nipples.

"Be careful. If I get wrinkled, the *Signora* Giuditta will be quite angry."

Carlo hesitated for a moment, remembering that the woman who had become such an unreasonable and despised taskmaster as his housekeeper had, when she was as young as Rubina, fulfilled his sexual fantasies almost daily.

He eyed Rubina's voluptuous form and reached for his chair. "You may sit here."

She obeyed his order, and he stood before her. She methodically unbuttoned the front of his trousers and took his manhood in her soft hands before bringing it to her lips.

Ecstatic, he groaned once, then again, and three more times, faster and faster until it was over.

"My lovely Rubina," he said huskily. "You have become too proficient at this. I would like to last longer and enjoy entering you more often."

As she re-did his buttons, she said, "I would love to have you inside me, but you must be gentle. Your child grows in me now."

Dark brows raised, he grunted, "I was not aware." He rubbed his hand over his face. "You were to have taken measures to prevent such a thing."

"Sir, the *pessario* failed. It was not reliable." She winced, lashes fluttering nervously before adding, "I promise, sir, the baby is yours. I have been with no other man."

His tone lightened. "Don't worry, my sweet Rubina," he said. "It is not a problem." He put his hand on her shoulder. "I shall take care of you." Caressing her breasts one last time as she got up, he said, "I am happy about this. After my poker game tonight, we shall celebrate with fine *spumante* and whatever foods you desire."

"You are kind. I will be here awaiting your return." She wiped the remains of his explosion from her mouth using the back of her apron. "I love you, Carlo." She kissed him on both cheeks and left.

As the door closed behind the maid, Mocenigo picked up the phone, dialed three digits, and waited for the telltale click of an answer. "Gianni, come here, *subito*!" he ordered.

The man who entered through the door a minute later was huge and mean-looking, with a broad, open face damaged with pockmarks. His voice resonated in his barrel chest as he spoke. "At your service, *padrone*."

"I have a task for you," Mocenigo said in a precise manner.

"As you wish."

"Luscious Rubina has become a problem. I should say she is carrying a problem inside her."

The big man nodded. "I understand, sir."

"She will be in this room awaiting me tonight after poker. I expect that, as usual, she will be asleep on the divan." Mocenigo smoothed his curly hair back with his hand. "Leave the light off when you enter. I want you to take care of her, so there is no trace. You may take her first, from the rear, if you wish. She will think it is me." Gianni grinned crookedly as his boss continued. "I do not want any hint of her left. Use those strong hands. No blood and no evidence. She was never here, understand?

"*Sí, padrone,* I will be careful."

"Take the boat and sink her body into the lagoon. Not in a canal where a gondolier's oar might discover it. Use a canvas bag and stones, c*apisce?*"

Gianni nodded.

"Good. Now, have you been following my wife?"

"Yes, sir. Just as you asked, every day this week."

Mocenigo leaned forward over his desk. "Tell me, where does she go?"

"Always the same places. To Mass, usually to the basilica, but lately, the *Madonna dell'Orto*. Maybe for the art, the church of Tintoretto, you know, but maybe for a miracle."

"Bullshit!" Mocenigo scowled. "There are no miracles. Where else?"

"To the markets, the *piazza* to shop and stroll."

"It sounds so innocent. Have I married a saint?"

Gianni shrugged, glancing at the ceiling.

"Is this all?"

"As before, she spends time at *Contarini del Bovolo*. You know, the studio of your young friend Max."

Mocenigo said matter-of-factly, "She buys frocks from him. Nice ones he designs. You know how those faggots have a knack for such things."

"Yes, sir," replied Gianni, "Sometimes she stays for more than an hour?"

"To have fittings. Completely harmless. I believe Max is the lover of the notary Leonori." Mocenigo grunted. "Just the same, continue to keep me informed."

* * *

With the canvas top of his sporty roadster down and wind tousling his thinning hair, Enzo Noschese drove across the *Ponte Littorio,* the motor vehicle access bridge to Venice opened by Mussolini only months earlier. The reporter pulled into *Piazzale Roma,* a large parking area across the Grand Canal from the train station. Once he had secured his automobile like a doting mother hen attending a favorite chick, he arranged for a water taxi to take him to a hotel near the Rialto bridge. It was one of the most active locations in the city and perfect for socializing and collecting stories for potential articles. It was not as busy as *Piazza San Mar*co, but he knew that would turn impractical with the arrival of the two dignitaries.

The driver eased his boat into a dock at the *Riva della Fava* and gave his passenger directions to *Il Leone d'Argento*, a small *albergo* he recommended for its comfort and proximity to the Rialto. When Noschese arrived there, he was greeted by Mario, the desk clerk, and shown to his room by a young bellhop. Noschese immediately settled into the soft, down-filled bed, expecting to nap before going to dinner and exploring the nightlife of Venice.

Unfortunately, after a few minutes of drowsy stupor, the insanely recurring thoughts about Sepp bubbled to the top of his consciousness. "Why was Karper impersonating a university professor? What was he doing in Venice?" His thoughts turned to the redhead. "Who is she, and why did both Karper and Ravelli contact her?" The echoes in his brain continued until, finally, he sat upright against the headboard, stretched his arms and legs, and convinced himself that he did not need rest. At the washstand, he splashed his face, dried it with a crisp linen cloth, smoothed his suit jacket and trousers, and left. In the lobby, he asked Mario if he could help him locate some friends also visiting Venice.

"Certainly, anything you wish," the clerk said eagerly. "I can try. Do you know possibly the name of their hotel?"

Admitting he had no idea where the people would be stopping, he pulled out his pad and pencil and wrote three names: Sepp's, the cover name of Austrian professor Höbling, and the name of a Mrs. Markham. He added a few descriptive comments and gave the paper to Mario, who promised to make inquiries. A generous gratuity from Noschese sealed the deal.

The *Calle dei Stagneri* leading to the Grand Canal was narrow, dark, and ominous, but when Noschese saw the lights of the Rialto, he became excited at the prospect of some much-needed social contact. As he picked up his pace, the cumulative effects of his days of inadequate rest and almost nine hours of driving caught up with him. He faltered and grabbed a railing. Barely managing to stay upright, he conceded there would be no hobnobbing and celebrating this night. Walking tentatively, he returned to the *Leone d'Argento*.

Monghidoro, Italy

While exploring the tree-covered hills of the picturesque village, Sepp and Martha found a small *osteria*, and considering the amount of food they had consumed earlier, stopped for a light meal. Despite their intentions, the repast delighted their palates and was far more filling than either had anticipated. The delightful meal was paired with some of the best wine either had ever tasted. After turning down dessert, they left the eatery and walked under a star-filled canopy back to the highway and their hotel.

On the way, Martha paused, took hold of Sepp's arm, and pointed almost directly above to a bright star. "Look, Professor Alex, is that Vega?"

Sepp went on instant alert and began dredging up the astronomical facts he had fed his brain for the past few weeks. "Why, yes, it is." Echoing the words of professor Graff, he added, "It is one of the brightest in the night sky." However, when he tried offering a comment that would end the discussion of astronomy, he stumbled. "In the constellation Libra." By the time he realized his mistake, Martha had caught it.

"You mean Lyra," she corrected.

Nonchalantly, Sepp went for his package of cigarettes and offered her one. "Of course, Lyra, the harp. Libra is the scales. It must be the wine."

Martha waved off the cigarette and added, "I remember it because it was the lyre made by Hermes—you know, Mercury."

"Have you studied astronomy?" he asked.

"Astrology. It was all the rage at Vassar."

He recalled the professor telling him how astronomers use the constellations to map the skies and identify stars and let the topic drop. Lighting the cigarette and gazing up the road, he happily announced, "Look, there is our hotel."

Venice, Italy

Carlo Mocenigo descended the grand marble staircase and entered the game room on his hotel's first floor just as the porcelain and gold clock on a carved wall shelf chimed eleven. Decadently decorated, the chamber had three round gaming tables, a billiard table, and a small, well-stocked bar. He poured himself a large scotch, splashed in some seltzer, and joined the three players already seated at one of the felt-covered tables.

Dominating the scene was a dark-haired cow of a woman wearing too much makeup and stroking the Pekingese dog almost lost in the folds of her lap. Countess Adelaide Albini was delicately selecting and passionately devouring *Gianduiotti,* a chocolate and hazelnut candy. At poker, she was as eager about winning as she was about demolishing her supply of sweets.

To her right was Giulio Leonori, a wealthy Florentine notary and unabashed homosexual. His *Palazzo Leonori* on the Grand Canal was one of the oldest and most beautiful in Venice, known for its eccentric furnishings and what some considered scandalous décor.

A social misfit, Leonori was more interested in what was for him the rare camaraderie of the evening than in winning money. Amiable to the point of adulation, he joked, laughed, and carried on like a court jester. That and the lire he always left behind in the pockets of the others ensured a return invitation from his host.

The player Mocenigo feared most was Max Klemperer, a sandy-haired young man he had concluded was romantically involved with

Leonori. Max's luck at poker was unwavering and his ability to read the other players uncanny. His father, a famous Jewish writer, had moved his family from the Fatherland to Switzerland in the 1920s. Classically educated and gifted in the arts, Max quickly tired of the pastoral life in the Alps and moved south to Venice. There, he took over a lavish apartment kept by his aunt, Katherine Hermann, in the *Palazzo Contarini del Bovolo*. Although a talented artist, couturier was an ideal profession for him. As word of his fashions spread and his business grew, he began having affairs with his more delectable clients. One day, when Claudia Mocenigo entered his emporium, all thoughts of other women vanished. He had found his soul mate. Unfortunately, she was already married to the ogre sitting across the table from him.

"Let us begin," said the countess. "Who deals?"

Max pointed. "Our host, of course."

With expert ease, Carlo shuffled the cards and distributed the first hand.

It turned out to be a harbinger of things to come. Max won the game comfortably and triumphed at most of those that followed. After less than two hours, he had all but depleted the host's funds and put a severe dent in the stacks of the other players.

On Max's turn to deal, Mocenigo found himself holding three queens along with the two and three of clubs. He opened with a bet of five-hundred lire and, after his fellow players matched it, discarded the two losers and received replacements. Max dealt requested cards to the other players and took one for himself.

Mocenigo inserted the new additions into his hand, drained the last of his whiskey, and slowly fanned out the cards. Three queens greeted him first, but they were backed by a nine of diamonds and a four of hearts. Smiling broadly, he exuded the confidence of a man who had received precisely the spread he wanted. He then proceeded to commit a *faux pas* when he left the table holding onto his cards and went to the bar.

"Carlo, you opened," said Leonori. "What is your favor?"

"Three thousand," Mocenigo replied as he freshened his drink with one hand and reached under the bar with the other.

"I'm sorry I asked," Leonori responded and threw his cards down in disgust.

"Oh, why not," said the countess with a shrug. She contributed to the pot and stroked her little dog for luck.

When Carlo returned to the table with his drink, Max announced, "I'll see the three thousand and raise another five."

Carlo smiled and pulled a wad of bills from his pocket. "I think I can afford it, my young friend." He was almost jovial as he counted out and contributed the raise amount.

"I'm all done," said the countess. She set her cards face down, and went for the last of the *Gianduiotti*. The Pekingese was allowed a bite with its saw-like teeth before she tossed the remainder of the sweet into her mouth.

Ignoring the countess's disgusting act, Mocenigo taunted Max, "Now, it is only the two of us, boy. Would you like to go higher?"

The young man spread his cards just enough to see each suit and denomination. They were all hearts: the ten, jack, queen, king, and ace—an unbeatable royal flush. Calmly, Max replied, "I guess I can go for another five thousand, *Signor* Mocenigo." He pulled several notes from his winnings and tossed them onto the stack.

Mocenigo laughed. "It will cost more than that to see my cards, boy." He extracted a ten-thousand lire note and ceremoniously added it to the pot.

From his position of supreme strength, Max could have raised again, but decided against it. He matched the ten-thousand lire bet. "Okay, let's see what you have."

The host proudly spread out his hand on the table. "The cards tell the story." There they were, four queens, including the impossible queen of hearts.

Mocenigo had cheated and Max was at once angry and frightened. He buried his reaction in the assumed demeanor of a defeated dupe. "I guess you hold the winner, sir," he conceded as he mixed his hand with the other discards. He knew better than to reveal his host as a cheat. Rumor had it that men had disappeared for lesser offenses against the brute.

Before the countess could gather up the deck to deal, Mocenigo deftly returned the card he had replaced to the pile and palmed the offending queen of hearts, which he slipped into a coat pocket.

In the end, Max did not need to betray Mocenigo. Following the four-queens episode, the host began betting wildly and losing incessantly, continuing the earlier trend with most of the winnings going to Max.

In another part of the hotel, Gianni entered his master's study to find Mocenigo's young paramour asleep on the sofa. He put his hand on her luscious raised rump and shook her.

"Rubina. Rubina, you must wake up."

She stirred. "Lift my dress, Carlo, I am ready for you, but go carefully."

"Rubina, please," he said, his gruff voice as loud as he could risk.

She looked at him, "Gianni, what are you doing? Where is Carlo?"

"Pay attention! You must come with me."

"Why, where is he?"

"He would have me kill you. Please, you must never see him again." He scooped her up like a rag doll. "You leave Venice now, tonight, and never return. Your life depends on it."

* * *

At almost three in the morning, with his pockets packed with lire and his soul full of joy, Max walked happily home through the dank, deserted streets of Venice. Memories of the poker game quickly faded and his thoughts turned instead to the alabaster body of the woman he had enjoyed in his bed at the outset of the evening. "Claudia Mocenigo," he said her first name lovingly, but grunted the surname that stuck in his throat. "Mocenigo!" He grimaced. "How can such an angel be married to a bestial bastard like him?"

Chapter Eighteen

Thursday, 7 June 1934

Monghidoro, Italy

It wasn't yet five in the morning when, on the balcony outside his room, the crisp mountain air sent a shiver up Sepp Karper's spine as he waited for the sun's warming rays to defeat the effects of his fitful sleep. Worries over the delay getting to Venice and his choice to travel by auto instead of the train had haunted him throughout the night.

By contrast, Martha slept dreamlessly until after six. As she awoke and gathered herself, reviewing the events of the previous day, one thing insisted on bothering her. "How could such a noted astronomy professor confuse Libra and Lyra?" She shrugged. "Oh, well, maybe it was the wine."

Later, during a breakfast of coffee and rolls, to which Sepp added thin slices of prosciutto, they made small talk about the town, the weather, and their hopes of a quick return to the road. Because the temperature had dipped overnight, the hotel fireplace was becoming uncomfortably warm for Sepp, who was wearing a Loden jacket. Small beads of sweat grew on his forehead, and he pulled a white linen handkerchief from his pocket. He removed his glasses and laid them on the table before wiping his face.

"My, you don't look so studious without these, professor," Martha observed as she went for the spectacles. "Let me see what they do for me."

Sepp instantly grabbed the glasses before she could reach them. "Please, I wouldn't want them to strain your lovely eyes," he said with a stiff smile.

Martha shrugged. "Okay, I was just wondering."

"I am so sorry," Erno apologized as he came to their table. "I have worked long and hard, but the motor has defeated me." Responding to their questioning looks, he continued. "It will take more time to repair. You see, the cylinder was scored. I could not see it until I removed the piston."

"What does this mean?" asked Sepp. "When will it be finished?"

"More work means more time," Erno replied with a glum expression. "We may have to re-bore the cylinder. If so, I will need to use a larger piston and rings. It means another trip to Bologna."

Sepp's chin fell to his chest. "Another day, lost."

"Possibly, *Signore*," Erno said with a shrug. "We shall see, but I must go now." Erno left Martha and Sepp commiserating about their plight.

The gloomy talk lasted only a few sentences before Martha, ever the optimist, said brightly. "Well, it gives us more time here, and for a photographer, that's always an opportunity. How about coming along as my assistant, mister?"

As he looked into her eyes, something stirred inside him. "It would be an honor."

Venice, Italy

Content that he had finally secured help with his quest for Karper, Enzo Noschese had slept deeply without the aid of alcohol and did not stir until 09:48 the next morning. The room was dark, except for the few rays of light streaming through the slits in the closed shutters. As his grogginess dissolved, his obsession with the Austrian agent resumed. He went quickly to the washstand.

"Good morning, *Signor* Noschese," said Mario when Enzo entered the lobby. They traded pleasantries before the clerk admitted he was unsuccessful at locating the persons Noschese was interested in finding. "I have contacted my friends at other hotels and those I know among the gondoliers and merchants. No one has heard these names or seen anyone resembling your friends." Seeing his guest's disappointment, Mario added, "I did wonder why, sir, there are three names and only two descriptions."

Noschese considered several explanations before revealing

what he thought he knew about Sepp and the suspicion that he is an Austrian agent in Venice to make trouble during the meeting between Mussolini and Hitler.

Mario listened thoughtfully and promised to redouble his efforts to locate the couple who were the focus of so much concern.

* * *

Detective Sergeant Isadoro Bianchi was a fleshy man with a handlebar mustache, thick lips, and a bulbous nose. He was an unlikely representation of a highly capable police detective, and yet, that is precisely what he was. Some ten years younger than the man with whom he was proud to serve, Bianchi had become Luigi Petrin's closest confidant and the first line of defense against the inspector's notorious excesses with alcohol. It was after one in the afternoon, and he had spent the morning poring over the files from Chief Bocchini. He was now reviewing phone messages taken at the central police desk over the past twenty-four hours. Bianchi was more than halfway through the stack when he spotted a familiar name: "Karper."

"Inspector," he rushed into the office adjacent to his desk. "I may have something."

Petrin was standing at a map of Venice holding the Mussolini-Hitler visit schedule in one hand and sticking map pins in the locations where the two leaders would appear. With a supply of pins between his lips, he turned and gestured for more information.

Bianchi announced that one of the foot-patrol officers had reported inquiries about a possible Austrian agent named Karper. "It is the same name as the one identified in an anonymous telephone call to Bocchini," he explained, pointing to the boldly stamped *Polizia di Stato* file on Petrin's desk.

The inspector spit the map pins into his hand. "I recall Bocchini's note, but be cautious because he also thought it might have been a crackpot call." Petrin shrugged and added, "Just the same, we still need to look into it. Where was it?"

"In the Rialto sector near *Riva del Carbon.* Possibly one of the boatmen."

Petrin checked his service revolver, returned it to his shoulder holster, grabbed his suit coat, and hustled out. Bianchi gathered himself and followed.

A series of interviews led the two detectives to the *Leone d'Argento,* where Mario was in his usual place at the desk. "*Buongiorno signori.* How can I be of service?"

Petrin and Bianchi showed their badges, and the inspector asked for Mario d'Benedetto. The clerk's eyes went wide as he admitted to his identity and asked why they were looking for him. "We understand you are attempting to locate a man named Karper. An Austrian."

"Yes, sir. A guest asked me to help find him. A task at which I failed."

The next series of questions revealed that the person who made the inquiry had left several hours ago. Bianchi took notes as Mario described Enzo Noschese and recounted his suspicions about an Austrian plot.

* * *

Convinced that Karper would have to come to *Piazza San Marco* if he had any plan of disrupting the Hitler visit, Noschese intensified his search. He had looked into hundreds of faces for one resembling the Austrian agent but found none. There were red-haired women in the square and under the arcades, but none so glorious as Karper's companion. Certain they would eventually turn up, he took a table at *Caffe' Quadri.* The coffee shop, which had been there for three centuries, was nestled under the long arcade known as the *Procuratie Vecchie.* Its tables spilled into the open air of the square. Noschese ordered a coffee, which he sipped slowly as he observed the passersby.

As the day wore on, he switched to Cinzano and soda, hoping it might buoy his spirits. As he raised his glass for a first taste, he spotted two men who appeared to be searching the *piazza.* Could they be Austrian? Were they cohorts of Karper? He tried to convince himself otherwise until one of them checked a piece of paper, pointed in his direction, and the pair headed his way.

Noschese slithered out of his chair and eased away from the table. As he moved into the shadows of the arcade, he saw the men pick up their pace. One of them again pointed in his direction, and they broke into a trot. Simultaneously overtaken by nausea and adrenaline, he began running. Veering right, he raced through the *Piazzetta San Marco* then left to the *Riva degli Schiavoni,* where rows of boats were moored. Desperately, he jumped aboard a motorboat and waved a wad of lire at the boatman, shouting, "Please, you must save me. My life is in danger!" The boat came to life and raced from its slip moments ahead of the arrival of Petrin and Bianchi.

"Fast! Go fast!" Noschese shouted. "Those men are trying to kill me."

The boatman complied and charged his craft into the open waters of the lagoon. "Where do you want to go?" he asked.

"Anywhere safe. They are murderous Austrians!"

When Noschese looked back and saw his pursuers at the dock, he again insisted on more speed. The boatman pushed the throttle lever to its limit, and they were almost halfway to the *Lido* when the engine's roar suddenly quit and the boat began to drift.

"What happened?" Noschese shouted. "What did you do?"

"Look!" The boatman pointed to two approaching police launches with lights flashing and sing-song sirens blaring. "Help is on the way."

Monghidoro, Italy

It was late afternoon when Sepp and Martha headed back to the hotel. On the way, they called at Erno's shop for a status report and found the two mechanics in the process of lowering the engine into the Fiat.

Erno looked up, his face shiny with sweat and grease. "My friends, I have good news. It will take some time to remount the engine, but the difficult work is done. You should be able to leave in the morning."

"Why not right away," asked Martha?

"*Signorina*, we must test everything to be assured all is well," Erno explained. "I could not let you leave otherwise. Part of the engine is new, and I know you would not want it or something else to fail along the road."

Accepting Erno's logic, Sepp and Martha returned to the hotel. Continuing to make the best of the situation, they sat at a table on a veranda sipping wine in anxious silence. Each was trying to calm the growing anxiety of idling while their arrival in Venice was already a day overdue.

Finally, Sepp verbalized what they were both thinking. "I can't stand this waiting. Let's get the car and carry on. We can make Venice before the night is out."

"Fine! I'll meet you at the desk in five minutes."

As they went to check out, Erno arrived with another report. "I regret to say that while the engine repairs are fine, the clutch slipped during a test drive. We attempted an adjustment, but I believe it needs to be replaced. It will never serve you on the hills. Please, give me until morning."

Venice, Italy

Enzo Noschese sat stiffly and silently before Petrin's desk. The inspector leaned back in his chair while his partner paced, and they both interrogated the reporter.

Bianchi waved the prisoner's press credentials at him. "You are a reporter for *Il Messaggero*, but it does not explain why you ran when you saw us. What are you hiding, *Signor* Noschese?" he demanded. "You must tell us. We are prepared to stay the night until you do."

"Please," Noschese pleaded, his eyes brimming with tears. "As I have said, I am completely innocent of everything. I saw you and feared for my life because I took you for Austrians who are here in Venice plotting to kill someone. Maybe the German chancellor. Maybe me!"

"Okay," Petrin interceded. "We have been down this path before. You are neither Austrian nor German, yet you feared for your life and ran from us." He hammered a fist on his desk. "It makes no sense!"

"I can only say what I believed, sir," Noschese replied. "My motives are pure and honest. You must trust in that."

Bianchi took over. "Let us suppose this Karper is a real person working for the Austrians. Do you actually believe he is here to kill Mussolini? Or, Hitler?"

Noschese shook his head. "Certainly not *Il Duce,* who is a friend of Austria and Chancellor Dollfuss."

"Good," said Petrin sarcastically. "So, we have narrowed it down. You are saying he is here to go after Hitler."

Wide-eyed, Noschese shrugged. "Maybe. I don't know. I don't know what I am saying. But he is in disguise, an agent of Austria, and here in Venice."

"Do you have any proof?" asked Bianchi.

Noschese shook his head, "Only that I believe he is Karper and not this professor."

Petrin proceeded to inform him that, for his own protection, they would keep him at the jail overnight while they looked into his claim. Noschese was too frightened and confused to object.

Chapter Nineteen

Friday, 8 June 1934

Monghidoro, Italy

With their luggage in the back of Dante's truck, Sepp and Martha were on the way to the garage. As they rode, Martha recounted to herself the Lyra incident and compounded it with what had occurred regarding the professor's glasses. She concluded that, after days spent together, she had no idea who the man riding next to her was. A thought broke through. "Maybe, what I forgot to do on the morning we left was forego the companionship and drive to Venice alone."

"There she is," Sepp pointed to the Fiat shining in the morning's glow. "Looking fit for the open road."

Their forced stay in Monghidoro was over and, once again, they were on the way to Venice, full of promise and uncertainty.

Venice, Italy

The door of the small cell in the police station clanked open, and Noschese woke with Petrin and Bianchi standing over him.

"I expect you have slept well, *Signor* Noschese, but be aware, we never sleep," said the inspector.

Detective Bianchi followed up with the news that they had contacted all local police resources, including the *carabinieri* and state police, and determined that no one with the name or appearance of Karper was currently in Venice.

"What about the name Höbling?" asked Noschese as he pushed himself up into a sitting position on the bunk.

Petrin replied, "An inquiry of the University of Vienna revealed he is a professor under Doctor Kasimir Graff, head of their astronomical observatory."

"And, the woman? This *Signora* Markham?" Noschese persisted, rubbing the grit from his eyes.

"A photographer for America's *National Geographic* magazine," Bianchi responded. "She is due to arrive at her hotel soon."

"What hotel?" asked Noschese.

Petrin grabbed the reporter by the collar and pulled him to his feet. "We don't want you harassing guests of Venice, is that clear?" He let go and backed away dismissively. "You may go, but we will be watching you. I would much prefer that our paths never cross again."

Bianchi held the cell door open for Noschese. "There are papers for you to sign at the desk."

The wiry reporter stepped into a corridor, fighting the urge to run.

The Road to Venice

Martha's Fiat hummed contentedly as she guided it over the flat topography that greeted them beyond Bologna. In Ferrara, they shared a cozy picnic lunch before starting the final leg of their arduous journey along the *Padana Superiore*, the main highway across northern Italy that would take them to *Ponte Littorio* and Venice.

As they traveled, Martha kept the conversation light, hoping to find out more about this man who alternately evoked in her uncertainty and passion. Cautiously, she asked about her companion's past and present life, searching for his real character; however, Sepp cagily drew from the biography of Professor Graff for answers. He was so convincing that, by the time they entered Venice, Martha was satisfied that Alexander Höbling was genuine.

Venice, Italy

"Well, Professor Alex, we have finally arrived," Martha gleefully announced as they entered *Piazzale Roma*. "Now, we must rely on the canals to get us to our hotels."

Sepp produced a paper from his inside jacket pocket. "I have directions," adding as he unfolded the note, "I don't know what to make of them. It's the *Palazzo Contarini*." Acting like he had not burned the name and location into his brain during mission preparation, he suggested, "We may need to inquire somewhere."

"*Contarini*?" Martha echoed, "Which? *Contarini della Porta di Ferro* or the *Contarini del Bovolo??"*

"Bovolo," replied Sepp.

Martha's smiled, "I know it well. It is famous for its amazing staircase. Like a snail shell. Ergo, the moniker *'del bovolo.'"* As she said it, she made a winding gesture with her finger.

"So, you are a student of architecture as well as art."

She smiled. "Professor Alex, in Italy, architecture is art." She locked onto his gaze. "You will know it immediately. It's on my list to photograph while I am here." As she drove toward a parking space, a policeman in a white uniform and helmet stopped them.

She cranked down the window. "Yes?"

"*Signorina*, do you plan to leave your car here for long?" he asked.

"I do," she answered sweetly. "For a week or more. Why do you ask?"

The policeman frowned, "I must request that you go to the other end of the *piazzale*. You see, we have distinguished visitors arriving soon, and we need to control this area." He pointed to the end of the vast lot. "If you would move there."

"Certainly, thank you."

The policeman nodded, smiled, and saluted as she proceeded to follow his directions.

Martha pulled into an empty space. "That was interesting. Do you think it meant *Herr* Hitler will be coming this way?"

Sepp shrugged and offered her a cigarette, which she declined. Taking one for himself, he explained, "I don't know, but I expect we will need to remain flexible and alert."

"Speaking of which," Martha prompted, "I suggest we don't leave anything in the car.

Sepp looked about at the dozen or so police officers in the *piazzale*.

"It does appear quite safe here, but neither of us can afford to lose equipment."

"Exactly, the camera gear is my livelihood."

He scratched his beard. "Well said. While this particular telescope isn't part of my everyday existence, it is crucial to what I wish to accomplish here in Venice."

"Then, it's decided." Martha made a dragging motion. "We *schlepn*."

"Schleppen?" Sepp looked puzzled. "How do you know this word?"

"My *nonna* uses it when she refers to moving something from one place to another. I assumed it was Yiddish."

"It is close to German. Yes, we must *schleppen* quite a lot."

As they went about the task of unloading the car, two dark-eyed, olive-skinned lads approach smiling broadly. They were pulling a flat, wooden wagon with metal wheels and a pole for a handle.

"Benvenuti and welcome, *signorina e signore, a Venezia*," said the taller of the two. "We are here to serve you and would be most happy to transport your baggage."

Martha and Sepp exchanged glances, nodded, and made a deal for the boys to cart the luggage and equipment to a landing and their next mode of transportation.

Once at the edge of the Grand Canal, they were met by several boatmen, all bidding for their business. However, while the younger boy unloaded the wagon, the other one waved to a gondolier lolling in his boat across the canal. "Hey, Bepi. Come quickly, you have work."

The boatman roused, donned a hat, and grabbed his oar. As he worked his boat to the landing, Sepp gave the boys a five-lira coin each for which he received two huge grins and several "*grazie.*" As they wheeled their wagon away, Martha remarked, "You paid too much. You will spoil them."

Sepp shrugged and looked down at the pile of baggage and gear sitting between them. "Well worth it, I would say."

"Signore," called the gondolier as he brought his boat near. Martha gave him the names of the *Contarini del Bovolo* and the *Hotel San Moise*, where she would be staying. As she haggled a price, Sepp

realized that he hadn't asked her where she was stopping because he was fighting feelings for her that he could not afford to have.

"He will go by the *palazzo,* then to my hotel," Martha told him. The trip down the Grand Canal was leisurely, and the view appealing as some of the most exquisite old architecture in Italy drifted past. It was nothing like the romantic gondola rides Sepp had seen pictured in the brochures and on postcards, and for the moment, that pleased him. He held on to the wooden box, careful not to jar it, and Martha did the same with her rucksack of cameras and lenses. As they went under the *Ponte Rialto*, he promised himself to repeat the trip with her some evening, complete with candlelight and music.

Several hundred meters after the Rialto, Bepi eased the boat left into the *Rio di San Luca.* Minutes later, the gondola stopped at a set of doors topped by a pointed Moorish-style arch. The same motif was repeated in the windows and balconies of the building's elevation. "*Palazzo Contarini del Bovolo*," announced Bepi. "I apologize that this is a delivery entrance the merchants use. You will be inside much faster because the access to the front is difficult from here."

"That's fine," said Sepp, "so long as it is open."

"We shall see," the boatman replied as he set one foot on a small step inches above the water line and tried the handle. It worked, and one of the doors swung inward, revealing a landing and steps. "*Eccolo*," he declared.

While Bepi steadied the gondola, Sepp handed him his luggage and stepped onto the landing. Martha then passed him the telescope. As he took it from her arms, he turned his head to kiss her cheek and got lost in her fiery tresses and the scent of roses.

They were face-to-face for an instant, and seeing that certain look in their eyes, Bepi murmured, "Maybe I should have sung for you."

"Professor," Martha said as Sepp paid Bepi, "Remember, *Hotel San Moise*."

Sepp smiled. "How about dinner tonight?" he asked as the gondolier pushed off into the flow of the canal.

"That would be lovely," she replied as they floated farther apart. With her hand cupping her mouth, she added, "Phone me at the hotel. I may have a treat for you."

"Treat?" Sepp repeated blankly as the gondola got lost in the canal traffic. "What kind of treat?" His mind jumped to several possibilities, most of which involved some level of intimacy, and for a moment, his feelings for Martha superseded all thoughts of the mission.

Once he and his gear were safely in the *palazzo's* entryway, Sepp pushed the door closed and climbed to a level where he found himself in a dank, dimly lit hallway that led to a wine cellar. He continued to the midpoint of the corridor, and there he saw another set of steps that led to a large kitchen area with three doors. He was in the process of deciding which way to turn when, in the distance, he heard a faint mechanical noise similar to the clacking of the valves of an auto engine.

The sound eventually led him to a spacious room sumptuously appointed with furniture, paintings, and two huge tapestries depicting an ancient battle covering the main wall. There, Sepp found the source of the noise. A roundish woman was operating an electric sewing machine.

Closer at hand were three long tables, shelves piled with bolts of cloth, and a half dozen dressmaker models, four of which stood as silent sentries along a wall. A fifth was in the process of being draped in a light blue fabric by a dashing young man Sepp calculated to be Katy's nephew. He wore dark brown trousers and a tan vest over a white shirt, with sleeves rolled up, accented with a bright yellow tie. His appearance reminded Sepp of the fancy men he had seen in certain quarters of Vienna.

As the dandy picked up a bolt of material from a table strewn with drawings, he spotted Sepp. "Aha! My guest has finally arrived." He greeted him in German. "I am Max, and I take it you are poor Auntie Kate's professor." His tone lowered. "She wrote to me not long before … well, you know."

"Yes," replied Sepp. "I am so sorry for your loss."

"Our loss," Max corrected. "She was a wonderful and unique person."

"Since we are being honest about names," said Sepp as he reached to accept the greeting and found Max's handshake surprisingly firm. "I assume you know my true identity."

"Auntie told me quite a bit about you … and her."

"I see. She was quite irrepressible at times." He looked over at the busy seamstress, and his manner turned serious. He whispered, "Please, I am Professor Alex Höbling while I'm here."

Max regarded the woman in black. "Don't worry about *Signora* Costello. She can be trusted. She speaks no German and is usually quite wrapped up in her work."

"Fine," Sepp replied. "I do not wish to interfere with your business."

"Certainly," Max assured him, "but count on me to help." He posed, hands out to his sides. "Don't be fooled by appearances. I have a will of steel." He paused before adding, "And, because of the regard in which most people hold me, I get away with a lot, including claims of a poor memory."

"So," Sepp concluded, "like me, you are not what you seem."

"For Venetians, I am *Signor* Max, master of the House of Contarini," he said proudly with his palm to his chest. "You see, I adopted the celebrated family name for my business, and there is no one left to challenge it."

"Is business good?"

"I do fine," Max admitted. "My inaccurately perceived sexual tendencies serve me as well, both professionally and with the ladies, most of whom attempt to turn me back to the so-called proper side."

"You are a bit of a fraud."

"Please, *Herr* Professor, let me clarify," Max hastened to add. "I love wearing and designing clothes; however, when it comes to sexual appetites, I am blessed with a family trait with which I believe you are familiar."

Not wanting to pursue that line any further, Sepp asked, "Where will I be staying?" He looked around the vast room. "Something cozy would satisfy me."

Max grinned. "I'm afraid such cells can only be found in convents. Any *palazzo* worthy of the name will have spacious chambers."

"Then I shall be content with splendor," said Sepp with a smirk.

Max picked up his visitor's luggage. "Come, let me show you to your room."

As they approached the door, *Signora* Costello spoke up in Italian. "*Signor* Max, excuse me, but I believe we will need one more fitting before I can finish the dress for *Signora* Mocenigo."

"Excellent," Max answered. "I will so inform her." He thought for a moment and asked, "Is later today acceptable?"

"Very good, *signore*," she said with a twinkle in her dark eyes.

"*Signora* Costello, allow me to introduce a friend who will be staying with us for a time. This is Professor Höbling from Vienna."

She smiled warmly. "*Sí*, he is the one your blessed aunt sent us."

Max and Sepp traded surprised glances as the *Signora* returned to her work.

Sepp hoisted the telescope box, and off they went.

Vienna, Austria

Prince Ernst Starhemberg sat on a remote bench discreetly scanning the expanse of the *Volksgarten* from under the shadow of a broad fedora. As he caught sight of a group of chatty nursemaids in the distance, the syncopated crackling of footsteps on the gravel path behind him betrayed Colonel Joscht, limping his way to the bench.

Starhemberg stood. "Well, Paul, it was good of you to join me here. I know it takes some effort."

The colonel, dressed in street clothes, smiled with genuine warmth as they shook hands. "It's nothing, sir. There's no place better than this park to discuss certain matters."

As the two men sat, Starhemberg said, "There are, my friend, certain matters, to be sure." He pushed his hat back on his head. "What we are about could change the fate of Austria and possibly the entire world. And, it all falls to one man to accomplish. A good and capable man, but it does give one pause about having all of our eggs in this single basket."

"Yes, sir." Joscht nodded. "I harbor similar concerns but have decided the nature of the mission necessitates it."

"I am sure you have gone over this time and again. I want to be able to offer Karper assistance if and when the time comes."

"We have someone who is well-established in Italy. He has been reporting to me regularly." Joscht leaned on his cane toward the prince. "He knows about Karper."

Starhemberg cocked his head. "Does Karper know about him?"

"Not at all," Joscht assured him. "If contact is required, we have given them both a recognition phrase."

"And, I take it, we could not have used this local agent for the mission in the first place."

"As you know, Chancellor Dollfuss selected Sepp personally, and I agree with his choice. He is completely reliable. I have never seen anything deter him when on an assignment." Joscht reached into his coat pocket and came up with a folded piece of paper. "Besides, I wanted to follow security protocol by not revealing the agent's name, but if you feel you need to know, it is on this paper."

Starhemberg held up his hand. "That won't be necessary, Paul. I know you have the situation well in hand." He patted Joscht's good leg, now, let me treat you to a coffee and a sweet at the café." He led their way to the small group of buildings in the central section of the park.

Venice, Italy

The evening found Sepp Karper relaxing in one of the richly brocaded chairs in a cozy sitting room off the lobby of Martha's hotel. He was scouring the first few pages of a June third edition of the liberal German newspaper *Berliner Tageblatt* for information about the Hitler visit when Martha arrived and grabbed his attention. She was a vision in a pale green blouse with a revealing neckline and a mid-length dark green skirt complementing her fiery tresses.

She greeted him with a kiss that left his cheek tingling. "Good evening, Alex," she said, omitting his "professor" title and surname for the first time.

"Buona sera, Martha." As he took her hand and kissed it lightly, he sensed something had changed between them.

"Well, are you ready for my treat?" She winked playfully. "Some delicious food and conversation."

"Yes. A loaf of bread, a jug of wine, and thou. What more can a man ask for?"

"Why, I would never have taken you for a student of Omar Khayyam. A romantic."

Without making eye contact, he explained, "I know bits and

pieces of the *Rubaiyat,* and for that matter, many things. Mere trivialities—trifles." When he did look directly at her, he glimpsed the gold flecks sparkling in her blue-green eyes and added, "You do look quite lovely tonight."

"Another trifle, is it?" she asked.

"Not at all. Let me simply say it is a fact. A delicious fact. You seem to have an odd effect on me."

"Good," she made hypnotic movements with her fingers, "then my spell is working."

Feigning a trance, he confessed, "I am under your control, dear temptress."

Martha took his arm, "Then let's go. It's only a short walk. Like Florence, most places here are close by."

"I see. Then there will be no gondola ride," he chided with a smile.

"We'll save it for later. It's much too bright out now to be effective."

"My God," he thought, "what an amazing woman."

They walked to the *Calle Larga XXII Marzo,* where they crossed over the *Rio di San Moise.* When they reached *Calle Vallaresso*, Martha tugged him to the right. "This way. We're close." A minute later, they were standing in front of the unimpressive façade of an establishment with the unlikely name "Harry's Bar" on its windows.

"I make a point of coming here every time I'm in Venice. It is new by Venetian standards, but already quite the international attraction."

"It's a bar," Sepp observed flatly. "I thought you might choose a fine restaurant."

"Trust me, the food here is quite good, and the atmosphere, while a bit frenzied, is like nothing anywhere else in Venice." She reflected for a moment. "It's not as rowdy as one of your Viennese beer halls, but stimulating just the same." She looked directly in Sepp's eyes and added, "You do want to be stimulated, don't you?"

Once again, he labored for a response. "What are you up to?"

She shrugged. "Fun! After our ordeal in Monghidoro, we need a break, don't you think?"

He held the door for her, and they entered an atmosphere of

conversation and laughter mixed with the din of clattering pans, dishes, and glassware. Out from behind the bar came owner, Giuseppe Cipriani. "*Signora* Markham," he said as he kissed her on both cheeks. "It has been some time."

"At least a year. My work, you know."

"I very much enjoyed the photographs you made last time. It is good to have you here again." He glanced at Sepp.

Martha took the cue. "*Signor* Cipriani, this is Professor Höbling of the University of Vienna."

"We are honored, professor," said the host, giving Sepp's hand a single pump, then seating them at a table barely larger than a generous pizza pan.

"This is quite intimate," Sepp observed as he leaned in inches from her.

When she moved closer, he could feel her breath on his face, the scent of roses rising from her bosom, and her knees touching his. "Yes, isn't it cozy?"

When she rounded her shoulders, the neckline of her blouse dropped. Sepp sensed that, if he had lowered his eyes, the view would have left little to the imagination. He strained to keep his gaze firmly on her face as she continued, "More and more titled Europeans and wealthy Americans come here each year. Harry's has become what we in the states call 'the cat's pajamas.'"

"Something to do with sleep attire? Strange Americans," he said, shaking his head as the waiter returned to take their order. They decided to share a seafood dish of scampi and mullet prepared with shallots and white wine.

As the evening progressed, they revealed more and more about themselves: their likes, dislikes, secret desires, and innermost thoughts. Sepp was careful not to break cover as an astronomy professor, but identity aside, he shared more of himself than he had with anyone in years. Likewise, Martha omitted any reference to her mission for FDR but spoke frankly about her life, her children, and the tragic death of her husband.

By the time they had finished one of Cipriani's signature desserts, their earlier awkwardness was gone. Leaving Harry's, they stepped into a balmy, moonlit environment.

"Look," said Martha regarding the emerging stars in a darkening sky. "This might be a lovely time for that gondola ride."

With a maturity that comes from having tasted so much of life, Sepp looked into her eyes and said softly, "Do we really need it?"

Martha embraced him and shook her head. "I get a little seasick anyhow, and we wouldn't want that." Arm in arm, they strolled back to her hotel.

* * *

Enzo Noschese, frustrated that his search for Sepp and Martha had been for naught, settled in at one of the watering holes near the *piazza* and ordered his usual Cinzano. As he dolefully drained his second glass, inspiration struck. He ordered two bottles of *valpolicella,* and with them in hand, headed for the *Riva degli Schiavoni.* Brandishing the bottles, he addressed a group of gondoliers. "I am a reporter for the Roman paper, *Il Messaggero*, writing a feature story about the famous boatmen of Venice." Handing them the wine to share, he asked for their help as he took out his pad and pencil. After several minutes of inconsequential note taking and massaging their egos, he got to the crux of it. "Is it true you have many celebrities as passengers?"

Receiving a slew of positive responses, he pressed, "Have you had any recently? I had heard a certain ginger movie star arrived today."

The gondoliers shrugged at each other and shook their heads.

Noschese was considering a different tack when one of the boatmen in the back of the group piped up, "Not a movie star, but my friend had a redhead he thought was a model. She was with a gentleman who may have been a photographer. They had equipment with them."

Straining to curb his excitement, Noschese responded, "That is quite interesting. I would like to speak to this friend."

"Oh, he is not here," said the gondolier. "He usually stays by *Piazzale Roma*."

"Can you take me to him? It would make a good story, and I will use your name."

The man's face lit up for a moment, then turned serious. "You will pay the usual fare?"

"Certainly," Noschese agreed. "And, a nice bonus when we find him." He then asked cagily, "What is your friend's name?"

"Bepi."

* * *

Martha's hotel room was small but grandly appointed in the manner of Venetian Baroque. It had a sitting area with a carved table, two elaborate cushioned chairs, and an ample four-poster. An adjoining bathroom made the accommodation appropriate for an unaccompanied woman.

Oblivious to the room's décor, the two lovers kissed, groped each other, and fell onto the bed, swallowed up by a down comforter as they began removing each other's clothes.

Sepp stopped. "Wait," he said in a husky voice. "I have not come prepared."

"It's okay," she assured him. "I am just over my monthly visit."

The lovemaking that followed progressed from timid to torrid and rose to a level of euphoria. When it was over, they fell asleep in a romantic embrace.

About an hour later, Martha awoke, slid carefully out of Sepp's arms, and went to the bathroom to relieve herself and remove the diaphragm she had inserted earlier as a precaution. When she returned, she spotted the professor's glasses sitting on the nightstand and could not resist trying them on. Standing there naked except for the thick-rimmed spectacles, she made a shocking discovery. "Shit! These are plain glass." She took them off, enraged. "You bastard, who the hell are you?" Her jaw tightened, and her faced blanched. "Who have I allowed to invade my body?"

Suddenly, Harry's seafood dinner burned in her throat, and she rushed back into the toilet. A few wrenching minutes later, Martha returned to the bedroom, still fuming and holding the glasses which she threw at the head of the naked stranger in her bed. When they plopped harmlessly on a pillow, she prodded her sleeping bedmate with her foot. "Hey, professor, or whoever the hell you are, wake up!" Receiving only a groan and a mumble, she poked him again.

"God damn you, wake up!"

"Wha … what is it? What's happened?" Sepp asked groggily.

"Get up. I want you out of here and out of my life," Martha said with icy resolve.

Still foggy, Sepp asked, "But why. What did I do?"

"It's not what you did; it's who you are!"

As he went to get up, the glasses slid to him. He immediately understood. "I can explain. Please, it is not what it seems."

"Bullshit! You've deceived me for days, and now you have assaulted my body. Just leave!"

Sepp confessed, "I am neither a professor nor an astronomer."

"I should have suspected it when you mistook Lyra for Libra." She shook her head, "My God, what a fool I've been."

He again tried to clarify, "I'm Captain Sepp Karper of the Austrian state police."

"Of course you are. 'Karp,' isn't that what the priest called you?"

"Oh, that." He scowled.

"Yes, that. I was too foolish to know what it meant, even after that one-act play you and the priest put on. What a simpleton I've been." She pointed to the door. "Now, go!"

Pulling on his trousers, Sepp begged, "Please, I will leave, but you must never tell anyone about me. It is a matter of Austrian national security."

"I certainly do not intend to announce this embarrassment to the world." Her gaze oozed contempt.

"I am the person I said. I promise. I have no papers of my real identity because of the sensitivity of my mission." He stepped toward her.

She backed away. "Leave! Now!"

Sepp opened the door, and with his jacket and tie over his arm and shoes in hand, he stepped into an empty hallway where he finished dressing before going to the lobby. There, Enzo Noschese was having an animated conversation with the concierge.

"Her name is Markham," said the reporter. "She is a redhead and quite attractive. The gondolier told me he delivered her here earlier today." He tried to grab the hotel register, but the man behind the counter quickly closed it and placed it out of sight. "I'm sorry sir, I cannot reveal names, especially of beautiful women. This is a hotel, not a brothel."

Sepp watched from the shadows as Noschese produced a wad of bills from which he peeled off several lire. "Maybe, if I made it worth your while."

The concierge glared. "Neither am I a procurer." He indicated the door, "Do I need to have you thrown out?"

As Noschese exited the hotel grumbling, Sepp returned to the sitting room where his evening's misadventure had begun. While he waited for the prying reporter to leave the area, Martha dominated his thoughts. She was a fantastic woman and an ardent lover, but this was neither the time nor the place for any of that. She must not be allowed to affect his mission—a mission he may not survive. Why put her through that? He left the hotel with one dominant thought, "If it is to be, it will be."

Chapter Twenty

Saturday, 9 June 1934

Venice, Italy

Sepp navigated the Patriarchate's confusing hallways, guided by Father Tucci's descriptions of the hanging artwork that led to the office of Monsignor Virgilio Monaco. He was standing before a large, oak door with gilded lettering when he became aware of the sound of approaching footsteps.

The distinguished-looking man in a black cassock with a rose-colored sash girding his midsection asked, "Are you Professor Höbling?"

Sepp gave a slight bow and reached for the priest's slender outstretched hand. "Monsignor, it is my pleasure to be here."

As they broke their grasp, the priest added, "I am happy you have found my office. This is quite a beautiful building, with wonderful artwork and no signs. A place of baffling grandeur, not meant for visitors."

Sepp nodded, "For me, all of Venice is so. Confusing, yet breathtaking as it rises like Venus from the lagoon."

The priest smiled. "A most eloquent observation, but I suppose, as an astronomer, you are accustomed to visual marvels."

"I see Father Tucci has told you a little about me."

"Yes, he called and explained your need." The Monsignor opened the door. "Come, I have prepared the letter."

Monaco led Sepp into a large chamber; its walls hung with religious paintings by Tintoretto, Titian, and other lesser Venetian artists.

Sepp followed his host to a smaller room with a table and several chairs, all desperately neat and precisely placed. On a side wall was a large crucifix and a painting of the Blessed Virgin. An opposite wall held a portrait of Pope Pius XI.

Retrieving a folder from the tabletop, Monaco opened it on a letter with several lines of precise handwriting below the letterhead of the patriarchate. As he handed it to Sepp, he explained, "There are two provisos, professor." He raised an instructive finger, "First, you must understand that the Church cannot officially condone any glorification of Galileo."

Sepp nodded, "I saw an example of that same paradox in Florence. I mean, his tomb at *Santa Croce*."

"In the eyes of the Holy See, he remains a heretic."

Sepp regarded him quizzically and asked, "And, the second?"

"You must go to the office of the police commissioner-general for permission to access the bell tower. The police control its entrance despite the fact it belongs to the church."

"Is it going to be a problem?"

Monaco shook his head. "Not with that letter in hand. More of a formality, but one you must not overlook."

Sepp thanked the Monsignor and left, unwinding his way back to the palace's entrance. He headed immediately to the offices of the Commissioner-General of Police.

Following signs to registration and permitting, he turned left into a room resembling a hotel lobby with a long concierge counter. The group of four men gathered along the wall were familiar to him, especially the broad-shouldered husky whose head rose above the rest. He was the film crewman who had pulled him from the *Donnaukanal*.

At the counter, director Marcello Martone was shouting at a clerk. "We must have access to each of these venues. The document from *Istituto Luce* explains this. "

The milquetoast man behind the counter nodded sympathetically. "Please, give me a moment to confirm this."

"*Sí,* " Martone replied with a wave of his hand.

With his head down to avoid eye contact with the film people, Sepp approached the far end of the counter and presented the archbishop's letter to an agent with crescent eyes and an obsequious smile.

"*Sí, Professore* Höbling," fawned the clerk. "We have received a call from the Patriarch's office. You will only need to complete this." He handed Sepp a form and pointed to the pen and inkwell on the desk, adding, "Please notice, I have already entered most of your information."

Sepp placed an "x" in and initialed several appropriate boxes indicating the areas and structures to which he would require access. He finished by scrawling a signature.

"Splendid," the clerk gushed as he took the document. "Now, please take a seat while I obtain the appropriate authorization."

Sepp moved furtively to a bench and observed as the waiting crew members were called to the counter to sign papers. Handing the director and each of his troupe documents, the clerk instructed, "Show them to the guard each time you need to access one of the locations listed."

Martone immediately asked, "If I need to hire additional workers, must they come here?"

The clerk shook his head. "Sir, I have made provision for such a need. Here are three signed documents you may complete. Will that be sufficient?"

The director nodded and thanked the man. As the film crew sauntered casually to the door, Sepp's toady returned with a sour-faced, bearded officer. "Professor," the clerk said, waving Sepp over. "My superior, Superintendent Gizzi, would like a word."

Gizzi stepped forward. "Professor, it is not clear to me why you must use the bell tower at this particular time."

"You see, sir, I will be here for only a few days because I must return to Vienna to present an important paper on nebulae on 20 June." Ignoring the superintendent's questioning look, he continued, "I need to take measurements of the bell tower location where we will recreate Galileo's historic demonstration for the *Doge*."

"Yes, but that should take only a few hours, is this not true?" Gizzi demurred.

"Certainly, sir. However, I also need to calibrate the telescope, noting readings. That will take some time."

"I see," the inquisitor nodded.

"And, most importantly," Sepp continued, "I must determine

the effects of the ringing bells on the accuracy of the instrument. Vibrations, you know. History tells us the great scientist used the tower for more than a week before his presentation, and I must know if the bells might alter the accuracy of the scope. I will then return to Vienna with my information and prepare for the presentation in August."

"The bells can be silenced for special occasions." Gizzi appraised Sepp once more before nodding to his underling and leaving.

The clerk stamped and signed the document and handed it to Sepp. "There you are, professor. Enjoy your time here in Venice."

Sepp quickly left the building and had gone no more than twenty paces when a voice from behind called, "Captain Karper."

Marcello Martone caught up with him. "I thought I recognized you," said the director. "When I pictured you without the beard and glasses, I was quite certain."

"*Signor* Martone, I assume you are here for your command performance. Are Hitler and Mussolini your stars?"

"Exactly. It is why my company and I require certain privileges." Martone explained, "My job is to record the movements of the two strutting peacocks. For this, I will have cameras in several locations. Primarily the *piazza*, but I will also be at *Villa Pisani*, the Grand Hotel, and generally everywhere they go." He looked Sepp in the eyes and asked, "Tell me, my good Captain, why do you require such access?"

Sepp's response was close to the truth. "I am assisting a friend, a photographer for the National Geographic. She is documenting the art and monuments here, which often necessitates special entry. I will be accompanying her."

"Did I hear the clerk call you professor?" asked Martone.

Stroking his beard, Sepp replied, "A ploy, I'm afraid. My role as a bogus art professor will help us gain access to certain areas not seen by the public."

Martone regarded him suspiciously. "A coincidence then that you are in Venice in time for the arrival of the German chancellor?" Looking askance, he continued, "Are you not here for that Jew-hating bastard?"

Taken with the man's frankness, Sepp explained, "My friend is freelance, so she may choose to cover the event."

Martone smirked, "Certainly." Adding with a nod and a wink, "If you require assistance, feel free to call upon me. I believe we may have mutual ends in mind." He left, adding as he went, "*Ciao*, my friend."

Sepp immediately began replaying their conversation. Was his mission compromised, or had he found an ally? Only time would tell, and he would have to prepare for either eventuality.

Chapter Twenty-One

Sunday, 10 June 1934

Venice, Italy

The two bronze figures known as "Moors" atop the clock tower were striking seven as Sepp Karper entered *Piazza San Marco,* carrying the telescope box over his shoulder. The square was deserted save for the churchgoers scurrying to Sunday mass, the ubiquitous pigeons, and two uniformed policemen guarding the elaborate bronze door of the *Loggetta del Sansovino* at the base of the *Basilica di San Marco* bell tower. He approached the one who, by the decorated epaulets of his uniform, was the more senior, and plied his best Italian. "Excuse me, but I must go up into the tower."

The graying officer frowned. "No visitors for the next week, please go away."

Sepp retrieved papers from his inside coat pocket. "These grant my admission, sir." He held out the authorizations from both the archbishop's office and the police department.

The man sneered as he perused the documents. Eyeing Sepp suspiciously, he challenged, "If you are this Professor Höbling from Vienna, then you must prove it. Where is your identification and what is in the box?"

"A telescope," Sepp responded as he produced his Austrian passport. The guard compared the photo to the person standing before him, flipped through the pages, and handed it back with a shrug. He said to his younger companion, "Officer Gallo, check the box, and please, speak to this poor soul in his language, so he no longer murders our beautiful Italian."

Gallo saluted and addressed Sepp in passable German, "Sir,

please open it for inspection."

Sepp felt his collar tightening around his neck as he was about to experience the first real test of Tropp's invention. "Here," he complied. "You see, it is a telescope for a ceremony commemorating its demonstration to the doge, as it says in the papers."

Gallo looked to the older guard and asked. "Sergeant Masciarelli, do the papers authorize a telescope?"

His partner answered impatiently, *"Sí, Sí,* hurry up.*"* He made a hand motion telling Gallo to get on with it.

The young guard performed a cursory inspection of the instrument. "You may close it."

As Sepp did so, the senior guard barked, "Accompany him and be quick about it." He grumbled, "I want to be enjoying breakfast before seven-thirty. Understand?"

Gallo saluted and beckoned for Sepp to follow him. As they entered the *loggetta*, Sepp remarked, "My, the exterior is much more impressive."

"Yes, sir," Gallo agreed, assuming the role of a docent. "This was the design of Jacopo Sansovino in the sixteenth century." He added wistfully, "A shame that, except for a few pieces, the original was destroyed when the tower collapsed in 1902."

"And yet, here it is today."

"*Sí*, for ten years they rebuilt it accurately, both the *loggetta* and the *campanile*. It has been reinforced, but to the eye, there are few differences." Gallo added with a smile, "And, thank the Lord, inside the tower, there is now a lift."

"You are quite well informed, Gallo."

"Sir, my job is as a policeman, but my passion is the history of our wonderful city."

"Then, you understand the importance of my visit here."

"Yes, sir. Galileo's telescope, he worked it for the Doge, Leonardo Donato, in 1609, three hundred and twenty-five years ago."

Sepp marveled at the young man's knowledge, which also alerted him to avoid detail as it could reveal his own shortcomings.

Gallo added, "But the demonstration was in August, and it is only June."

Sepp gave his practiced response. "I will do my research and return to Vienna to draft the final scenario. Then, we will conduct the ceremony with actors representing the doge and others in August. Maybe you can participate."

This evoked a big grin. "I would be honored to be present, Professor."

"You could be posted as a guard or possibly one of the scientist's assistants," Sepp said, knowing the ceremony would never take place.

As they reached the far end of the *loggetta*, Gallo held open another set of doors, and they entered the tower's base. Off to one side, Sepp saw a ramp.

Noting his interest, Gallo explained. "It is said that Napoleon rode his horse up the incline of the old *campanile* to observe the city he had conquered. We don't speak of it much, and some think it brought a curse that caused the tower to collapse." He indicated the open door of the elevator. "The ramp is rarely used."

On the ride up, the policeman made excuses for his superior. "Professor, please, you must forgive my sergeant. He is usually at a desk in the headquarters, but because of the Hitler visit, he feels this assignment at the tower dishonors him."

"Is the entrance usually unguarded?"

"It is under the domain of both the state and the Church and is most often controlled by those involved with tourists. Otherwise, it is locked. Sergeant Masciarelli, that's him, he believes such would suffice now, but the chief is determined to take extra measures. The sergeant is especially resentful of being placed with a novice like me." Before Sepp could ask, Gallo explained, "I have been a policeman for less than a year."

Exiting the elevator, they entered the *loggia* dominated at the center by its five large bells. Sepp carefully set down the box and went to the outer railing. *"Wunderbar!"* leaped from his lips as a marvelous panorama greeted him. He could see it all: the rooftops and façades of Saint Mark's Basilica, the boats on the lagoon, the islands large and small, and through a haze, the distant Lido. Moving to the opposite side, he took in a grand view of the main *piazza*, arcades, and the galleries. He was mentally calculating distances and possible shot angles when Gallo interrupted.

"Sir, I must go now. Masciarelli expects me back so he may have breakfast. The regular lift operator will arrive soon, and you need only to press the buzzer button to have him come for you."

"Very good. I expect to be here for some time, so that should be fine."

"And, sir." Gallo pointed to the lagoon, "History tells us Galileo aimed his telescope in that direction. Out to the islands and the sea."

Sepp nodded and watched the elevator door close on the policeman. Alone and anxious to get started, he removed the telescope and stand from its box and set up the instrument in the direction of the *piazza*. As excitement and anticipation welled up inside, Sepp made his initial review of the square. At first, he observed the movements of people and horse carts as if he were viewing stars and planets. Then, encouraged to see more, he released the trigger mechanism and began tracking prospective targets in the scope's crosshairs. He lit a cigarette and pushed the scope to its limits when he zeroed in on a pigeon well across the square. He imagined what it would be like to draw a bead on a human. The thought disappeared when the elevator motor came to life. Quickly, he stored the trigger and moved the telescope to the lagoon side, where he began casually observing boat traffic and picking out landmarks. The elevator door opened, and a towering figure emerged carrying a bulging rucksack. As the man came into the light, Sepp recognized the brute from the Vienna film crew. "Hello," he called.

"Captain Karper." The big man's face lit up. "Director Martone said I might find you here." After an awkward silence, he added, "Don't worry. He has asked me to help you with your mission in any way I can."

"You can begin by referring to me as Professor Alex Höbling of the University of Vienna."

"You are the professor, and I am Bruno, a member of the film crew." He set down his rucksack. "Right now, I must check for camera positions, and I see you are doing something similar with your fancy telescope, if that is what it is."

"No, you see …"

The big man put a hand on his shoulder. "It is okay, Professor Höbling. I understand."

As Sepp reset the stand facing the *piazza*, *La Marangona,* the largest of the five tower bells began to toll, announcing the beginning of the Venetian workday.

Bruno went about his tasks marking with chalk positions for his camera and focusing his lenses. When he was finished, he repacked his gear and excused himself. "*Addio,* professor, I must go see to other locations."

Sepp remained, acclimating himself to the ear-splitting tolling of the bells. He considered using wads of cotton in his ears, but that would tend to isolate him from the *piazza's* ambience and could dull his instincts. Besides, it was not unlike the bombs and cannons he had endured during the war.

Peering into the telescope's eyepiece, Sepp began calculating optimum kill zones from both the *piazza* and lagoon sides. The day wore on well into the afternoon.

Meanwhile, below in the *Piazetta dei Leoncetti*, the small square next to *Basilica di San Marco*, Martha Markham was taking advantage of a rose-tinged beauty light to capture photos of the church's imposing side elevation. As she aimed her camera for a shot, a fishmonger caught her elbow with the smelly cart he was pushing, just as she was about to press the camera's shutter release.

"Oh, hey! Pardon me!" she exclaimed as the vendor trundled on to the *piazza*, the disgust in her voice complementing the lingering stench of his cart. Without turning around, he responded with an obscene salute.

"Since when are Italians so rude?" she wondered, unaware that the offender was an itinerant Bosnian who had little respect for anything outside his own culture.

She tossed off the uncouth man's distraction and went into the main square, where she took several more shots of the church's Byzantine façade. Then, aiming in the opposite direction, she opened the camera lens wide, steadied herself against a pillar, and took odd-angle exposures of the bell tower. As she did so, the view of the structure stirred in her resentment and disgust over the episode with Alex. Intent on not letting the thought ruin an otherwise good day, she picked up her camera bag and headed into the square to the *Caffe' Quadri.*

There, Martha searched for a friendly face, hoping that some of the American press might have arrived early to cover the Hitler visit. She was about to give up when, in a quiet corner under the arcade, a shock of ginger hair caught her eye. It belonged to a man she had met through her contact with outspoken reporter Dorothy Thompson, whom he had replaced as Berlin bureau chief for the New York Evening Post. Now, as luck was with her, there he sat, correspondent Hubert Renfro Knickerbocker, hunched over a notepad.

"Red," she called out as she approached his table.

He looked up, instantly all smiles. "Marti, what are you doing here?" His voice was mellow and tinged with a charming Texas drawl. He stood, and they hugged. "It's so good to see you and completely unexpected." He held her at arm's length as he added, "The last you wrote, you were doing work for magazines." His face turned somber. "I was happy to know you had at least begun to get beyond … well, you know. Ronnie was a good man, and nobody deserves that kind of hurt." He smiled away the dark mood. "How's the photography working out?"

"I love it," she replied as they both sat. "Capturing the beautiful places of art."

"Looking at her with a broad grin, he asked, "Can I get you something? The coffee here is top drawer." He signaled for a waiter and indicated they needed two cappuccinos. "Well, I guess taking pictures could be a challenge, but then again, I've never done much of it."

"Photography is a lark for me, but there's a lot that goes into it. Setting up, getting the light and camera adjustments right, and because the venues I frequent are often so popular, one has to work around the crowds, sometimes in spite of them."

"Heck, I never considered any of that. So, this has nothing to do with the Hitler visit."

"Well, maybe." Her response was interrupted by the arrival of the two coffees. She raised her cup to him and took a small sip. "I could use a break and am interested in finding out what it would take to cover this meeting as a news photographer."

Red explained, "As you might guess, security is pretty tight. I don't think *Il Duce* is any great admirer of the German chancellor, but he certainly wouldn't want anything to happen to the son of a …" He caught himself. "Excuse me, Hitler is a sore subject with me. I was there at the beginning and observed his rise to power. I've also seen what he's done with it and fear there is going to be a war." He took a swallow of his drink and reset his mood. "To answer your question outright, you will need press credentials and police permission for access."

Martha pursed her lips. "Oh. Unless my papers for getting into museums and churches count, I'm afraid I have neither."

"I need to go to police headquarters for my papers. I'll pick up applications and meet you back here, say at five. Maybe I can help you get over the hurdles."

Feeling a calming sense of relief, Martha turned their conversation into one of catching up on family matters, the status of friends, and conditions in the United States.

From a nearby table, Enzo Noschese sat feigning nonchalance as he sipped his drink and kept an ear cocked. He did not recognize the man with her now, but because they both had red hair, he guessed they were related. "Possibly her brother?" he wondered. After some time, the gentleman looked at his wristwatch and excused himself. Seeing Martha remain at the table organizing her camera bag, the Italian reporter made his move. Appearing before her, he bowed. "Excuse me, please. You are Mrs. Markham, yes?"

Martha regarded him with a wrinkled brow. "I am, and who are you?"

"*Scusamis, signora.*" Uninvited, he took a seat. "May we speak *italiano?* My *inglese* is not good."

"*Sí,*" she replied, and their conversation continued in his native tongue.

"My name is Enzo Noschese, and I am a reporter with a Roman newspaper."

"And, what is it you want from me, *Signor* Noschese?"

"Oh, nothing from you, *Signora,*" he assured. "Except, I would like information about the man you were with."

"You might know him." She indicated the chair where Red had sat. "That was H.R. Knickerbocker, quite a noted American journalist. A Pulitzer winner."

“Oh, no. I do not mean the gentleman who was with you a moment ago. I mean the one in Florence, and with whom you traveled here. The professor, as he is called.”

“The professor? I know little about him,” she replied frowning. “We met only a short time ago, and because we both needed to come to Venice, we motored together. Nothing more.”

“Do you know him as a member of the Austrian police?” he pressed.

“Certainly not.” She glared at him. “He is a professor from Vienna University. An astronomer.” She closed her camera case deliberately. “I really must be going now, sir.”

He pushed back from the table and stood. “Excuse me, *signora*. I must be mistaken about the gentleman.” With a head bow, he bid her *Buona sera* and left.

Martha fumed. This thing with Alex, or Sepp, or whoever the hell he is, would not go away. She made a mental note to ask Red what he knew of Noschese.

* * *

Evening shadows cloaked the alleys of Venice by the time Sepp set out for the *Contarini del Bovolo,* having completed his first checks at the *Campanile di San Marco.* As he made his way, it seemed the canals had become particularly malodorous. He hadn’t noticed it before, maybe because of the scent of roses he experienced when he was with Martha.

“Huh! She might well have been the source of that pleasant waft, and possibly everything else good,” he muttered, concluding nothing seemed quite right since she rejected him two nights ago.

He took a route back to the *Contarini del Bovolo* along *Piscina San Moisè* that went right by Martha’s hotel. Once there, although he had not planned to do so, he found an obscure niche opposite the hotel’s entrance and waited, observing the passersby. Fifteen minutes passed. Then twenty. Sepp was about to leave when he saw her. She wasn’t alone. The lanky man with her carried her camera case, and they were lost in conversation. Sepp’s heart dropped. “What the hell could have happened in two days?” At the hotel, the man turned over the camera case, gave her a peck on the cheek, and left.

Sepp wanted to stop her before she entered the hotel, but thought better of it, reminding himself that the mission must come first. As she disappeared into the lobby, he continued on to Max's *palazzo*.

* * *

The luxury of the *Contarini's* bedchamber paled against the naked loveliness of *Signora* Claudia Mocenigo, a lithe, porcelain-skinned beauty sitting at a set of vanity mirrors brushing her long, black hair.

"Must you leave so soon?" asked Max from the bed, rumpled by their passion and scented with her lavender water.

"Come now, Maxie. You know, Carlo is already suspicious, so we must be doubly careful. I would hate to think what might happen if he ever found out."

"I understand, but I don't like it." He said as he rolled out of bed and brought his nudity to her. "Maybe if you let me pleasure you once again," he offered as he let his fingers slide down her pert breasts to the slight, soft bulge of her abdomen and into the damp warmth below.

She allowed his touch to continue for a few seconds before playfully slapping his hand. "Please, I would love nothing more, but I must go."

"Claudia," he insisted as she pulled away, "I love you and I want us to be together forever."

"I feel the same, *mio caro*, but we must be patient." She stroked his hand. "He will toss me aside, as he has the others, and then I will be yours. I told you, marrying him was not my will but that of my father. The Mocenigos once ruled Venice, and papa believed it would improve our family's standing."

"So you must suffer an arranged marriage." He wriggled into his shirt and searched the bed for his underwear. "Darling, this is 1934. The world has experienced the war to end wars. Things have changed. Does your father not know this?"

"Please, my Papa is not an ogre. He is a kind, gentle man who has the interests of our family at heart." She slipped into her dress and fastened the front buttons, adding, "Things do not change so easily here in Venice." She went to him as he finished dressing. "My dear Maxie, I do not do this happily, but I do it willingly to please Papa."

"Your father may not be one, but he made you marry an ogre."

"Carlo is a brute, of this there is no doubt, but I can control him well enough." At the door, she added, "I very much fear the consequences should he discover our secret."

"If ever he harms you, I will kill him."

"We must make certain it never comes to that."

He joined her, and they descended the steps to the ground floor. As they reached the foyer, the door opened and Sepp arrived carrying his big wooden box.

"Professor," Max exclaimed, preempting any chance of Sepp revealing his true identity.

Sepp caught the cue. "Max, I'm pleased to report that my arrangements are going well." He set the box down and walked toward them.

Max turned to Claudia, "*Signora Mocenigo*, I wish to introduce Professor Alex Höbling."

"The great astronomer Max has told me about," she said as she extended a hand.

Sepp grasped her delicate fingers lightly and bowed over them, as he replied. "Max does me too much honor, I assure you, madam."

They made a minute of small talk before Claudia bid them goodbye. Sepp and Max were alone.

"She is quite remarkable," observed Sepp.

"That she is, my man, but it sounds like you aren't doing so badly yourself," said Max, attempting to return the compliment.

"I'm afraid that's over," Sepp replied glumly.

"What happened? When you arrived, she was all you could speak of. Now, two days later …"

"Two evenings ago, she found me out a fraud. We had a wonderful romantic interlude, but then, she made a ruinous discovery when she tried on these phony glasses of mine." He yanked off the spectacles. "There ensued a terrible row and she threw me out."

"From passion to rejection, all in one evening. It's ironic, happening after she opened herself to you, or to who she thought you were. Is that why you made yourself scarce yesterday and this morning?" He sat next to Sepp.

"It is. I couldn't face anyone." He rubbed his beard. "I somehow have managed to fall in love with this amazing American widow, and my life has been turned upside down."

"Sepp." Max said as he patted Karper's knee. "Being in love with someone can do such things. You certainly have been there before."

"What your aunt and I had together was different. We were two people dedicated to our work. Our intimacy was quite incredible, but the job came first." He made a fist. "The mission must always come first."

"Even now?" asked Max.

"Especially now, but this is the last of it for me. My mind is made up. I want Martha to be the future. A future I have now fucked up terribly."

Max nudged Sepp. "Let's have a drink and talk about it." He got up and headed for a door to one of the anterooms, "I have a fine old scotch."

Sepp followed him. "I don't see what alcohol will do, but I think I may need some."

Max poured three fingers worth for each of them, and they settled onto one of the brocaded settees scattered about the grand room.

They touched glasses. *"Prost,"* said Max. "Now, let's see how we can untangle this web you have woven for yourself."

"I saw her minutes ago in the company of another man," Sepp revealed. "He carried her case for her and kissed her cheek when they parted."

"That may not be anything," Max concluded.

This time, the quizzical look was on Sepp's face. "Are you mad? It was terrible."

"A kiss on the cheek? My God, it means next to nothing here in Italy. Forget about this other guy. You need to get back in her good graces on your own." Max sipped his scotch. "There is hope if you confess. Make a clean breast of it, as the Americans say."

"Tell her everything?" Sepp considered another sip of the potent liquid, frowned, and set the glass aside. "My identity? My mission?"

“Everything. Regain her trust by showing that you are the man she thought she knew, and the one for whom she had feelings.” Max pointed to the half-full glass, and when Sepp shook his head, he poured its contents into his own. “My guess is she still has those feelings, so you need to do whatever you must do to make her realize that. Reveal yourself and don’t hold anything back. She will understand that you are trusting her with your life.”

Sepp shook his head. “Oh, God, this is such a distraction. I don’t know. I can’t allow anything to affect the reason I am here.”

“It already has. You said it yourself,” Max reminded. “The mission will be part of the past. Martha is the future.”

Chapter Twenty-Two

Monday, 11 June 1934

Washington, DC

It was after seven in the evening when President Roosevelt returned to the White House proper from his office. With the help of one of his aides, he made his way to a private library where he met with James Farley and Davis Walsh, a fellow Democrat from Massachusetts.

Walsh, a large man and flamboyant dresser, had once served as governor and was now his state's first Irish-Catholic senator. He had been summoned to the White House because Roosevelt wanted to be sure he was in line with the New Deal before his bid for re-election in November.

After fifteen minutes of friendly and often jovial conversation, FDR concluded that, while Walsh was undoubtedly no lap dog, he would not attempt to derail the administration's policies aimed at relieving the devastating consequences of the Great Depression.

Before Walsh left, he assured FDR, "Mr. President, we need to get America going again, and you can count on my support."

Once the senator was gone, Roosevelt turned to Farley. "Well, Jimmy, what do you think?"

"I say he's on board," Farley concluded. "He may be hanging over the side throwing up, but he's not about to abandon ship."

"Good," Roosevelt slapped his hands and clasped them. "Now, the matter of the Hitler visit. What's the latest?"

"I can only say what I read in the papers," replied Farley. "Not much more from the embassy, and as planned, nothing yet from our curious butterfly over there."

"We don't know much," concluded FDR.

"By design. There is to be no contact until it's over unless she runs into a problem." Farley's tone was mollifying.

"I understand all that. I don't necessarily like it, but I guess I'll have to live with the situation for the sake of deniability."

He leaned toward his friend, "Jimmy, what about the meeting in general? I read the newspapers too, and I'm still not sure what to make of it. Why Venice? Why now? I get the feeling the German is up to something, but I cannot fathom Mussolini playing the fool."

"Some say *Il Duce* didn't want to grant Hitler the honor of a full state visit in Rome," Farley advised. "He's a man of pomp and circumstance like the days of the Romans, so this certainly could be the case. You know the Eye-ties are more show than go."

FDR nodded. "I give him credit though."

"As for the timing, I think Hitler is planning to tighten his grip on the reins of power in Germany. Hindenburg is failing. Once he goes, it's Katie bar the door."

Roosevelt shook his head. "And, I am left to rely on the observations of a woman photographer for information. What the hell was I thinking?"

"Hold on there," Farley said as he raised his hand. "We agreed she was a perfect choice because of her ability to blend in. We know she's got the intellect for it, and I expect she'll give you a view of all this you could never have had otherwise, barring being there yourself."

Farley looked into Roosevelt's eyes. "Let's not doubt this. Just hold your breath for a few days and it'll be over. We'll get her report, and you can decide where to go from there."

"Entirely logical, but I have to trust my gut as well. Venice has traditionally been a place of intrigue, and I'm feeling it in my bones." He regarded Farley with a grin. "How'd you like a vacation?"

"Even if I could get there in time, what would I do?" Farley countered. "I'm sure to be recognized." He pointed. "Look at this face. It's been in newspapers and magazines for years."

"To be sure," FDR said in a convincing Irish brogue. "And it's the sort of face only a mother can love."

They both laughed, and the tension over the Mussolini-Hitler meeting dissolved in the air like the smoke from the cigar Farley lit before wheeling the president to the dining room.

Chapter Twenty-Three

Tuesday, 12 June 1934

Venice, Italy

After completing another day of planning and measurement taking at the tower, Sepp returned to Martha's hotel, determined to speak with her. He had decided to take Max's advice and confess everything, hoping she would forgive him. As he ground out a cigarette and dropped it into a receptacle, Martha appeared carrying her camera bag and looking uncharacteristically bedraggled. He rushed to intercept her as she headed for the elevator. "Martha, please. Please, we must speak."

She regarded him coldly. "I'm sorry, have we met?" adding with mock discovery, "Oh, wait! Aren't you the man who lied to me for weeks? The one who invaded me and …"

Sepp took her arm. "Please, I want to explain everything."

"Explain?" she pulled out of his grasp. "Explain what? That by knowing you, whoever you are—Karper—Höbling—Satan, you have put me, my two children, and possibly my entire family at risk."

"I love you!" he declared.

She went silent.

He continued, "I am in love with you." As she settled, he added, "Now, I beg you, can we go someplace where I can tell you everything?"

She set down her case and folded her arms on her chest. "What's wrong with right here."

"Too public. You will understand when you hear what I have to say."

"Not my room. You will never see the inside of it again."

"Maybe we can have a stroll or go to a quiet café."

She looked around the busy lobby, reluctantly left her case with the desk clerk, and stiffly accompanied Sepp from the hotel.

With the narrow streets and alleys crowded with revelers, Sepp offered, "This isn't working. Maybe we can go to my friend Max's place. He won't be there and we will have perfect privacy."

"Way too private for my liking."

"Nothing will happen, I promise. You have my word as a gentleman."

"The word of a liar!" Martha corrected, her voice full of scorn.

"It is the word of an Austrian patriot. Please believe me."

During the minutes it took to get to Max's, she barely spoke and would not let him take her arm or touch her in any way as they walked. They entered the courtyard of the *Palazzo Contarini del Bovolo,* and Sepp escorted her in. As he had hoped, the place was deserted.

Attempting to assure Martha their meeting would be open and safe, Sepp led the way to a sitting room with a table and several chairs. She took one and he sat across from her.

"Can I get you something to drink?" he asked.

Her disgust still had not run its course. "I want to stay as clear-headed as possible in anticipation of your amazing revelation."

"I had in mind some mineral water."

Receiving a second negative response, Sepp began. "What you discovered, you should never have learned." He bowed his head and rubbed his hands together before looking directly at her. "My true name is Sepp Karper. I am a military member of the Austrian state police with the rank of captain. I am on a special assignment, under direct orders from the chancellor of Austria."

"Dollfuss, isn't it?" she asked. "I've seen his name and photograph in the Times. A little fellow."

"To be sure, but powerful and quite a patriot."

"Is Austria an entire country of patriots?"

Sepp took the remark on its face and responded, "Unfortunately, not. There are internal enemies: the Bolsheviks, the National Socialists, and others who want to claim Austria for themselves or *Deutschland.*"

"So, if things are so bad at home, why are you here?" Martha asked.

"My mission is to somehow neutralize the single biggest threat, the Nazi leader." He stared directly into her eyes.

"Neutralize, huh!" she leered. "You mean kill, don't you?"

"There may be a second option. Abduction."

"Who makes that choice?" she asked.

"It is complicated, and my commitment is to follow orders no matter the consequence. Even death." Sepp ran his fingers through his hair. "Martha, I simply don't know all the details yet."

"You have the telescope, and you plan to be up in Saint Mark's bell tower at a most opportune time, I suppose."

"That is part of it. You see, the telescope contains a rifle. I can use it to carry out an assassination, but the rest is unclear. The abduction may only be a pipedream."

"So, is it all up to you?"

"The choice is not mine. Right now, I am to kill Hitler. Should that change, I will be contacted."

Her look was one of genuine concern. "You are but a single pawn."

"I hope to get help, but that too is vague." He reached across the table and took her hand in his, and she did not withdraw. "Martha, I have said too much. The more you know, the more vulnerable you become." Locking his eyes on hers, he added, "As it stands, what you know could topple an entire government and lead to the assassinations of the leaders of my country."

"I would never say a word," she assured him.

"I know." He smiled warmly. "I not only love you, but I also trust you." He leaned back. "Are you still passing on that drink?"

"Maybe a gin and tonic. Easy on the gin." Her words were pleasant, as was the smile that followed.

"Your wish is my command," he promised as he headed for the door.

Martha spent the moments alone carefully weighing every word Sepp had uttered as she tried getting comfortable in the stiff chair. By the time he returned with the drinks, the ambiance of the entire place seemed a bit more hospitable and lighter.

"So, here I sit with a man who is on a mission to either kill or kidnap the chancellor of Germany." She took a sip of the drink he handed her. "And I'm still here! Am I a fool, or am I also a patriot?"

Sepp shrugged. "I don't know, are you? A patriot, I mean."

"May I remind you, I come from a land founded by patriots." Her light mood turned serious. "Look, Alex … Sepp. I have something of my own to come clean about."

"Don't tell me you're not Martha Markham."

"That's me, alright. American widow and mother, freelance photographer, and a patriot of a different sort."

It was her turn to look him in the eyes. "You see, I too am here at the request of my country's leader."

Sepp's brows went up. "President Roosevelt?"

"The same," she let the words hang for a moment before adding. "I don't know him directly, but my father is in politics. He was once an ambassador. The president wanted to have someone be his eyes and ears for this Hitler-Mussolini meeting. He won't show any interest publicly, but I suspect he is concerned about the outcome."

"And, well he should be. The Nazi is bent on world domination. Anything else?"

"That's as much as I know. I, too, am on my own. I am to observe, and when it's over, someone will contact me for a report."

"And, here I sit, in the presence of an American spy. Should I flee?"

"I'm no such thing!"

He grinned. "I was joking, but I must ask, what is your motivation for doing this? I assume you could have refused."

"I left out something. My mother and her side of the family are Jewish. I fear what that bastard Hitler may do to our people, so I wanted to experience him close up. Curiosity, I guess, more than anything."

"So, you wouldn't mind if he were taken out of the equation."

"Not at all." She drained her drink. "Now, what about all this lovey-dovey talk you spouted earlier?"

"It was my revelation of a fact I cannot deny. I am in love with you. I know it is sudden, but in the little time we have had together, you've changed my life. When this is over, I would like the opportunity to show you."

She reached over and took his hand. "First, let's get through this, together."

Vienna, Austria

Prince Starhemberg hummed a phrase from *Die Fledermaus* as he strode down the hallway and entered the office of the chancellor. Immediately, his mood changed when he saw Engelbert Dollfuss nervously pacing back and forth before his desk. "Engel, what concerns you so much? Your Italian friend is about to put the mad German in his place and see to it that Austria remains free."

Dollfuss stopped and stared at Starhemberg. "You've seen the reports, Ernst. Nazis regularly bomb us from our own country, and God only knows how much of it has been supported by the *Reich*."

"I am well aware of it," Starhemberg agreed as he slumped into a seat. "We must remain firm and resolute. Confident the German is no match for *Il Duce.*"

Dollfuss resumed pacing. "I don't know about Mussolini. He seems to be ignoring me and Austria."

"We have no alternative but to trust him," Starhemberg countered. "His years in power say he knows what he's doing. Besides, he would never turn against Austria because of your close friendship and his desire to keep the Germans off his border."

"If Benito sees Austria as no more than a buffer state, then he can be seduced by assurances from Hitler that he will never attack Italy." The chancellor paused. "You have said so yourself. When you were around him in the twenties, Hitler was one of the most persuasive and devious men you had ever met."

"I know what I said, but we must trust that we are doing everything possible to protect Austria."

"Which brings us to the kidnap plan." Dollfuss took a seat behind the desk. "Where does it stand? Hitler arrives in Venice in two days, and our opportunities are limited."

"We believe Karper is ready," assured the prince.

"And help for Sepp?"

"Will remain in the shadows unless it becomes absolutely necessary to engage. We don't want this to point back here, so we'll keep exposure to a minimum."

"I assume Sepp has identified the points of greatest opportunity, correct?"

"His training would tell us so. We have had no direct contact; however, we know he is both methodical and resourceful."

"That's the Sepp I know," Dollfuss slapped his hands together. "Completely reliable."

Once the meeting had ended, Starhemberg went directly to the Ministry of Defense and made his way secretly to the basement office of Paul Joscht. He found the colonel at his desk perusing a stack of intelligence reports. Joscht looked up and immediately rose.

Starhemberg waved him back into his chair and took a seat himself. "Is there anything new I should be apprised of, Paul, particularly as related to Venice?"

Joscht pointed to a small pile of papers. "I receive intelligence related to Hitler's visit, but little about Karper. One indication from the Italian state police is that a reporter with little credibility claimed to know Sepp as an Austrian agent and reported seeing him in Venice. The police were unable to confirm it. They even contacted Graff at the university, and he backed up Sepp."

"Are you certain it is of no concern?"

"I am, sir," assured Joscht. "There was also some mention of an American woman, a photographer. That too went nowhere."

"How is this woman involved?"

"She drove Karper to Venice. It sounds like he found a convenient way to get the weapon transported. Nothing more."

"Then, the plan, my plan, is still intact."

"Yes, but what about the abduction? Does Dollfuss continue to promote it?"

"He clings to the fantasy that we can somehow kidnap Hitler." Starhemberg chortled. "I doubt Hitler would want to go on that way as a captive, don't you agree?"

"I think he might prefer death," Joscht replied.

The prince slapped the arm of his chair. "Exactly! And we shall be happy to accommodate him."

Both men laughed, but their merriment was cut short by the buzzing of Joscht's desk phone. He answered it. "Yes, I see." He hung up. "Sir, your office received a call from Count Ciano. He would like you to contact him at your earliest convenience."

Starhemberg looked around. "May I have the room for a moment?"

"Certainly." Joscht got up and limped to the door.

"Paul, please have them get the count on the phone for me." The prince added, "And, ensure the call is not transcribed."

"Yes, sir. What about Karper? Do we need to contact him?"

Starhemberg shook his head, "For now, let's see that he is allowed to succeed or fail on his own."

Venice, Italy

Attempting to cover all possible threats during the visit of *Il Duce* and Chancellor Hitler, Inspector Petrin forced himself to go over his security plan one more time before ending his long, thirsty day. Peering through smudged reading glasses, he examined rosters of the men assigned for the three days of the visit.

Marino had been most supportive, clearly under pressure from state police chief Arturo Bocchini, and had made available every resource. Veneto police were sent to bolster the Venice force, and agents had come from OVRA, the secret police controlled directly by Bocchini. In the end, however, Petrin was, as Bocchini and Marino had wanted, left to his own devices.

Fighting to control the quivering hand brought on by a lack of alcohol, he double-checked all the venues the two leaders were expected to visit as well as the routes they would travel. An "x" marked each location, and a notation told the time the dignitaries were expected to be there. Included were the airport, the site of the Biennale art festival, the golf club, the Doge's palace, Stra, and *Piazza San Marco*.

Petrin sat back, looked at the ceiling as he had countless times before, and decided the *piazza* was the location of greatest vulnerability. He grumbled, "The goddamned *procuratie* with their arcades and balconies. Impossible to properly control. Then, there's that fucking bell tower!"

He tossed the plans aside. "Who knows where else the strutting politicians will venture?"

"Sir, why are you still here?" His sergeant asked, leaning in from the office doorway.

"Just going over some details, Bianchi," Petrin replied, indicating the papers.

"Something concerns you?"

"Everything concerns me. I'd be a fool if I said otherwise."

"Inspector, you are a fine detective, able to foretell every eventuality. You will see to it nothing happens, I'm certain of it."

"Thank you, but we won't know how well we have done until it is over. Before then, we must consider every detail and stay informed and focused. "

"Please, leave with me. Your day has been long enough."

"No, you go ahead. I'm not quite finished."

Bianchi shrugged. "Then, good evening, inspector."

"Until tomorrow." Petrin returned to considering where impromptu visits by the two leaders might occur. His focus was on the latest version of the event schedule when the phone rang. He picked up the handset. "*Pronto*."

There was no response.

Not trusting the instrument that had been installed only days earlier, he shook the handset and repeated, "*Pronto.*" Again, there was nothing. He was about to hang up when the sound of sobbing caught his attention.

"Gia? Is that you?" he asked, thinking it might be his ex-wife who had left him two years earlier for the arms of another man. The pain of the breakup still haunted him daily.

"Gia?" he asked again, hopefully, but after a few seconds, the line went dead.

"Was it really her?" he asked himself, wondering why she might have called. Was she alone again or caught up in nostalgia for their past? He shook his head and continued reading.

Presently, the phone rang again. This time, Petrin answered, "Gia, my love, are you okay?"

"I'm fine," said a masculine voice, "but who is this Gia? Aha ... Petrin, are you still pining for her?"

"Excuse me, Prefect Marino. I thought . . ." Petrin stammered, red-faced.

"Don't worry, my friend." Marino's words were calm and understanding. "These things happen to ordinary mortals. Now, please tell me where we stand with the security coverage. Is everything under control?"

"I would say so, sir. Although, as you know . . ."

"Yes, we never know until it is over." The prefect completed the thought. "The problem, my dear Petrin, is if things go wrong, we could find ourselves confined in some remote place. The islands are stunning, but views from inside a prison are far less pleasant than the freedom of a beach, don't you agree?"

"I promise, sir, nothing will go wrong. *Il Duce* and his precious German guest will be safe throughout."

They spoke a few moments longer, and when the call ended, Petrin went to his office window, pulled it open, and watched as the sun sank into the horizon and squealing seagulls followed returning fishing boats. He pondered what it would be like to fly above it all and never suffer the pain of disappointment and defeat. Petrin went to a metal cabinet and reached far in the back, feeling for a particular bottle as he salivated in anticipation. He came up empty, exclaiming, "Bianchi! You are too fucking thorough."

* * *

As he had done for days, Gianni hung out in the shadows, smoking a cigarette and watching the entrance of the *Palazzo Contarini del Bovolo*. Earlier, he had followed the *padrone's* wife Claudia as she went to the *Basilica di San Marco,* lit a candle, prayed for a few minutes, then continued on to the *Contarini*. It was a journey she had been making quite regularly of late, sometimes varying the church she visited but always ending up in the same place—the studio of *Signor* Max. He was there for almost an hour when there was activity at the *palazzo's* entrance. *Signora* Mocenigo said goodbye to *Signor* Max with a handshake and walked through the forecourt directly toward him. As he took in her graceful beauty, he unconsciously came out of the shadows, and she spotted him.

"Gianni, what are you doing here?" Her smile was warm, melting his heart, just as it always did. "Are you looking after me for some reason?"

He stumbled on his words before admitting, "In fact, I am *signora*, at the request of *il padrone*." She frowned and he continued, "He has me look out for your welfare."

"My welfare or my whereabouts?"

"Both. He becomes quite concerned when you are away from the hotel."

"And, I suppose you report my every move to him."

Gianni rubbed the side of his face. "Well, not all I might. Only basic facts. You go to the church to pray, you shop, and you come here to see *Signor* Max for your beautiful costumes."

She tested him. "Do you think there is more to it than that? Lighting candles, praying, then selecting materials, or having a fitting?"

"I would never think that." He shook his head once and stopped. "But the master might, and that would not be good."

She moved closer to the large man, "You would never allow it to come to that, would you?"

"Never, madam. Never. You know I so admire you."

"I do, Gianni, and I admire you as well." Her smile warmed him. "Would you like to accompany me back to the hotel?"

"As you wish," he said, joining her as she resumed her walk.

Chapter Twenty-Four

Wednesday, 13 June 1934

Riccione, Italy

Villa Margherita, a beautiful but simple two-story structure with lower arcades and a single square turret rising above the roof level, had a lush garden with a path the led directly to the beach. For the past several years, the villa had been a favorite vacation spot of the Mussolini family. A point of pride for *Il Duce* was the fact that they rented the place just as any typical Italian family might. He was so delighted with this detail, he had written to Gaetano Manzoni, the Italian Ambassador in Paris, telling him to inform his detractors in the French press he did not own the villa at Riccione or one at any other seaside location. At the time, he was utterly unaware his dear *Donna* Rachele was scheming to buy the vacation retreat. At the suggestion of *Il Duce's* secretary, Alessandro Chiavolini, she confiscated copyright earnings from articles about her husband in the U.S. magazine *Fortune*. The money initially earmarked for charity would be used for a down payment on the property.

Ignorant about his wife's dealings, *Il Duce* enjoyed a pleasant visit to the beach accompanied by his two younger children, Anna Maria and the precocious Romano, along with a small retinue of bodyguards. The beach was suitably remote, but crowds cheered him enthusiastically from a distance as he enjoyed frolicking in the sand and surf with the *bambini*. Feeding a need to be the center of attention, he had guests Fulvio Suvich, undersecretary for foreign affairs, and Achille Starace, Fascist Party Secretary, summoned to watch over the children while a boat took him to the deeper waters. There, onlookers along the shore and in craft nearby watched and cheered as he demonstrated his skill and stamina as a swimmer.

When *Il Duce* led the others back to the villa, he was greeted by his daughter Edda, son-in-law Galeazzo Ciano, and their children. Six-month-old Dindina was asleep in her mother's arms, but three-year-old Fabrizio ran to his beaming grandfather, shouting, *"Nonno, nonno!"* The Ciano family was on hand because Mussolini had asked Galeazzo to motor with him to Venice for the Hitler meeting.

When they later sat down for the midday meal, Rachele, who had seen to the preparation of a decidedly modest repast, announced boldly, "Today, salad, vegetables, and lunch meats. Nothing heavy."

"What! Why?" asked her husband as he broke off a piece of fresh-baked bread, aiming to take the edge off the ravenous appetite he had worked up. "I have a great desire for your wonderful risotto."

"Not today. You are about to drive to Venice, so you must be awake and alert for the trip. There will be no grand feast and no nap afterward." She wagged a finger at him like a strict school teacher. "And, definitely, no wine." She snatched a bottle of *Chianti* from the table, knowing her husband would be content with his usual milk.

It was approaching 14:00 hours, and Mussolini stood in the villa's driveway next to a red roadster as it idled impatiently. The Alfa Romeo 6C 1750 Gran Turismo Spider was the very same car he had driven on an April day in 1932 when, by chance, he encountered Claretta Petacci for the first time as he motored from Rome to Ostia. A two-seater with a long hood housing a straight-six, supercharged engine, accommodated a driver and passenger but had little space for transporting luggage. That would be handled by the three large, black vehicles sitting further back on the driveway. The cars also held Suvich and Starace as well as bodyguards, none of whom relished the idea of trying to keep up with the speed demon they were assigned to protect. They knew he would do everything he could to outrun and outmaneuver them along the way.

The lead security man approached. "*Duce*, are you certain you want to personally drive? One of my men could do that for you."

Mussolini frowned. "I am most certain. And, don't try leading me." He lowered himself into the driver's seat and added, "Allow me plenty of roadway."

Ciano trotted out of the villa and dropped into the seat next to his father-in-law, who nudged him with his elbow.

“Well, Galeazzo, we are off. I love such motoring adventures.”

Il Duce and Ciano waved to their spouses and family leaning out the windows of the villa as the impatient driver adroitly moved the shift lever into first gear. Mussolini engaged the clutch, causing a hail of pebbles, and the car lurched forward, leaving behind a hanging cloud of dust.

The Road to Venice

The small convoy traveled along the Adriatic state highway, slowing to negotiate turns and avoid the carts, buggies, and various livestock along the road. Residents recognized the driver of the eye-catching automobile and broke into cheers and chants of, *“Duce, Duce!”* As the four-plus hour trip unfolded, Mussolini was greeted similarly at the towns overlooking the sea: Rimini, Bellaria, Cesenatico, Cervia.

After more than an hour after they had left Riccione, the nourishment from Rachele’s light meal had long faded. As the car sped toward Ravenna, Mussolini announced, “Galeazzo, we must stop and have a proper meal.”

“What about security? Your men will surely advise against it. The risk!”

“I’ve known you many years, and your father, the naval hero, is a good friend. He is an accomplished and intelligent man. I’ve always admired him very much.”

“Your esteem is been reciprocated, sir,” Ciano assured him, not knowing where this path of words was leading.

Mussolini continued, “As a hero, did he not teach you that risk is a great part of leadership? Without it, there would be few victories.”

“Quite so.” Ciano nodded. “He instructed me in many such things.”

“Well, I am still hungry for pasta, and I know of a wonderful restaurant here. Any risk will be worthwhile, I promise.”

Ciano shrugged at his father-in-law’s convoluted logic. “As you wish, *Duce*.”

When the Italian leader headed the car into Ravenna, he remarked, “You remember, I was born and reared in Predappio, not fifty kilometers from here. I know these towns well."

Il Duce guided the roadster over a series of back roads, confusing the drivers of the automobiles following him. "They know to await us ahead."

Minutes later, Mussolini and Ciano were seated in a small, simple *trattoria* with fewer than a dozen tables, each covered with white cloths and adorned with red napkins. The husband and wife owners, working to overcome their astonishment at *Il Duce's* presence, scurried about as their other patrons gawked. Ciano cautiously eyed everyone and everything. The wife brought two green-covered bills of fare to the table.

Other than comment that the color combination matched the tricolors of the Italian flag, Mussolini ignored the menu and asked, "Do you still prepare the wonderful risotto with *melograno*?"

"Yes, Excellency," the woman said deferentially as she stood erect.

"And, your best *Chianti*, please."

"Without looking down at him, she replied, "We are at your service, *Duce*."

Ciano opted for the *tortellini*, and as the gawking and whispering from the other tables subsided, Mussolini and Ciano continued their conversation.

Il Duce's thoughts had landed on what he considered a relevant piece of local history. In this beautiful and historic city in 476 A.D., the last Emperor of the Western Roman Empire, Romolus Augustalus, was overthrown at the hands of Flavius Odoacer. This event marked the end of the dominance of Rome and ushered in the Middle Ages.

Leaning over the table and speaking softly so as not to be overheard, Mussolini asked, "Do you think Hitler's barbarians will test your *Duce* just as Odoacer and his rabble did Romolus?"

Caught off guard by the question, Ciano thought for a moment, shrugged, and asked, "In what sense, Duce?"

"In the sense, they too will want to win it all."

"I suppose it is possible, but I do not know. What do you think?" Ciano was careful not to show his cards regarding Hitler as he didn't want to give his cagy father-in-law any hint of the plan revealed to him by Starhemberg.

"You are most tactful. You answer a question with another question. I think your current role as head of the press and propaganda has made you even more evasive and slippery than when you served as a diplomat. Whereas I, the leader of fascism and this wonderful country, I pull no punches. I give straight answers, and I expect to receive them. Maybe in the future, I will have to think of something different for you. Is this what you want?"

Sensing it was a rhetorical question as well as a veiled threat, Ciano answered, "Whatever you wish to do with me, I will always succeed."

"You know, I have no love for the little German bastard. I do not need to meet with him to learn this. I know him like I know my own hand. Who can say? Maybe, in the next few days, I will come to despise him completely."

Ciano nodded. "I understand, *Duce*, truly I do."

"Nevertheless, we still have to act delicately in order to lure him out. To further open him up and see what is inside. Any advice you may have in this area, my tactful son-in-law, I will appreciate. We must always remember Austria lies at our northern border."

Il Duce's last sentence grabbed Ciano's attention. "Yes, but we are the friends of Austria, and they with us," he observed.

"Now! But who can predict the future?" Mussolini sat back and allowed the woman who had arrived with a basket-wrapped bottle to pour wine into a crystal goblet and set it before him.

She regarded Ciano. "And, for you, sir."

"San Pellegrino, please," replied the count politely.

As she left the table, Ciano again leaned into *Il Duce*. "When?" he asked.

"Soon. Hitler will reclaim the land of his birth. In his book of rants and platitudes in which he describes what he calls his struggle, he makes Austria a primary goal."

Ciano regarded his father-in-law and wondered whether the powerful autocrat had already raced ahead of everyone and planned it all out. He was a master at managing situations and making the best of those not in his favor.

Seeing Ciano's concerned look, Mussolini assured him, "Do not worry, Galeazzo. I am not ready to concede anything, not a single condition or meter of land. However, we must prepare for what could happen if that monkey successfully re-industrializes Germany. It would violate Versailles, but he has little respect for the treaty. He claims the Kaiser was coerced into surrendering far too early in the great war and promises to make Germany once again a power to be reckoned with. We don't want him sitting on our northern border."

It suddenly became clear to Ciano that the meeting with Hitler had more to do with positioning Italy for the most significant advantage vis-à-vis the Germans than with saving Austria. "When will Hitler attempt the annexation of Austria?"

"He will likely move immediately after this meeting."

"And, not before?"

"Certainly not. He does not want to draw attention to his plan and will do anything to avoid the subject. I don't expect many specific answers to my questions about it. Like you, he will respond with questions. Anything he says will be generic and vague."

"But *Duce,* you make it seem the meeting is a pointless farce."

"Not so. I agreed to it so the German worm could experience *Il Duce* at the height of his power. He needs to respect us so, whatever the future holds, that respect will form the basis for his decisions. From afar, he may see us as weak, a future target, but tomorrow he will learn otherwise.

"I see," Ciano said as he glanced across the room. "Look, *Duce*," he said, drawing the leader's attention to a table where a family was dining. The man and woman conversed as they ate, while their son of no more than three or four years, stood next to his chair at rigid attention facing Mussolini's table. He smiled at *Il Duce* and raised his arm in a fascist salute.

Mussolini saluted back and pointed to the boy. "Now, you see, that is the power I speak of. It will be years before Hitler achieves it." He nodded once more to the child and then returned to the conversation at hand. "However, we Italians must play our game."

"What is that?"

"Deceit! We must carry on the pretense of being friends with the Germans."

"Pretense?" Ciano paraphrased. "Is that what you are about?"

"Exactly. And, we must strengthen our weapons and tighten our friendships with France, the United States, and even England. Do you know Churchill has always admired me? Remember, in 1927, when he was here for a meeting, he told reporters, if he were Italian, he would be a fascist. Churchill believes I have saved Italy from the chaos of possible civil war and the communist threat."

So that was what *Il Duce* was up to, Ciano thought. Very clever, but also tricky because there were many variables and unknowns. He became increasingly aware, deep in the recesses of his mind, a more immediate solution was at hand—one that could be accomplished immediately. However, as he was about to offer it, the chef approached the table with a large plate of a pinkish risotto with red pomegranate seeds, and a dish of *tortellini* in a red sauce. Following him, the wife carried a grater and a chunk of parmesan cheese. As the plates were laid, both *Il Duce* and Count Ciano accepted the offer of extra cheese.

As Ciano watched Mussolini attack the *risotto,* his thoughts returned to what he would dare to suggest to him. He swallowed his first mouthful of *tortellini* and drank some sparkling water. "*Duce*, I have something I must say. It may be an alternative to the plan you propose."

Mussolini, in the process of devouring a mouthful of rice, responded, "What is it? I am all ears."

There was no turning back. Ciano downed another forkful, sipped more water, and cleared his throat. "Why not simply get rid of Hitler? Defuse him before he can build Germany into a threat."

Il Duce's eyebrows shot up. He held up his glass of wine and proclaimed, "Well, well. You do know about risk." He took a sip and looked directly into Ciano's eyes. "How do you propose doing such a thing?"

Worried he had said too much, Ciano recoiled. "I am not sure of details, *Duce*, but it would be a simpler solution."

Mussolini set down his glass. "And, what would the world say of such an event happening here in Italy?"

"Sir, I think the greater concern would be who committed the deed, not where it occurred."

Mussolini stroked his chin thoughtfully as he looked up at the ceiling.

Ciano pressed his point. "What if a foreigner perpetrated the incident with no ties to you, fascism or Italy?"

Again, *Il Duce* mulled the idea. "We should not be seen as having arranged any of it." His face hardened as he added, "The criminal must be apprehended and identified immediately so as not to throw a shadow on us or this country."

"Exactly," is all Ciano got out before his father-in-law slapped the table and exclaimed, "It is a pipe dream! We have no time to arrange this, and at this late hour, we risk a shoddy operation doomed to fail."

"*Duce*, I believe I know of a perfect solution that is already in place," Ciano offered. "I verified it with a telephone call only yesterday."

Mussolini raised his hand in Ciano's face, halting further comment. "I want to know none of it. If you have something which meets all the criteria we discussed, then I leave it to you to make the appropriate arrangements. I must have no ties to it."

Il Duce returned to his meal, and Ciano played with the pasta on his plate as he considered the steps he would need to take to make this pipe dream a reality.

Chapter Twenty-Five

Thursday, 14 June 1934

Venice, Italy

It was not yet 05:30 by the *Junghans* alarm clock sitting on a nightstand, and sunlight was already seeping through the cracks in the shutters across the room. Martha carefully slid her naked body out from between the bed linens and stood stretching for a long moment. Her pale skin, sprinkled with freckles, and the glow of her red hair created a vision to behold. One that she paused to admire in the dresser mirror before collecting the clothes she had worn the night before. As she picked up a lacy camisole, she was interrupted by incoherent, masculine grunting coming from under the sheets next to the spot she had just vacated.

"My love, I'm sorry," she said as she pulled up a pair of silky step-ins.

"Hrmph," was Sepp's groggy reply.

"I didn't mean to wake you." She buttoned her blouse and proceeded to slip on a skirt.

"I always wake up when a beautiful woman attempts to leave my bed."

"Well, this woman needs to get going," Martha said as she finished donning her clothes and picked up her handbag. "It's the big day today."

"Come back to bed. I need you next to me. Besides, according to the schedule, the Germans don't arrive until ten."

"Red is picking me up," she explained, adding with emphasis, "at my hotel."

"So early?" Sepp ran his fingers through his hair as he regarded her, and the lust of the previous evening began returning.

"A girl has to make herself presentable, you know."

"You look fine to me." He licked his lips as he eyed her up and down. The pleasant ache inside him grew.

She kissed his cheek lightly. "A boat has been arranged to take us to the Lido. I'm his photographer for the next few days. As we say in the States, 'the early bird gets the worm.' Besides, they won't be allowing traffic to cross the lagoon after a specific time. Red has it all figured out."

Sepp reached up and pulled her on top of him. "What if I can't let you go?"

They kissed passionately before she slowly extricated herself from his grasp as she covered his face with playful pecks. "I would love to stay and make love all day, but we both have jobs to do, and we must get to them."

"You will be busy, but I doubt there will be any opportunities for me today. According to the schedule, they spend most of the time at Stra or at Hitler's hotel." He held on to her hand as she stood next to the bed. "The word is they may attend a concert in the *piazza* tonight, but who knows if it's correct?"

He let go of her hand, allowing her to go to the door. "I'll see you later. Right now, I have this interesting and bright ginger reporter to pal around with."

"Are you trying to make me jealous?" he asked as he rolled and sat on the edge of the bed.

"Maybe." She blew him a kiss and left.

Sepp was wide awake and it was only 05:35. *"Scheisse!"* he muttered. "You have allowed a woman to get in the way of your mission." He let the thought roll around in his brain—the doubts, the fears, the questions about the future—before concluding he would gladly do it all over again. After all, what harm has it done? "None!" He told himself as he swore to do everything to keep it that way.

A thought oozed in from the past in Austria. When he and Katy were about to go their separate ways for the sake of their missions, she would remind him that one could not have his cake and eat it too.

"Well," he said to the empty room. "I shall have Martha and achieve what I came here to do as well." With perfect logic, he concluded, "After all, the two are not mutually exclusive."

Sepp grabbed a pillow Martha had laid her head on and put it to his face. The smell of rosewater and her essence made him feel warm all over.

* * *

Martha carefully opened the main hotel door and tiptoed into the lobby, thankful a doorman had not yet come on duty. She silently passed the snoring desk clerk and climbed the stairs to her room. Once inside, she immediately began shedding the clothes she had slipped into minutes earlier. Appreciating both her nudity and the afterglow of Sepp's lovemaking, she drew a bath, hoping wistfully it would help her ignore the fact that she had fallen for an assassin. She stepped into the tub, determined not to let her feelings for Sepp interfere with her mission for President Roosevelt.

The room phone buzzed just as Martha was completing her toilette. A groggy clerk announced that a *Signor* Knickerbocker awaited her in the lobby.

Wearing dark slacks and a wool jacket against the early morning chill, Martha descended the stairs to the ground floor. With her hair pulled into a bun atop her head and hidden under a sloppy brown fedora, Red barely recognized her.

"Marti, you look so …"

"Masculine?" She finished his sentence. "I'll be out there with a flock of male vultures."

"I see." Red checked the lobby clock showing 06:37 and observed, "A press *vaporetto* arrives in ten minutes. They will close the lagoon to boat traffic at seven." He assured her, "We should be okay."

With little more than a sketchy schedule to go by, neither of them knew with any certainty what to expect for the remainder of the day.

* * *

Sepp Karper had decided to give himself ten minutes to lie in bed and savor the pleasures of the previous night; however, when he felt the reverie consuming him, he forced himself to rise short of his goal. By 06:45, he was dressed and focused on one thing—the mission to kill Adolf Hitler.

He found *Signora* Costello in the kitchen, laying out a traditional Austrian breakfast of freshly baked bread and sweet rolls, jams, cold cuts, fruit, and of course, plenty of milk and butter. Not only did she excel at the sewing machine, but she was also an excellent cook, and he had gotten used to enjoying her hearty morning meals and her other fare, both Austrian and Italian.

They traded "*boungiornos*" as she poured coffee for him and asked if he would like any eggs or sausage. Turning them down, he asked, "Is the boss about yet?"

"No, *professore*," she replied. "*Signor* Max must have worked late into the night. I found two completed pieces this morning. For *Signora* Mocenigo." Seeing that her guest had settled for a crisp roll and butter, she added, "I must return to my machine now." She swigged a last bit of coffee and went to the door.

"Thank you for this, *signora*. You are a fine baker."

"Oh, *professore*." She blushed and scurried out.

Sepp checked his watch, and as he was draining his cup of coffee, his host arrived.

"*Guten Morgen,*" greeted Max, barefoot and yawning.

Sepp returned the salutation as his host padded by, leaving the aroma of musky lavender in his wake.

"Do you have time for a coffee with me?" Max asked.

"Just a quick one," Sepp conceded, holding up his empty cup. "Then I have to go. I need to be ready for anything once they are here." As Max served, Sepp commented, "I really do appreciate your fine hospitality, as well as your advice and understanding."

"My pleasure," he said as he eyed Sepp. "I am especially glad you are once again in the good graces of your Martha."

"In the end, love can overcome anything. I have never known such bliss, even as I prepare for this impending mayhem."

"We are fellows in that regard." Max took a roll and stuffed it with cold cuts.

* * *

Martha and Red sat at one of the makeshift canteen tables set up primarily for the thousands of military and paramilitary troops taking part in the airport arrival activities. They and other members of the press were also invited in and were now relishing the fresh rolls and boiled coffee offered as a *piccola colazione*—a small breakfast.

As they chatted, she mechanically tore a piece off a roll and dunked it.

"I'm certain you didn't learn that at Vassar," observed Knickerbocker.

After swallowing the dripping morsel she had just slurped into her mouth, she replied, "Actually, I did. The roll cools the God-awful hot coffee and adds a nice yeasty flavor."

"And, makes a mess of the roll."

"Oh, but it is quite yummy." Her luscious lips dripped with coffee.

"I stand corrected. I guess I learn something new about you every day."

As she went for another sloppy bite, her focus went wider. She froze. "Oh, no. Not him," she grumbled.

Red followed the direction of Martha's gaze to a group at the serving line. "Not who?"

She wiped her face and looked at Knickerbocker directly. "He's a reporter and a damnable snoop." Red's brow shot up as she continued. "We ran into him in Florence, and he seems to be following us ever since."

"Us?" Red focused on Martha's plural reference. "Is there someone else?"

"Have I not mentioned my traveling companion?" she asked. "A Viennese professor I met in Florence. We motored to Venice together. I truly enjoy him. You might say we have become something of an item."

"I see," Knickerbocker responded, a smile masking his disappointment. "Is he at the same hotel?"

"He is staying with a friend at the *Palazzo Contarini del Bovolo*."

"I know it," Red said, assuming a more positive manner. "I'd like to meet him and learn more about the conditions in his country. I haven't been there since Hitler became chancellor. Did you know

I had to leave Germany when the Nazis took power? I see them and Hitler in particular as a real threat to peace."

"Yes," she agreed. "I've read some of your articles on the subject. You've made quite a study of it all. So, you think the Nazis are that terrible a threat to Europe?"

He answered in a low voice. "To my mind, Hitler is a jingoistic madman. There is no end to the evil he may cause." He leaned back in his chair. "Now, tell me more about your prying reporter over there."

"Not much to add. He has gone so far as to accost me and claim my Austrian friend is an agent here up to no good."

"Well, is he?" Red asked matter-of-factly.

Fighting off gagging on the swallow she had just taken, she cleared her throat and managed, "I really . . ." Her answer was mercifully cut short by Noschese coming toward them.

"*Che cos'è questo*? *Signora* Markham?" he exclaimed. "Is that you?" With a toothy grin, he added, "A wonderful surprise, this is."

Martha grunted, shrugged, and forced a smile.

Ignoring her chilly reaction, Noschese continued, "Do you mind if I join you?"

"We were about to leave," she replied, irritated that the conversation with Red had been so rudely cut off, yet relieved she would not have to explain her professor further. She drank the last of her coffee and got up. Red took the cue and followed, but before she could get away, Noschese grabbed her arm. "I am glad to see you are now in the company of a gentleman and not with the deceitful Austrian."

As Martha escaped his grasp, Red looked like he was about to take a swing at the slimy reporter. They strolled in silence for several minutes before he reminded, "You know, you never did answer my question about your friend."

To which she employed the distressed damsel gambit. "Please, Red, the entire subject upsets me. Can we not talk about it?"

"It's probably a good idea to get over there early anyhow." They made small talk during the short walk to the receiving area located in front of large hangars. True to his word as a gentleman, he never raised the subject of the Austrian professor again.

They arrived at the grassy area and joined members of the press and dignitaries waiting there. Red introduced her to two reporters she had not met before, and the foursome traded light talk for several minutes before the sound of a military band and tromping boots overtook the ambiance.

Benito Mussolini appeared proudly leading a squad of black-shirted paramilitary followed by companies of the regular armed services units. It did not seem to matter to *Il Duce* that, unlike his usual public appearances, there were sparse cheering crowds and very few doting fans. The guests in attendance were mostly military, along with a group of fascist officials, diplomats, and security personnel. Much of Italy, including the population of Venice, had been kept in the dark about the meeting, although it had been reported on and spoken of in most other corners of the world. The same was true for Germany where, despite the fact it was to be their chancellor's first official visit to a foreign country, Nazi-controlled media carried no announcement of the historic event until after Hitler had departed the Fatherland that very morning.

Lacking a crowd to play to, Mussolini passed the time chatting with senior officers and diplomats on the scene. His disdain for his guest showed itself several times in the form of jokes and disparaging references to the German chancellor. However, when three Junkers Ju-52 tri-motor aircraft broke through the lingering haze of the morning sky, he assumed a proper official behavior.

The planes were part of the *Deutsche Lufthansa* inventory available for the *Führer's* use. The lead plane, with the registration D-2600, was Hitler's personal aircraft designated "Immelmann II" after the aviation pioneer and legendary German flying ace. Hitler's pilot, Hans Baur, set the plane down with smooth precision and taxied it to the area where the reception party waited. As the side cabin door came open, two members of the Italian ground crew moved steps up to the egress point. A moment later, Adolph Hitler appeared wearing a well-used tan raincoat over a dark business suit. Doffing a gray fedora as he bent to clear the plane's doorway, he descended onto Italian soil. He immediately raised his right arm in a salute before shaking the hand of the man he had idolized for much of his political life. *Il Duce* returned the greeting, using the German phrases he had learned while living and working in Switzerland.

Meanwhile, photographers bobbed in and out of the assemblage attempting to capture images for the historical record. Martha was among those stooping under the D-2600's fuselage. Working for a dramatic point of view, she managed to get several clear shots with her Retina camera.

Red Knickerbocker watched from several paces away, observing and recording nuances on his pad. His first entry began with the unusual silence when Hitler emerged from the aircraft with a hat he seemed unsure whether to put on or carry, and wearing a rather shoddy coat. He also noted how the German chancellor appeared uncomfortable in his diplomatic attire, especially when he saw Mussolini's sharp military garb. Most every Italian was in uniform while every key member of Hitler's party wore civilian clothing.

The two delegations came together, mingling and shaking hands. Among them were Konstantin von Neurath, Hitler's foreign minister, and his Italian counterpart, Fulvio Suvich. The greetings were interrupted by the playing of a triple fanfare, followed by *Marcia Reale*, the anthem of the Kingdom of Italy. Throughout, all present stood in silence except for a few enthusiastic photographers.

Martha chose to observe quietly during the anthem as she evaluated the expressions on the faces of Mussolini—confident, and Hitler—regret bordering on anger. "Perhaps," she told herself, "this may turn out to be quite a bit more interesting than I had expected."

The two world leaders then moved on to a review of the troops. To the sound of rousing march music, they strode past Italian military units standing stiffly at attention. Hitler walked with his hat in his left hand and gave the Nazi salute with his right every third or fourth step. Mussolini strutted and smiled like a conquering hero.

After more pomp, the pair of grandees arrived at a dockside where sleek motorboats awaited to whisk them and their entourages off to Venice proper. Sensing *Herr* Hitler's uncertainty with protocol, Mussolini prompted his guest to board first. After other dignitaries had joined them standing aft in the open air, off they went across the lagoon. The second boat followed carrying the lesser luminaries of both countries. Other watercraft transported Hitler's various aides and support staff. Wilfred Metzger was among them, sporting a full beard and a determined frown.

Il Duce's boat progressed at speeds far below its capabilities and, as arranged by the host, traveled past a line of Italian warships before heading toward the *Isla San Giorgio Maggiore*, with its magnificent church standing as a sentinel by the entrance of the Grand Canal.

From the bell tower, Sepp watched the procession approach. He knew from past tests that the boats would come close enough for a chance at a shot once they had sailed past *San Giorgio* and moved on to the tip of the *Punta della Dogana* with its picturesque basilica of *Santa Maria della Salute*. As the craft came closer, Sepp peered into the telescope and opened the lever that released the trigger mechanism. He was so completely focused on his mission, he failed to hear the whirring of the elevator motor.

Scanning the optimal kill zone from the *Canale della Giudecca* to past the *Punta della Dogana*, he saw the lead boat come into view. He tracked it in the eyepiece, waiting for it to move closer. There they were among the group standing in the stern. Mussolini was smiling and waving to the crowds along both shores. The chancellor returned the greetings with an occasional nod and Nazi salute.

Using the crosshairs, Sepp zeroed in on the head of Adolf Hitler. Suddenly, the elevator door opened.

"*Ciao* professor," called Officer Gallo. "Do you see them?"

Scheisse! Sepp grumbled as he stowed the trigger and watched his target disappear behind a building. Pulling away from the eyepiece, he forced a smile. "The instrument offers a perfect view, but I am afraid they have already passed."

Gallo walked toward him and shrugged. "Maybe I will have a chance when they come to the *piazza*. How did they look?"

"I only saw them for a second or two. Your *Duce* appeared happy. I'm not sure about the German."

* * *

Martha and Red arrived at the *Riva degli Schiavoni.* "What do you say we skip the Grand Hotel, Marti?" suggested Knickerbocker. "Hitler and Mussolini will attend an early luncheon there. I wouldn't expect anything of substance as the first talks won't occur until Stra, which is where Mussolini will go right after the meal. It's less than thirty miles on the way to Padua."

She responded brightly, "I say we head there."

"We can go there directly if we hire a water taxi."

"I have a better idea. My car is parked in the *piazzale* by the train station. We can motor to Stra. It is sure to be faster, and we can stop for something to eat on the way."

"Wonderful. I'll arrange a gondola to your auto."

Stra, Italy

The early afternoon sun beat down relentlessly on the crowds filling the treeless grass forecourt of the *Villa Pisani*, an eighteenth-century mansion once owned by Napoleon Bonaparte. The site had been chosen by Mussolini to impress the German chancellor; however, as arrangements for the meeting progressed, the extent of disrepair in the once magnificent mansion became clear. The facilities required to properly host so important an event were sorely lacking. Barely more than a week before Hitler's arrival, an army of artisans, technicians, and tradesmen came from Rome and other locales to refurbish and furnish the rooms, install modern comfort facilities and communication equipment, refresh the artwork, and enhance the gardens.

What once suited Emperor Napoleon had been sufficiently revitalized for fascist and Nazi royalty. Having traveled to Stra directly after lunch, the Italian leader was quite pleased with how well the villa had been transformed. Fortunately, the swarms of mosquitoes that would later rise from the *Brenta* canal to attack guests were not yet in evidence.

Il Duce strutted about the luxurious rooms of the villa full of optimism that all would go well and confident he would prevail in discussions with the German novice. Egotistically sure of his facility with the chancellor's language, he had decided to meet privately with Hitler without the aid of an interpreter.

Outside, a *carabiniere* waved Martha's Fiat past the forecourt entrance and pointed to a line of vehicles parked farther down the same roadway she and Red had taken from Venice. As planned, the two Americans had stopped along the way for an early meal knowing it might be hours before they would have the chance to eat again.

Martha eased her car behind an Alfa Romeo and shrugged. "I suppose parking right out front would have been too much to ask."

"At least they didn't send us over to the other side of the canal," Red observed. "I don't see a lot of convenient ways to get across." He pointed to a pathway leading to the villa entrance. "Let's walk there and get away from the roadway."

They arrived at the courtyard and joined a group of reporters and photographers gathered on the right side of the main façade. Along the way, Martha studied the faces of the onlookers who had come from all over the Veneto to honor their *Duce* and get a glimpse of the German who was suddenly the subject of Italian news reports. She noticed many in the crowd gazing expectantly up at the empty balcony directly above the main entrance. "Do we have any idea when the two of them will appear?" she asked Red.

"Following the private meeting, I would say." He scanned the few vehicles parked along the villa's facade. "*Herr* Hitler isn't here yet."

His words had barely faded in the air when three large touring cars entered the driveway. Alert and determined, Martha waded through the sea of adoring Italians with her camera held above her head and moved as close as she could get to the entrance. At the same time, the lead car came to a stop, the villa doors opened, and a group emerged. The crowd roared when they saw Benito Mussolini in a business suit and sporty white yachting cap. He walked smartly to Hitler's car and greeted the German chancellor as he emerged from the vehicle. The two men shook hands and the Italian leader again invited Hitler to precede him as they entered the villa. Before disappearing, both men spent a brief moment acknowledging the cheers of the multitude.

Martha rejoined Red, who was jotting notes on his pad. "Well, that was a bust."

"Why's that?"

"I attempted two shots, and both times I was jostled so badly, they are sure to be blurry."

"Too bad, but there should be other less hectic chances."

"How so?" she asked.

"I believe Count Ciano will come out and say a few words.

He usually tries to keep the press informed on such occasions. It's generally a lot of gilding the lily, you might say. You know, the usual fluff, with maybe a morsel of solid information here and there. You should learn more about picture taking opportunities then."

"Will we be allowed inside?" she asked.

He shrugged. "Doubtful, but it's anybody's guess."

Several more minutes of waiting and wondering passed before, under an elaborate archway to the right of the main façade, the entrance to the villa's gardens opened. Immediately the cheering and waving Italians moved to it, but they were kept away by a squad of guards motioning for the members of the press corps to enter. Once the media representatives were inside, the gates were closed on disappointed masses. The reporters and photographers were ushered across a lawn to a freshly landscaped pathway where an enthusiastic Galeazzo Ciano met them.

He spoke first in Italian and then in English, painting a positive picture of the growing camaraderie between *Il Duce* and the German chancellor and inviting the group to observe as Mussolini and Hitler strolled the garden paths with their aides.

His father-in-law was actually putting on a show—appearing jovial as he indicated to his guest the magnificence of the gardens, the outbuildings, and sculptures. Generally unfamiliar with the grounds himself, Mussolini repeated facts he had been briefed on only minutes earlier.

Red Knickerbocker noticed that the German seemed to be having difficulty staying interested. He nudged Martha. "I think Hitler just wants to get on with it—the meeting that is."

"That should begin soon, yes?"

"At four o'clock." The count mentioned it when he went over the schedule with the press folks at the Hotel Danieli last evening. It was rather late when I phoned your hotel to invite you, but apparently, you were either out or sound asleep."

Martha quickly changed the subject. "So, we may not see them again for hours."

Red nodded. "Exactly."

The guards herded the journalists and photographers back across the lawn and out the gates to the forecourt.

Meanwhile, Hitler and his party were shown to rooms where they could refresh themselves. Once inside, the Nazi leader boiled over, releasing his frustration on his foreign minister. "Neurath! I detest the situation you have put me in! You are losing my favor!"

Visibly shaken by the chancellor's outburst, Konstantin von Neurath replied, "Excellency, I do not understand; however, I will do everything I can to ease your discontent."

Hitler glared at him. "First, you allowed me to come here as a diplomat, which I am not! Nor do I aspire to it. My role is that of *Führer*, but I cannot comport myself as such because of this attire you were so convinced would be appropriate."

Hitler slapped the arm of the chair, causing Neurath to wince. "I do not want to be appropriate! Understand? I must prevail! My ideas must prevail!"

"Excellency, I understood it had all been quite cordial and friendly."

"You comprehend nothing. While I have the deepest respect for Mussolini and all he has done in the name of fascism, I am wary of his motives and suspect they work contrary to my own." His knuckles whitened as he grasped the chair arm. "He is attempting to impress and placate me at every turn, trying to lull and control me." He again glared. "Is that what you want? That the Reich be dominated by Italy and their *Duce*?"

"Of course not, sir." Neurath pulled up and sat in a chair next to Hitler's. "You will triumph for the sake of our entire country."

"Do you have another of your suggestions as to how I might accomplish this?"

"You must pacify him and create the appearance of concord between our two countries." Neurath was relieved to see that his *führer* was considering his advice.

Hitler summarized, "Only the appearance until we are strong enough to prevail: rewrite Versailles, attach Austria, bring the people of the *Sudetenland* into the fold, cleanse our race . . . all of it!" His eyes glazed over as he stood, raised his fist, and declared. "The thousand-year Reich will not be established using diplomacy, but through the application of deception and extreme power!"

"Excellency, your appearance as a diplomat is part of the ploy.

You are a wolf in the clothing of a sheep."

Neurath's comment brought a welcome grin from the German chancellor.

At 15:00, the Italians held a social in a large salon with arched windows and doorways, niches filled with flower arrangements, and a grand chandelier at its center. *Il Duce,* with his delegation that included leaders Starace and Suvich, made brief welcoming comments. He eased the gathering's formality by inviting everyone to relax and enjoy the sparkling wines, tasty Italian fruits, and finger foods prepared for the occasion. Then, the Italian leader announced that smoking was an option and indicated a side table holding an array of cigars and cigarettes.

Accompanied by his usual associates—Von Neurath, Von Hassell, and the other Germans—Chancellor Hitler passed on the wine and smoking and was happy to receive a goblet of mineral water as an alternative. In all, there were some twenty men in the room. Working to defeat his general discomfort with the situation, Hitler mingled but purposely avoided contact with Mussolini. That would come later, and neither he nor the Italian premier gave any indication of the topics they might cover during the private talks to follow.

As the occasion ended, the two men left the room and went to a library where they could speak privately and take a measure of each other.

Out in the courtyard, the crowd and the reporters milled about seeking relief from the heat and boredom. Noschese was among them, but he had been avoiding Martha and Red ever since the run-in at the airport.

Knickerbocker checked his wristwatch. "Marti, I guess we're just gonna have to fill in the blanks later on." He ran his hand over his wavy hair. "You know, the press gets criticized for not always getting it right, but often, especially in these totalitarian societies, we end up simply repeating or paraphrasing what spokesmen like Ciano feed us, or writing about staged events such as the one we witnessed in the garden. It goes out over the wire services, and generally, every U.S. newspaper carries the same stories. It's the kind of thing I have always disliked and worked to avoid."

"It is so different than in our country, isn't it? You reporters get to see and write about everything."

Red held up his hand, "Whoa, hold on a minute. That's not exactly true, especially with old FDR. He keeps quite a few things off the record and out of the public view."

His words immediately reminded Martha of her mission. She nodded and went silent.

Inside the villa, the Mussolini-Hitler discussion had moved from the Treaty of Versailles, which the German leader demanded be changed to allow his country to develop its industry, to *Il Duce's* imperative for Germany to return to the disarmament talks in Geneva. It was a demand Hitler did not like, and Mussolini allowed it to drop without receiving any kind of commitment from the German. They then took up the independence of Austria.

"On this point," Hitler stated unequivocally, "I can assure you that I have no such designs on my native country."

Mussolini countered with a reference to *Mein Kamph*. "Chancellor, in your book, you speak of how, as a boy, you yearned to see Austria reunited with Germany. Has this changed?"

Hitler seemed to be waiting for such an opening when, in a heartbeat, he responded, "I believe Germans are Germans no matter where they are. In this regard, I ask that there be free elections in Austria, and if National Socialism gains power there, that such a choice by the people is respected."

Mussolini could handle casual conversation in German; however, his limited fluency with the language of diplomacy made it difficult for him to understand his guest's somewhat convoluted answer. Nonetheless, he gave the impression of complete comprehension.

As for the German chancellor, he pressed his case well beyond the boundaries of the ersatz diplomacy he had promised von Neurath. At one point, he bragged that he could take France in a matter of days. Again, the Italian leader was noncommittal. He had fully understood Hitler's boast but chose to treat it as the idle rambling of a madman.

Hitler was also quite clear regarding the Jewish question. "You see, *Duce*, I deeply admire and respect you for all you have accomplished. However, a great fungus has grown on your fine fascist tree, and it will impede and eventually stunt your growth. The Jews have too much control over everything. They permeate society and move it in directions neither you nor I wish to go, often toward Communism. I ask you to consider adopting the policies we have instituted to control these vermin. Our two countries can then unite in the establishment of empires that will last for centuries."

"I will give this serious thought," replied the Italian, having gotten the gist of Hitler's words and not liking any of it. The thought of treating Italian Jews in such a manner disgusted him, and when they took a break a bit later, he was seen by some reporters gesturing by a window that Hitler was a maniac.

Outside, Martha and Red were having a discussion of their own.

"Do you think there is any chance the two countries will form a pact?" she asked.

"Hitler is quite persuasive, and *Il Duce,* for all his strength, may underestimate him. If they do reach a concord, I predict the eventual downfall of the Italian. Either the Germans will get rid of him or convince the Italian populace to do so. Hitler will share neither the spotlight nor the seat of power with anyone." He sat next to her. "Take it from a guy who has lived in Berlin and witnessed the birth and wayward development of this lunatic."

"What are the English saying about it all?" asked Martha,

Red shook his head. "After reading their newspapers, I have concluded they haven't understood Hitler at all. They seem to be convinced a friendship with Germany will bring stability to Europe. They need to realize such appeasement will never work. I say so in my latest book. I promise when you do read it, you will understand why I think *Herr* Hitler is dragging the whole world into a devastating bottomless pit. It will be much worse than the war to end all wars."

Martha pulled her jacket tight around her. "Just the thought makes me shudder." She paused for a moment. "I must say, I don't expect this kind of conjecture from a Pulitzer winner."

"It is far more than conjecture. The lunatic is establishing quite a track record, rendering the result predictable."

At that moment, the crowd stirred, and their roar announced something was happening. The glass-paned doors of the balcony over the entrance were being opened.

Red again checked his watch. It had been almost three hours since they last saw the two dictators. "This must be it," he shouted to

Martha over the cheers of the masses.

Above them, Mussolini and Hitler came out onto the balcony, acknowledged the crowd's wild roars, and almost as quickly as they appeared, headed back through the doors. When the horde persisted with chants and waves, the two showmen returned for a curtain call. The entire appearance lasted only about a minute, long enough for Martha to take several photographs but still barely worth the wait; however, just as Red had predicted, Ciano appeared on the balcony and read an official communiqué of the event. It contained nothing more than facts already known.

"Will Germany annex Austria?" Shouted a reporter from Turin's *La Stampa* paper.

Ciano ignored the question, waved, and returned inside.

He had no sooner reached the hallway when one of Hitler's aides caught up with him, "The *Führer* is happy to leave here. Your damned mosquitoes are becoming a menace."

Ciano smiled, "I do apologize for the inconvenience. *Il Duce* will also be relocating to Venice. Excuse me." He continued down the hallway to Mussolini's quarters, where he found the Italian leader with his valet.

"So, Excellency, do you believe Germany will try to annex Austria?" he asked.

"He claims he will not, but I don't trust the conniving bastard," replied Mussolini. "He has grand plans for everything. He even claims he can defeat France in a day or two. It would mean the start of another great war when all I want is for the powers of Europe to sign a pact to avoid conflict for at least a decade." He walked up to Ciano. "And, Jews are his obsession. Hitler is crazy."

"Shall I proceed with the plan we discussed in the car?"

Mussolini folded his arms before him and replied, "I know nothing of any such plan."

"I see," said Ciano.

Vienna, Austria

It was early evening when Prince Starhemberg entered his plush office through a rear door following a boisterous luncheon with several high-ranking members of the *Heimwehr*. As he took a seat behind his wide, oak desk, his prim secretary, Elise Krause, entered through the main office door.

With a writing pad in one hand and a pen in the other, she told him, "Sir, excuse me, I saw you arrive and knew you would want to know, while you were out, Count Ciano telephoned. Shall I return his call for you now?"

"Yes, please do, Elise. Did I have any other messages?"

"No, sir, but Major Fey is waiting to see you."

"Please beg Fey's forbearance for a while longer. I will use the telephone first."

"As you wish, sir." Elise left Starhemberg pondering what Fey might want.

He went to a side table and shot some seltzer water into a glass, hoping it would calm the effects of the spicy food he had eaten earlier. He was downing the bubbly potable when the telephone ring beckoned him to his desk.

Meanwhile, in the outer office, Major Fey sat uneasily, deciding that the uncomfortable chairs were Starhemberg's way of discouraging visitors. He was also upset by a general feeling of being left out of the chancellor's inner circle. As his suspicions grew, he was considering ways to discover what the prince was up to when Elise's voice entered his consciousness. She was on the telephone saying in Italian, "Yes, please put me through to Count Ciano. Prince Starhemberg is returning his call."

Once she had made the connection and notified Starhemberg that Ciano's office was on the line, Fey went to her. "Elise, I need the current personnel status report from the military liaison office. Could you please go there and pick that up for me?"

"Of course, sir. It will take only a minute or two."

"I would appreciate it very much."

Once the secretary left, Fey carefully lifted the telephone handset.

Prince Starhemberg belched, held his stomach and undid two vest buttons as he waited for the count to come on the line.

"Ernst, are you there?" a familiar voice sounded in his ear. "Galeazzo here."

"Yes, my friend," replied Starhemberg. "Do you have news?"

"I do! Rather amazing. You see, I have carefully evaluated the situation here and can report without reservation that the meeting is not going well."

"I see," said the prince. "So, you recommend we go ahead as planned."

"Absolutely. As you indicated over tea, the Dollfuss plan to abduct the German is impossible. Have your man proceed. Hitler must be eliminated for the good of our two countries and all of Europe." There was a pause during which neither man spoke, then Ciano continued. "You understand this cannot reflect on Italy or *Il Duce*. As I had mentioned, your agent, whom we will identify as a Bosnian, will pay the ultimate price."

"Such is the cost of patriotism," replied Starhemberg.

Ciano closed with "*Buona fortuna,*" and there was a click on the other end of the line.

When Elise returned with the papers the major had requested, she was surprised to find that he was neither there nor in with the prince.

Fey was standing in front of the chancellor's desk, staring down at Dollfuss. His words were precise and clear. "I am saying your wishes have gone for naught. They intended to kill Hitler all along."

The chancellor's face reddened. "The way this was so cleverly hidden enrages me more than the aim of the plot. There is no doubt Austria would benefit from Hitler's demise, but that I have been undermined in the process is most disquieting." He stood and slammed the desk with his palm. "I will not abide it!" Taking a deep breath to calm himself, he continued, "There have been no reports of assassination, so there is still time to stop it."

Leaning over the desk and looking into Dollfuss's eyes, Fey promised, "I shall notify Colonel Joscht at once. We have a reliable agent who may be able to get to Karper." Assuming a stiff military stance, he added, "I also learned that if this killing happens, they will identify Karper as a Bosnian dissident and kill him."

Eyes wide, the chancellor shouted uncharacteristically, "I will never allow it! Sepp is a good man. Go now! Time is our greatest enemy."

As Fey headed for the door, Dollfuss picked up his phone handset. "Have Prince Starhemberg join me immediately."

Venice, Italy

Darkness had just chased away the last of the twilight, and the glow of a cigarette revealed Gianni, who was once again watching the comings and goings at the *Contarina del Bovolo.* He knew he would not see Claudia Mocenigo as she and Carlo had gone to a special event for Hitler. Still, he wanted to gather more information about the Austrian professor. Earlier, he had seen an attractive red-haired woman enter and assumed she was a customer of *Signor* Max. When, some ten minutes later, the professor went to the *palazzo* door whistling a familiar waltz, the big man decided to keep his vigil awhile longer.

In a drawing room named for the three Venetian scenes by Canaletto on its walls, Max was fixing a Negroni cocktail for Martha when Sepp strode in.

"Hail, all," he greeted them cheerfully.

"What in hell do you have to be so happy about?" asked Max.

"You must have had a successful day," Martha guessed.

"No, not at all," explained Sepp. "But on the way back here, I realized that come hell or high water, it will all be over soon." He turned down a tumbler of Scotch offered by his host. "As a matter of fact, I had a wasted day. I never counted on any early opportunities, and I was right. The good fortune I had hoped for never materialized."

"What about tonight?" Martha asked.

"Wagner?" exclaimed Sepp. "I can take an opera when I must, but his music is deadly. Either boring or so overstated, it does violence to the Austrian ear."

"He is a favorite of *Herr* Hitler," Max said, "but I'm not sure his music is exactly the *Duce's* cup of tea either. He would probably prefer something provocative and lively. You know, Verdi or Rossini." He shrugged, "I will get a full report from Claudia as she and Carlo were invited to attend. The evening will be much more suited to him than her."

"He is a beast, isn't he?" Martha asked. "Poor woman stuck going with him to Wagner; although I must say, the Doge's palace is quite beautiful." She sipped her drink. "After the long day we had, Red and I decided to let it pass. For me, the lighting would have been impossible, and Red prefers jazz to opera."

Max turned to Sepp, "So then, you've paused your quest, good professor?"

Sepp smirked at the use of his cover name. "That telescope of mine is a blessing and a curse. I can't very well use it as a decoy anywhere but in the tower."

Max offered, "I could have helped with another weapon."

"Somehow, those things are always traceable back to the source, and I wouldn't want to involve you or any other innocent bystander."

"Innocent? Me? Really?"

"Besides, the security at the Doge's appeared to be very tight. Not worth the risk of upsetting my original plan."

Martha chimed in, "Tomorrow will be much more interesting, I'm sure. Several opportunities." She looked at a wall clock, "Which reminds me. I have another early day." She took one more sip of the cocktail and set the glass down. "Thanks for the hospitality, Max." She motioned for Sepp to accompany her out the door.

As they walked the hallway, he stopped and took her in his arms. "I don't suppose there is . . ."

"Wait!" she cut him off. "I need to get some sleep, and so do you." She kissed his lips tenderly, leaving him yearning for more.

Gianni watched the redhead leave, made a note on his pad, and strode off, satisfied there would be nothing more for him that evening.

Chapter Twenty-Six

Friday, 15 June 1934

Venice, Italy

Sepp arrived at the bell tower as military units marshaled into the areas surrounding *Piazza San Marco*. As usual, he was met by officer Gallo at the entrance.

The young policeman held up his hand for Sepp to stop. "I am sorry, professor. I have strict orders not to allow anyone except the *Istituto Luce* film crew up there this morning," said Gallo. "Masciarelli is off having breakfast. He will kill me if I disobey."

"But my friend, you know me well. I must have access. My equipment is up there. Everything I have worked for." Sepp's words did nothing to soften Gallo.

"Sorry, sir, but I do have my orders."

Sepp thought for a moment before offering an option he hoped would work. "Only members of the film crew, right?

"Yes, sir." Gallo granted. "With proper documents."

Sepp quickly waded into the sea of soldiers standing by the gates of the *Loggetta del Sansovino.*

* * *

In his office, Inspector Petrin was reviewing piles of notes and photographs, attempting to ensure he had not missed even the smallest security lapse when the phone rang. "Petrin," he said confidently into the mouthpiece. His face paled when the operator informed him the caller was state police chief Arturo Bocchini.

"Put him through immediately." When the hum on the phone line changed pitch, he took a breath. "Petrin here."

To his surprise, Bocchini's tone was genial. "Well, well, Luigi, I am pleased you were the man Marino had in mind. It has been far too long, hasn't it?"

Petrin's mind immediately answered, "It could never be long enough," as he recalled an incident in 1927 when Bocchini stole his glory for solving a case involving a series of murders in Venice. He took a beat and moderated his reply to, "Why yes, chief, it has been years, and I am honored to speak to you now." He cleared his rapidly drying throat and continued, "May I ask how I can be of service?"

"You are as dedicated as ever, my friend," Bocchini said with a smile in his voice. "As you know, I like to keep a close watch on such events as this Hitler visit."

"Sir, I am this minute going over all the details. I don't believe we have missed a single threat." Petrin nervously ran his fingers through his hair.

"Luigi, I would expect nothing less. I do have a favor to ask of you."

"Yes, sir. Anything."

"I know you have posted guards at the San Marco bell tower restricting access."

"That is correct, sir."

"I would like you to keep the guards there and bar anyone you like, but please also allow the Austrian professor to pass. I believe his name is Höbling."

"But sir, an Austrian?"

Bocchini's voice gained an edge. "We are excellent friends of the Austrians, are we not?" He didn't wait for a response. "Someone we both hold in great admiration is close to their chancellor."

Maybe it was the change in Bocchini's tone or the fact that he had been without alcohol all day, but Petrin felt his body tremble. "I will see to it immediately."

Bocchini's softness returned. "Thank you, Luigi, and let's talk again soon. Maybe a nice *dolce* at the *Florian* when I next visit Venice."

The line went dead. Petrin slumped onto his desk for a moment before clicking the phone cradle to make a call.

* * *

After seeking help from *Luce* director Martone, Sepp arrived back at the tower entrance armed with a film crew access document. This time, Sergeant Masciarelli, who had joined officer Gallo, stepped forward.

"Professor Höbling," said the sergeant cheerfully, "may I inquire how you are this morning?"

Sepp was taken aback at the sergeant's uncharacteristically friendly manner. Cautiously, he replied, "Just fine, sir," as he proffered the film crew document signed by director Martone only minutes earlier.

"What's this?" asked the sergeant before he examined the document and handed it back. "Professor, it is unnecessary. You are welcome to enter the tower, as always."

Sepp shot Gallo a questioning glance to which the officer gave a wide-eyed shrug. Without further conversation, Sepp thanked Masciarelli and headed into the *logetta*.

"Gallo, go operate the elevator for our friend."

On the short ride up, the young policeman apologized. "Professor, I have no idea what happened to change him. Maybe he got laid for breakfast. Who knows?"

"Let's just take it as a piece of good fortune," concluded Sepp.

As Gallo pulled the gate and opened the door, he asked, "May I come later and see *Il Duce* through your instrument."

"Certainly," Sepp agreed as he exited.

Bruno, who was attaching the film magazine to his camera, greeted the Austrian professor with a friendly scold. "Where have you been?" He checked to see that the piece was secure and added, "I thought your plans might have changed."

"Not at all, but when I first arrived, the young policeman barred me. I then went to *Signor* Martone for a film crew access pass only to discover that I didn't need it. The sergeant all but begged me to go up. Something I did not expect, and it concerns me."

"Do you think they're trying to catch you at something?"

"I don't know what to think, and we would do well not to speculate. It might simply have been a matter of Gallo misunderstanding his orders." As he spoke, Sepp knew it was an unlikely option.

Bruno shrugged and returned to his camera as Sepp began scanning the view that had become so familiar. He selected a position on the extreme right of the *piazza* side of the mezzanine, uncased his telescope, and set it on its base. Looking down, he tried aiming with the scope and found the reviewing stand would not offer a good target as it was too close to the tower. The severe angle made a shot anywhere but the extreme edges of the platform impossible. His only hope, he reckoned, was to get Hitler as he approached or departed the scene.

Shortly before 09:00, the German chancellor and his entourage arrived. Mussolini joined him, and they walked to the stand together. As Hitler came closer, Sepp directed the telescope down and to the left. He had his target in the crosshairs and was about to trip the trigger mechanism when the chancellor was suddenly obscured by waving banners and swastika flags mounted on the stand. The target reappeared and ascended the platform steps, but the telescope could move no further vertically. Hitler quickly went out of view.

Pulling away from the eyepiece, Sepp saw Mussolini leave his guest and entourage on the stand. "Damn," he muttered, "Is it possible that, after all the preparation, I may fail?" He frowned. "Never!"

Minutes later, military music blared and the flamboyant Italian leader reappeared, strutting before a company of black-shirted fascists arriving in the square.

Following his show-stealing entrance, Mussolini joined Hitler. The military display that followed was grandiose, impressive, and for the German visitor, quite dull. Hitler dutifully stood next to his Italian host and worked at looking interested. Still, he barely tolerated the seemingly endless procession of black shirts, fascist youth, militia and regular army and navy units passing in review for the better part of an hour.

When it ended, Sepp was poised at the telescope awaiting a departure opportunity that never came. He leaned out over the mezzanine wall and searched the stand. Two guards remained posted, but both Hitler and *Il Duce* had disappeared along with their minions. Surmising they had exited in the other direction away from the *piazza*, Sepp moved quickly to the opposite side of the mezzanine and scanned the crowd. He saw a group moving through the masses, but could not be sure of his target. *"Scheisse!"* he exclaimed as he went to the telescope and removed it from the base.

"There will be another opportunity," reminded Bruno. "Much more to your liking, I believe."

"If you mean the speech by *Il Duce* at eleven, are you certain Hitler will be there? It is shown on the schedule as an address to the people of the Veneto."

"That is so, but according to Martone, Hitler is expected to attend. I think maybe *Duce* wants to impress him with the adoring crowd overflowing the *piazza*. And the time has been changed to six this evening. *Signor* Martone believes *Il Duce* made it late in the schedule to leave a lasting impression on his guest."

"Your director is quite astute." Sepp cocked his head, "I suppose you can even tell me exactly where they will be standing?"

Bruno nodded, "*Duce* will speak from the center of the *Ala Napoleonica* directly across from us." He pointed to the far end. "I know this because my job is to film him using my long lens. Your scope should work well."

Sepp eyed the distant balconies and smiled, feeling a sense of relief he hadn't experienced since the escapade began.

* * *

Meanwhile, in the *Piazzetta* under the tall columns of Saints Mark and Timothy, Mussolini and Hitler parted. The former heading for a military boat to take him out to visit Navy ships moored in the lagoon; while the latter and his following were escorted to the *Biennale* art exposition.

After hours of boredom, the *Führer* welcomed the promise of a change of pace. He was delighted when the vivacious Elisabetta Cerruti, wife of the Italian ambassador to Berlin, joined them. They were followed by a group of reporters and photographers that included neither Red nor Martha. The pair chose to pass on the art event and claim an early vantage point on the Lido where Hitler and Mussolini would come for lunch and a second and final round of private talks.

Hitler's group entered the exposition's main hall where *Biennale* president, Count Giuseppe Volpi di Misurata, greeted him. For the first time, the chancellor appeared genuinely pleased to be there. He fancied himself a great artist, even though twice as a teenager, he had been rejected by the Academy of Fine Arts in Vienna. They ruled his style tended more toward the architectural, and he did not do well depicting the human form. He was once heard to remark that after he had rebuilt Germany into a great power, he would return to his paints and canvases.

As they toured the rooms of the main hall, *Signora* Cerruti guessed the expression on Hitler's face said he was repulsed by the modernist works that seemed to dominate the exposition.

The chancellor went impatiently from room to room and at one point remarked, "What we see here are the works of degenerates. There is no place for such rubbish in the Third Reich. Classical themes honoring the Aryan heritage is what I want."

Signora Cerruti simply nodded as she considered how easily this egotistical man could condemn these artists who worked in the genres of Mueller, Chagall, Dix, Klee, Munch, and Picasso.

The group passed through the final section of the hall and moved out to the sprawling gardens where elaborate pavilions hosted by various countries dominated the landscape. Napoleon first developed the area as part of his program to make Venice a cultural center as well as a naval power. Enterprising Venetians carried that same goal forward when they established *La Biennale di Venezia* in 1895.

Hitler confided to *Signora* Cerruti, "What I have seen thus far disgusts me. I wish to visit the exhibit of my own country."

"As you wish, Excellency."

She looked to their guide, who nodded his understanding.

The German pavilion was at the far end of the gardens from the main exposition hall, and the art there was more to the *Führer's* liking. To Elisabetta, the works lacked heart or soul and appeared to be painted over photos. As she watched Hitler happily examining the pieces, she decided they were much like the man himself—odd and, in a sense, coldly surreal.

Leaving the German pavilion, Hitler turned back. "You know," he said to von Neurath. "I must have Professor Speer look at this and make it grander. More worthy of the Fatherland, with powerful symbols of the Reich."

The German group finished exploring the exhibits and returned to the main hall, where Count Volpi proudly presented the chancellor with a painting by the artist Fioravante Seibezzi, depicting an impressionistic view of Venice.

Hitler scowled and said flatly. "This does not please me at all. There is too much nuance. I prefer crisp, clear images."

Immediately, *Signora* Cerruti suggested a depiction of boats by Tuscan artist Mino Varaggini. Hitler appeared quite satisfied with the piece she recommended, and she quickly arranged an exchange of gifts.

Soon afterward, the entire group went to their boats and traveled to the Alberoni Golf Club on the Lido. There, a luncheon sponsored by the Italian delegation was set for the club's lush garden area. Once Mussolini returned from his naval excursion, everyone took their places at the beautifully laid table.

Hitler was seated between *Signora* Cerruti and Countess Marina di Valmarana, both of whom served as translators for the German chancellor. Across from Hitler sat Mussolini in the company of Ilse Von Hassell, wife of the German ambassador in Rome. Among the guests were many distinguished Venetians, typically from families that had influenced the culture and politics of the city for many decades. The group included Carlo Mocenigo and his wife.

As this was the first social event with ladies present, the conversation tended to be light, trivial, and spiced with gossip.

"Did you see?" said Countess Valmarana, "The daughter of President Roosevelt, Anna, is about to divorce her husband, Curtis Dall."

"Yes," agreed Ilse Von Hassell, "I read in the paper she has just left for Reno, Nevada, where she can get a divorce in a very short time."

"If I am not mistaken," added Elisabetta Cerruti, "Roosevelt's first son, Elliott, divorced there just last year and remarried within an embarrassingly short time."

"Divorce is such a cruel conclusion," opined Mocenigo grimly. "Maybe death is preferable."

Il Duce cut the silence that followed the depressing remark. "Are we to conclude that important Americans are unreliable and not to be trusted?"

"Not at all!" said the German chancellor. "I can count a number of influential admirers of National Socialism in the United States."

"Excellency, who are these Americans?" asked Countess Valmarana.

"Randolph Hearst, the press baron, and Irenee du Pont of the chemical family. Even the heroic pilot Charles Lindbergh. They are all my honest supporters." As was his habit, the German chancellor droned on for several minutes regarding the support he enjoyed from influential Americans. His detailed discourse caused eyes to gloss over and lace handkerchiefs to hide stifled yawns, but finally, he seemed to have reached a coda. "And, remember, Germany now hosts many of the largest American corporations such as General Electric, Singer, and the bottling giant, Coca-Cola, which has a plant in Essen."

"I love that cola," announced Elisabetta Cerruti, hopeful the *Führer* was done.

Unfortunately, her comment prompted Hitler to further remark, "Thomas Watson, through his IBM subsidiary Dehomag, is providing us with special card machines to automate a national census." Hitler's gaze intensified as he looked around the table. "So you see, there are certainly good Americans we can count on."

Mussolini quickly took the opportunity to close out the subject when he turned to his guest, raised his glass of white wine and proclaimed, "A toast to the Americans. *Prost!*"

Relieved by the change of pace, all present joined in as the luncheon entered its final phase of dessert and coffee.

Carlo Mocenigo remained silent following his divorce comment. His thoughts centered on the nagging suspicion that he was being made a cuckold by the woman next to him. He scowled as he wondered who in the group privately thought him a dupe. When the event ended, he took Claudia firmly by the arm and guided her out of the clubhouse.

Mussolini and Hitler also left together, going to an open area where, while their associates stood by at a distance, they resumed their confidential conversation. Once again, *Il Duce* carried on without an interpreter.

On the topic of Austria, Hitler proposed a list of points that avoided the question of *Anschluss* but focused on replacing Dollfuss. He pressed the idea of having free elections. Barely suppressing his disdain for the Austrian chancellor, he told his counterpart, "If the election results give the National Socialists a majority, then I expect one of their number will be made the new chancellor."

Mussolini, who had been very clear with him about his resistance to the idea of Germany annexing Austria, made the tactical error when he asked, "Is there someone you have in mind for that position?"

Hitler replied in the negative, skirting the impression he was controlling the Austrian Nazi party. Still, *Il Duce's* response led him to believe that the Italian was warming to an overthrow of Dollfuss.

The two men went on to other topics during the next hour—primarily those related to the Versailles Treaty and the restoration of German industry. As was the case earlier, they found little common ground before pressing on to a subject they had not yet visited.

"I would like to pursue the matter of the Vatican," said Mussolini.

"Is there a need to address the Vatican?"

"I should say so, Chancellor. Consider your current attacks on Catholic parties, such as *Zentrum* and *Bayerische Volksspartei*. I can assure you, the Pope is upset by all of this, and I need not remind you, over thirty percent of your people are Roman Catholic."

"I was raised a Catholic," replied Hitler. "But now, the state of my country must come first. Popes have no concept of what it takes to win favor and rebuild an entire nation. They simply inherit the power and riches of the Church." He regarded his host. "I serve the gods in my way."

Mussolini decided it was another subject that would not be resolved at this confab or possibly ever. The two dictators ended the meeting with empty words of geniality and returned to the clubhouse.

* * *

The Mocenigo speedboat arrived at the hotel's wharf where Carlo and Claudia debarked. The ogre stopped before entering the hotel.

"I would like to have a nice drink with my wife now in my study." Pulling her close, he groped her breast. "And, maybe something more."

"My darling," she responded with a smile, "I would love it, but I can stay for only one drink—in the bar. You see, I have an appointment for a final fitting with *Signor* Max. It shouldn't be long, and we can enjoy each other's company when I return. I shall model my latest frock for you."

"And you must allow me to remove it slowly, piece by piece."

"Whatever pleases you, my dear." She stroked his face.

"I will keep you to that, dear Claudia," he vowed. "I have not enjoyed the full passion of your love lately."

As they entered the hotel, she replied, "Dear Carlo, you know women have certain times when it is not possible, but today is not one of them. I promise."

* * *

It was almost 17:30, and Sepp Karper was once again in his bell tower aerie. Following the military review, workers had added to the *piazza's* décor. In front of the imposing façade of *Basilica San Marco* waved three large banners. At the center was the flag of the city of Venice with its iconic winged lion, while on either side stood the red, white, and green Italian tricolors. There were garlands and banners all around the grand *piazza*, from the terraces of the clock tower, the double row of windows of *Procuratie Nuove* and *Procuratie Vecchie*, and along the left and right galleries. From the marble balustrades hung drapes of red velvet and damask bordered with gold and embellished with coats of arms.

Unlike the earlier event, this display was public, drawing a crowd of more than seventy thousand that filled the square to overflowing. Learning of the meeting from Italian radio and journals only a day earlier, the people had flooded Venice via train, bus, bike, boat, and on foot. It was a testament to the irrepressible love so many Italians had for their *Duce*. Besides the *hoi polloi*, there were groups of fascist representatives from various regions of the country, the Federal Directorate, the Veneto, and multiple institutions, all flying their respective banners.

In front of the *Procuratie Nuove* stood more than a thousand soldiers at parade rest awaiting the arrival of their supreme commander. Across the way, university students in hats and colorful neckerchiefs passed the time joking and harassing each other playfully. Farther down were the men of the *Legion Morosini* decked out in blue and white, honoring those instrumental in the Italian reunification. While next to them, standing as proud as peacocks, were the elite fighters of the *Bersaglieri* noted for their characteristic hats with black plumages hanging down the sides. The horde of onlookers was comprised of commoners: workers, shopkeepers, artisans, priests and nuns, young parents, and old grandparents, all visibly excited over the prospect of seeing their *Duce* and hearing his words.

The reviewing stand had been moved to the center of the *piazza* and now held a small orchestra doing its best to project patriotic songs and classical music over the ear-pounding roar of the crowd.

* * *

Claiming she had to go prepare for her fitting, Claudia left Mocenigo at the hotel bar where he had already consumed several glasses of *Amarone*. Once she was gone, he picked up a phone on a small side table. "Have Gianni join me in the bar immediately."

Moments later, his burly henchman arrived. "*Sí, padrone*, how may I be of service?"

"I do not want you to follow the *signora* today. She will be going to the *Contarini*. I will go there and discover the truth for myself."

"But sir," Gianni scrambled for an alternative, fearing for the fate of the woman who had touched his heart. "Sir, you have always relied on me, and now . . ."

Mocenigo got up unsteadily. "You have been a good and loyal servant, but there are things I must see for myself."

Gianni tried another approach, one that played on his master's lust. "*Padrone*, the new girl, Regina, the one who replaced …"

"Yes, yes. I know. Regina with the ample tits."

"You asked to see her when she came in today."

“How is she?

“Very ripe, like a tender peach. She knows her place and understands certain liberties accompany her duties here.”

Mocenigo thought for a moment before his testosterone won out. “Fine, send her to my study and tell her nothing.”

Gianni nodded and hurried down the rear stairs to the maids’ dressing room.

Having ascended the long, marble staircase to his first-floor study carrying a partial bottle of *Amarone*, Carlo pushed open a paneled door. Setting the wine on a desk, he retrieved a crystal goblet from a wall cabinet and filled it to the brim. Savoring a mouthful slowly, the thought of following Claudia slipped to the back of his mind as anticipation of a new sexual conquest took hold. He rubbed his crotch and was loosening his belt when there was a tapping at the door. A small voice asked, “Sir, may I come in?”

“Yes, Claudia. Please do.”

The comely young girl wore a form-fitting black and white uniform that did little to conceal her sensual body. “Sir, my name is not Claudia. I am Regina.”

“No, my dear. For this moment, your name is what I say it is.” He began unbuttoning the front of his trousers. “Now, come here, Claudia.”

She obeyed.

* * *

Gianni arrived at the *Contarini del Bovolo* and searched for his master’s wife. The clatter of *Signora* Costello’s machine drew him to the studio, where he found the seamstress working alone. Moving back to the main foyer, he heard soft, sensual murmurs coming from an upstairs bedroom. There, Max and Claudia were locked in an embrace on a rumpled bed.

Boldly, he interrupted, “Please, you must listen to me.”

Claudia covered her nakedness with a sheet as Max shouted, “Gianni! What is the meaning of this?”

“There is little time. The *padrone* is coming here, *Signora*. You must leave at once. Please, do not let him find you.”

* * *

From his vantage point on one side of the bandstand, Inspector Luigi Petrin observed with the eyes of an eagle, his brow wrinkled with concern and determination that nothing would happen to the head of the Italian government or the German visitor during his watch. To this end, he had stationed men strategically to monitor and control those entering the square. Uniformed police, plainclothes detectives, and agents blended into the sea of people while marksmen sat on the two *procuratie* roofs. Yet, with all the precautions, Petrin felt he had not done enough.

He mentally revisited the subject of the professor and determined that the Italian government may want to demonstrate to Germany its friendship with Austria. Could it be that *Il Duce*, a master of tactical surprises, might mention the presence of the Austrian visitor during his speech? Petrin's lip curled in a sneer. "That would upset the German bastard."

* * *

Carlo Mocenigo climbed the spiral staircase to the first floor of the *Palazzo Contarini del Bovolo* and could hear the cheering and music coming from *Piazza di San Marco*. "Mussolini," he grumbled, "a usurper of power. He deserves none of this."

He tried a door and found it locked. Forcing the latch to no avail, he immediately climbed the flight to the next level, where another locked door defeated him. Abandoning the idea of a stealthy entry, he rushed down the steps and barged in the *palazzo's* main entrance and immediately commenced searching for his wife. He looked into several chambers and found them all deserted. Returning to the hallway, he followed the clattering noise to Max's studio where *Signora* Costello worked at her machine while Max, with a decidedly effeminate flair, draped a mannequin in blue satin and velvet.

"Has she been here!" Mocenigo roared, startling them both.

"Why Carlo," Max slathered his words, "what a nice surprise."

"Where is my wife?" Mocenigo demanded.

Remaining pleasant, the couturier responded, “She was here briefly for a fitting but left quite a long while ago.”

“So, it is only the two of you now? And, the Austrian? He stays here with you, does he not?

“He does, but not at the moment. He is in the *piazza* doing something related to Galileo.” Max smiled at how nicely he had managed the situation. But the look on the irate intruder’s face told him he needed to say more. “He is at the bell tower preparing a special re-creation of the telescope’s demonstration to the Doge.”

Apparently satisfied, Mocenigo asked, “Are there others here?”

Max toyed with him. “None of the ladies who come for my creations are here now.

“And, no one else?”

“No one, I can assure you, Carlo.” Max made an expansive gesture. “You are welcome to see for yourself.”

“I damn well will,” Mocenigo grumbled and left. He climbed an inner staircase back to the first floor, where he again began checking rooms. On his third attempt, he located a chamber with a messy bed. When he felt its silky sheets, he caught the distinctive aroma of lavender—a scent he had so often enjoyed on his wife. There it was! Proof of her infidelity.

Blinded with rage, he stormed out of the *palazzo* and rushed back to his hotel, where he bombarded the staff with demands and inquiries but got nowhere. Claudia was not there. Desperate to defend his family honor, he came to the only conclusion that made sense, having eliminated Max as a suspect—it had to be the Austrian.

* * *

There was no better vantage point than the loggia of the bell tower to get a full 360-degree view of Venice. Officer Gallo was using binoculars as he moved from one side of the mezzanine to the other. Cameraman Bruno was focusing his long-range camera lens, and the man they knew as Professor Alex Höbling was working at positioning his Galileo replica.

Below in the *piazza*, Inspector Petrin consulted his pocket watch. It was fifteen minutes before 18:00, and the crowd was consumed with anticipation at seeing the man considered the father of the new Italy. Petrin climbed the side steps of the bandstand for a better view and scanned the crowd.

On the other side of the stand, Martha and her camera were working as one as she made her way through the crowd. She paused and focused on a young lad dressed as a *Balilla*, a member of the fascist youths dedicated to Mussolini. He wore a black shirt, short gray-green trousers, knee socks, a blue neckerchief, and a green fez hat. Not more than eight or nine years old, he was clearly unhappy to be there. She guessed the boy was either frightened by the daunting public display or simply missing his mother. When he began crying, she went to him and showed him the camera. "Would you like me to take your photograph? You may be in the newspaper. Wouldn't that be an honor for your family?"

The boy's pout became a big grin. He wiped his face with his sleeve and posed proudly for her.

Enzo Noschese, taking notes for his weekly feature, slithered his way about the *piazza*. The meeting of Hitler and *Il Duce* would be interesting, but he was looking for a different viewpoint, something that would set his piece apart from all other news reports of the event. Suddenly he found himself staring at the American photographer as she hugged a young *Balilla.* "There it is," he shouted. "My angle." He decided he would make her the focus of his article, viewing the events in Venice through the eyes and the lens of an American. Once Martha helped the boy rejoin his group, Noschese approached her. "Excuse me, *Signora* Markham. A moment, please."

"I am very busy. Perhaps later."

He grabbed her arm. "Please, I have a wonderful idea that includes you."

"Me?" she said through tight lips. "I have no time." She yanked herself away and tried to move on, but the crowd trapped her in place.

"I want to write a story about your coverage of this meeting."

"I could never agree to such a thing," Repulsed by the slimy reporter, she was also concerned that such publicity would destroy the secrecy of her mission.

"Maybe it can also include your professor friend, or the

correspondent Knickerbocker," he persisted, ignoring her words. "I will do it with or without your permission. Is it not better if you cooperate?"

That did it! She grabbed Noschese by his lapels and pulled his face close to hers. "Look, you creep! Attempt any such thing, and I will have you arrested for harassment. I'm sure my friend Red would love to have a word with your publisher. Your career will be over. Do you understand?"

Wide-eyed and trembling, the reporter nodded, indicating comprehension.

"Now, get lost and make certain I never see your ugly face again." She let go of his jacket, and Noschese disappeared into the seething mass of humanity.

Inspector Petrin looked up at the loggia of the bell tower and called out, "Bianchi, come here." When the detective sergeant arrived from the other side of the stand, he told him, "I am not convinced we have done all we could to protect the tower."

"Sir, we have two men there: Gallo and his senior, Sergeant Masciarelli."

"I know this, but there are others, are there not?" asked Petrin.

Bianchi nodded. "The film cameraman from *Istituto Luce* and the professor."

"The Austrian," Petrin grumbled. "I don't know what connections he has, but I was ordered by Chief Bocchini himself to leave him alone. Maybe, you should go there and make certain there is no hint of danger to *Il Duce* or the German."

"Yes, sir." Bianchi left and fought his way toward the tower.

* * *

With all bells in the *piazza* silenced for Mussolini's speech, the *Torre dell'Orologio* clock marked time with a single gilded hand pointing to the numeral VI.

Almost simultaneously, at the other end of the square, *Il Duce* stepped out onto the central balcony of the *Ala Napoleonica*. Behind him were Attilio Teruzzi, the Militia Chief of Staff, Achille Starace, and Galeazzo Ciano.

A loud, sustained roar echoed off the *piazza's* arcades and loggia, as did thunderous applause and cries of welcome. Hundreds of white handkerchiefs waved their greeting as the orchestra played, and singing swelled up throughout the crowd.

Count Ciano leaned forward and said into Mussolini's ear, "Duce, you have exiled our visitor. Is it not demeaning?"

"Absolutely! Hitler has much to learn about managing real power. Maybe he will understand better from that vantage point." Mussolini smirked. "Besides, I don't want that monkey siphoning off my glory."

"It looks like he has gained some of his own," said Ciano as he pointed to the crowd below Hitler's balcony.

Il Duce grumbled, "A pittance."

Sepp was homed in on Mussolini's entourage directly across the *piazza* from the bell tower. Searching the group, he shouted, "Hitler isn't there!"

"Not with Il Duce, but I believe he may be with us, Professor Höbling." offered Bruno, his movie camera grinding away as it captured the scene on the far balcony.

"Where? I don't see him."

"Look at the activity down on the left." Bruno pointed to a group waving swastika flags as they saluted and shouted up at a balcony at the far end of the *Procuratie Nuove*.

Sepp turned the telescope on that part of the crowd then raised it to reveal brief glimpses of Hitler's head bobbing in and out of sight while his hands and arms waved back and saluted the Nazi revelers below. "Impossible! The angle is too severe."

"We had no idea the German would be there," Bruno admitted. "Our cameras were not set up for this, but I am certain director Martone will assign someone to capture reaction shots of him from the *Procuratie Vecchie* across the way. You might go there."

Sepp considered waiting to see if Hitler would lean out far enough over the balcony then decided to take Bruno's advice and move. Avoiding the complication of removing the rifle, he packed the telescope and base in a *Luce* equipment bag and slung it over his shoulder. Checking his pockets for the film crew credentials gotten earlier, he headed for the elevator.

"Buona fortuna!" called Bruno.

Film director Marcello Martone, wearing a light linen suit and a slouch Panama hat tilted rakishly on his head, was leaning against an arch looking casual but boiling inside as he awaited a report.

Finally, a young man broke through. "Sir, all is well. Toto will film from there," he pointed to a balcony behind them as he continued, "and he knows to focus on the German during the speech, just as you ordered."

Martone slapped his hands together. "Excellent! I hate the Nazi bastard, but I'll need shots of him to intercut with *Il Duce* and the reactions of the people."

"Yes, sir."

"Now," Martone continued, "Go and fetch me a *dolce* from the *Quadri*. Something from my beloved *Napoli*. And, get one for yourself." He gave him a handful of lira coins, and the lad was gone in a flash, slipping through the crowd like a salmon making its way upstream.

* * *

Sergeant Bianchi's struggle through the surging masses finally ended at the tower entrance, where he checked in with Sergeant Masciarelli and learned there was little happening of any consequence.

"The only ones up in the tower at present are the *Luce* man and my assistant, Gallo," Masciarelli informed Bianchi.

"What about the Austrian?"

"He just left. He might be headed for the *Procuratie Vecchie,* if he could ever make his way through this crowd. He was carrying a case." He shrugged.

Bianchi gazed up at the tower. "I will go up just the same, to satisfy Inspector Petrin."

* * *

As the roar and handkerchief waving continued unabated, from the far balcony, Starace and the others with Mussolini raised their arms in a fascist salute that had the effect of quieting the crowd. When the storm in the *piazza* calmed, in a clear, baritone voice, Mussolini began. "Camicie Nere!" His first words were a salutation for his fellow fascists. He continued by reminding all it had been eleven years since he last visited Venice and spoke to the people in that very square. His delivery was precise, slow-paced, and included tactical pauses in anticipation of the inevitable wild applause and roars of the crowd.

Sepp was able to make his way through *Il Duce's* attentive audience, and once he passed the *Caffe Quadri,* he paused and surveyed the arcades for access to an upper balcony. That's when he spotted Martone. The director was just finishing the last crispy curls of a *sfogliatella* as Sepp worked his way to him. The pair carried on a broken conversation amid the loud reactions to *Il Duce's* speech. "Well, Professor, I suspect you were as unaware of this surprise as I," Martone said as he pointed to the balcony holding Hitler and his party. "You were wise to move."

"You understand me well, *signor direttore*," Sepp replied.

"It appears you have come prepared," Martone said, nodding at the *Luce* case.

"Maybe, you know me too well."

"Nonsense, Captain," Martone assured him. "I am on your side." He regarded Sepp quizzically. "How did you know I would have a camera there?"

"Your man Bruno anticipated it," Sepp replied.

"This is why he will someday make a fine director." Martone grinned and continued, "When I saw what was happening, I had to react quickly." He pointed to Hitler's balcony then pivoted toward the *Procuratie Vecchie*, "You will want to be up there."

"Yes, it is precisely where I wish to be. Can you help?"

"Do you have your *Luce* authorization?"

Sepp nodded.

"There may be nothing, but in case you are questioned, let me take you to the portal and arrange your access." Martone put his hand on Sepp's shoulder and guided him to the entrance.

As they made their way, the director added, "I am certain I can offer a plausible reason, and I do enjoy a share of respect. After all, I am Marcello Martone."

Neither man was aware of the figure in the crowd trying to catch up with them.

* * *

Coming from south of the *piazza* along the mouth of the Grand Canal, the Hotel Mocenigo speedboat growled into a slip at the *Riva degli Schiavoni*. Two crewmen secured the craft and laid a gangway by which a resolute Carlo Mocenigo quickly debarked. He instructed the crew to await him there as he felt for the dagger in the breast pocket of his coat. Immediately upon entering the sea of humanity, he began a struggle to traverse the area to the bell tower, which took several minutes. He was met by Sergeant Masciarelli when he arrived at the *logetta.*

"I must go up there," the ogre demanded.

Masciarelli held up his hand. "Wait a minute, sir. No one is allowed in the tower at this time."

"Do you know who I am?" He regarded Masciarelli with a scowl. "I am Carlo Mocenigo, heir of seven Venetian doges."

"Sir," the policeman replied firmly, "you may be the reincarnation of Marco Polo himself. I cannot allow you in the tower."

"Yet, you permit an Austrian access. He is up there now," Mocenigo claimed.

"If you mean the professor, he is not in the tower," countered Masciarelli.

"I was informed he would come here today," the angry hotelier insisted.

"He was here earlier, but he is gone."

"Where? Where did he go?" Mocenigo pressed.

"He disappeared in the crowd." Masciarelli shrugged. "He may have left the *piazza.*"

Mocenigo's face reddened. "You cannot tell me more?"

"Only what I saw, sir," Masciarelli replied. "He was here, and now he is gone."

Mocenigo hesitated for a moment then moved on.

* * *

Inspector Petrin observed the tens of thousands of faces turned up with their eyes focused on a single point: *Il Duce*. He could also see Hitler and his entourage watching like university students taking a course in dictatorial power and presence. As was the way of the German chancellor, he would learn from this experience and use it to his advantage in the future.

The people listened attentively to the words of Italy's head of the government as he promised a secure and prosperous future so long as he remained in power.

Petrin scanned the roofs and balconies surrounding the square with his binoculars. On the left side, above Hitler, he spotted two of his men precisely where he had ordered them to station themselves. He pivoted and examined the opposite roof with the same result. Content that he had done his job, he retrieved a flask from his coat and took a large swallow. Savoring the drink and its afterglow, he resumed his observations. Just above an entrance to the *Procuratie Vecchie,* shutters and windows came open, and drapes were pulled aside. His binoculars revealed movement in the room, but nothing much different than the many other windows packed with onlookers.

* * *

Leaving the room dark, Sepp had set the telescope back away from the window, making it virtually invisible from the outside. Carefully, he released the instrument's trigger mechanism and watched the scope's crosshairs come into view. He adjusted the eyepiece and zeroed in on the head of Adolf Hitler. At last, he was about to achieve the success that had been eluding him. As he put pressure on the trigger, he was interrupted by a voice from the shadows behind him.

"*Sed tantum dic verbo*."

Instantly, Sepp eased off the trigger and responded, "*Domine, non sum dignus*."

With the code key complete, the figure stepped into the light.

"Tropp!" Sepp exclaimed. "I had no idea!"

The toymaker's face was grim as he delivered a message that

would change everything. "You must end your attempts to kill Hitler, Sepp. Dollfuss himself has ordered this."

"What? I thought ..."

"You have been under the influence of Prince Starhemberg and Colonel Joscht, both of whom want Hitler dead, but our chancellor has no stomach for murder. He desires that the Nazi merely disappear. If it is not too late, you must implement a plot to kidnap him. We will help you."

"We?"

"Father Tucci is with me. I needed to come here quickly, and a train trip was out of the question. I went to him because I knew he had a car and was on our side."

"Where is he?" Sepp asked.

"Waiting in the *piazzale* by the train station."

"How did you gain access here?

"A harmless old man offering lire coins usually works," Tropp confided with a mischievous smile.

* * *

Having concluded the crowd in the *piazza* made it impossible to pursue the Austrian, and with his rage temporarily in check, Carlo Mocenigo ordered his boat crew to return to the hotel. As he watched the *palazzi* along the Grand Canal slip by, he recalled his family's former greatness, their prestige, their holdings, and now his need to protect the honor of the name Mocenigo. Recounting to himself his recent legal research on avenging unfaithful spouses, he was sure of what he must do.

* * *

Max picked up a red bolero from *Signora* Costello's table and began fitting it onto a buxom mannequin. "I don't know; it seems small."

Signora Costello frowned. "I made it precisely to your pattern, is that not what you wanted?"

"*Signorina* Bosco is quite well endowed and should never attempt wearing such a piece, but as a customer, she must be satisfied. Make it larger so she can move easily."

As Max removed the bolero, Claudia entered and ran to him. "Oh, my dear Max, you are safe." They embraced.

"We are fine, my darling," he assured her.

"Did Carlo come?"

"Yes, and he found nothing, but I fear he is still searching for you. It is best you not be here."

"Certainly." She backed away and looked at dresses on the rack. "Are any of mine ready? I can take one to soothe his suspicions."

"Yes, of course." Max looked to *Signora* Costello, who picked out a pastel violet creation.

As the seamstress folded and wrapped the dress, Claudia took Max's hand. "Please, come with me. I need your strength."

"Whatever you wish, my darling," Max assured her. He accepted the package from *Signora* Costello and they left.

* * *

Hurriedly debarking his boat, Mocenigo entered the hotel and went directly to the front desk.

"Santino, has the *Signora* returned?" he asked.

"No, *Padrone*, I have not seen her pass this way," replied the prim, bespectacled clerk.

"Well, has she, or hasn't she?" grumbled the boss.

"I have not . . ." he glanced up and saw Claudia coming through the door with Max. "Ah, here she is now, sir."

Mocenigo turned. "Claudia, where have you been?"

Her answer was direct and touched with enough truth to make it convincing. "I went for a fitting, then to the church of *Madonna dell'Orto*." She took the package from Max. "I returned to *Signor* Max's to bring you my latest fashion, and he accompanied me back because the streets are crowded with revelers."

"My friend," Mocenigo addressed Max, "You are a gentleman. Thank you."

"It was my pleasure." Max shook the ogre's hand and left.

The hotelier absently put his right hand to his face and caught the scent of musky lavender that caused him to recall the rumpled bed at the Contarini. Everything came into focus for Mocenigo, and he grabbed his wife's arm and grunted, "Come, you must model your new frock for me." He ushered her up the lobby's marble staircase.

The desk clerk waited for them to reach the top and dialed the phone. "Gianni, this is Santino."

As the Mocenigos entered the study, Carlo demanded, "Now, my dear, loving wife, show me this latest creation." He waved his hand with a rolling motion, "Please proceed."

Fighting nervousness, Claudia stripped down to her undergarments.

"You are quite lovely like that," he leered. "I can understand why so many men desire you."

"But Carlo, I am yours alone," she assured him.

"Oh, really? Am I to be comforted by your lies?" he asked as he poured himself a glass of *Amarone*.

"Why doubt me?" She was on the brink of tears. "What can I do to convince you?"

He swallowed a mouthful. "Nothing. Nothing at all, you bitch." He set down the glass and approached her.

With tears in her eyes, she asked, "Darling, what is it? I don't understand."

"It was I who did not understand until now." He grabbed her by the hair. "I sensed what you were doing, that your love was no longer mine, but I finally realized it was with the bastard I had considered an effeminate sodomite." He tightened his grasp, pulling taut the skin of her face, and shoved his right hand to her nose. "Do you smell that? Do you smell your own essence?

She screeched, trying to shake her head no.

He shouted, "At first I concluded it was the Austrian. But now I know differently, and you will both pay in the name of Mocenigo honor." He pulled the knife from his pocket, shook off its sheath, and was about to stroke the blade across her throat when two massive hands grabbed his head from behind and twisted it violently to one side. Mocenigo's neck gave a sickening crack, and he went limp like a marionette whose strings had been cut.

"You are safe now, *Signora*," said Gianni as he let Mocenigo's body drop to the floor.

Claudia hugged the big man. “Oh, Gianni, you saved me. I will never forget this.”

He accepted her embrace awkwardly then held her away from him. “Now, you must leave. Do not remain in the hotel. I will take care of this. No one will ever know what happened here.”

As she rushed from a hotel side door, Gianni began executing his cover-up.

* * *

In the *Contarini* studio, Sepp Karper was introducing Max to his compatriots from Florence. “These men also support the cause of Austria.” Sepp put his arm over the shoulder of the white-haired craftsman. “This is Reinhard Tropp, toymaker extraordinaire.”

Tropp gave a slight bow and turned to the priest. “This is …”

“Father Tucci, an unfortunate acquaintance of both these men.”

They settled into small talk about Venice, Florence, and Vienna when their conversation was cut short by the arrival of Claudia, distraught and shaken.

“My God, what is it?” asked Max.

Eyeing the two unfamiliar men, she lied. “Oh, I am simply upset by the crowds filling the streets. Carousers and ruffians.”

“Why did you come back here?” Concern painted Max’s face.

She shrugged and embraced him. Max held her close as he introduced Tropp and Tucci and explained their presence. None of it was strictly true, but at that point, it didn’t matter to any of them. Feeling Claudia quivering in his arms, he suggested, “Let’s go to the Canaletto room for a drink to welcome our new friends.”

* * *

A police officer interviewed the Hotel Mocenigo desk clerk. Meanwhile, a sergeant, Gianni, and a doctor stood over the body of Carlo Mocenigo, lying at the base of the marble staircase. The head was twisted grotesquely to one side.

“A tragic accident, I would say,” opined the doctor. “The smell on his breath tells me he had been drinking heavily. He must have slipped on the steps."

"Yes," agreed Gianni. "He loved his *Amarone,* especially at this time of day."

"Did you witness the fall?" the policeman asked.

"No, sir, I came later and found him as you see him now," answered Carlo's former henchman.

"Did anyone see what happened?" the officer persisted.

"The lobby is quiet at this time when the tourists go for their early dinner," Gianni said. "Maybe Santino, the clerk, knows something."

The officer called to the policeman at the desk, "Anything to report?"

The other man shook his head. "He was absent from the desk at that time. He saw nothing."

The sergeant shrugged. "So, we have an obvious fall and no witnesses. Is this enough for you, doctor?"

"I believe so," replied the medical examiner. "I shall enter it in my report as an accident, plain and simple." He turned to Gianni, "The family should be notified."

"There is only the wife, and I will see to her," the big man promised.

The policemen covered Mocenigo's body, pending its removal, while Gianni went to the desk and spoke with the clerk.

"Santino, I am sorry the errand I sent you on was so poorly timed. Possibly, you might have been here to come to his aid."

"I don't think it would have mattered," the clerk said. "I had no love for the man, so maybe I would and maybe I wouldn't have tried to save him. An accident is an accident. What more is there to say?"

"Yes," Gianni agreed as he walked to the hotel entrance. "What more is there to say?"

* * *

Minutes later, Gianni stood before the group in the Canaletto room, his head bowed and hands folded before him. "I am sorry to tell you, *Signora* Mocenigo, there has been a terrible accident at the hotel." Looking directly at Claudia, he added, "Your husband has died in a fall on the steps."

Claudia dropped the glass of Amaretto she was holding and shrieked as she shed tears not of grief, but relief. She collapsed in Max's arms.

Signora Costello, brought there by the cry of the stricken wife, asked, "What has happened?"

Sepp explained, "The *Signora*'s husband has died."

"Oh, my God," the seamstress crossed herself. "I will go light a candle."

Max carried his lover to a chair and offered her another drink.

She waved him off. "No, I will be fine. I need to go back and make the appropriate arrangements. He was a brute, but a powerful and respected man just the same." She looked up at Max. "Please come with me."

He helped her up, put his arm over her shoulder, and gently ushered her to the door, comforting her with soft words as they went. "Come, we will get through this together." As they passed him, Father Tucci blessed them.

Once they were gone, Sepp observed, "How sad, and yet poetic." He regarded the others. "So, this beauty Claudia was the wife of a beast." He scanned the selection of liquor on the table. "I believe I need a drink."

"Karp, what happened to self-imposed abstinence?" Tucci asked.

"Temporarily dispensed with, along with my sanity."

* * *

When Max returned to the *palazzo,* he found Sepp, Tropp, and Tucci sipping cognac and reminiscing about the past.

"How is Claudia doing?" asked Sepp.

"She will be fine, eventually, but the way she is balancing grief and relief tells me it may take some time."

Tucci asked. "Is there anything I can do?"

"Not at the moment, Father. She knows I am here for her no matter what the future holds." He poured himself a drink.

Tropp smiled. "Tomorrow will be brighter for both of you once this dark cloud clears."

"One can only hope," said Max. "But I think maybe there will be much water flowing through the canals before that happens. Besides being widowed, she has inherited an empire to manage. She was prepared for neither."

"Just the same, I say it deserves a toast." Sepp raised his glass.

The others followed suit and declared, "Prost!"

"Well, well," Martha said from the doorway, still dressed for the formal event she had been covering. "The Florentines are here." She hugged Tucci and Tropp then kissed Sepp. Adding, as she curled her arm around his waist, "So, what are we celebrating?"

Max replied, "Carlo Mocenigo is dead."

Martha's face registered surprise. "When? How?"

"Earlier," Max explained. "He fell down a flight of marble steps at his hotel."

"Awful!" She looked at Tropp and Tucci. "And, you are now toasting the accidental death of the man. How ghoulish."

"Totally inappropriate," agreed Tucci.

"Actually, not," Max explained. "Claudia told me the whole story, and it isn't what you think."

"Come, spill it," Sepp said.

Tropp volunteered, "You have our word, we would never betray any confidence."

Max looked to Tucci, who reminded, "I'm a priest."

"He died while trying to kill Claudia," said Max matter-of-factly.

"My God!" Martha put her hand to her mouth.

"Somehow, he had discovered our affair." The couturier looked to Sepp. "At first, he said he suspected you, believing women were not my preference."

Sepp shrugged. "Me? I did nothing! You played your role too damn well."

"He had planned to come after you, but then he deduced that I was the guilty one. He had a dagger and was going to kill Claudia then me."

"What stopped him?" asked Sepp.

"Not what—who. Gianni grabbed him from behind and twisted

his neck," Max replied. "Then, he staged the fall at the base of the steps."

"And, the *signora* knew of it when she first came here," concluded Tropp.

"Yes," Max confirmed.

"That explains her upset," said Tucci.

Max agreed. "She may have been in shock. Likely, she still is. I'll need to watch her."

"It has been quite a day." Sepp regarded his compatriots. "At least some good came from it."

Martha nudged Sepp. "I knew you weren't celebrating your success. The German chancellor was in my sight all evening."

Sepp shook his head, "I'm afraid my mission has failed."

"Maybe not," she said coyly.

"What do you mean?" asked Sepp.

"I've had quite an evening myself. It began at the Grand Hotel, where the Germans hosted a dinner honoring Mussolini. Then we moved to a gala at the Excelsior on the Lido. In the process, I made a friend of Elisabetta Cerruti."

Max asked, "The ambassador's wife?"

"Exactly," she confirmed.

"But how?" Sepp questioned.

"Well, I finagled my way onto the boat to the Lido, and she recognized me from somewhere—the airport or *Stra*—and I suppose she was fascinated with my being a woman photographer. We struck up a conversation."

"She does love to talk," Max said. "I had her here for fittings about a year ago. She works with words the way I do fabrics. Quite attractive, I might add."

"You didn't, you know ..." wondered Sepp.

Max waved him off. "Oh, no, no." He immediately added, "Please, let's hear from Martha."

"Well," she continued, "I guess *Signora* Cerruti was bursting to tell someone the latest about *Herr* Hitler, and I was handy, so ..."

"And?" prompted Sepp as Max and Tucci shrugged at each other.

"It seems she had seen that *Herr* Hitler was quite unhappy with the *Biennale*, so her husband proposed showing him the art at the Basilica early tomorrow morning. The Germans left the Excelsior after barely an hour, so I hitched a ride because I thought you'd want to know. Would it be possible to use the telescope then?"

"Things have changed," said Sepp. "The mission is now an abduction," his tone brightened, "I think we may have a chance at it."

"What time is the visit?" asked Max."

"Six in the morning. It will be quick. Hitler's flight leaves at eight."

"We must act immediately!" exclaimed Tropp. He added cautiously, "It will not be easy, but it is possible that we can fulfill Chancellor Dollfuss's directive after all."

Sepp looked at Tucci. "Since assassination is off the table, I assume you are willing to participate."

Tucci relented, "A caper at the basilica. I believe I can support that."

Questions, ideas, and suggestions filled the air before being distilled into a single approach, albeit one fraught with danger and requiring a measure of good fortune.

Sepp would go to the basilica as a visiting priest seeking to celebrate an early mass. Max, posing as a Nazi agent, would assume the guise of a docent for the basilica since he had studied the great church's art and architecture in detail before becoming a couturier. His role was particularly apt since he was fluent in Italian, English, and German.

Martha reminded the two men they would need convincing disguises, and immediately offered her help. Max volunteered that he and *Signora* Costello would make whatever costumes they might need.

Father Tucci stepped forward. "I can supply a cassock for Karp." With anticipation in his eyes, he continued, "And, I have an idea how we can swiftly take our package away and back to Austria."

"My God, *Padre*," said Sepp. "You still have a penchant for scheming."

"Piety, my friend, is what I too have temporarily suspended."

"Okay, so, we have a plan, but we need to develop specifics,"

Sepp concluded. “Let’s get on with it.”

“It is best to work backward from the end, the successful abduction, to the beginning, as we decide every step along the way,” Tropp suggested. “It will ensure greater feasibility and a better chance for success.”

The group agreed, and Tucci stepped forward. “First,” he raised his index finger. “Our goal is to take the package to Austria and turn it over to Dollfuss’s people. Am I correct in that?”

“Precisely!” said Sepp before following up with, “So backing up, once we have him—this package—how exactly do we do that?”

“My automobile can easily make the trip, and it has plenty of room,” Tucci assured them as he raised a second finger. “Next, we need a fast boat and a safe place to rendezvous before the motor trip.”

“The hotel has a ripper of a speedboat,” Max announced. “I can arrange that.”

“What about a transfer point?” asked Sepp.

Tucci wasn’t done. “When I lived here, I used to like to fish, and one of my favorite spots was *Fiume Dese*, north of here. There is a landing and road access less than a kilometer up that river. I can be waiting there with my auto.”

“Okay, a good exit plan,” said Sepp. “Simple and feasible. Now, we need to get this package onto the boat.”

“I have an idea,” said Max. “Something else from the hotel. They have these enclosed luggage carriers. We can use one as transport.”

Sepp frowned. “Now, for the most basic question. How do we take him?”

All business, Tropp offered, “It should happen in the basilica. Lead him away from the ambassador and drug him. Out a side door and into the carrier. It will require some sort of distraction to separate the two of them.”

“Hey, fellas. Here I am,” Martha said, striking a pose with one hand on a hip and the other buried in her hair behind her head. “And,” she added, “I just happen to have access to photograph the basilica’s interior for a pictorial spread once the visit is over. So, I show up slightly early, what will it matter?”

Sepp shook his head. “Martha, I really don’t want you taking such a risk. And besides, I thought you would be covering the departure scene at the airport."

"Right," agreed Max. "Won't it look odd if you are missing?"

She shrugged. "I'm one of many. Only Red would notice. I'll telephone him and make my excuses." She squeezed Sepp's arm. "It'll be fine, I promise."

With the basic approach roughed in, they assigned specific tasks and committed to meeting again at midnight to finalize the details for what could be the most crucial abduction of the century.

* * *

Slouching and stone-faced, Adolph Hitler returned to his suite after hosting the dinner in honor of Mussolini. "I am immensely relieved to have this ordeal end so I can return to the Fatherland," he said to foreign minister von Neurath who had accompanied him into the room.

Tactfully, the diplomat observed, "But Excellency, you have made great strides with *Il Duce*. You effectively presented the points you came here to express, and I am certain he is quite impressed with you."

"You would speculate as much," Hitler snapped as his aide Brückner helped him off with his suit. "You who thought it perfectly fine to come here as a diplomat and be outplayed by the Italian."

"Sir, it was the proper thing to do, I assure you," insisted von Neurath. "Maybe you are merely too tired to see all the positive aspects of this visit."

"Tired? Of course I am tired," the Nazi leader grumbled. "And, I will get little rest until we have returned home."

"*Mein Führer*, may I get you a sedative?" asked Brückner.

"Something weak as my torment is not quite over. I must rise with the chickens." Hitler glared at von Neurath. "You allowed me to stupidly accept Cerutti's offer to show me about the basilica at six tomorrow morning."

"But Excellency, you did agree, and the place is quite wondrous. It is sure to please you, unlike the rubbish of the *Biennale*. I believe Byzantine art is more in line with the Nordic legends of our great heritage."

Hitler shrugged and grunted. "I am inclined to call it off."

Von Neurath immediately cautioned, "Excellency, you gave your consent to a representative of Mussolini."

"I will claim I am infirm," countered Hitler as he slipped off his shoes and went to a side table where he poured a glass of mineral water from a carafe.

"Illness shows weakness, and you need to look fit for your departure," reminded the minister. "I must recommend against such a ploy."

Hitler waved off von Neurath's words. "Who will have any interest in the basilica at such an early hour? Certainly not the drunkards of the press corps."

"That sort of thing always finds its way to the reporters. I beg you to reconsider."

Hitler growled, "No more! I am in no mood to discuss this any further."

"Ja, mein Führer," Neurath said obediently. He wished the chancellor a restful night and left.

Hitler thought for a moment then picked up the small white tablet Brückner had left on a plate and swallowed it with a sip of water.

"Brückner, get me Metzger."

Chapter Twenty-Seven

Saturday, 16 June 1934

Venice, Italy

The light of a new day had chased away the lingering darkness by the time Sepp, Martha, and Max arrived in the deserted *piazza*. After a final review of their plan at the basilica's main doors, Martha entered with her equipment while the two men remained outside.

Max, looking positively Aryan with his blonde hair, blue eyes, and neatly tailored dark suit, had added a small goatee to complete the deception.

Also thoroughly transformed, Sepp's hair was now dark brown, he had shaved his beard down to a neatly trimmed mustache, and his glasses were gone. He wore the black cassock and sash of a Jesuit.

It was a few minutes before 05:30 when Sepp and Martha entered the magnificent church, while Max lingered by the doorway awaiting the two dignitaries.

Once inside, Sepp helped Martha set up her lighting and camera equipment adjacent to the main altar near the *Pala d'Oro,* a gold, gem encrusted altarpiece from the twelfth century.

A smile played on her lips as she told Sepp, "If it doesn't work," she fluffed her hair, "I am prepared to seduce him right here in this holy place and do whatever is necessary to make this a success."

"Martha Hughes Markham, you are a dangerous woman." He gave her a wink, wishing it could have been a kiss, and followed a memorized diagram to a side exit of the church. Going north then west, he entered the atrium leading to the *Porta dei Fiori.* He tried the latch securing the two large doors. It clicked, and when Sepp swung them open, there stood Reinhard Tropp, a common laborer, by a luggage *carretto*. They traded nods, and Sepp reclosed the doors.

At the entrance, Max ran the details of the abduction over in his head as he observed his surroundings. Across the way, a small gathering at the center of three towering flagpoles was growing steadily along with his concern. With almost fifteen minutes to go before the expected arrival, he entered the basilica and reported his apprehension about the flagpole group to Martha.

"I very much doubt word of this has gotten out," she assured Max. "I just happened to learn of it because of *Signora* Cerruti." She paused for a moment, then added, "Although, she is a terrible gossip, so anything is possible."

Her eyes drifted across the nave, where she saw Sepp heading for a side chapel carrying a tray with a covered chalice and small decanters of water and wine.

"There he is," Max said. "Should I tell him?"

"No need for that." Martha touched his arm gently and smiled confidently. "I am certain we will be okay."

When Max returned to his position by the front entrance, he was happy to see that the flagpole group had not grown appreciably. Many of the onlookers were waving small red, white, and black swastika flags.

Beyond them, at the base of the bell tower, Officer Gallo was about to unlock the doors of Sansovino's *loggetta* when Sergeant Masciarelli came running and barking orders. "Don't bother opening it. Come with me. We have a special duty." Masciarelli headed into the *piazzetta,* and Gallo raced to catch up with him.

"What is it, sir?" asked the young officer.

"Inspector Petrin and his partner Bianchi were to be here to meet the German."

"Hitler?" asked Gallo. "I thought he was leaving."

"A last-minute tour of the basilica," the sergeant explained as they rushed by the two tall columns. "Bianchi called to say Petrin had taken ill and that we were to go in their place."

"Sir, this is the most important job I've had since joining the force."

"It would be best not to muck it up," chided the sergeant as they reached the *Riva degli Schiavoni* where Hitler was expected to arrive.

"You keep watch!"

Not ten minutes had passed when Gallo cried out, "Look, there," as he pointed toward the *Basilica di Santa Maria della Salute* and the mouth of the Grand Canal. "Here they come."

Once the speedboat was secured in a slip, Chancellor Adolf Hitler and Ambassador Vittorio Cerruti stepped onto the dock.

Sergeant Masciarelli went to them and bowed. "Excellencies, we are here to see you safely to the basilica."

Cerruti thanked them, but Hitler waved the policemen off. "I do not believe we will need these brave men."

Gallo translated for the sergeant, "He says he doesn't need us."

"He may not need us, but we need him," Masciarelli responded. "We must stay with them." He and his partner fell in behind the pair walking apace to the front of the basilica. There, Hitler gave several limp-arm salutes acknowledging the cries of *"Heil Hitler"* and *"Sieg Heil"* coming from the group at the flagpole. Masciarelli and Gallo eyed the exchanges carefully for any hint of danger to the chancellor.

When the dignitaries approached the church's entrance, Max greeted them. "*Mein Führer,* I am here to serve as your guide," he explained, carefully masking the Austrian nuance in his German.

The chancellor regarded Max. "You are one of us, yes?"

Before Max could answer, Cerruti objected, "Please, we are on a very restricted schedule." With that, he tried to brush past, but Max stepped in his way.

"This is precisely my purpose, Excellency," he said to Hitler. "I am well-schooled in the art and architecture of this lovely church and have been directed to be your guide."

"I was not informed of this," Cerruti demurred sternly. "Who sent you?"

What began as a frown on Hitler's face morphed into a sly grin. "Was it Putzi? Did he somehow find out about this and decide to surprise me?" He looked at Cerruti. "Were you a part of this, Vittorio?"

Cerruti shook his head and shrugged, "Not at all, Excellency. I assure you."

Max took the confusion as a cue to usher both men into the

basilica.

Masciarelli told Gallo, "He is safely inside with one of his own. I believe we have done our job and can hold here until they return."

Gallo agreed and they took up positions on either side of the entrance.

"My God, look at the gold!" Hitler exclaimed the instant they entered the grand church's nave. He appeared spellbound as Max explained the mosaics of the three major cupolas while he led the way toward the main altar.

"This center one, Excellency, is a representation of the Ascension of Jesus Christ with Mary, angels, and the twelve apostles. You will note the sixteen allegories between the cupola's windows."

"Yes, I see them," Hitler said, hands folded in front of him and staring directly up. "The figures are quite large and understandable. Not like the interpretative trash at the art exhibit." He looked at Max, "When was this made?"

"In the late twelfth century, *mein Führer*."

"Very old, *Herr* Cerruti, and still, I am inspired," Hitler commented as he looked toward the main altar. "We do well to remember the past. Otherwise, how would we understand the future?"

"Quite so, Excellency," responded the Italian ambassador.

As they progressed down the main aisle, Max narrated, "That impressive piece behind the altar is the *Pala d'Oro*. Very famous and often photographed." He indicated Martha, who was working under the cloth hood of her camera.

At the rail, Hitler regarded the superb altarpiece for several moments before grunting, "I believe I wish to see more of the large figures."

"If you please, Excellency," said Max as he indicated the north transept.

Before the group moved on, Martha came out from under her cover and asked in Italian, "Gentlemen, may I record the momentous event of your visit? Perhaps a photo before the altar."

Max translated, and Hitler responded, "I am sorry, *Fräulein,* but I do not have the time."

Catching his meaning, Martha gave a small curtsy, smiled and turned to Cerruti. Leaning forward, displaying cleavage and a most alluring gaze, she gestured at the iconostasis, "Ambassador, if you would, maybe a photo with this magnificent backdrop. Something for the newspapers, perhaps."

Cerruti was nonplussed. "Why, I …"

Max whispered in Hitler's ear, "*Mein Führer*, she would like to know if the ambassador might have his photograph made." The chancellor gave his approval with a dismissive wave, and he and his docent continued on toward the Chapel of Saint Isadore. Cerruti, clearly taken with Martha, was happy to accommodate her.

* * *

The lobby of the *Hotel Leone d'Argento* was dimly lit and deserted except for the figure speaking with the desk clerk.

"Is it here?"

"Sí, signore, your gondola awaits," said Francesco, "but it is such an early hour."

"I want to board the first press boat to the Lido, well before the chancellor leaves," replied Enzo Noschese. "I find I can gather some interesting stories from the other reporters and guests that way."

As the slimy journalist left the desk, harboring the hope that he could still vindicate himself regarding Sepp Karper, the clerk called after him, "Good luck to you, sir."

* * *

While Martha made a contrived fuss over posing Cerruti, in the north transept, Max and Hitler stopped under the cupola of Saint John the Evangelist. Solemnly, two women in black came from the atrium and scurried past to join the group attending mass in the nearby chapel of St. Isadore. As Max described the mosaics for Hitler, with hands clasped piously, Sepp strolled past the chancellor and his guide and went into the north atrium.

Moving on from the St. John mosaics, Max led Hitler into the same atrium Sepp had entered, but when they arrived, the bogus priest was nowhere in sight.

Under the first of four domes, Max explained the representations overhead of the life and tribulations of Moses during the Exodus.

In the shadow of a pillar, Sepp pulled a small bottle typically used for holy water from his pocket. He sprinkled a half dozen drops on a linen cloth, taking care to avoid breathing in the sweet-smelling chloroform.

Hitler was gazing up, commenting on his own struggle, as told in *Mein Kamph,* when Sepp struck. He held the chancellor across the chest and put the anesthetic-doused cloth to his mouth and nose. The German struggled mightily for a few, long seconds before going limp.

Silently, the two abductors carried the unconscious chancellor to the basilica's *Porta dei Fiori* doors that Sepp had checked earlier.

Sepp peered out at the *Piazzetta dei Leoncini* and saw that Tropp had moved the luggage carrier closer to the exit and had its hatch open. They quickly deposited Hitler inside. Max removed his suit jacket and false whiskers and threw them into the wagon then donned a workman's cap and jacket. He crawled into the *carretto* and pushed open a small access panel in the wagon's roof as a breathing hole in case Sepp had to administer more chloroform.

Sepp traded places with Max, and Tropp closed the hatch. He and Max rolled the high-wheeled vehicle onto *Calle Canonica.* They drew scant attention from the chatty vendors and workers they passed along the way.

After Martha took a final photograph of Cerruti, the ambassador excused himself and hurried to catch up with his guest. Finding no one in the transept or atrium, he entered St. Isadore Chapel, where a priest was reading a gospel to the worshipers. There was no sign of Hitler or the guide.

When Cerruti's searches of other chapels and areas of the transept were equally fruitless, he rushed to the basilica's front portal, where he found the two policemen soberly eyeing the Nazi gathering across the way. With panic defeating his customary diplomatic aplomb, the Italian ambassador shrieked, "Hitler is gone! The chancellor is not in the basilica!"

"How could that be?" wondered Masciarelli. "It has been only minutes, and no one has passed here."

Fighting for control, Cerruti added, "There is no sign of either his

Excellency or that Nazi tour guide."

"It is a vast space, sir," Masciarelli said in a placating tone, "there are many places they could be."

"I know what I saw!" Cerruti cried out. "I observed where they went, and moments later, nothing."

"Is anyone else there?" asked Gallo, drawing a glare from the sergeant.

"Mass is going on, and there is a woman photographer, but I doubt she is part of it. She was with me when the chancellor went missing. I believe the German guide is the culprit."

"Call the station," Masciarelli barked, "We need units here immediately! Petrin will have our heads if we fail to stop whatever plot is afoot."

"Yes sir, the telephone at *Caffe' Quadri* is closer than the call station."

"Too early! Use a boat radio at the *riva*."

Gallo saluted and took off running back to the pier, where they had first greeted Hitler and the ambassador.

On the bridge over *Rio del Palazzo de Canonica* canal, Tropp and Max labored to move the luggage wagon up then down its broad, deep steps. When they reached the other side, they went right and overcame more stairs as well as a railing along the water's edge. Max pointed to a break in the low wall where he had moored the Hotel Mocenigo speedboat. Once there, Max opened the back of the wagon as Tropp went for the boat's controls. He started the engine, unaware of a passing gondola carrying the ubiquitous Enzo Noschese on its way to the docks at *Riva degli Schiavoni*.

The reporter appeared nonchalant as he took in the passing scene. His indifference suddenly disappeared when he spotted a shock of white hair and a face he recognized from Florence at the wheel of the boat they were passing. "What is that fucking toymaker doing here?" he asked himself in a hoarse whisper. Shouting at the gondolier, he demanded, "Slow down, you are going too fast! And give me your hat."

The boatman stopped working his oar, allowing the craft to move with the flow of the canal, and handed the straw hat to his passenger."

A moment later, Noschese saw Sepp Karper emerge from the *carretto*. The Austrian agent's garb as a priest did nothing to hide his identity from the reporter who now saw him clearly without the glasses or beard of the professor. It was Karper alright, the same person he had met at *Il Duce's* security conference the previous Summer.

As the gondola drifted on, Noschese watched warily from under the hat's brim as Sepp and another man transferred what appeared to be a body into the boat's cabin.

"Max, take the wagon back and await Martha," Sepp told his friend. "If she does not return soon, use your contacts to help her."

Max saluted, "*Ja, mein Führer,*" quickly adding, "Sorry, something rubbed off while I was his guide." He waved to Tropp as he labored to navigate the wagon back over the bridge.

Sepp joined Tropp at the boat's controls and took the wheel from the older man.

"I shall cast off," volunteered Tropp.

"Good," said Sepp. "Then, see if our guest needs attention."

"Will do."

Once free of its bonds, Sepp merged the boat with the canal traffic.

Noschese crouched low and watched as the suspect craft, its engine growling like an angry dog, trailed his gondola.

Without incident, Sepp guided the boat under the famous Bridge of Sighs noting to himself its history as a symbol of prisoner desperation. The thought was fleeting as the *Riva degli Schiavoni* bridge was quickly upon them. He stooped low as they went under and was happy to see the lagoon directly ahead. Moving cautiously, until they reached open waters, he pushed the Mocenigo boat's throttle as far forward as it would go. The craft lurched and roared off, trailing a plume of white foam.

Meanwhile, Cerruti and Masciarelli had returned to the basilica, where the police sergeant began questioning Martha. With wide-eyed innocence, she reported her version of events, including where Hitler and the other man had gone. Deciding her description added nothing new, he and Cerutti began rechecking the basilica's interior. Long, empty minutes passed before the quiet of the immense space was broken by the excited return of officer Gallo.

Breathlessly, he reported to his sergeant, "Sir, while calling headquarters as you ordered, a speedboat emerged from the *Canonica* canal and sped off across the lagoon."

Masciarelli shouted, "It may carry Hitler!"

"I have a boat waiting at the *riva*."

"Good work." Rushing back to the water's edge, Masciarelli. asked, "How did the chief react to your call?"

"Quickly. The regular force, the secret police, and *carabinieri* are all being informed. Unfortunately, they will also notify Petrin."

"Merda!" grumbled the sergeant.

* * *

Petrin sat at a table of a deserted waterfront bar that was an afternoon hangout for members of the police force.

"Luigi, you must have this, please," pleaded the barman as he delivered a second *macchinetta* of syrupy black espresso coffee.

"I only want to sleep, and it will be over," slurred the drunkard.

"Your career may also be over, and you are so close to the finish. Please, sir, don't let the alcohol defeat you," advised the barman as he served a cupful.

"It never has, and ..." Petrin's head wobbled to the table, and he cradled it in his arms.

Bianchi burst through the doors. "Inspector! He is missing!"

Petrin looked up, his head bobbing. "How foolish Bianchi, I am right here."

"Sir, I just heard on the boat radio. The German chancellor has vanished."

Petrin regarded Bianchi blearily. "If you mean Hitler, he is fine. We saw him last night, and today he gets on the airplane and our mission ends."

"Listen to me. It seems that he's being taken by boat across the lagoon."

"*Certo!*" Petrin shouted. "He's going to the airport. That's where we will go to watch the bastard leave."

Frustrated, Bianchi shouted in Petrin's face, "Please listen. Remember, we were to join him and Ambassador Cerruti when they went to the basilica early this morning, and now he's missing. We should have been there but were not because of your condition." The inspector's unfocused gaze told him he wasn't getting through.

"We couldn't fail," mumbled Petrin.

"Please, we must leave immediately."

Petrin shook his head. "You go. I need more coffee."

Bianchi watched his boss drain the cup of espresso then grabbed his arm. "No, I refuse to let it end this way for you." The detective dragged Petrin out the door to the dock where a police boat was tied up. The boatman helped him deposit the inspector in the craft's cabin.

"This is a state emergency," Bianchi barked. "We need to go now! A boat is escaping across the lagoon. We must intercept it."

"Aye, sir," responded the boatman. Once they had cleared the dock, the boat pitched back as they gained speed, cutting through the water.

Several minutes had passed when, through binoculars, Bianchi spotted a craft flying across the water. "That must be it. Go after them!"

The boatman checked his spotter glasses and reported, "Sir, it has police markings. I believe the one you want is ahead of it."

"Go after it, now!" Bianchi ordered.

Tapping every bit of the craft's powerful engine, they fell in less than 300 meters behind the other police pursuers. Farther ahead, the Mocenigo boat veered sharply to port as it went around the eastern end of Venice at *Sant'Elena*.

Sepp called to Tropp, "That should help us. They can no longer gain an angle of intercept. Now, it is simply a matter of who is the swiftest."

At the controls of the first police craft, Masciarelli shouted, "Can't this thing go faster?" Pushing the accelerator lever so hard it bent slightly, he grumbled, "Whoever that is behind us, I don't want them stealing our glory. This is our hunt."

Veering to starboard past the tip of *Isola la Certosa*, Masciarelli tried to close the gap with the suspects and widen the one with the trailing police boat. "We can win this, Gallo," he proclaimed. "No bastard can make fools of us."

“Sir, there are red markers ahead,” the young policeman hollered, but his warning went unheeded. By the time Masciarelli realized what was happening, they had run aground on a sandbar off the island.

At the same time, Petrin’s boat continued to gain on Sepp and Tropp. The experienced police driver skillfully navigated the lagoon and brought them within 200 meters.

Meanwhile, Bianchi was in the cabin, trying to coax the inspector out of his stupor. Thanks to the coffee, he was more awake and aware, but still talking nonsense.

“Must we go so fast?” Petrin asked. “He isn’t due to depart for hours.”

Ignoring the question, Bianchi bent his boss over with his head between his legs to send more blood to his brain. Five minutes of that treatment seemed to have had a positive effect.

“How long Hitler is missing?” Petrin managed to slur.

Bianchi heard the boatman yell, “I believe we are in range, sir,” and went on deck. Leaning on the cabin to steady his weapon, he aimed at the Mocenigo boat speeding some 150 meters ahead.

A triple crack sounded, and two of the bullets went wild. A third struck the wood of the Mocenigo’s cabin, splintering it.

Attempting more speed, Sepp adjusted the choke, but when the engine began to cough, he called to Tropp, who was busy administering another dose to the captive, “Can you refine the carburetion?”

With Sepp keeping the craft reasonably steady as it darted over the water, Tropp removed the engine cover and turned two needle valves until the roar rose audibly and black smoke poured from the exhaust.

Tropp stuck his head up and, catching his breath against the rush of air hitting his face, shouted, “We now have greater speed. It will burn more fuel, but there is plenty to spare. Time is at a premium.”

Two more shots exploded from Bianchi’s gun, but both were well off the mark, and the separation between the pursued and the pursuer widened.

Sepp checked the chase boat waning in the rear-view mirror and shouted triumphantly, “We may now be able to end this.”

Tropp emerged from the cabin, “Our guest is sleeping like a baby.”

Sepp pointed to the myriad islands and canals scattered further starboard past the isle of *Massorbo*, "I think we can lose them in there."

Bianchi called to the driver, "If we get too far behind, they will be impossible to catch."

"I am doing my best, sir," the boatman assured him as he grasped the wheel tightly. "These waters are tricky and they are outpacing us."

A few minutes after they entered the maze of islands, Bianchi scanned the waters for a sign of the Mocenigo boat. It had vanished.

* * *

Shortly after Masciarelli and Gallo left the Basilica, more than two dozen officers and detectives from the various agencies descended on the scene. Most searched the church, while two concentrated on interrogating Martha. The group by the flagpoles were also questioned, and, to a person, their stories were consistent with each other and with what Martha had described. Having nothing substantial to go on, the police took down contact information and allowed them all to leave.

* * *

After winning the wild chase across the lagoon, Sepp cut back the boat's speed and kept its compass pointing north by northeast. Once he had navigated around more islands, he headed for the mouth of *Fiume Dese*. It was just as Tucci had described. In less than a kilometer, the right bank revealed a familiar auto and a waving priest.

* * *

At 07:13, Petrin's boat was making its way to the Lido when a call came over the police radio. The message was clear and, at the same time, confusing. "Stand down. Stand down. All officers engaged in actions related to an abduction at *Basilica di San Marco* are ordered to stand down and return to normal duties."

"What the hell was that about?" asked Petrin, who had regained most of his faculties.

"Sir, it seems we were misinformed," Bianchi explained. "We may have been chasing a speeding craft, manned by persons unknown, heading for an indefinite location, for no good reason."

"Reacting to surmises and guesses," Petrin grumbled. "Piss poor police work. We are damned lucky it did not end in disaster." He frowned. "What a fucking waste."

The boatman called from the bridge and pointed, "Look to starboard. The craft that ran aground."

There sat the stranded police boat they had once trailed with the two policemen, Masciarelli and Gallo.

"Pick them up," ordered Bianchi.

Petrin added, "Then, we must go see the German get back on his plane. My ordeal is almost over."

Bianchi frowned. "I hope you do not plan to celebrate any further, sir. Your successful mission has been sufficiently toasted."

"Absolutely," Petrin responded. "However, one day soon, we shall drink to my retirement. My most happy retirement."

* * *

It was 07:43, and the D-2600 Ju-52 Junkers aircraft stood ready to receive its honored passenger and his party. Mussolini's entourage gathered at the Nicelli flight line along with hundreds of troops and scores of witnesses, including dignitaries, the press, and the police. Red Knickerbocker, Luigi Petrin, Isadoro Bianchi, and the two bell tower policemen were among the host of those awaiting Hitler and the final event of the visit.

* * *

A radio played fascist music as Martha, Max, and Father Tucci sat at the *Palazzo Contarini del Bovolo's* kitchen table doing a post mortem on the morning's events.

"I don't understand," said Martha. "It's been hours. I would have expected reports of chaos by now."

The others agreed, but their conversation was interrupted when the voice of a news commentator broke into the broadcast. “We have a report from the Lido. At 08:00, at the Nicelli aerodrome, German Chancellor Adolf Hitler was seen off by the head of the Italian Government, Premier Benito Mussolini. The occasion ended most amicably.”

“How in hell is this possible?” said Max, expressing what they all were thinking.

Martha stood and with hands on hips. “It simply can’t be. We cannot have failed.”

“Could he have been rescued at the last minute?” wondered Max.

Tucci shook his head. “Everything went according to plan. I was waiting with the automobile, and the transfer went off without a hitch.”

“Could they have caught up with Tropp and Sepp after you left?” wondered Max. “It would explain why there have been no further repercussions.”

“I guess that’s possible,” conceded Tucci, “but I saw no signs of it when I returned. The only odd thing when I arrived at the *Riva degli Schiavoni* was the police waiting there with this scarecrow of a man. A news reporter, I believe. He was pointing at our boat and ranting about seeing an Austrian agent dressed as a priest leave in it carrying Hitler.”

“That worm Noschese, no doubt,” muttered Martha.

Tucci continued, “You can imagine his confusion and bewilderment when a priest showed up with the very same boat looking nothing like Sepp. They took him away, babbling.”

* * *

As the German plane passed over Venice, Hitler watched the ancient structures and canals crawl by below. “It is a glorious city, to be sure, Neurath, but it is old. The Reich is new and will be even more magnificent. Like Venice, our buildings shall stand for at least a thousand years.”

“Excellency,” said the foreign minister, “I wish to apologize once again for misleading you regarding the diplomatic attire."

"Nonsense," replied the *Führer*. "It made no matter, and all went exceptionally well. I was able to achieve precisely what I had come for."

"But sir, I thought ..." von Neurath said with a blank look.

"Mussolini is a most intelligent leader," Hitler went on. "He understood the validity of my words, and in the end, we achieved concord."

Von Neurath could only nod at his leader's pronouncements.

Hitler continued, "Your document citing the general conclusions of our talks will include none of the private details, but enough to convince the world of the amity that now exists between our two nations."

The Road to Austria

Sepp drove Tucci's Lancia along a winding back road heading for a border crossing in the *Friuli-Venezia Giulia* region of the Dolomites. Meanwhile, in the back seat, Tropp monitored the consciousness of their bound guest. He had shaved off the captive's mustache and changed the unconscious man's attire to a workman's cap and jacket.

"You have been quite efficient, Reinhard," said Sepp as he looked in the rear-view mirror. "I would never know him. Too bad there was no time for papers."

"I doubt any guard along the way will recognize our guest, and I think we can do without the papers," Tropp responded. "The Italian guards will not care who is leaving their country, and I am certain the Austrian border will be no problem. If necessary, a phone call to the *Ballplatz* should suffice."

As they motored on, their captive opened his eyes and glared at them. Tropp quickly retrieved a bottle of chloroform and dripped some onto a cloth, but before he could administer it, the man he believed to be Adolf Hitler muttered scornfully, *"Ihr seit alle Narren."*

"You are all fools."

Epilogue

On the morning of 16 June, German radio reported that Chancellor Hitler had arrived in Munich aboard his Junkers Ju-52 aircraft from Venice, Italy.

A day later, Martha was approached by John Ravelli as she was photographing the interior of *Basilica di San Marco*. He debriefed her on the events she had observed during the historic meeting and predicted that President Roosevelt would be pleased by her insights and the photos she promised to submit. She never said a word about her knowledge of or involvement in the plot against Adolf Hitler.

After turning the package over to the Austrian secret police, Tropp drove Sepp to Vienna then continued back to Venice. A day later, Sepp reported to the *Ballhaus* offices of Engelbert Dollfuss, where he gave the chancellor a detailed report on his exploits in Italy. He ended his narrative by assuring the chancellor that, despite reports of Hitler returning to Munich, the kidnapping of the German leader had succeeded. Dollfuss responded that although a *Doppelgänger* may have been involved, he was confident that the man confined in Tyrol was the real German chancellor. They never discussed the subject again.

During the same meeting, Sepp announced his intention to resign his commission to marry the American woman with whom he had fallen in love. Happy at the news and sympathetic to Sepp's needs, the chancellor asked Sepp to stay on for several weeks while they evaluated the Nazi threat. Neither could have known that *Anschluss* would not come until March 1938 when Germany annexed Austria.

On 25 June, in a reign of terror which came to be known as the "Night of the Long Knives," Hitler turned against his longtime supporter and catalyst for his rise to power, Ernst Röhm and his

Sturmabteiling (SA). Röhm. other SA leaders, and many of their underlings were arrested and killed or made to commit suicide. With their ranks decimated, the stormtroopers were later used to carry out attacks on Jews. Filling the void, Himmler's *Schutzstaffel* rose in status and power and eventually became the most potent paramilitary unit of the Third *Reich*.

Exactly a month later, Austrian Chancellor Engelbert Dollfuss was mortally wounded and left to die during an attempted *putsch* at the *Ballhaus* by Austrian Nazis. Prince Ernst Starhemberg served briefly as Acting Chancellor and later redirected his interests to concentrate on supporting the Fatherland Front.

On a bright July day at *Villa Donat*i in Florence, Father Guido Tucci performed a wedding ceremony to unite Sepp and Martha. Those attending included the bride's two children, her parents, grandmother Donati, and an ebullient Reinhard Tropp, who brought gifts of carved toys for the youngsters.

When Weimar Republic President Paul von Hindenburg died on 2 August, Adolf Hitler quickly merged the offices of *Reichskanzler* and *Reichspräsident,* giving himself total dictatorial powers. He would use those powers to build Germany's industries and military strength to levels well beyond the limitations imposed by the Treaty of Versailles.

In the ensuing years, Hitler's dominance of *Il Duce* and Italy led to changes in that country's racial laws. As anti-Semitism grew, Italian Jews began leaving their homeland. Among them, Marcello Martone relocated to Hollywood, California, where he would rise to prominence as an award-winning movie director.

Max Klemperer's relationship with Claudia never survived the trauma of Carlo Mocenigo's attempt on her life. The young widow suffered deep psychological scars that Max's love could not surmount. She sold off her husband's estate, put the proceeds into a fine arts memorial endowment, and joined a convent in Siena.

Max tried breaking into America's burgeoning fashion industry, but the dark memories of the *Contarini* haunted him and destroyed his taste for dressmaking. Refusing to accept failure, he applied his skills and creativity as art director of an emerging advertising agency on New York's Madison Avenue.

In Connecticut, Martha and Sepp enjoyed an idyllic life with their children. Sepp made a successful bid to become a shooting coach for the United States team preparing for the 1940 Olympics. The games, originally scheduled to be held in Japan, were redirected to Helsinki, but unfortunately, they never happened due to the war.

When America officially entered the hostilities in late 1941, Sepp joined the U.S. Army and was appointed the commander of a sniper training unit.

As the German menace overtook Europe, Martha turned her camera on the United States. Her photos and stories of everyday life in the towns, cities, factories, and farms of the country would become a series of popular books.

Slightly more than eleven years from the time Hitler and Mussolini first met, the world celebrated their deaths as World War II wound down.

With the collapse of Italian fascism during the German occupation, the people turned against Mussolini. In 1945, he and his mistress, Claretta Petacci, were executed and hung upside down from a girder in a Milan square.

As the war in Europe was ending, the man the world knew as Adolf Hitler and his bride of one day, Eva Braun, died in a Berlin bunker.

The Tyrolean captivity that had been sustained by a secret endowment ended in 1945 when the prisoner escaped during Austria's liberation. During the decades that followed, there persisted rumors and reports of Hitler sightings.

§§§

Authors' Note

The Dollfuss Directive focuses on the June 1934 meeting of Hitler and Mussolini in Venice and the related concerns of Austrian Chancellor Dollfuss regarding his country's continued independence. We have combined facts about actual venues, documented events, and real people with fictional characters, conversations, and circumstances. As part of the writing process, we studied documentary films, news reports, books, and myriad other documents to create believable, thrilling, and entertaining scenarios. We hope you have enjoyed this product of history and our imaginations.

Our previous work, *The Other Eisenhower*, is a novel based on an actual security breach just before D-Day that could have doomed the plan to invade Normandy and free Europe from the Nazis.

For more information about us and our works, please visit us at campana-ditillo.com.

Made in the USA
Columbia, SC
11 November 2020

24329522R00163